CLAIMED BY THE WINTER REALM

CLAIMED BY THE SEVEN REALMS COLLECTION ONE

AIDY AWARD

xoxo
~Aidy Award

Copyright © 2022 by Aidy Award

All rights reserved.

No part of this book may be reproduced in any form or by any electronic or mechanical means, including information storage and retrieval systems, without written permission from the author, except for the use of brief quotations in a book review.

Cover by Danielle Doolittle of Doelle Designs

PROTECTED

CLAIMED BY THE SEVEN REALMS - BOOK ONE

For everyone who went to see the Nutcracker Ballet at Christmas, all wide-eyed and excited, dressed in your pretty holiday clothes.

Who then also thought, how is this not a romance?

And then wondered what the hell happened to the plot after the first fifteen minutes.

I like the plot of the Nutcracker - not at all.

— PYOTR ILYICH TCHAIKOVSKY

SAME. So I wrote my own version.

— AIDY AWARD

THE MAGIC OF CHRISTMAS

CLARAMARIE

*N*ervous energy whizzed through me, swirling like the blowing snowflakes outside. I wanted this role, and I wanted it bad.

I was freaking perfect for it. Who better to play a chubby, rosy-cheeked, life-sized dancing doll than a chubby rosy-cheeked plus-sized ballerina?

I knew the choreography. I could provide my own outfit, so the costume department didn't have to get all outraged over having to make one for me on short notice, since I didn't fit into anything they had on the racks already. This was one of the few dances in Frau Hoffman's studio's repertoire for a ballerina without a partner, and none of the guys would even consider lifting my right thigh, much less all of me. Most importantly, I was available to perform this part tonight.

I didn't exactly have the evening free. I was supposed to be at my family's annual Christmas Eve party. If I scored a part, I would still be there, only as a performer instead of a hostess.

Wouldn't that surprise the shit out of my stupid brother. He'd probably have an aneurism if he even knew I was here trying out at all. The dance performance was supposed to be a surprise for my family and our guests, but Drosselmeyer had given me a whole host of clues to make sure I would be here for the audition this morning.

"Group three, you're up. Let's go, ladies." Frau Hoffman clapped her hands and five of us made our way to the center of the studio for our turn.

I tried to take the spot in the middle, but Louisa gently pushed me aside with a whisper. "Not this time, ClaraMarie."

I rolled my eyes and took the place beside her just to piss her off. She and I had been dancing together since we were little kids. She was the beautiful one with the ballerina body, the one who always got cast in all the parts. I didn't have it in me to hate her. Louisa wasn't a typical mean girl, and we were sort of friends. She tried to be kind to me, in her own way, while most of the other dancers wouldn't give me the time of day.

But when it came right down to it, she wasn't going to let me get in her way. Especially now that I had a shot. She'd get a starring role for sure, probably as the toy ballerina. I rarely even got to be a back-up dancer. Not this time. I was going to get a part if it killed me.

When it was my turn, I gave the small pendant I always wore a squeeze, sending up a wish to my long-dead mother for a little luck from above.

The music started up and I bowed my head. The tinny notes that sounded just like a music box pinged from the speakers and I pasted the perfect fake dolly smile on my face. My arms rose as if on marionette strings and my legs and feet followed suit. I pirouetted, arabesqued, and pas de bourréed just as good or better than the other girls, throwing myself into the role of a wind-up dancing doll come to life until the music stopped and the other dancers politely clapped.

My heart beat with the exhilaration of getting to dance and I couldn't help but smile for real this time. I totally nailed that audition. Louisa knew it too, if her irritated pout was any indication. Of course, she quickly covered it with a smile and a pat on the back for me. Even Frau Hoffman gave me an approving nod as I padded off the floor and back to my seat.

"Parts will be posted within the hour. We'll start rehearsals at ten o'clock sharp and perform this evening at seven. If your name is on the list, expect to be here all day. I don't want any last-minute excuses about having to spend time with your family on Christmas Eve. This is paid work, people. Don't accept the job if you can't fulfill the responsibilities of the role."

No one said a word, probably because we all knew each dancer chosen for tonight's performance would be paid more for one hour of work than most made in a month. Nothing but the best in entertainment for the Stahlbaum Christmas party.

Not that we could afford a penny of it.

If I got the part, I'd be doing the family a favor because Fritz certainly wouldn't hand even a single dollar over to me.

I dug my bag of grapes, half a hard-boiled egg, and lemon water out of my bag. If we were going to be here all day, I needed some energy. Before I opened the baggies of food, I turned my back on the rest of the room. Dancers were weird about food at the best of times. I was weird about it all the time. I'd die before I'd let any of them see me eat.

I'd been called Clara Cow, or worse, enough times to know better. Didn't matter if I starved myself or ate two large mushroom and sausage pizzas, I pretty much stayed the same weight always and forever. I could dance eight hours straight, sweat buckets and the scale would still say the exact same two hundred something pounds, like the asshole that it was.

I guess I shouldn't care what I ate or who I ate it in front of, but like a dummy, I did. I wished that I didn't but wishes weren't worth diddly squat.

Forty-five minutes later, Frau Hoffman posted the list. Everyone else rushed up in a big mob to check whether they'd gotten a role or not. I stayed where I was, closed my eyes, and willed the universe to give me this chance to prove I was as good a dancer as the rest of them. Just this once. Any of the roles. I didn't care which at this point. Just—something.

Call it my Christmas wish. Miracles could happen and if I believed hard enough, maybe it would come true for me.

I wasn't delusional. I knew I'd never be a professional ballet dancer, but this wasn't exactly *Swan Lake*. These were little vignettes based on fairy stories, just like the ones Drosselmeyer told me and Fritz as young children. I especially loved the one about the Vivandiere because she was a strong warrior princess who took no guff from anyone. That wasn't me. Honestly, any part but that one would be better.

When all but five other dancers were gone, I stood, crossed to the list, and gave my fist a couple of clenches to keep my hand from trembling in front of the others. Please. Please. Let me get a part.

I ran my finger down the hand-written names.

Harlequin - Frania

Soldier - Astrid

Columbine - Daphine

Vivandiere - Marea

Ballerina - Louisa

I blinked and looked at each role one more time, taking an extra-long stare at each name. One of those parts were supposed to be mine. Mine.

But not a one had my name.

There had to be a mistake. I'd nailed the audition. There was no good reason to give the part to what's-their-faces instead of to me.

I marched over to Frau Hoffman, right past Louisa and the other girls who'd been cast. Four of them gave me stink faces, but Louisa stepped away from the rest and into my path. She took me by the shoulders and whispered, "ClaraMarie, don't do this. Frau Hoffman isn't going to change her mind. Some of the new girls have real talent, and this could be the start of a career. You don't want to ruin that for any of them, do you? I didn't think you were the kind of Stahlbaum who was spiteful."

Well, crap on a cracker. Why'd she have to go and put it that way? She could have said anything else and I would have ignored her, kept on my righteous path to get what I wanted, but dammit, I refused to act like my brother.

I swallowed hard and felt my future drop through the floor and skulk away as if it never existed. Why did I even try so hard? I wasn't ever going to get a part. I was too fat, not pretty enough, and not talented enough to make up for my other shortcomings. "You're a good friend, Louisa. Thanks."

My self-righteous anger oozed into a glob of green jealousy sitting in the pit of my stomach. Maybe if I had told myself that I wasn't going to get the part anyway, like I usually did, this wouldn't feel so damn bad. Just this once I—never mind. I'd be a lot smarter, if not happier, if I quit dreaming of being a dancer, even for fun, and got on with real life.

Tonight's Christmas Eve party was the perfect place to start, I guessed. There was no getting out of it now. No avoiding Fritz and his machinations. No avoiding Drosselmeyer and the commitments I had to fulfill. Not anymore.

I eyed the trash can on my way out the door of the studio. My dance bag wouldn't fit in the opening, but I imagined a dramatic toss of it as I walked away forever.

As soon as I got home, I'd put my dance bag in the back of my closet, never to be seen again. I had expensive tap shoes and other high-end dance gear that was worth a lot of money. I should try to sell it. A bitter burn rose up the back of my throat. That might be more heartache than it was worth.

I didn't have to decide right now while I was still upset. I could decide later. It's not like Fritz or my father would know, and the few hundred dollars I might make wouldn't make a dent in our debt anyway.

No, there was only one way I could truly save my family from ruin. And by ruin, I meant complete financial bankruptcy and social humiliation.

A very heavy weight, like a cartoon anvil, sank down onto my shoulders. Tonight was truly the end of any dreams of my own. It was time for me to do the right thing and save the Stahlbaum name. By becoming a Drosselmeyer.

I snuck in the kitchen door at the back of the house hoping to avoid Fritz. It was still early enough that he might not even be up. No such luck.

"If you ever try to serve this garbage to me again, you'll—" Fritz threw a piece of toast on the floor at our cook's feet, and I have no doubt he would have smashed the plate too if he hadn't caught sight of me out of the corner of his eye. "Where are you sneaking in from?"

"My, you are wound up today. Throwing a fit because you're not getting any presents from Santa this year?" I stopped being afraid of Fritz's temper tantrums a long time ago. He might be the head of the family since Father's dementia had gotten worse, but he still acted like a spoiled little boy.

I'm not sure when my own brother began hating me, but I saw it written across his face, and deep in his eyes. This was much more than simple sibling rivalry. He genuinely despised me and everything I did. At the same time, he was always too concerned with appearances to let the servants see the deep ire for me in his soul.

We hadn't liked each other since Papa got sick and Fritz had run the family business into dust with his stupidity. I sighed. I shouldn't think that way. It's not as if I could have done any better. What did I know about market economics and financial forecasts? Nothing, zilch, nada. Fritz was doing his best. It was just that his best had us all on the verge of bankruptcy.

"I would appreciate it, very much, dearest sister, if you could do something to help the family tonight, instead of…" He glanced over at the kitchen maid cleaning up and narrowed his eyes at her. He lowered his voice so only I could hear his sneering words, "being your usual Miss High and Mighty."

"I'm doing plenty, you've seen to that." I didn't wait for any more of his chastisements and went up the back stairs to my room. Even there I couldn't escape my future.

In the corner, hanging in a long poofy garment bag, was my wedding dress. While I hated everything the dress represented, the gown itself was beyond gorgeous. The one and only time I'd tried it on, I'd almost hoped I would look like a frumpy, over-dressed, fairy godmother. As it turned out, I'd felt like a fairy princess.

Outside of ballet class, I wasn't one to stand around and look at myself in mirrors all day. I'd been told one too many times growing up how I was a little too chunky and needed to lose some of that baby fat not to look at each part of my body with a hyper-critical eye. The day I'd tried on that dress at the fitting, I'd stared at my own reflection for probably longer than all the other times in my life combined. I'd felt uniquely beautiful that day. At least Drosselmeyer could give me that, if not true love.

A little self-confidence and some financial security would have to do.

Both of those were better than unrequited dreams, anyway. The sooner I learned that lesson the better, and today was the day to start learning my place.

I showered and changed into jeans and a long-sleeved t-shirt. There was still plenty of prep for tonight's party I could help with. I wasn't looking forward to the engagement announcement part of tonight's festivities. I was more excited for the gift giving and receiving, just like in my childhood.

When we'd had more money than we knew what to do with, Father had upheld the long tradition of giving presents to all the children of the families who attended. In the last few years, Drosselmeyer had helped us continue with that by providing a supply of beautiful artisan toys from his renowned shop. I never could resist any of his automatons or dancing dolls.

It had been a while since I'd gotten a gift myself, aside from the singular Christmas gift, but I enjoyed seeing the delight of the younger generation when they opened a new surprise. My own collection of hand-crafted dolls had gone to younger girls except for one particular fairy ballerina in a red and blue Vivandiere costume. The very same make-believe soldier girl in a story set in a fantasy land that didn't exist. I should have given her up long ago, but still she sat on the corner of my vanity, even though she hadn't done her little dance in years.

That would be me someday too. A pretty but worn-out toy of Drosselmeyer's.

I headed downstairs and immersed myself in wrapping presents, decorating the tree, and making sure the house sparkled for the coming guests. It was strange to think I wouldn't even be living in this house next Christmas.

The big grandfather clock in the great room clanged the hour and the front door crashed open, a chilly wind blowing in, bringing with it snowflakes and the scent of sugar and pine trees. "ClaraMarie, my dear, hello. It's almost time."

Drosselmeyer bustled into the room and threw his hat and jacket on the bench near the door. He carried a gift wrapped in pretty blue paper under one arm, and a smile on his face meant for me.

I wanted to love this man who would be my husband, but I didn't. I wasn't ready for a life as nothing more than an eccentric rich man's wife. "You're right. I should hurry and get dressed. Please make yourself at home and I'll—"

I didn't finish my sentence as I quickly hurried up the grand staircase and rushed to my room. I almost slammed the door behind me, but caught it at the last second, letting it click softly shut. Then I put my back to it, stared up at the ceiling to contain the tears threatening to fall, and sighed.

"Don't be silly. He'll treat you well and you'll never want for anything." This wasn't the first time I'd chastised myself for not wanting the life I was destined for. It wouldn't be the last.

Best to keep myself busy so I didn't think about it more than I had to. The long red dress I'd selected for the party was already laid out on the bed by one of the staff. It was pretty, but I'd hoped not to be wearing it tonight.

I'd dreamed of being something different, someone new for just this one time in my life. A beautiful dancing flower, a doll, or even a soldier girl. Anything other than who I really was.

THE NUTCRACKER SWEET

CLARAMARIE

There was something different about tonight. The scents and sounds around me crackled and felt crisp, as if the very molecules in the air were here to celebrate the arrival of Christmas with the Stahlbaums one last time. Even my stroppy mood couldn't combat the magic and excitement of children dressed in their party dresses and suits, the adults in all their finery, and the feeling of comfort and joy all around me.

The string quartet played a pretty piece of music that could barely be heard over the din of the crowded party. We did not expect this many people to show up this year. The last couple of Christmas Eve balls hadn't been well attended. It was like society knew that we were down and out and just pretending to keep up appearances.

People could get a whiff of gossip like gingerbread cookies baking, and yet not a one had given me a sideways glance or whispered an unkind word. Even Fritz looked as pleased as a partridge showing off in his pear tree. Even if this wasn't the life I wanted, I was determined to enjoy myself tonight and begin anew tomorrow.

With the position and wealth marrying Drosselmeyer would afford me, I could probably make a difference in the world, even if it was a small one. I knew better than to allow any big dreams to seep in again, lest they be quashed.

I smiled at every boy and girl, greeted every man and woman, and even said Merry Christmas to Fritz and meant it. "Just for one night, Fritz, let's be on the same side."

He surveyed the room from the position he'd taken up next to the enormous tree. He responded without even looking at me. "Fine. I supposed we won't even see each other much in the new year once you're married. I'm looking forward to the announcement of your engagement. It will be quite amusing to see everyone's reaction."

Sigh. "Yes, it will. Now wish me Merry Christmas and I'll go make my rounds to gather the children for the gifts."

He rolled his eyes, but there was a little bit of a twinkle in them. Even Fritz liked presents and he knew there was one under the tree for him as well. There always was. I wondered what Drosselmeyer would give us this year. We were well past the age to be part of the tradition, but still he had some trinket or other for us every Christmas Eve.

"Merry Christmas, ClaraMarie. Now off you go. Check on Father while you're gone."

I nodded and smiled, even though I'd already been to see Father after I'd dressed and before the other guests arrived. He didn't have very many good days, but tonight his eyes were bright and filled with happiness. He'd said I looked just like the princess I truly was. He even insisted I go back and put on the necklace with the sparkling gold and ruby crown pendant left to me by my mother. The one that I had thought too old and tarnished to wear to the party. I did as he asked, because it matched the Christmas-red dress, and no one would be looking at me anyway.

I promised to have some hot chocolate and some sugar plums brought up for him later. So heartbreaking how he'd gone from a hale and hearty gentleman to a frail invalid almost before my eyes. This was the first year he wasn't well enough to attend the party. He'd gone downhill so rapidly that now he didn't even have the capacity to know that it was going on right below his feet.

He was the real reason I'd promised to marry Drosselmeyer. I could live without the house, the servants, the fancy clothes, and the easy life, but without a steady income, we couldn't pay for Father's care. I'd sit by his side and feed him every meal, take care of all his needs, if I could—and on his good days, I did. On the bad days, though, when his mind turned on him, he became more than belligerent. He was a danger to himself and to others. He'd once pulled a sword off the wall above his bed and brandished it at me, spouting something about never succumbing to the queen of the mice.

That was the day I finally agreed to the arranged marriage I'd resisted for almost a year.

It didn't take me long to get each and every child to gather around the Christmas tree. They all knew they were in for a real treat. Even the adults quieted down as the ballet troupe rolled out the giant boxes decorated with shiny paper, ribbon, and bows. I, of course, knew who and what hid inside each person-sized box, but the rest of the assembled crowd had no idea.

The lights lowered and a spotlight shone down on the first box. The four sides dropped, the lid falling to the back, and out popped the first dancer, Frania, as the Harlequin. The children giggled and laughed at the silly dance she did pretending to be a wind-up toy, and I bit the inside of my cheek.

The Columbine's dance was next, and I very carefully

studied the ornaments on the tree while Daphine performed the part perfectly, I'm sure. When I looked back, Drosselmeyer caught my eye and gave a small frown. He nodded toward the performance with a look that said I should be paying attention.

He'd been the one who hinted that the performance tonight would be a ballet version of his fairy stories, knowing full well dance was my passion. I went to that dumb audition because of it. I was torn, wanting to hate him for being an instrument in dashing my dreams, and at the same time thank him for being kind enough to schedule an entertainment designed to delight me.

I did turn back to watch the next dance. Marea and Astrid popped out dressed as the soldier and Vivandiere. Only the dancer in the soldier's uniform, with the rosy cheeks painted on, had a sword by his side. Yeah, *his* side. A man had taken over Astrid's role. What had happened to her?

I wasn't even sure he could dance. Not that he really had to.

He simply stood there as Marea pirouetted around him, and all the while he stared directly at me. His bright blue eyes sparkled, but his face was set in that same stern, blank expression of the soldiers who guard Buckingham Palace. Tingles flew from my chest to my belly and settled between my legs.

I glanced around to see if I was just imagining that he was focused on me. On one side of me was the tree, and on the other Fritz. I supposed he could be watching my brother with the intensity of a winter's storm, but if he was, Fritz hadn't noticed. He was picking at a piece of lint on his cuff looking bored.

No, no. I was being ridiculous. The soldier was simply playing his part in the performance. I backed away, my feet brushing against the presents under the tree and my dress knocking the ornaments on the lower branches. Shoot. There was no way of escaping without being noticed.

Fine, then. I stared right back at the dancer who was far too good-looking for his own good. He didn't even have a dancer's build. His thighs were muscled under the blue tights, but not in the lean, lithe way of a danseur. His physique was bulky and strong, like someone who worked ridiculously hard for a living. Almost like a real soldier might.

When Marea finished her performance, she and the soldier stepped to the side and the final box rolled forward. Louisa as the ballerina doll would be inside and this one, I simply couldn't watch everyone ooh and ahh over her. "Excuse me, Fritz. I need to freshen up quickly before we give out the presents."

He smirked at me but stepped a few inches to the side to let me by. There wasn't even close to enough room for my head, much less my hips to get through, especially not in this dress. I rolled my eyes at him and gave him a little shove. Butthead. He was already mesmerized by Louisa.

I picked my way around the other people watching and was met at the edge of the great room by Drosselmeyer. I hadn't even noticed he'd excused himself from the festivities too, but it made sense. He never was much of a crowds person, and he clearly preferred children's wonderment to adult disenchantment. He did his duty, showing his face about town and at his business, but apart from that, he mostly stayed in his studio where he wrote his stories, made his toys, and kept to himself.

I'd spent many an hour there fascinated with the pretty toys, the gears, the springs. Drosselmeyer's workshop always had a special magical feel about it. It was the stories he told us about the enchanted Winter Realm and the adventures of the fairies who lived there that kept me coming back for more. Even before I wanted to be a ballerina, I'd spent hours pretending to be a dancing fairy soldier girl.

Drosselmeyer waved me over. There was no avoiding him this time. I felt bad for even wanting to. I sucked in a slow, calming breath, pasted on a smile, and joined him near the grandfather clock on the opposite side of the Christmas tree and away from the performers.

The show was almost done anyway. The harlequin, columbine, and vivandiere were already back in their boxes. In a few minutes we'd do presents for the children, so it wasn't like we had to spend much time together anyway. Although after that came the engagement announcement, which of course meant a lifetime together.

But not yet.

"ClaraMarie, your dress is quite perfect, and I'm glad to see you're wearing your mother's necklace. Although I worry you'll be cold." Drosselmeyer touched the sleeve of my gown, rubbing the lace between his fingers.

I gently pulled away. Someday I would have to submit to his touch, but not tonight. Not yet. "With so many people here tonight, the rooms are pretty warm."

"Ah, yes. Well, still. Be sure to keep a cloak handy. Now, I'm glad we have a moment together. I've got a special present for you this year." He pulled the blue-wrapped box I'd seen earlier out from behind his back. I wasn't sure where he'd been hiding it up till now.

"Thank you." I took the gift and was more excited to open it than I let on. I wasn't a silly little girl who played with dolls anymore, but the shape of the box indicated that would be exactly what was inside. "You really didn't have to. You've done so much for the family already."

"Have I? Hmm. I feel as though there is much left to do. As if I haven't prepared you nearly enough." He glanced over at Fritz who was no longer watching Louisa dance but narrowing his eyes at the two of us. Probably just jealous because he hadn't gotten his gift yet.

I lifted the paper from the box, where one corner was already a bit torn. Instead of a pretty doll, I was met with the sparkling blue eyes, rosy cheeks, and red coat of the soldier. "Oh, Drosselmeyer. What a beautiful nutcracker."

I didn't say the words because they were merely what was expected, but in true awe of both the clear craftsmanship of the toy and because it bore an uncanny resemblance to the man who'd played the dancing soldier. I lifted the nutcracker out of the box and got that same strange tingling in my chest and belly as before.

"Oh, is that what's in the box? Hmm. I'm glad you like him. He took long enough about finding his way to you."

I must have stared into the toy's eyes for far longer than I realized, because the next thing I knew, Fritz was grabbing it out of my hands. "ClaraMarie's a bit old for dolls, don't you think, Herr Drosselmeyer?"

"No more than you, young Friedrich." He handed a smaller, flat box over to Fritz and gave me a little wink.

"Silly," Fritz said, but ripped the paper off anyway. He popped the top off the paper box and found a pair of silvery cufflinks, shaped like miniature Christmas trees, dotted with tiny gemstones as baubles. "Thank you."

Fritz was an ass more often than not, but he did have enough manners to thank someone for what was clearly an expensive gift. Drosselmeyer knew exactly how to please a spoiled brat.

"Now, ClaraMarie, put your dolly away and let us attend to our guests. It's time for the gifts to be given out." He grabbed the nutcracker from me, but I'd been prepared for his little snatch and grab and held on tight. I should have just given him what he wanted. In the tussle, Fritz half got it away from me. We fumbled for the toy and it fell to the ground with a crack.

"Oh, no. Fritz, why did you have to go and do that?" I bent and carefully picked the nutcracker up. His right arm was cracked at the elbow, destroying Drosselmeyer's fine work.

"It's only a toy, ClaraMarie. Grow up." Fritz didn't give me or his mess a second glance and marched back to the tree and our guests.

Drosselmeyer tutted and tsked and pulled a handkerchief from his jacket pocket. He gently wrapped it around the nutcracker's arm and over his shoulder just as if he was creating a sling for a real soldier. "He'll need to heal before going back to the Winter Realm."

I cradled the nutcracker in my arms. "I used to love those stories. Fritz is right, though. It is time I grew up. Time to stop playing with dolls and believing in fairy stories."

"Ah, but the stories are real, and time is a funny thing. So are irritating brothers. Don't pay too much attention to either."

The stories are real. What a strange thing for him to say to me. "I'm not a child any longer. If we are to be married, you mustn't treat me like one."

Drosselmeyer smiled down at me, and it was neither patronizing nor romantic. "Right you are, ClaraMarie. Forgive me. My dear, I have never lied to you, nor will I ever. The stories are real, and you'll do well to remember them. You'll need everything I've taught you soon."

What in the world? For a brief moment, I wondered and worried that maybe Herr Drosselmeyer was also developing dementia. Was that to be my lot in life? To take care of two old men? Was he even older than my father? He was certainly much older than me, but he'd always seemed ageless to me, even as a child.

I opened my mouth to ask him, but Fritz's voice rang out through the room. "Attention everyone, honored guests and children. It's time for the presents."

Squeals and clapping rang throughout the great room. There was a mad rush toward the tree and when I looked back, Drosselmeyer was no longer standing next to me. He must have slipped into the fray to help the boys and girls find the presents with their names on them. There was one for each of them, and anyone who'd gotten a Drosselmeyer toy before knew better than to open one that wasn't intended for them. He had an uncanny ability to make exactly the right gift for each child. To get any other by mistake would be pure disappointment.

I doubted I would be able to find him again until after all the presents were given out. At least I'd already gotten mine. Even if it was broken, I would cherish it forever as a final symbol of the end of innocence for me. No matter what Drosselmeyer said, I did need to grow up and get on with my adult life.

Many a child rushed over to show me their gifts and thank me for hosting the party. I showed them my nutcracker in return. Nobody commented on how he resembled the danseur from the performance, but they all noticed his broken arm. I sent each one off to make sure they talked to Fritz as well because a little thanks and praise went a long way in keeping him happy.

Before long the guests began gathering their coats and their tired children, saying their goodbyes with little ones sleeping on their shoulders. Only when there was not more than a handful of revelers dawdling did I realize we'd never made the engagement announcement.

Well, that was something we'd have to deal with tomorrow. The paper already had the information and picture to print, so it wasn't as if the whole town wouldn't know in the morning anyway. Perhaps they wouldn't even care since it would be Christmas Day. I could only hope.

"I'm going up to check on Father, and then to bed. See the rest of the stragglers out, won't you?" Fritz faked a yawn. He was a master at getting out of anything he didn't want to do.

I didn't mind being the last one about. I'd love a little peace and quiet to enjoy the lights of the tree on my own without the hustle and bustle of the party. There were still a few hours until the holiday was officially rung in by the old grandfather clock. "Yes, of course. Goodnight. Merry Christmas."

Fritz didn't bother to reply and took the stairs up two at a time, in quite a hurry.

I grabbed a pillow from one of the chairs and set it in front of the tree, dropping down onto it. My feet were sore from all the standing and I slipped my shoes off. I wanted to rub my toes, so I set the beautiful nutcracker down under the nearest branches. I hadn't wanted to let go of him while there were so many people about who might jostle him and damage him even more.

I stared up at the twinkling lights of the tree and sat in silence, loving the first quiet and calm of the day. I must have been more tired than I thought because the next thing I knew I was waking up with my head half off the pillow and the blur of the lights shining in my eyes.

I guess I'd fallen asleep staring at the tree. What had roused me?

"Princess Clara, wake up." A deep, insistent male voice filtered into my waning and waxing consciousness.

I blinked a few times and sat up. Staring down in front of me with one hand extended to me was the nutcracker, or was it the danseur? I must still be dreaming.

He took my hand and a rush of warmth swept through me, from my fingers all the way to my spine and back again. He blinked as if he felt it too, but shook his head and looked over his shoulder toward the tree. "We must hurry. The Winter Realm is in grave need of you."

THE BATTLE WITH THE
MOUSE KING

NUSS

The princess was so much more beautiful than I ever could have imagined. How she'd hidden in this strange human world without being discovered was baffling. She outshone any of the women or men gathered in her home. Perhaps on some basic level they did know she was special among them, and that's why they were here to celebrate her on this most magical night.

We had only a few moments before the portal between our realms opened and I could guide her back to the Winter Realm, back to her destiny. Or so we all hoped. That same portal could allow the Mouse Queen's army into her world, which meant we needed to be ready and waiting to avoid them.

"Please, come with me, quickly. The rest of your Nutcracker protective guard await." I extended my hand to her, willing her to accept it and me.

"What a strange dream you are. I must have sipped a bit too

PROTECTED

much eggnog. Either that, or I am dreading my marriage more than I thought to have conjured up someone as handsome as you. Who are you supposed to be?" She blinked up at me like a precious porcelain doll with her big eyes, soft rosy cheeks, and springy blonde curls that begged to be stroked.

She was mine to protect, not bed. My head knew the drill, my cock did not. Why did she have to be so sweet and beautiful? One touch of her and I'd splinter. I called upon every bit of my training and willpower. Not only did I need them both to keep her safe from her enemies, but from my own need of her. No one told me my heart would be stolen by her at first glance, my blood would sing, my need would pound. "I'm the captain of the Nutcracker Guard and it's our sworn duty to protect you, Princess. I promise to explain everything once we're safely in the Winter Realm."

She took my hand and rose from her soft pillow. A whoosh of her magic ran through me and straight to my cock. I gritted my teeth to keep from pulling her into my arms and claiming her right then and there. She wasn't only mine.

The release of that small bit of her power propelled her forward and she ended up tucked against my chest with my good arm wrapped around her. "Oh, oh my. This is a very nice dream."

Her face flushed as if we were standing in front of a roaring fire and her eyes sparkled up at me. The pretty bow of her mouth opened ever so slightly, and she licked her lips.

The lost princess of Spirit and Magic, our one real hope to defeat the Mouse Queen, wanted me to kiss her. She stared deeply into my soul, just as she did when the dancers performed their entertainment for her and her guests, when I hid in her gift from the Fae magician. In only those brief moments I'd already fallen in love with her.

But it was her concern and kindness when the toy was

broken that confirmed she was indeed the lost princess for whom our band of nutcracker soldiers had been searching.

"Your arm. Does it hurt? Can a sexy, talking toy in a dream heal, or are you injured forever?" She touched the makeshift sling over my broken arm, and I flinched.

The sensual spell surrounding us broke, and I was able to step away and remember my place. I felt as though I'd already failed her as a protector and guard.

Unfortunately, a glamour didn't protect me from being hurt, no matter the form. I could hide my true identity with a bit of Fae persuasion—humans were easy enough to manipulate—however, it appeared the princess saw right through it all. "My apologies, if there had been another way to sneak in without the Mouse Queen's army detecting me, I would have taken it. I would never let anyone see or touch me but you."

"A mouse queen sounds horrible, but one with an army is even worse. Perhaps we can placate them with cheese. I think there is some left over from the party in the kitchen."

"I promise, if you're hungry, the marzipan pixies will provide. Right this way, if you please, my lady." I took advantage of her still-disoriented state to pull her toward the tree. "At the stroke of midnight, the portal will open."

The magician's clock ticked and the first peal of the Fae-made bells inside rang through the room, awakening the magic. The lights on the tree glowed brighter and the scent of snowflakes, pine, and aromatic sweets from the Winter Realm drifted around us.

"Ready, princess?" Her entire world was about to change. Mine too, if I was lucky.

She glanced over at the clock, then back to me and shook her head and smiled. "Not in the slightest."

"Don't worry, I'll be here to protect you every step of the way." I squeezed her hand and together we took the first step forward.

But instead of being drawn into the magic of the portal, we were met with the sword of the one person I'd been doing my best to avoid. Konig, the Mouse Prince.

"Good try, Nuss." He eyed the princess like a prize. "The queen has commanded me to capture her and bring her back to the Winter Realm."

I dropped Princess Clara's hand and drew my saber from the scabbard at my hip. "You'll have to go through me first, and I will never allow you to take her anywhere near that despot you call queen."

The princess' mouth fell open and she gaped at the two of us. "You're going to fight over me? This is a strange dream. I might need to seek out some serious psychological analysis in the morning."

Konig grinned at her like she was the sweetest of sugar plums and he was going to eat her up. Princess Clara smiled right back at him, and a shiver went from my skin to my spine. She knew nothing of Konig's treachery. I would not allow her to be tempted by his good looks and charm.

"Not on my watch, traitor." I raised my sword and stepped in front of the princess. For the briefest of moments, I thought I saw hurt flash in Konig's eyes. Good. The way he betrayed us all should cause him infinite pain.

"Seems I have no choice, once again." He lifted his weapon and eyed my bandaged arm. "En garde, Nutcracker. Do your worst."

I advanced with three fast, hard blows. If I could back Konig up far enough, the princess and I could make a dash for the portal. He retreated all right. Too easily.

He always was the most cunning among us. I slashed at him again, and he jumped away, leading me further from the princess and hardly tarrying himself. This was a mouse trap if ever I saw one, but I knew how to push his buttons too. "Fight, you bastard. You're not going to let an injured Nutcracker best you, are you?"

"You're the bastard, not me, remember?" For the first time in the fight, he struck at me and grazed my already-injured arm, drawing some blood, but not doing any real damage.

I deflected his blade and spun to check on Princess Clara's safety and position. Fuck.

She squealed and jumped away, kicking at the little beasts that were gathering near her ankles. "I don't like this part of the dream. Shoo, you dirty little things, shoo. Get away."

The princess was surrounded by dozens of mice who were trying to shepherd her toward the portal. If they pushed her through, who knows where she'd land in the Winter Realm.

Konig advanced on me with renewed efforts now. If his minions took her through the portal, he alone would be able to find her on the other side. Dammit. I would not let the hopes of the entire realm be dashed before they even knew we'd found the lost princess.

"She's practically in the arms of the queen already, Nuss. I thought you'd try a bit harder to save her than this. Perhaps you want her to be controlled. Is that your dark fantasy, or are you too much of a bright shining snowflake to desire her that way?" His blows hit hard and with only one working arm, it was a struggle to keep my balance.

His sword wasn't the only thing wounding me. He knew I already had a deep need for the princess. His animal senses could sniff out emotions just as well as if he were reading my mind. I may not be as pure as a true guardsman should be, but he could use Princess Clara's sweet innocence against her.

"You have no idea how I feel about the princess, and you could never understand what we all want from her. Neither you nor your queen will ever have command over her." I couldn't let that happen. With redoubled effort, I jumped forward, crashing our swords together and shoving Konig back across the room. I spun and ran toward the princess, hoping to gather her up and jump through the tree's portal before he could catch me.

Konig wasn't going to let me get anywhere near her to set an intention on the portal to guide us to my home and the meeting place of the other Nutcrackers in the Land of the Snowflakes. He jumped high into the air, like only a shifter from the Land of Animals could, grabbed onto the chandelier, and propelled himself through the air to land right in my path.

A chill blew through me seeing I'd been bested by that damn rat. With one easy move, he could grab her and take her to his queen. I charged forward with no concern for my own safety. It wasn't a gentleman's attack and that was my only advantage now.

Konig dodged and fell back into the tree, sending his minions scattering in multiple directions. An idea formed in my mind that could save her from being kidnapped. Almost instantly, I discarded it.

No. I couldn't send her through on her own. That could be catastrophic. Madness. She knew nothing of our world and would be alone in the snow, lost. That would be even worse than allowing her to go with the mice. At least someone would know where she was if they took her.

What choice did I have? None. I jumped up onto the closest chair, and then the table, doing my best to gain an advantage over my opponent. We'd trained and fought together. He knew my moves and strategies just as well I knew his. There was no way he'd allow me to escape with the Princess.

The only option was sending her on her own, but without a clear intention on her part, she could be captured, or worse, before we found her. Damn and blast. I should have explained how the portal between realms worked, but I hadn't thought she'd need to know. The best I could do now was give her a mental picture.

It would give away the location of the Nutcracker resistance, but I had to trust that my fellow guardsmen could keep her and the rest of the oppressed safe when the Mouse Queen inevitably came for them. I hated the idea of not being there with her, but this was the closest I had to a plan, even if it was a shitty one.

"Nice try, Konig. Don't worry, the Princess will use her own intention to get to the rest of her Guard." I pushed my voice out loud so that she would hear me and hopefully understand. Even putting the thought into her head to focus on my brothers in arms could help her arrive safely in their castle keep. Or so I hoped.

Princess Clara caught a stray mouse with the toe of her dainty little shoe and flung it straight into the tree. The magic of the portal fizzled and fritzed as the animal was sent back into the Winter Realm. Her eyes went big and round like fluffy snowflakes, and she snorted with surprise. "I will?"

"Yes, Princess. Visualize the rest of your Guard." I had no choice but to reveal who they were. If the Land of Animals didn't already know who they were battling, they would now. "The Sugar Plum and Dew Drop Princes, the Gingerbread Viking, they are all waiting for you. Go quickly through the tree and into their care. Save the Realm."

I jumped off the table and shoved her toward the tree. She needed only to touch even one needle for the portal to open and take her to her true home.

"Not as long as I am under the command of the Mouse Queen." Steely white light flashed in Konig's eyes and he charged toward me with an animalistic war cry piercing the air and my very heart. He threw his sword like a long dagger, spinning end over end, directly at the tree.

If he destroyed the portal, he would trap us all here. I

couldn't allow that to happen. It had taken help from a powerful magician to get me through the veil before the portal opened and the spell wouldn't work in reverse. I couldn't allow that to happen.

I threw myself in the path of the dagger, hoping I wouldn't have to sacrifice my life to get the princess back to the Winter Realm. I so wanted to be there to support her through the trials she would have to endure and overcome to reclaim the seven crowns.

A flash of red whooshed in front of my eyes, my heart stopped, and the world slowed as if frozen on a cold winter's night. Instead of the ripping of flesh or wood, the sword tore through the billowing skirt of Princess Clara's dress, as she flung herself right in its path.

The sword clattered to the ground, the sound restarting my heart. Princess Clara shook out her skirts and spun around. "Well, that's one way to get pockets in a ball gown."

The Mouse Prince was still advancing upon us, that same icy look in his eyes. The mice that had been scattered to the far corners of the room stampeded, surrounding us on three sides. Konig, however, had made a critical error. There was nothing now standing between us and the portal to the Winter Realm.

"Go, Princess Clara, go, go, go." I grabbed her hand and pushed her into the tree. I stepped into the magic with her and set my intention on the Land of Snowflakes and the waiting guards. Just as the lights and scent of the tree overwhelmed my senses, the tip of the Mouse Prince's sword slashed at my broken arm, tearing a gash from shoulder to elbow, then continued on and ripped open my leg.

The pain seared right through my intention and the portal swirled and spun us, not knowing where we wanted to go. Princess Clara screamed and her hand was wrenched from mine. A moment later, I fell, bloodied and battered, into the soft snow, surrounded by a huge forest of Christmas trees that stretched as far as the eye could see.

"Nutcracker? Are you okay? Oh God. You're bleeding. Help. Someone help us, please." She shouted into the night, but there was no answer.

STRANDED IN THE CHRISTMAS TREE FOREST

CLARAMARIE

*M*y words echoed through the crisp and chilly night air. The Nutcracker and I were very clearly the only people in this entire forest of sparkling Christmas trees. There must've been someone here at some point to have decorated them with the twinkling lights and shiny stars. So where had they all disappeared to now?

I was so over this dream sparked by Drosselmeyer's fairy stories from my youth. I wish he hadn't reminded me about them today.

The bit with the two incredibly good-looking men fighting over me was fun, but when the rodents showed up and the Nutcracker threw himself in front of the deadly flying sword, I was ready to wake up. I did not remember any of Drosselmeyer's stories having horrible creepy mice. Yech.

I must have left a window open in my room where I was fast asleep, because I was really feeling as if I were standing around in a winter wonderland, but there was no time to rub my arms or do a few jumping jacks to get my blood flowing, not as long as the nutcracker's blood was spilling into the snow. I didn't want to dislike the delicious warrior who'd been trying to kidnap me, but it turned out he was the bad guy in this dream scenario.

Why were the hot ones always the most evil?

"Nutcracker, wake up." What had the other warrior called him? Right. "Nuss, can you hear me? Please don't be dead."

I looked around again, hoping against hope that a Red Cross unit dressed up as Santas might come dashing through the snow in a one-horse open sleigh. No such luck. What I did see were little yellow eyes peering at me from the nearest trees. Not just one pair, or even two. The longer I looked, the more I saw.

Eek. There were some kind of animals staring at us. I hoped they weren't scavengers or carnivores who were attracted by the scent of blood. The Nutcracker had lost his sword and I had nothing more than some hairpins to defend us with.

"Shoo. Go away. I don't have the time or energy for you. Shoo, shoo." I waved my hands at them. For a moment, the eyes disappeared, and I thought they'd gone away.

Wrong. The little beasties or whatever they were just dropped down from the branches they were hiding in, to the ground. Some even ventured further into the snow. It was too dark even with the lights on the trees for me to see what they were, but the way they slowly crept toward us didn't feel safe.

I scooped up some of the snow around us and made myself a quick pile of snowballs. I had fairly good aim and a great arm. If I had to, I'd at least surprise them, and at best scare them off. "Don't you come any closer."

How I wished I had a fire. That would keep them away, and warm us up at the same time. Nuss groaned and I took my eyes off the little buggers for just a moment to check on him. Thank goodness he wasn't dead. I gave him a gentle shake on the shoulder to see if I could rouse him, but he only made a pained noise.

I was on my own, taking care of someone else. Not like I hadn't felt that before. When I looked up again, the creatures had come closer and were surrounding us. They were small and I cringed at the thought that they could be more mice. Eek.

These snowballs had better work. I picked one up and cocked my arm back, ready to let fly. What would be even better is if I could just freaking wake up. I'd had darker and scarier nightmares than this before and I'd always woken up in a fright. Why couldn't that happen right now?

I pinched the sensitive underside of my arm because I'd read that people did that to wake themselves up. Didn't do anything but make my arm hurt.

Shoot. What else could I do to get out of this? Wait. I'd also read that people who realized they were dreaming could then manipulate the dream world around them. Turn a nightmare into something more fun even. I had my doubts about that. I hadn't been able to control anything else since Nuss appeared to me in my sleep. Although, it's not like I had lots of other options. It was worth a shot.

Okay, think positive. Those aren't little monsters with mouths full of sharp teeth who want to eat us. They are...uh...bunnies. Soft, fluffy bunnies. I narrowed my eyes at the creatures coming closer and closer, willing them to be soft and squishy balls of fluff.

One of them hopped forward into the halo of light around the tree I was under. Holy snowballs. It worked. The bunny rabbit tipped its head inquisitively and looked up at me like I was the most fascinating thing it had ever seen. Wait. Rabbits don't climb trees. They live in hutches under the ground.

The little animal shook itself and piles of fluffy snowflakes fluttered into the air. I was surprised enough to see a fluffy bunny come bouncing into the light, but I was gob smacked when it turned into a tiny pink pixie hidden under all that snow. Holy shit snacks, this dream kept getting weirder and weirder.

I had no idea if the pixie would understand me, but there was certainly no one else to ask for help. "Hello, there. Can you help us?"

The pixie flew up in a loopty-loop and then dive bombed into the darkness, where their friends or family were waiting. A whole rainbow of colors went crazy with activity, flying this way and that, gathering something and bringing it over to us.

"What in the world are you doing?" I watched them flit and flutter about and began to lose hope that they could help us or be able to contact someone who could.

The same pink pixie flew right up to my face, bowed, and held out an arm solemnly as if presenting royalty. Into the circle of light came a whole multi-colored crew of their kind, carrying an intricately carved wooden tray above their heads. On the tray were two wooden mugs, decorated just as beautifully as any fine china, filled with some kind of steaming hot drink.

They carefully guided the tray, setting it down in front of me. A blue pixie made some insistent squeaking noises and pointed to the cups. Perhaps this was a curative potion for my poor injured Nutcracker.

"Thank you." The pixies who'd brought the tray over all went into fits of excitement and clapped their hands madly at my words, then stopped and stared when I picked up one of the mugs and brought it up to my nose to smell, clearly waiting to see if I'd drink it.

This better not be like *Alice in Wonderland* where I shrink or grow from eating and drinking stuff. I'd rather it didn't turn me into a mouse or fairy or a pixie, either. I took a long whiff of the hot drink and was met with the most wonderful chocolate scent.

The pink pixie flew up and looked inside the cup, then at me, and made an encouraging motion to drink it. I nodded at them. "Okay, I'll try it."

I blew on the steam and then took a tentative sip. An amazing explosion of flavor like nothing I'd ever tasted before went through my mouth and down to my stomach, warming me from the inside out. "Whoa. How did you do that?"

I smiled at the pixies and took a longer, deeper drink. This hot chocolate definitely had something special in it besides milk. I wasn't the slightest bit cold anymore and that, just as much as anything, revitalized me. My fears melted away, along with the chill. If a simple drink from some pixies could do that, I couldn't wait to have something to eat.

"You are clever little things. Thank you. I'm glad you're on my side." They buzzed around excitedly, and I found it cute and adorable how they responded with so much joy whenever I praised them. "Now let's see if we can help my friend, the Nutcracker."

If I was cold, he probably was too, even if he was unconscious and couldn't feel it. His face was ashen, even in the dim light. I lifted his head, doing my best to prop him up in my lap. The other mug still steamed, and I was sure even if I could get just a little into him, it would help.

From this awkward position I wouldn't be able to put the cup to his lips without spilling it all down the front of him. Even if I could, I didn't know if he could swallow it. Perhaps if I just wet his lips with it.

The thought of even touching his mouth gave me that same tingling feeling in my belly. How shameful of me to be feeling turned on, even thinking about kissing those soft, sensual lips of his, when he was dying right in front of me.

ClaraMarie, pull yourself together. Stop it.

My little self-chastisement didn't help my inappropriate thoughts, but it got me moving. I grabbed the second mug and brought it close so as not to spill any. I dipped my fingers into the hot chocolate and brought the drops to Nuss's mouth as quickly as I could, just painting his bottom lip with it.

The liquid glistened there, but he didn't move. Of course not, silly. He didn't get it in his mouth where it could do any good. I swallowed and tried again.

This time I pressed the very tips of my fingers into his mouth but went no farther than his teeth. The drips seeped in and instantly some of his color returned. Emboldened by his improvement, I did it again, this time a bit more brazenly, pushing two of my fingers covered in hot chocolate onto his tongue.

His mouth moved and he swallowed, almost sucking on my fingers. It was getting hard for me to breathe, and I had to consciously pull the air into my lungs and push it back out.

The pink pixie buzzed about and as far as I could tell, she was urging me to give him more. She didn't have to twist my arm. I dipped my fingers into the chocolate again and repeated my actions. Nuss swirled his tongue over my fingers and swallowed again. This time, when I went to withdraw them, his hand flew up, grabbing my wrist and holding it steady as he sucked off every last bit of flavor that could possibly be on my skin.

If I had ever been cold in my life, I couldn't even remember it now. Heat radiated from him, into me, and all around us. I wouldn't be surprised if the snow beneath us melted.

His eyes fluttered open, and he stared up at me. He rolled his tongue beneath my fingers again and released the hold his mouth had on me, but I forgot to pull away. The little pink pixie landed on my hand, looked up at me, back to the Nutcracker, and back again. Then it giggled and did a little pirouette.

What a funny little thing. I shook my head and pulled my hand away to swirl the liquid in the cup. If he was awake, maybe I could get him to take a drink on his own. I certainly didn't pull away because I needed a minute to compose myself and stop thinking about what else Nuss could do with his tongue. No, not at all.

I took several deep breaths, to uh, blow on the cup of hot chocolate, not to keep myself from kissing him. I was just looking out for him. I didn't want him to burn his mouth. Or his lips, or his tongue.

I bit my own lip and smiled at them both, and very carefully I pressed the cup to Nuss's mouth. "Take a sip if you can. I don't really know what's in it, but I think it will help you feel better until I can find more help."

He did as I asked, but a little dribble escaped and ran down the side of his mouth. I really should lick that up. Ack. What in the world was wrong with me? Nuss's own tongue darted out to lick up the escaped drip and I just stared at him.

His eyes drifted shut again, but his breathing was easier, some of his color had returned, and when I checked, his wound didn't appear to be seeping any more blood into his clothes and onto the snow. Thank goodness.

I carefully removed his head from my lap, but even before I could settle him onto the ground a dozen more pixies came over and created a makeshift pillow out of the soft under-branches of the big pine tree. He would be much more comfortable that way than just in the snow.

"Thank you again, my new little friends. Now, let's see if you can help me find someone more my size who can explain where we are. Barring that, maybe some better shelter than under a tree, somewhere I can build a fire." I stood and brushed off the skirt of my dress. The brilliant red material was soaked both from the tumble in the snow when we first landed here and from sitting in it with Nuss. The fairies' drink may have warmed me for now, but wet clothes in a deserted winter forest with no shelter was a death knell.

My life up to this point had not exactly prepared me for

surviving in the wild. I knew how to argue with my brother and politely ask the cook to make me some dinner, not make a shelter and give a dying man first aid. I didn't know much of anything other than how to dance and say please and thank you.

I walked a few paces in one direction, then circled back and walked the other way just to see if there were any indications of human life. Nothing, but I did find a small clearing where tall spindly trees formed an almost dome-like canopy overhead, protecting the ground from quite so much snow. It was the closest thing I'd found to shelter, and I did a little dance around in a wide circle feeling a modicum of joy that we could at least sit on dry ground here.

I rushed back to Nuss and found the pixies dancing and twirling around too. They'd been joined by another fanciful being. While the little pixies were quite androgynous, this slightly larger golden creature had distinctly female features and wings more like that of a bird than the butterfly-like ones of the fairies. She reminded me of the angel that sat on top of the Christmas tree.

The golden girl floated down as if on a gentle breeze and landed on Nuss's chest. She held a piece of paper in her hands and nodded and tipped her head to me as if she wanted me to take it. Nuss's name was scrawled in heavy block print across the front.

Someone knew we were here. Or at least that he was. I spun in a slow circle and peered through the trees to try to see who might have sent this messenger. Whoever it was, they had to be nearby to have seen us spill through to this place, but I saw nothing besides more trees, more fairies, and more angels. "Please, if you're hiding, come out. Nuss is hurt and unconscious. He can't read your note."

I waited but no one came. Fine. Maybe the note would give me directions or a clue as what to do next. I gently took it from the tiny angel and lifted the flap of the envelope. Inside, on a card, were five little words written in the same rough hand. *Where the fuck are you?*

I turned the card over and there was a neater, slightly more flowery scrawl that read - *And do you have the princess?*

THE IRE OF THE MOUSE QUEEN

KONIG

I knelt in humble submission before the Mouse Queen of the Winter Realm. I had failed her, failed to bring her the lost princess of the Land of Spirit and Magic, failed to carry out her orders.

All of which I would be punished for. Yet it wouldn't be through receiving any lashes, or reduced rations, or being sent to sleep out in the frigid winter storm that her ire would be brought down upon me. No, my punishment would be to watch my people suffer in my place.

Had I been able, I might have stayed in the gentle human world where at least my kind could scavenge table scraps and crumbs, and sleep in the walls of warm, opulent houses. Like the one Princess Clara had been hidden in all these years.

Deserting those who depended on me to defend the realm and bring peace was never an option. Princess Clara's allure had made me forget that for a brief shining instant, but no, I would never give up my place as the Mouse Prince, not even for one delicious moment with her.

The Queen remained quiet, and that more than anything else foreshadowed the severity of what was to come. If she'd yelled and screamed and thrown chairs at me, rather than stewed in silence, I'd have been happier.

Her voice started low and at almost a whisper, but there was no mistaking the command in her tone. "You will not fail me again, Konig. If you do not bring Princess Clara to me by the time the magician's clock next strikes twelve, you'll regret you were ever born."

As if I didn't already.

"Get out of my sight. I don't even know if I can count on you anymore." She dismissed me with a wave of her hand, as if I was the most insignificant thing to cross her path today. She signaled to one of her attendants and though she whispered, I could still hear her say, "Bring the boy to me, when that pathetic creature has gone."

I knew better than to think her disdain for me was anything but feigned or that I'd escaped her wrath. I pitied whoever this boy was that she was summoning. Perhaps he would serve her better than I ever had.

"Oh, and Konig. Send me twelve of your best warriors. One for each day of Christmas, until you either bring me Princess Clara, or the portal closes. I'd like to have a little fun with them." Her voice was all sweetness and light. Her meaning— death and despair.

Shit. There was the punishment I'd been waiting for. She'd destroy our army one by one just to hurt me. "If you take my best warriors, it will take me longer to capture the princess."

The Mouse Queen leaped from her throne and landed behind me. I could have turned and defended myself, but that would only bring more consequences. She extended the claws she normally kept so well hidden and scraped one across my throat.

If it wasn't the coward's way out that would leave my people without a barrier between them and her fury, I'd tell her to kill me now. I already lived a half-life as her pawn as it was. The image of Princess Clara in her Christmas party dress, hearty and hale, so full of spirit and magic, helped me keep my mouth shut.

"Don't ever call her that in my presence again. She is no princess of this realm, she has no claim to my throne. She is nothing more than an empty symbol to the rebel Nutcrackers and I won't dignify her with even the title of such a position." Her furious protests rang through the empty halls of Christmas Castle, echoing off the barren walls and spotless floors.

We both knew her denial was false, yet how harshly she clung to it. "Of course not, my Queen," I murmured.

"Now go. Take your warriors with you, and know that if you return empty-handed again, their lives will not be the only ones forfeited." She released me and marched back to her lonely throne.

She hadn't always been this way. Once upon a time, she'd been a stern but still loving mother to so many. Now there was only me, and memories of the day the Winter Realm froze her heart.

I hurried off to the barracks that had once belonged to the soldiers of the Nutcracker Guard. I'd been so proud the day I'd first walked in to find my bunkmates already fast friends. Five princes of the Realm, all born on the same day, choosing service over the easy life.

Now, the stench of urine, moldy bread, and unkempt bodies, smashed together in the only serviceable building left standing after the last rebel attack, made the quarters a shadow of their former glory. Still, I would cram more in to give them shelter from the storms ahead.

I gathered six of my most trusted warriors together near the entrance, where the air was fresher. I would not ask those with families to join me on this mission. If they had nothing and no one they loved, it was harder to hurt them. "The lost princess is here somewhere in the Winter Realm, but we have no good indication as to where the portal spit her out. She didn't have a solid intention on where it should take her, so she could be anywhere."

"Is it possible she's been taken by the rebels?"

I could only hope. "They are likely on the search for her as well. The faster each of you can get to one of the lands, the sooner we'll know what we're up against. I'll take the Land of Snowflakes."

They looked at me like I'd grown a Christmas tree on my head, but I ignored them. "Divide the other lands up amongst yourselves and use the mice to send me a message when you're sure she isn't being hidden by the locals there."

I got a round of *Yes, sirs* and more than one look that said they knew what I was doing. Yes, we all knew she was most likely to be in the Land of Snowflakes because that's where the rebels were operating from. We knew that. The Queen, however, did not.

We also knew it meant I was the most likely to be captured or killed in a battle against the elite trained Nutcracker Guard who'd sided with the rebellion. So be it. With the princess here, getting captured might be my best chance to infiltrate the rebel alliance of the other lands from the inside. One way or another, her presence here after all these years would bring this war on Christmas to an end, and someone would have to die to do it. If it had to be me, I was willing to make that sacrifice.

"Go, and Godspeed." With their dismissal, each of them shifted into their animal forms and a moment later, I did the same. It was faster and easier to travel this way. One of the only advantages of being one of our kind.

I sped through the snow and cold to the northernmost land in the realm. I would have to pass through the Land of Comfort and Joy and their Christmas Tree Forest to reach my destination. The marzipan fairies would provide even me with a respite from the journey.

I ran and ran, pushing my body as hard as I could. A more leisurely pace would give me too much time to think. Better to push myself to the point of exhaustion. If I couldn't consider what I had to do, it would be easier to carry out my duties.

The edge of the forest came into view and the first thing I noticed was a flurry of activity where normally all should be quiet. The messenger angels were all aflutter, and the marzipan fairies were glowing with their joyful light that came from serving someone who appreciated them.

It couldn't be the princess. That would be too damn easy. Yet that was exactly whose scent I caught. Princess Clara. She smelled of cinnamon, licorice, and fate.

I'd found her.

It couldn't be just luck, and what's more, she appeared to be all alone. She was dancing in a chapel of birch trees, and I was fucking mesmerized.

I shifted and hid behind one of the trees, watching her, wanting her. She twirled and smiled, filled with a joy I would never know. I selfishly wished for the gash in her dress to tear open further to give me a glimpse of her shapely legs.

What I wanted to do to her with my face between her legs wasn't decent. I grew hard thinking about hearing her cry out as I gave her orgasm after orgasm and had to grind my hips against my own hand. My pants became distinctly uncomfortable with visions of wrapping her hair around my fist and pushing my cock deep into her mouth.

A princess like her would never get on her knees for a prince from the Land of Animals. One of the Fae princes maybe, the Gingerbread Viking prince perhaps, but never the lowly Mouse Prince. I shuddered at the thought. It made my fantasies all the more taboo and delicious.

Now, what to do with her? I was sworn to bring her back to the Mouse Queen. However, the queen made a mistake when she didn't specify that I do that immediately. She'd given me far too much time to comply with her commands.

No one else even knew where I was, nor would I be missed for several days. I could so easily kidnap the sweet princess and have her all to myself for a while. She would learn to love how a beast could make her feel like a dirty plaything.

The princess halted her twirling and scurried back into the light of the Christmas trees. Fuck. I'd missed my chance to nab her because I'd been too busy daydreaming about having her all to myself.

I stalked quietly through the trees, following her, and discovered her sitting on the ground next to Nuss. The snow around him was stained with blood, but he wasn't dead. I refused to feel guilty about his wounds. He and the other princes betrayed me and my people so deeply. I would never forgive them.

Not even now that they'd finally found the princess and brought her back to the Winter Realm. No, now it was a race between us to see who would help her access the powers of the seven crowns and, ultimately, who would get control of the Winter Realm.

Never again would I allow my people to be subjugated by those who thought they were superior.

Even as I thought this, the Fae princes I'd once called friends appeared, riding their steeds through the snow like an avenging cavalry. How had they also found her so quickly, with Nuss unconscious?

Princess Clara had a message in her hands, and a messenger angel sat on Nuss's chest. I looked up and saw the trail of gold the angels had left in the air along their paths. Sneaky bastards.

They'd sent him a note and then followed the angel as she searched him out to deliver it. Very clever.

I should have killed Nuss when I had the chance. Even an angel can't deliver a message to a dead man. Then I'd have the princess to myself, and they could all get fucked. Instead, they would now also have the opportunity to make her theirs.

Nuss was too pure of heart to sully her with his own carnal needs, but the Fae princes—too fucking good-looking for their own good, unmatched in beauty by anyone but Princess Clara —weren't. They would seduce her just as easily as they would any man or woman in their path, although unless they knew where the broken crowns of their lands were, it would all be for naught.

Without the Gingerbread Viking here, and Nuss too injured to fight, I had a chance at beating them and capturing Princess Clara. It would be a close fight, but I always was better with a sword than either of them. I had to be.

I drew my weapon and snuck closer, looking for the right opportunity to take them down and grab the princess. I could have dived in at once, if my feet hadn't been swarmed by an entire platoon of mice. Mice that were under the queen's control, not mine.

THE THREE HORSEMEN OF CHRISTMASPOCALYPSE

CLARAMARIE

The sound of galloping coming toward us caught my attention. I looked around, wondering if I'd see humans riding horses or mythical beings like centaurs. It turned out to be two ethereal men, who were far too pretty to even look at, charging toward us astride their horses.

Fae princes. Like in Drosselmeyer's stories.

I was starting to question my sanity when they stopped just a few feet from us, looking more like gods than men. They practically glowed, one with a violet aura, the other dewy green, and don't think I missed their pointy ears under their long flowing locks. Were they some kind of grown-up fairy men? Were the little pixies who'd worked so hard to help me and Nuss their children?

"Princess Clara. Forgive us for taking so long to find you. Are you well? Have you been injured?" The man who glowed with a soft green aura jumped off his horse, pulled me into his arms, and kissed me frantically.

Those same tingles that skittered through me when I first saw Nuss and then the warrior with the mice warmed me once again. The way he explored my mouth as if kissing me was his dying wish, and the feeling of this being so incredibly right, made me forget for a good long minute that I didn't know him, and he certainly hadn't asked my permission to get so up close and personal.

When he broke the kiss, I felt as though I'd been drinking delicious dandelion wine. He placed a hand on my cheek, then I was whisked into the other man's arms and the tingles started all over again. I looked up into eyes that were as purple as a ripe summer plum. He stared back down at me like I was the most beautiful girl in the world.

"You are even more delectable than I imagined you would be." He lowered his mouth to mine, and where the other kiss had been excitingly frenzied, this one was slowly sensual, intoxicating, and sweet. He literally tasted like sugared fruit and brandy.

If this was about to turn into a sex dream, I was so down for that. I still liked a good fairy tale, but if it was much dirtier, I could confess my sins at church tomorrow. Tonight, I would happily revel in this male appreciation and passion. It's not like I had much of that in real life. That's what dreams were for, right?

He broke off the second kiss far before I was ready, but I looked forward to what might happen next. I'd admit, only to myself of course, that I'd occasionally had naughty fantasies about being taken by two men at once. I was even more sure now that all of this was a clear manifestation of all the things I longed for but would never have once I married.

Drosselmeyer would dote on me, but I could never feel any real passion for him. I never should have agreed to the arrangement in the first place. Perhaps in the morning, I would use the quiet Christmas day to consider whether there was another way to save the Stahlbaum name and help my father.

"Luscious princess, where is Nuss? Why has he delayed your arrival? You two haven't—" He waggled his eyebrows at me.

"What? No. Oh, no, *no*. Nuss was injured in a fight. A warrior with an army of mice said he had come to kidnap me." I was thoroughly embarrassed that I'd gotten so distracted by these handsome men and their kisses that I hadn't immediately directed them to Nuss. They might have first aid supplies, or at least be able to take us somewhere with a doctor.

The green fairy immediately dropped to the ground beside Nuss and ran his hands over the injuries from the sword, and his broken arm. "I see you've started the healing process. Apologies, did we interrupt you?"

"Me? I didn't do anything but give him a bit of the hot chocolate these nice little pixies brought us. I was hoping you'd know some first aid or where the closest doctor is located." I glanced between the two men and saw they both had surprised looks on their faces.

He rose and cupped my cheek. "Then the stories are true. You truly don't know who and what you are."

The stories are all true. Drosselmeyer's characters from his tales of adventure in the Winter Realm were repeating his own words back to me. I got a strange uncomfortable feeling like pins and needles, but inside my brain.

"I know exactly who and what I am." That was a lie straight from the pits of Hell, but it felt good rolling off my tongue. I was many things to many people…a daughter, a bratty sister, a fiancée, someone to be pitied, someone to be picked on…yet none of those was the real, authentic me. Here in this dreamland, I could decide who I wanted to be and make it so. Tomorrow morning my life might go back to whatever it was before, but tonight, I was an adventuress like never before. "I am ClaraMarie Stahlbaum…and I am a dancer. Now if you don't mind, I'd like you to explain how I can help Nuss here, since he almost sacrificed his life to save mine."

The purple Fae prince's eyes went dark and sparkly. "I'd very much like to see you dance, ClaraMarie Stahlbaum, but you are so much more than that here in the Winter Realm. You are the lost Princess Clara, of the Land of Spirit and Magic. More importantly, you are the one woman who has the power to defeat the evil Mouse Queen and free us all from her despotic reign."

Lost princess, huh? Nuss had also called me a princess. None of Drosselmeyer's stories had a princess in them, only a warrior woman who fought alongside her consorts. That clearly wasn't me, so I guess I'd conjured up a more appropriate role for myself. Not as interesting as the Vivandiere, but close.

I remembered these men from the stories, but how did the Fae princes know me? "I'm sorry, I recognize you as Fae royalty, but who exactly are you?"

The two of them gave each other a look communicating something without words. "More apologies, my lady. We assumed Nuss would have filled you in, but we now see that with the troubles getting you into the realm, he was unable to do so. I am Zucker, Fae Prince of the Land of Sweets."

"And I am Tau, Fae Prince of the Land of Flowers, at your service." The way he said service gave it a very naughty connotation.

Kissed by two princes, fought over by two warriors. What was next, being carried off and bedded by the first-born Viking from the stories?

Oops. I shouldn't have said that.

A third horse pounded in through the trees, sending the pixies and angels scattering. A huge mountain of a man with an axe strapped across his back and a braided red beard jumped to the ground, scooped me up, threw me half over his shoulder, and strode back toward his mount.

"Put me down. Let go and put me down." I kicked and pounded at his back, but I got a slap to the ass for my troubles. If he wasn't so big, with more muscles than I'd ever seen in my entire life combined, I would have worried he would drop me. No one had ever picked me up before. Not since I'd been a small child, anyway. Here he was toting me around like a fluffy marshmallow.

"Come lads, I've seen the footprints of our little mouse friend Konig about. If he's here, the Queen's army won't be far behind. Let's ride and get our prize to safety." His voice boomed with a slight accent and the self-confidence of no one I'd ever met before. Not like Fritz's blustering arrogance. He was simply the alpha in the room, and everyone knew it.

I also understood from what he was saying that he was on Zucker and Tau's side. That emboldened me enough to chastise him. "I am not your prize, and I'm not going anywhere without Nuss. So. Put. Me. Down."

"She's a fiery little thing, isn't she?" He turned back to the Fae princes, and I got a mouthful of horsetail. "We'll need that to melt the hearts of the realm."

"Leb, put the princess down before she melts you. She's already formed a loyalty to our captain here, and I for one would prefer if he didn't die just yet." Tau dashed over and stopped the giant before he could climb on his horse.

"Yeah, what he said," I yelled while trying to right myself. From my upside-down position, the world was wonky, but I noticed things I hadn't before. Like the tiny homes that must belong to the pixies, that looked like little mushrooms tucked around the base of the trees. I also spotted dozens of mouse footprints in the snow.

Out of the corner of my eye, something dark flashed, getting closer, streaking from one tree to another. Yech, I hoped it wasn't more mice. I might just climb up on top of the Viking's horse myself, if we had to fight off the squeaky little monsters again.

But maybe it was the dark warrior. That shouldn't excite me so much. He'd wanted to kidnap me and do terrible things to me. I shivered, and it wasn't from the cold.

"What?" The Viking turned again, and I got another mouthful of horse tail. "Princess, why have you not healed him yet? He needs nothing more than your magical kiss."

"Put me down, right the hell now, you delicious-smelling brute." You'd think being slung over someone's shoulder, only a few inches from their strong muscled buttocks, would mean that the last thing you'd want to do is take a sniff. In fact, I hadn't meant to, but all three times I'd yelled to be let down, I had to suck in a good amount of air into my lungs, and along with that air came not gross man-butt smells, but rich, mouth-watering spices like freshly baked gingerbread and strong Turkish coffee.

Before I could spend much more time contemplating whether he would taste as good as he smelled, my body was dragged back across his shoulder, then down, down, down his tall, built, half-naked, did I mention built, torso. When I landed on my feet, I was out of breath and looking right up into his chocolatey gaze. Without taking his eyes from me, he grinned and said, "You hear that, lads, she thinks I smell delicious."

"Oh, my fucking flowers, we'll never hear the end of this." The eye-roll was clear in Tau's tone. The three of them had obviously spent a lot of time together and were tight friends.

"Leb, will you stop trying to seduce her with your sheer size, and let her heal Nuss?" Zucker gave me a wink and waved the Viking toward the tree where Nuss was lying. "Then we can be on our way."

"Save a kiss for me, my lady." He lowered his head to mine and brushed his lips over the very corner of my mouth so gently that I found myself reaching for his touch. That a giant warrior could be both sweet and gentle, as well as dominant and grabby, was frying my brain cells.

The fact that I was letting him almost kiss me after manhandling me and calling me a prize was something I was going to attribute to my deepest, darkest fantasies coming to life in a dreamworld. The longer I stayed asleep, the more I wanted this to be my reality, and begrudged ever waking up.

I blinked a few dozen times, trying to get my mind out of the gutter where it was currently rolling around in the snow with three sexy men, and back focused on my task. It didn't work until Leb grabbed me by the hip and shoulder and spun me away from him. He gave me a little shove and I stumbled toward Nuss.

Right. Heal him with a kiss. "I'm just supposed to kiss him, and his injuries will magically disappear?"

I suppose it worked in Sleeping Beauty, why not in my fairy tale of a dream? Although that was a true love's first kiss. Nuss had stirred something inside of me, but I barely knew him. I certainly didn't love him. "Should I say a spell or something? I don't know how this is supposed to work."

Zucker knelt next to Nuss and held out his hand to help me down. "You're the princess of the Land of Spirit and Magic, and you have more power than you know. It's simply been suppressed while you have resided in your temporary shelter in the human realm. Believe, look within yourself, and it will reignite."

I had spirit, all right. That's what had gotten me through the years of dance classes when no one wanted me there or thought I could do it. I'd be depending on that same part of me in the future to see me through years of a loveless marriage. Magic? That was a stretch.

I wasn't sure, even in a dream, I could believe I had that kind of power. I'd never known magic. That wasn't the life fate bestowed on me.

Even without belief, I had to try to help Nuss. I wrapped my hand around the necklace at my throat and closed my eyes, trying to imagine the pendant was more than a last gift from a mother I'd never known. Instead, I conjured up the fairy stories Drosselmeyer told me as a child about a magical realm filled with snowflakes, sweets, flowers, cookies, and crowns for everyone.

Tau's voice whispered in my ear. "Yes, that's it, Clara, whatever you're doing is working."

"Look at her glow. I wonder if she'll do that when I'm giving her magical fucking orgasms too." Leb's dirty words broke my concentration, but when I opened my eyes, a halo of red light did indeed surround me.

Okay, here goes. I brushed a lock of hair from Nuss's face and leaned forward to kiss him.

"Don't move another inch, Princess. You're all under arrest, by order of the Mouse Queen, for inciting rebellion in the Realm."

I snapped my head around to see the same dark warrior who'd injured Nuss in the first place, brandishing his sword, threatening me and the three men who'd come to my rescue. Damn it. This part was not in the stories.

Leb pulled the axe from his back and swung it over his head. "Your so-called queen has no authority over us anymore, Konig. Feel free to surrender now and perhaps Princess Clara will go easy on you."

Me? I didn't even understand why they were fighting in the first place, never mind how I was a part of it. It's not like I knew how to fight anyone, unless they challenged me to a dance-off.

"Don't make me enter into combat with you, Leb. I will have no choice but to kill you and take Princess Clara with me." He glanced over at me and once again I was sure I saw regret in his eyes.

Zucker and Tau jumped up and placed themselves between

me and the fight. They drew their weapons and Tau pointed his arrow at the warrior. "You chose the wrong side in this battle."

The warrior didn't answer the men but looked directly at me. "Don't even think about kissing that Nutcracker, Clara."

The way he said it was very strange. Not quite a warning, more like a dare. One that I was taking. I squeezed the crown pendant at my throat one last time and laid a big, slightly sloppy kiss right on Nuss's lips.

I'd meant for it be fast, but before I could pull away, Nuss wrapped his good arm around my back, then brushed his hand up into my hair and kissed me back. He licked his way across the seam of my mouth, urging me to open my lips for him, and I did.

I heard metal clashing against metal but couldn't pull myself away from the duel of my tongue with Nuss's. He tasted of hot chocolate, peppermint, and pure sexuality. I could happily die while kissing him and have no regrets.

"Glad to have you back in fighting form, Captain. Care to join the fray or would you two prefer to have a thousand mice watch you get it on?" Leb shouted.

Nuss pushed my tongue down with his and then nibbled my bottom lip. "I would stay here and kiss you all day if there wasn't a battle raging around us, my Princess."

"What battle?" The sound of swords clanging and fierce war cries from both Fae princes rang through the air. Oh, right. That one.

"It is my sworn duty to make you mine and keep you safe. Once I've done the latter, we'll get back to the first. That, I promise you." Nuss stood and shook out his legs and good arm. The other was still in the sling and when he moved his shoulder, he hissed and grimaced.

Guess I didn't believe quite enough. Although Nuss was up and about as if he hadn't been dying ten seconds ago, so that was something. "Great, you're fine and going into battle. Wow, dreams are so strange."

Nuss frowned at my words, but then a mouse crawled up his leg, I squealed, and he sent it flying into a tree, where a whole rash of pixies covered it in snow. He gave me a wink and then jumped into the fight. Leb threw him an axe that he literally pulled out of somewhere below the belt.

Okay, so it was gonna be that kind of dream, where men have weapons in their pants.

Why did that give me tingles all over my body?

THE GINGERBREAD VIKING

LEB

I could be having my cookies frosted right now by Princess Clara, but no. Fucking Konig Maus had to show up and pick another God-damned fight with us, even though he knew I was going to whip his ass. Again. Then again, he also knew we were both going to have fun doing it. One on one, we were close to evenly matched, and that made the fight all the more worth it.

The Fae princes and the Nutcracker captain were good warriors. Great, even. It's why I threw in with them and joined the Nutcracker Guard all those years ago. Still, none of them matched Konig's ferocity in battle. He'd always had a chip on his shoulder and could go berserker as well as any Viking from the Kingdom of Gingerbread.

He'd even bested me a time or two, but never when it mattered.

Now that the Princess Clara was back in the Winter Realm, I was going to kick Konig's ass all the way back to his mama.

Then I was taking the princess back to mine. Because Clara was absolutely my perfect match, with all those curves and sass. I wouldn't crush her with my brawn when we were in bed, and she wouldn't allow me to crush her heart.

She suited me perfectly. I wasn't exactly the gentle giant with bodies or emotions.

"It's high time we faced off again, Maus. I've missed beating you to a pulp in battle." I swung my axe in a figure eight, not just for show, but as a shield against his freaky little mouse army and their tiny attacks. Those suckers fucking hurt when they bit. I had more than one chunk of flesh missing because of their sharp teeth.

"I'm not here for you or any of the Guard. Just give me the princess and I can go." He twirled his sword, fully prepared to go through me to get to Clara.

"Never gonna happen. So, let's get this over with so I can get on with giving her the orgasms she needs and desires." I brought the axe up and over my head and yelled my favorite war cry. "For kingdom and cookies!"

How I loved the feeling of my blood boiling in battle. Our weapons clashed, I slashed, Konig dashed. I swung and he jumped away, spinning, and then brought his sword around, aiming for my ribs. I deflected with a turn, but his blade still cut a thin line across my back.

"You may have drawn first blood, Mouse Prince, but I'll draw the last." I parried again and Konig met my blow with his sword, holding his own against me. He'd developed his skills since our last clash.

"Not today, cookie." He attacked again, raining down fast and hard blows, three in rapid succession.

While defending against him, I caught a glimpse of the rest of the battle. Four of his lieutenants and a sheer shit ton of mice had joined the fray. When the hell had they gotten here? The Fae were on the verge of being overwhelmed, Nuss was backed up against the tree, defending the princess, and she was throwing balls of snow at battalions of mice.

Smart girl.

Dumb Viking.

Konig was a sly rat. He'd focused on me to keep me distracted while his hidden army laid waste to the friends I'd come to call brothers, and our savior, my future bride. Damn. He'd known exactly what he was doing baiting me, and I'd fallen right into his trap.

Fuck him and his queen.

I ran straight for him, not to deal a killing blow that he could deflect, but to employ a tactic not seen in any books. I barreled right into him, using the momentum of my body to toss him through the air and into the trees.

That gave me enough time to turn and sprint toward the princess and rally the troops. "I'm coming, princess. Don't hit me in the balls with your snow."

Instantly, I was surrounded by a mountain of mice. They crawled up, and up, and up, over my torso and chest, and then poured over my shoulders as if they could tackle me to the ground with their sheer numbers. I will admit, it slowed my progress, having to slog through hundreds of their little wiggly bodies. The resilient bastards were nigh on impossible to kill, even if someone as big as me stepped right on them. Shifter magic was some weird stuff.

Clara's snowballs pelted my legs, knocking away some of the mice, but still leaving her vulnerable. The blood-curdling scream she let out when a fresh wave of them crawled up her skirt, swirling like a tempest around her waist, then running up her arms and down her legs, would echo in my ears for the rest of my life.

"Hurry lads, save the princess." I sank deeper into the sea of mice. There was little I could do beside chopping off my own legs with my axe to get them off me. I watched Zucker and Tau disappear as if buried under a thousand rodents, still I pushed forward. We'd only just found our girl and gotten her home to the realm. I'd be damned to hell before I'd let her get taken by the mouse army.

Nuss was looking knackered but still valiantly slashed through the mice and holding back the warrior trying to slice and dice him. There was a good reason he was our captain. If I could make my way to him, our combined power might be enough to save the princess and escape.

Where, I wasn't sure. If we'd been found this quickly, it meant the mouse spies had infiltrated all the lands. Where there was one, there were always more. Except in the Gingerbread Kingdom. No mouse had ever found their way to the hidden pass that led to our mountain stronghold. We were the last bastion of freedom in the Realm, and the only land not to give in to the Mouse Queen's demands.

Could I risk taking Princess Clara there? It would expose my people, my family, my kin to invasion. I shook my head. No, if I had the chance to help her escape, I had to try to take it. It might be our last hope to keep the Princess safe and start her down the path to usurping the queen. My mother, brothers and sisters would help me deal with the consequences. Clara was worth it.

"Get off of me, ew, ew. Ouch. Help, help," she screamed again, sweeping the mice off her arms and flinging them out of her hair. The wee little marzipan fairies even tried coming to her rescue, dive bombing the ones on her shoulders, then tossing them into the branches of the Christmas trees.

But we were losing the battle.

Konig whizzed by me, using his shifter speed. In a last-ditch effort I flung my axe with all my might, praying that the Icing Valkyries would guide my blade to its mark in the middle of Konig's traitorous back. My prayers went unanswered as he turned and grabbed the axe out of the air, jumped over Nuss's head, and swooped the princess into his arms.

He crushed his mouth down on hers, kissing her possessively. I found a new surge of energy and exploded out of the horde of little beasties, rushing toward the two of them, yelling with all my might. I scared a good half of the mice away, but it didn't take them long to circle back.

Nothing was stopping me this time. Touch my girl, and out came my berserker. The pounding of my blood filled my ears, my vision tunneled until I saw only Konig and Clara, and I sprinted forward. I pulled a dagger from my belt and gripped it like a stake. I would cut Konig's heart out before I let him ravage the princess.

She tore her mouth from his and he said something I couldn't hear through my berserker rage. Then my sassy woman smacked him right across the face, kneed him in the walnuts, turned on her heel, and ran.

That's my girl.

Konig dropped to the ground, his mouse army falling and flopping about him as if they too had been kicked where the snow didn't fall. While I still wanted to kill Konig for his crimes, this was the perfect chance to save my friends and get all five of us the hell out of here—hopefully to live and fight another day.

I snatched up my axe from the ground and hurled it at the closest warriors. It took down one and sent the other running. One look at the remaining two and they fell to their knees, hands behind their heads in surrender. "Face down on the ground or I'll split you in half and tell the pixies to sew you back together with mismatched parts."

They dropped and I resumed the search for my brethren and the princess. She was still running, and I whistled to get the horses to return to me after dancing away from the onslaught of rodents. I had to hurry to get ahead of Konig and his army. It wouldn't take him long to recover. Shifters healed much faster than the rest of us. Unless of course we got a kiss of our own from the princess.

I'd make sure to give and take plenty of kisses to help her forget any other mouth but mine, the Fae Princes', and Nuss's had ever touched hers.

I continued my sprint, bypassing Konig rolling around on the ground grabbing his junk and pointing at him as I regained my wits. "That's what you get for being a rat, Maus. Be prepared to have your bollocks cut off if you ever even look at the princess again."

"Have no doubt, I'll be coming for her in more ways than one, cookie." He croaked the jab out, and if he could talk again already, it meant we were running out of time.

I fucking hated retreating. She might be the only one I would forfeit a good death in battle for. My stride was significantly longer than hers and it didn't take me long to catch up to her, throw her up onto my stallion, and jump up behind her.

"Please, Leb, we have to go back for the others." What a courageous heart she had. No wonder she was the one prophesied to save the realm.

"Don't worry love, we aren't going anywhere without the rest of your Guard." I grabbed up the reins of the Fae princes' horses and hurried them over to the last place I'd seen them in battle.

Tau was scratched all to hell and bloody, but conscious. Marzipan pixies were fussing over him, but he moved his way over to Zucker and laid his head on his lover's chest. "He's breathing."

Clara squirmed, trying to get down. "I'll kiss you too. I promise, I believe. Leb, let me down, let me at them."

"There's no time." Groups of mice were rousing and gathering together again. "Tau, can you get him onto the back of your horse while I get Nuss on the other?"

I hadn't spotted the captain yet and I worried the mouse army had carried him off into the forest, until I saw him drop down out of the nearest Christmas tree. The sling on his one arms was shredded and it hung limply at his side. His clothes were half eaten by the mice, too, yet somehow, he still looked like a prince and the captain of the guard.

I slid off the horse, picked him up, and laid him across Zucker's mount. It was probably not good at all that Nuss had fought and been injured to the point of unconsciousness twice in one day. I would have to have faith in Princess Clara's magic to heal them all.

Once we had Nuss and Zucker secured, I jumped back up behind Clara and gave my stallion the command to ride like the wind ahead of a winter tempest. In no time we put a good long distance between the flattened mouse army and ourselves. Until we were in the mountains of my home, resting safely under the watchful eyes of Mother Gingerbread, I wouldn't relax.

"Where are we going?" Clara shivered in my arms, and I pulled her tight against my chest.

"To my home. We'll be safe there for a time and can rest and recover before we start out on your quest to find the seven crowns of the realm."

She remained silent for a long moment, then turned her head to look over her shoulder at me. "This isn't a dream, is it?"

"A dream? No, lass. I know our lands may feel different and strange to you, having grown up in the human realm, but this is your true home. We're no dream, just as the home you left behind isn't either."

She turned back and stared off into the night, but I caught a whisper she meant only for herself. "The stories are all true. They're true."

THE STORIES ARE ALL TRUE

CLARAMARIE

I didn't understand how it was even the slightest bit possible, but all this time, I hadn't been dreaming.

This.

Was.

Not.

A.

Dream.

"When did I realize this?" the crazy side of my brain asked.

"Oh, well, you know, when ten thousand mice crawled up my dress and bit me like I was the tastiest piece of cheese ever presented at the mouse Christmas party," the other crazy part of my mind replied.

"But thousands of mice crawling all over me sounds more like a nightmare than reality," Crazy Brain said.

"Sure. Until it fucking hurt so much, I couldn't do anything but scream," other Crazy Brain growled back.

"Yeah. I suppose if I were going to wake up, that kind of pain would do it, where a little pinch to the underarm might not."

Leb tucked my head against his chest and stroked my hair. "Shh, lass. Everything is going to be all right now."

Wait. Had I said all of that out loud? Great. Now the hot Viking thought I was crazy too. Maybe I was. I'd have to be insane to believe I'd gone through a tree and landed in a wintery land filled to the brim with men who kept kissing the Christmas lights out of me, pixies with curative hot chocolate, angels who delivered messages, and thousands of ferocious attack mice.

Even if I had gone off my rocker, it appeared I was living in a reality where I could be injured or even killed. I needed to find my way out of this story and back home. Back to my pampered, if boring and subservient, life. Back to where Father, Fritz, and Drosselmeyer controlled my destiny, not nutcrackers, princes, cookies, and mice.

My stomach churned as if I'd eaten too many sweet mincemeat pies. Having a permanent bellyache was still safer than staying here. Who knew when we would be attacked again?

One of those crazy voices in my head said I could be just as hurt living the life the men back home had laid out for me.

The horses slowed a bit as we came out of the forest and to the edge of the foothills of some tall, snowy mountains. I could definitely imagine Vikings living here. "We're not far now. Just sit tight a little while longer and you'll be safe and sound in the arms of Mother Gingerbread."

Aha. That's what Leb smelled like. Gingerbread. "Mother Gingerbread? Who is she?"

He guided the horses up a spindly path across the hills. "The matriarch of my family and leader of the Gingerbread Kingdom. She's been waiting on you for a long time."

"Why would that be? She doesn't know even know me."

"Princess, we all know you, or at least of you. You're the hope we've been waiting for nigh on a century."

A century seemed far too long. I wasn't even a quarter as old as that. "You all keep saying I'm some sort of lost princess and that I'm here to do something for your realm, but how can that be if I didn't even know this place existed before today? I barely know how to cook myself breakfast. I'm certainly not going to be able to save you from some creepy rat queen. You need a warrior woman, not a dancing princess."

Where was the Vivandiere from the stories? She's the one who could save them, not me.

"We shall see, my sweet. Whatever is going to happen can wait until tomorrow. Tonight, we'll rest and heal and prepare for the inevitable invasion." He turned and gave a hand signal to Tau, who pulled out his bow, notched an arrow, and shot it into the snow beside our horse.

A ragged little mouse went flying and splatted onto a nearby rock. Leb's warning about an invasion wasn't exactly making me feel safe, never mind a mouse trailing us. A life of loneliness in a loveless marriage was sounding better and better.

Leb cupped his hands around his mouth and shouted up into the dark, craggy rocks above us. "*Heil!*"

Another man with a red braided beard who was definitely related to Leb popped up from behind the rocks. "*Heill*, Leb. You've got a stream of mice following ya."

"That I have. Send an angel up the mountain to let Mother know there will be trouble."

The head disappeared back behind the rocks and a moment later, a sparkling golden angel fluttered up and caught a breeze, taking her up the hill. A few moments later she and her trail of golden sparkles disappeared from sight.

"Where did she go? She's not injured or shot down or anything, is she?" I was already tired of seeing others getting hurt because they thought I was going to be some savior.

"No, but we can't be letting the Mouse Queen or her minions find the path to our mountain stronghold. We don't have magic like yours, but we have a few tricks up our sleeves. You'll see."

We continued along the twisting path. I never saw any more people, but occasionally an arrow would fly past us and I'd hear a death squeak. When we got to a precipice about halfway up the side of the hill, I was sure we'd gone as far as we could on horseback, and wasn't looking forward to climbing up and over rocks in my dress.

But Leb didn't stop and get off. He urged the horse forward. I held tight to the animal's mane, worried we were about to go over the edge, yet at the same time trusting Leb to keep us safe.

I didn't even close my eyes. If I had, I would have missed the thin slab painted and decorated to look like trees and rocks on the edge of the cliff. Leb steered the horse behind the slab and into a short, hidden tunnel. As we passed through, the distinct scent of iced gingerbread filled the tunnel as if we were inside a cave made of the cookies.

I reached out and touched the wall, expecting to feel rock or even tree trunks, but got instead a handful of crumbs. Holy cookies, the slab, the tunnel, and the decorations were all made of gingerbread. We continued to make our way out of the darkness. At first there were trees overhead that blocked any view of the sky, but then the canopy opened into a huge, bowled valley with high mountain peaks all the way around. The landscape quite literally made my mouth water.

There were dozens of gingerbread houses, a group of gingerbread Christkindlmarkt booths where more men and women with varying shades of red hair were shopping, and tucked away in the furthest corner, a gingerbread Viking longhouse. I stared at one building, then another, and another. Every piece of architecture in this hidden mountain village was made of dark but sturdy cookies, held together with thick lines of white icing.

Leb pressed his mouth to my ear and whispered, "Welcome to my home, Princess."

A half dozen men and women crowded around us, and several more surrounded the other two horses. Leb directed his people with quick orders. They clearly looked at him as a leader. "Take them to the longhouse and prepare a space for us all to bed down."

Within moments, they had Nuss and Zucker on stretchers and carried them toward the longhouse. Tau brought his mount up alongside the two of us and took my hand in his, pressing his lips to my fingers. "I'm glad you're safe, my lady. If you'll forgive me, I want to check on Zucker. He didn't look well."

"Oh, of course. I'll come with you and see if I can do the healing thing again." I could believe in magic if it helped Zucker and Nuss.

Tau shook his head. "You need rest, too. You've already used a good deal of power today. Go with Leb and meet Mother Gingerbread first. I'll take care of Zucker and Nuss until your magic is recharged." He coaxed his horse into a gallop and sped off after the others toward the longhouse.

I hadn't thought that magic could be used up and recharged. Tau made it sound sort of like physical energy. After a big dance practice, I knew to drink, eat, and crawl into bed, but how was I supposed to recharge magic?

Leb kept a steady pace through the town greeting each person by name. There were so many, I couldn't keep track of them all. "You sure know a lot of people. Is it because you're the, uh, prince of gingerbread town?"

"Gingerbread town. I like that. This is the Kuchen stronghold, and yes, I know every single person here, man, woman, and child. Most of them are my brothers and sisters."

He must mean they were like metaphorical family to him.

There was no way he could have that many actual siblings. "Just how many of these...uh...brothers do you have?"

If they were all big and brawny like most of the guys who'd greeted him so far, we might have a chance against the army of mice he said would invade.

"You'd have to ask my mother that." He shrugged. "I lose count. Maybe thirty or so."

Thirty? "And sisters?"

"A bit more than that, I think." He chuckled and I felt his laugh go up and down my chest like a little bomb of lust.

"How can one woman have that many children?" She must have been pregnant her entire life.

"Many lovers."

Oh. Ohhh. Heat bloomed on my throat, and I felt it creep up my cheeks, I'm sure making me turn as red as if I'd had a bit too much wine. I hadn't even had one lover yet. I'd had more kisses today than in the entire rest of my life. I couldn't imagine what it would be like to have so many men lust after me.

Or maybe I could. No. Yes? I was so confused.

We stopped in front of the longhouse where an absolutely gorgeous woman stood in front the doors with her arms crossed, waiting for us. She had long red braids, thighs the size of the Christmas tree in our great room, a chest like king sized pillows, and both a scowl and a twinkle in her eyes. I could see exactly why she had her choice of lovers every night.

"Mother." Leb slid down off the horse and grabbed me around the waist and lifted me gently to the ground.

"Leb Kuchen. Who have ya brought me?" Her voice boomed, but somehow it was still warm and inviting. The affection she had for Leb was like a huge bear hug that even I felt the warmth from.

"You know as well as I do this is the Princess of the Land of Spirit and Magic." Why did Leb sound like he was proud of my erroneous title?

She looked me up and down appraisingly, and I felt as if I was being weighed and measured. Would I be found wanting? Eventually she smiled widely, spread the fur cloak around her shoulders open and drew me into a welcoming embrace. "So, you're the one bringing us all the trouble, are ya? Good. We've been sitting on our arses for a sight too long and I relish a good battle. Come in and let's get ya warmed up."

I had been in trouble since before I even landed in their realm. I'd have thought that was a bad thing, but this woman seemed to admire me for it. She didn't wait, and I found myself scrambling to get up the stairs and follow her into the longhouse. The scent of ginger, nutmeg and other Christmas spices was even stronger in here.

"We've set your men up near the fireplace. You'll be cozy with them there tonight." She pointed to the far end of the room, and Tau waved from a table laden with piles of food.

"I should go to them and try to heal Nuss and Zucker." I was anxious to see them and make sure they were okay. It was so strange how I felt much more for all of them than I ever had for my own brother. It was as if they were already family.

Truth be told, there were things I wanted to do with the four of them that had nothing to do with familial affection. It was weird. I wasn't in love with them. I didn't even know them. Still, there was something between us that went beyond friendship.

Like I had any idea what I was talking about. I'd never been in love. This was probably nothing more than lust and the adrenaline of surviving a battle together. I shouldn't expect anything more from them than I'd already been given.

"In a bit, lass. You and I need to talk woman to woman. Your men will be fine for a bit. Leb will see to that." She waved him off and pointed me toward a set of comfortable looking chairs with a much smaller table set between them. It too was piled high with food and a steaming kettle.

I was torn. I did want to talk to her and find out more about what everyone thought I was and what was expected from me. I also wanted to see if the Vivandiere would be showing up. Then maybe I could find out if there was a way home. At the same time, my heart was pulled to go with Leb to see Tau, Zucker, and Nuss.

Leb stepped close to me, lifted me up so our faces were level and gave me a sweet and chaste kiss. "Go, sweet thing, and have your chat. Our swords will be waiting for you when you're done."

He kissed me once more and then set me back on the ground, spun me around, and gave me a swat on the butt to get me going on my way. I fast stepped a few paces and caught up with Mother Gingerbread just as she was sitting down.

"Please, sit and rest your bones. Have something to eat." She reached for the kettle, and I flopped heavily into the other chair, not realizing how tired I was.

The second my bum hit the cushion, I felt something wrong. I jumped back up and from out of the folds in my skirt flew two tiny pixies, one pink and the other blue. They buzzed around me for a moment, then flew straight for Mother Gingerbread, snagging the kettle and the cup from her hands.

The pink one, with the cup, flew right up into her face and made a sort of buzzing tinkling sound. I think it was mad at her. "I'm so sorry. I must have accidentally picked them up in the battle. I don't exactly know what to do with them now, though."

Mother Gingerbread smiled and waved me back down into the chair. "It's all right, child. It's been a fair while since we've had any Marzipan pixies about."

The pink pixie brought the cup over to the blue one and they poured a fragrant brown stream, plopped two sugar cubes into it, and expertly swirled it all around to mix it up. They brought it over to me and floated right in front of my face until I took a sip. "Thank you. It's delicious."

Just like back in the forest they fluttered about excitedly, pleased at the praise. Mother Gingerbread watched with a funny grin on her face. "They're quite attached to you. I dare say you'll never be without a hot drink the rest of your days."

"This is the second time they've done this. What's that all about?" I watched as the blue one picked through the food, and after much deliberation, found a vine of bright berries, brought it over, and handed it to me with much ceremony.

Mother Gingerbread laughed. "What do you mean? That's what they do. Marzipan pixies live to provide comfort and joy, usually in the form of food and drink, but sometimes by supplying clothing, blankets and such. They're likely already judging the lodge harshly and will want to decorate it up with lights and baubles by morning."

"How lovely. Can you understand them? Do they have names? I'd like to thank them by name, if I could." The pink pixie flew in a little pirouette and landed on the edge of my teacup, tinkling and buzzing like before.

"This one says they are called Trost, and the other is Freunde." The pixies each bowed at me and then went to dig through the food again, arguing over a pile of cookies.

"You are an interesting lass." Mother Gingerbread took an offered cookie and dunked it into her own teacup. "So shall we see what powers are in ya, and how the Gingerbread Kingdom can help ya take down the Mouse Queen?"

"I'm not sure why everyone thinks I can do anything about this queen. I seem to have a little bit of magic that can heal people, but I don't know anything about how to overthrow an evil dictatorship." I didn't even have enough gumption to control my own life back at home. My brother ruled over us all there, and even with my small rebellions against him, I was nothing more than a blister under his big toe.

"You're a woman, lass. What more do you need? That alone gives you power."

I supposed to a woman like her, or to the Vivandiere, it might. Not me. "It never has before."

"Well, that's the strange land of the humans for ya. Patriarchal malarkey if I ever saw such a thing." She pounded her fist on the side of the chair, sending crumbs flying. "I do wish your lads had discovered where you'd been hidden away earlier. If you had been raised here in the Winter Realm with me, you wouldn't question your power."

I wished that too. The thought surprised me. Until a few minutes ago, I still very much wanted to leave the intrigue and danger of this place far behind. Now, there was something special here that felt right. It wasn't only Nuss, Zucker, Tau, and Leb either. She kept calling them mine and I didn't understand what made them such. Although the more I thought about it, the more I found I wanted them to belong to me, and me to them, very much.

I glanced over again to the area near the fireplace and found both Tau and Leb staring over at us. "What is it that makes me have these, umm, feelings for them?"

"Fate, love. Never before have six princes of the Winter Realm all been born under the same Christmas star. The same star as you. You've been connected all along. My goodness, did no one teach you anything?"

"Six?"

"Your four here, who've been raised in light and love. They swore a bond to guard and protect you and become your consorts. There are also two more born under that same star who've both been tainted by the Mouse Queen herself. Either could steal the throne for themselves because they hold no bond, only treachery and greed guide them."

"Konig, the Mouse Prince, is one, yes?" I knew I felt a connection to him. I'd heard the guys call him a traitor, but there was more to it than any of them understood. I knew that now. "But who is the other? We haven't met anyone else."

"Your twin, lass. The prince of the Land of Spirit and Magic. I'm sorry to tell you, we've gotten reports from others in the rebellion that he's been seen with the Mouse Queen entering Christmas Castle."

"My twin? I have a brother here in the Winter Realm?" Suddenly I wondered if Fritz was even my real brother. We'd always been at odds with each other, and I certainly never felt a connection with him. Perhaps I could save this long-lost twin of mine, too.

"No, lass. He too was hidden in the human realm." She shook her head sadly, like I was missing something important. "But somehow the Mouse Queen pierced the veil and has taken Friedrich to her bosom."

Fritz? A tainted prince?

Would he betray me? Abso-fucking-lutely.

THE DEWDROP FAE PRINCE FALLS IN LOVE

TAU

I could tell the moment Mother Gingerbread told our Clara about the betrayal of her brother and the Mouse Queen's alliance with the lost Prince. Greedy bastard. It was spies from the Land of Flowers that had risked their lives to bring us the information about the Mouse Queen's liaison with the lost Prince.

I battled with my guilt over not telling her myself. Now her pain was mine to bear as well. The surge of angry power was quite the opposite of the luscious swell of her magic I'd felt when I kissed her there under the glowing Christmas trees. Yet it had the same effect.

Even in her hurt, her beautiful soul could do no harm, and healed instead. Her magic sparkled across my wounds and bites. In an instant, my energy was restored, and with it, my lust.

"Whoa," Leb said. He looked at me and then at his own arms and legs where the bites had suddenly disappeared. He patted his side where the slash mark from Konig's sword had cut him open. There was little more than a thin white line left. "Fuck, she is powerful."

"That she is." Would Zucker and Nuss heal from that deluge of her magic too? Both my heart and my cock hoped so.

The sliding wooden door creaked along its track, opening to the room where we'd laid them both to recover while our Princess restored her powers before trying to heal again. Zucker filled the doorway, looking hale and hearty again.

I jumped up from my bench and wrapped my arms around him, holding him close, needing to feel his heartbeat strong and steady against my own chest. "I thought we'd lost you."

He nodded and brushed his stubbled chin across mine. "Me too, for a minute there. Where is she?"

"With Mother. She's just found out about her brother." Leb clapped Zucker firmly on the shoulder, enough to make him stumble forward. "Ah, here's Nuss again too. You need to quit dying on us. The Valkyries will become too fond of you one of these days and not send ya back."

Nuss leaned against the door frame, his one arm still hanging limply against his side, and he gave us one of his lopsided grins. "Even they could not keep me from the princess's side. If today has taught us anything, it should be that we've got a hard battle ahead of us. We have to make sure she's ready."

We wouldn't have nearly as much time to train her as any of us had hoped. Even in the worst-case scenario, we thought we'd have at least the twelve days of Christmas for her to grow into her powers. We'd have to do something drastic to help her prepare. "Leb, how long do you think we have before the mouse army breaks through the stronghold's defenses?"

"A day, day and a half, maybe. Those little rats will chew right through each home here. Might as well poison every slab of gingerbread for them." He spat on the floor, disgusted at the idea of his home falling to the mice.

"But we have tonight?" My mind was sketching out plans, examining them to see which was the best path forward. I kept coming back to the same one each time.

"Yes." He nodded. "Why, what is that strategic brain of yours thinking?"

Zucker sat on the edge of the table and pulled me to his side. He wrapped one hand around the back of my neck, and I leaned into him. After a close call like he'd just had, we both needed each other's touch, to feel the other was alive. "I know where your head is at, but she isn't ready. The human world has instilled strange, strict values in her. You saw how uncomfortable she was even though she craved our touch, each of us."

Nuss came forward and stared across the room at her. "She was set to marry a man there. I suspect he was a magician from the realm himself."

"Then you're saying she may not even accept us as her consorts? That's bullshit. I can win her over with a landslide of orgasms." Leb always was a confident fucker. With each of his conquests, he'd always said he was just practicing to get better at bedding women so he was ready for the day we claimed our princess.

It wasn't like any of us had stayed chaste for her. Well, except Nuss.

A grown Fae who couldn't fuck was only living a half-life. I knew once Zucker and I were with her, there would be only each other and her for the rest of our lives. Unless of course I could talk the pure and unspoiled captain of the Nutcracker Guard into fooling around with the three of us while Leb watched.

We'd all hung around the Gingerbread Kingdom long enough to know that when Vikings chose their bride, they dedicated themselves to one woman and one woman only for their entire lives. Leb had been able to talk us into adopting his cultural norm of one woman with multiple husbands when I was sure the other five of us…four now…would have torn each other apart to earn the right to become the sole consort of the lost princess.

Zucker shook his head and rolled his eyes at Leb. "You can't talk someone into letting you give them an orgasm by giving them orgasms."

"Maybe *you* can't." Leb folded his arms. In that moment, the four of us were all focused completely on our sweet princess.

Mother Gingerbread took her arm and we watched as she encouraged Clara to take a few deep breaths to calm down. I could still feel the heat rolling off her emotions and I did my best to push cooling thoughts back to her. Because we weren't yet bonded, I couldn't use my gifts to their full extent, but she still seemed to feel my calming presence and her powers ebbed and waned until she was breathing normally again.

Leb rocked from foot to foot. "It's killing me to sit and do nothing. I'm going to march over there in a minute and throw her over my shoulder and—"

Zucker held up his hand. "She'll come to us when she's good and ready. We're not going to bully her into being with any of us."

"Well, of course not. I'm a Gingerbread Viking, not an asshole." Leb huffed and puffed like all warriors of his kind, but he was a big fluffy bunny at heart. He'd no more hurt the princess than he would harm his own mother.

In another moment, the two women stood, and Mother Gingerbread took a necklace from around her neck and placed it over Clara's head. A small but brilliant flash of amber light zipped through the longhouse as the pendant first touched her skin. The Gingerbread Kingdom's piece of the crown was now hers.

Clara placed a hand over it and nodded to Mother Gingerbread. They exchanged a few more words and Clara's eyes went wide as she looked over at the four of us. My heart skipped a beat or two. Mother said something else, and Clara shook her head and put her fist over her mouth.

Whatever Mother Gingerbread was telling her about us, the princess didn't believe it. If what Nuss said about her being set to marry one man in the human realm was correct, I couldn't imagine what she might think about having four consorts. She was so sweet and innocent, as virginal as a snowflake.

I wanted nothing more than to see that bashful flush spread across her body as I did dirty things to every last inch of her.

From the tales I'd heard growing up, I was already half in love with her before I ever met her in person. I'd known my whole life that I would belong to her.

She, however, would only just be coming to terms with the idea, if I was correct in guessing that their woman to woman talk extended beyond explaining her quest for the seven crowns and our plan to usurp the Mouse Queen.

Clara asked Mother Gingerbread something more and I cursed the fact that the Viking matriarch had purposefully put us so far away from the conversation. I wanted very much to interfere and pledge myself to Clara right here and now.

Mother gave the princess a kiss on each cheek and a long, solid hug. Then she pointed Clara in our direction and gave her a gentle but firm shove. Clara stumbled a few steps, glanced up at us and I held my breath as I saw the indecision flash in her eyes. Behind her, Mother Gingerbread held up a finger, indicating that none of us should move. Clara had to make this decision on her own.

Fuck, how I wanted her to choose me, to choose us, this bond. The dangerous road ahead was forcing her hand, but her choice to be our woman would be all the sweeter if she truly wanted it, not merely felt she had to accept the arrangement out of obligation.

She licked her lips and sucked the bottom one between her teeth. If my cock wasn't already standing at attention for her, it would have arisen now. My pants were rapidly getting uncomfortable, yet I was so focused on the princess, I didn't notice Zucker's hand sliding across my thigh until he pressed it against the fastening of my trousers.

"I know," he said. "I feel her allure too."

At least if Clara didn't accept us as lovers into her bed tonight, he and I could lose ourselves in each other's bodies. Leb and Nuss would just have to suffer. I hoped it didn't come to that, though. I knew exactly how badly each of us wanted to bond with her and indulge in all the pleasures of the flesh that entailed. More importantly, if we had no time to train her, and would only be steps ahead of the mouse army in the quest to find the crowns, we needed to give her every advantage.

Quadrupling her power overnight was a boon we could offer her, but she had to accept us into her bed for the bond to work its magic.

I concentrated on sending positive, open vibes. She took a steadying breath, straightened her spine, and walked to us with new purpose in her stride. Whatever question she'd been deliberating, she'd claimed it and aimed it. My chest puffed up with pride in my future mate. Zucker leaned over and softly said, "I can hardly wait to see her riding my cock as I suck you off and she can watch as you come for us both."

I'd imagined that scenario, and about a dozen others, that had her over me, under Zucker, or that had him inside of her while I was inside of him, and so many more. I had to tamp down both of our libidos because if the society she was raised in was as strict as Zucker said, she wasn't ready even for gentle lovemaking, much less the dirty things I wanted to do to her. "I think we'll need to seduce her mind before we can get to her body."

"I suggest the opposite. Seduce the body and the mind will

follow. That's how I got you into bed the first time, remember? When you wanted nothing to do with me besides besting me in combat while vying for the right to be her consort."

That I couldn't deny. Thank flowers he had, too. The special bond between us was what had gotten me through our darkest days when Konig betrayed us all.

When Clara got a within a few steps, she gasped and ran the last bit of the way until she stood directly in front of us. She looked from Nuss to Zucker, then to me, and finally to Leb. "You...you're all healed. Who did it? Where is she? I need to have a talk with her and tell her to keep her lips to herself, thank you very much."

She spun her head looking around the great hall. My lust was already raging for her, but seeing her jealousy at the thought of someone else kissing us to heal us, my heart and soul ignited for her as well. It was too much to ask that she fall in love with us on sight. She knew nothing of us or our world, whereas we were all raised on stories of her.

I stood, dragging Zucker with me, and the two of us caged her with our bodies, so she couldn't unleash her ire on any poor passing Gingerbread warrior maiden. She didn't yet know how to use her powerful magic, and it was only going to get more powerful when she bonded with each of us.

"My passionate princess, you healed us. Your emotions are the key to your magic. If you'll let us, we'll show you." I ran the back of my fingers gently down her chin and to the two necklaces she now wore, tracing the chains down to the pendants that sat just above her breasts.

Her eyelids fluttered and the soft muscles in her chest flexed and contracted under my touch, but she did not pull away. "Oh, umm, I thought kissing was how I healed you. That's what you guys said."

"Yes." Zucker pushed a hand into her wild curls and used his grip to turn her face up to his. Her lips parted and her breath shuddered. Her magic was already swirling out from her to the four of us. He was right to suggest we seduce her body, letting her mind follow. "Lust is a powerful emotion, even more so than the anger you felt when you were talking to Mother Gingerbread about the state of the realm."

Leb joined us, taking up all the space in the room with his big bear of a body. "Lass, we don't expect you'll have feelings for us before the bonding of our souls to yours, and maybe not even for a while after that, but I promise we'll give you more pleasure than any man of the human realm ever has or ever could. We are yours, the four of us, Princess Clara, if you'll have us."

"I just don't understand. Why me? Mother Gingerbread explained about the Christmas star and all, but there's something missing in the stories I know about the Winter Realm, someone. Are you really sure I'm the one you're meant to be with?"

I nudged Zucker forward. Leb and I weren't getting the message across. He, however, had a seductive charm that could convince a Snowflake nun to give up her vows for him.

He took her hand and placed it over his heart. "I feel your spirit. Your magic has caressed me from the inside out. My body recognizes yours. But it's more than that with you. Clara, you are the only woman for me, for any of us."

Slowly he dragged her fingers down his torso until she was cupping the bulge of his cock pushing against his trousers. "I've fucked plenty of other men and women, and only one other has come close to making my blood pound the way you do. If you open your mind, you'll feel it is the same for all of us. We want you, Clara, with everything we have—hearts, souls, and bodies."

"You want to...I mean, shouldn't we...aren't you...but I...." Her fluster was as sweet as snowy honeysuckle. I wanted to lick it up and share it with the others. Yet this was only the tip of the petal for her.

Clara pulled her hand away and pressed against Leb's chest with the other one. I thought she was about to take us up on our offer. Instead, she pushed against Leb, not moving him, because no one could budge a mountain, but using the force to remove herself from the half-circle of our bodies around her.

"I won't be coy and say that what you're offering isn't tempting. It is. I just, I've never been near a situation like this." She ran her hands over her scalp as if she could push her reticence away. "Men don't even acknowledge me back home, and now you're all looking at me like you want to eat me up."

"We do," Leb chuckled, "in the most fun way you can imagine."

She blushed even more. On the one hand I could slay every man in her human world for making her feel unwanted, but on the other, I treasured the knowledge that we would be the ones to show her just how carnal and voluptuous she was. I couldn't imagine how strong and sensual she'd be once she fell in love.

I already had.

Nuss cleared his throat, breaking in when I thought we'd have to drag him kicking and begging. "Princess, we are all yours to do with as you like. We made a pact long ago to join forces to be together at your side upon your return. Bonding with us all will make you stronger and more powerful, but know this, the choice to do so is entirely yours. You say when, you say how, you say where, you get to decide what our roles are in your life and in your bed."

Fuck. That's why he was the captain, and we were jackasses. Of course she was the one in charge, but I'd stupidly assumed she knew that, and had tried to push her into something she didn't even understand. Zucker and Leb came along for the ride because we all simply wanted to be close to her, pleasure her.

She swallowed and gave the tiniest of nods, mostly to herself. "Okay. I just need...urgh. Dammit. I want to say I need a minute, that we should slow down, but that is what I would say in my previous world, and I'm trying to live in the here and now in this strange new place. It's just…it's incredibly hard for me to believe that you all want to be with me out of anything besides a sense of obligation."

There it was. This was why she was my perfect match. I'd feared myself she wouldn't want to be with me except out of duty. I didn't like that, and neither did she. "Princess, we each have made promises to our people, and indeed the realm that we would find you, return you to your proper home, and help you defeat the Mouse Queen to restore peace to the Winter Realm."

"Yes." She waved her fingers showing that she already understood that. "I get it. You have to serve me or whatever."

"Not whatever, Princess. I've been prepared, trained, and conditioned my entire life to be your consort. I love this land and the flora and fauna in it. We all do. What none of the other guards know," I held my arms out indicating Zucker, Leb, and Nuss, "is that I was worried about how I would feel about you once we met."

"You never told me that." Zucker tipped his head and frowned at me.

"I know, because I didn't want anyone to know that as much as I wanted to do my duty, I wanted to be more than simply a consort, someone who fucks the princess to seal the bond. That was never going to be enough for me. I hid my true desire from you all, because I wanted a love bond too." The words burned coming out of my mouth.

Zucker grabbed my shoulder, and I couldn't breathe at the hurt look on his face. "You know how I feel about you, Tau."

"Oh no," Clara's hands went up over her mouth. "Am I in the way of you two being together? If you've already found love with each other, I don't want to come between you."

I took Zucker's hand from my shoulder and squeezed it tight. We knew exactly what we were to one another. If there was no war, no Mouse Queen to defeat, and no stolen princess to bring us all together, I would have been content to spend my days adventuring with him and my nights wrapped in his embrace.

I loved him deeply, but we both knew there was something more for us.

Having Clara join us would only strengthen the bond he and I already had.

I led him the two steps to her. "No, sweet flower, that's exactly where I want you to be. We do have deep feelings for each other, Zucker and I, but without you between us, there's something missing. You. Being with you, falling in love with you, will only make our feelings for each other stronger. That's the bond I want with you."

Zucker wrapped his arm around Clara and grabbed my other hand, hugging her between us. "I am better at saying what I feel, and Zucker is better at showing it."

As if to prove my point, Zucker let go of my hands, grabbed me behind the head, and kissed me with as much ferocity as the first time we'd been together. Need and heat burst through me, and I let it course through the fledgling connection I had with Clara. Her breathing ratcheted up and her magic along with it, dancing just at the surface.

He broke the kiss far before I was ready, and looked into Clara's eyes, lust glazing his own. "Did you feel that Princess? Do you understand how I feel about Tau?"

"Yes," she whispered, wide-eyed and confused.

"Good, then feel this too." Zucker grabbed her the exact same way he'd done to me and crushed his mouth to hers. His tongue pushed past her lips and withdrew. He thrust in and out of her mouth, teasing her, giving her a taste of how he wanted to take her cunt with his cock.

He tore his mouth from hers just as abruptly as if punishing us both with his lesson. "Did you understand that?"

Clara stared up at Zucker from beneath hooded eyes, her mouth hanging open as if she'd forgotten how to use it for anything but kissing. She bobbed her chin up and down, but before she could vocalize her answer, Leb wrapped his arms around all three of us and picked us up with his brute strength. "I'll take that as a yes. Know that what they just said and made you feel, that's from me too, tenfold."

He spun us as a group and walked into the room. "Come on, Captain. We've got a love bond and a night of pleasure ahead of us."

WHAT IS LOVE?

CLARAMARIE

Who was I to say what love felt like? It wasn't like I'd ever been in love before. I'd certainly never felt these kinds of strange tingles and zips of energy rushing through my body in this way. Maybe this really was it.

Ugh, what a time to have absolutely no experience with either sex or magic.

Leb carried me and the two Fae Princes into the most beautiful, rustic room I'd ever seen. The walls and furniture were made from the same deep brown, fragrant material as all the buildings, but the walls here were decorated in swirls of white, with hundreds of tiny pastel jewels dotting the decorative lines. In the center was a huge bed covered in gorgeous fluffy furs and pillows galore.

The room was lit with soft light from multiple flickering candles, and it had a very wedding night kind of feeling to it. Up around the ceiling I caught the glow of the pixies. "Aww, did you two decorate for us? You're the best."

Trost balled up their little fists and vibrated with joy so hard they passed out and floated gently like a feather down into the furs. Freunde laughed and laughed, then flew down, picked up Trost, tossed them over their shoulder and gave a little wave as they flew away out the door.

"They've made it romantic for ya, lass. If I was less of an idiot, I'd have thought to do that myself while you were talking to my mother." He pushed one curl behind my ear and then tugged on another one. He was staring at my hair, not in my eyes.

Was my big, bad Viking feeling shy? I was the one who should be worried about what we were about to do. What I thought they wanted from me. "I don't need romantic."

As if I knew what I was talking about. I was nervous about, well, a lot of things. They'd all said and shown me they thought I was beautiful, but after a lifetime of being told I wasn't, I was still a bit worried about letting them see me without this big skirt that hid the size of my hips and butt, or the sleeves that hid the flabby bits under my arms. Maybe I could just keep them focused on my breasts. Guys liked big breasts, and I had those for sure.

He scoffed. "Need it or not, you deserve it."

Tau lifted my chin with one knuckle. "We have only the bond and our bodies to give you for now, but when this is all over, and the seven crowns of the kingdoms are restored to you, we'll give you a proper bonding ceremony with flowers and a banquet, and all the gifts your heart desires."

I still didn't have the same faith that they did that I could overcome this horrible queen, but somewhere along the way I'd finally decided to throw my lot in with theirs. If we didn't win, the human world I left behind wouldn't miss me much, and I trusted that Drosselmeyer would take care of my father.

If we did win, and I had a chance to change their world, that was more righteous than being a lonely hausfrau.

"I don't think I could handle falling in love and then losing you. What if I fail? What if I'm not up to the task?"

Maybe I didn't need to think about that right now. What mattered more was that they wanted to be with me. I had all kinds of crazy, jittery, lusty feelings for them. Back home, I would never even consider kissing more than one man. Meanwhile, I'd already kissed five from this realm and regretted nothing.

Zucker ran his thumb over my bottom lip, staring at it. "Do you think we'd give you up if that happened? Go off and find ourselves another chosen one?"

Yes, that's exactly what I thought. Perhaps if I just told myself it was more about the magic that this bonding was going to provide me with, and not about real intimacy, I could squash down the feelings I didn't understand, and frankly feared.

"Wouldn't you? To save your realm?"

Could I give my body to four men and not care about them? No. It wouldn't be like that. Each of them had already found their ways into my heart. Which was crazy. I'd known them for a hot minute, not a lifetime.

Unless I counted the stories that Drosselmeyer had told me when I was a girl. I hadn't thought about those silly children's stories for such a long time. Not until he'd whispered that they were all true. Had his tales really been about this realm and these men?

Strong hands grabbed my shoulders and spun me around. Nuss stood so close I could feel both his warmth and his cool breath. Tiny crystalline snowflakes hung in the air around his head, but there was fire in his eyes. "You break my heart with your questions. I have loved you since the day we were all born. I didn't know how much until I saw you standing among the mundane people of the human world, hiding the light within you so that others might shine. You don't yet love us, but never doubt the feelings we have for you."

Nuss pushed his good hand into my hair and brought his mouth slowly down to mine, watching my eyes. He seemed prepared for me to flinch away, but his passion had emboldened me too. When his lips were close enough, I stood up on my tiptoes to go the last ten percent of the way and kiss him.

I'd never been bold in anything but dancing before, but in this strange here and now I suddenly found myself wanting to be more than who I was with these four men. I didn't know if it was this place, the possibility of being more than what I ever thought my life was meant to be, or just the idea that I could experience something with a man...these men…that deep down I knew I wanted but would never have admitted.

His kiss was both sensual and needy at the same time. He didn't pressure me to open my mouth to his tongue, instead his tongue teased at my lips, leaving it up to me to take this a step further. There was no way I could possibly deny him.

I breathed him in, not just his kiss, but so much more. I felt like he was asking to touch my soul, and it felt incredible. I could live the fantasy, the one where not just one, not just two, not even three, but four...maybe even five…men worshipped me. Me.

They wanted me. I couldn't deny the lust in their eyes, the need radiating from them, or the bulges in their pants.

"Fuck me," Leb groaned. "I never thought I'd see a snowflake getting it on. If you two don't let us in on some of that action, I'm gonna have to go over here and come all over my own hand."

I thought Nuss would break the kiss when he, like me, realized there were others in our bubble, but he didn't. He deepened the kiss even more, slowly backing me up into them. I was surrounded by four huge, warm bodies, and I was melting.

Not because I was forced to, but because I wanted to. I wanted this more than anything else in my entire life. I wasn't willing to break the kiss, so I reached out and grabbed whoever was closest and pulled them to me. Someone pushed their lips down to the crook of my neck, and someone else nibbled their way up to my other ear.

Nuss groaned and withdrew just far enough to press his forehead to mine. "Tell me you feel this connection, not just between you and me, but with all of us."

"I do. I've never felt anything like it before."

"And you never will with anyone else, because we were fated to be together." He slid his hand around my waist and found the zipper to my dress and gave it a tug. "Your body joined with ours, your mind one with ours, our lives forever intertwined. This is what will bring both the magic back to your life, and to our realm."

He pulled the zip down, loosening the bodice. Zucker pushed one sleeve down, and Tau the other until the dress pooled around my waist. The top had been snug enough that I hadn't worn anything underneath it and now my chest was bare to them. I held my breath, waiting to see their reaction.

Nuss's gaze never wandered down even a centimeter. He took one of Zucker's hands and placed it over one breast, then motioned with his fingers for Tau to give him his hand and did the same thing with him, pressing his hand over my other breast. "Our bond is what will bring out the inner strength you've been forced to suppress for so long."

Zings of heat coursed from where their skin and mine met, down my belly, and pooled between my legs. I both wanted to squirm away and push myself closer, begging them to touch me everywhere. I couldn't do either, because my eyes were locked with Nuss's. I was mesmerized not only by his mere presence, but also the way he clearly commanded everyone's actions.

Leb groaned from behind me, yet still didn't move to touch me himself without his commander's permission. Nuss's gaze flicked up and he gave a quick nod, then returned his eyes to me. He didn't even flinch when Leb pulled my dress down in one fast yank, letting the fabric fall at my feet. It was as if he wasn't interested in what I looked like at all. Only in my reactions.

That made me love him even more.

Magic burst in my chest, swirling around and around my heart. I'd never felt the sparks of power inside of me like this, but somehow, I knew in a flash it was the magic I was born with and that I needed to feel love and be loved in return for it to ignite—

Oh, goodness. There it was. I loved Nuss.

I gasped at the feeling of the magic within me and let it grow. I glanced over at Tau and another burst joined the first and pooled in my belly. It felt amazing. I could hardly wait for more. I turned my gaze to Zucker, and once again the magic dropped into my core, heating me from the inside and melting away the fear and reticence holding me back from feeling the true pleasure of his lust for me.

I sucked in a deep breath and turned to look up at Leb. The magic rushed up and down my spine and bowed my body toward his. The amber necklace his mother gave me, his people's piece of the broken seven crowns, glowed and my magic pushed out until it filled the whole room.

Nuss's voice came from behind me, intoning as if he was performing a spell. "As you collect the broken pieces of the seven crowns from each of the lands of the Winter Realm, your bond with the consort representing those lands can be consummated, strengthening your magic, and their loyalty and duty to you."

As if the magic was pushing us together, I floated to Leb and into his strong arms. For the first time, he was wide-eyed and awed, losing a bit of his alpha vibrato. "My lady, I am completely overwhelmed by your beauty and grace."

He gathered me into his arms and brushed a soft kiss across my lips. He'd been so eager and forward about his sexual attraction to me that I had expected he'd be almost roughly enthusiastic. I smiled against his mouth and deepened the kiss with him, pushing my tongue forward to tease him.

He relaxed, his taut muscles releasing, and he smiled back, against my mouth. He opened his lips and our tongues dueled to see who got to taste the other first. I won and my magic surged up, intensifying everything. I shivered at all the sensations and allowed them to flow through me. Leb groaned and it turned into his hearty chuckle.

"I do love it when a woman takes what she wants from me for her pleasure." He picked me up under the knees and shoulders, carrying me like a real princess the couple of steps toward the bed. He laid me down and crawled up over me, his massive body blocking out everything from my sight.

On the periphery I could feel Zucker, Tau, and Nuss's spirits reaching for mine, but I couldn't quite connect with them in the same way I had with Leb. I could also sense one more wisp of a spirit searching for a connection, but it was lost somewhere dark and desolate.

The amber light of the crown pendant matched what I saw in Leb's soul, and it surrounded us, pushing the darkness away. I clung to his light and let it fill me.

The magic dancing between us emboldened me in a way I didn't know I had in me, and I reached for his belt. His chest contracted with tight breaths as I unbuckled the clasp and opened the fastenings of his pants. His cock was already pushing at the seam and my fingers brushed against his hard length.

"Fuck me, lass. Touch me again, I beg you." His words came out as a shudder that sent butterflies up and down my spine.

"I'll touch you, if you touch me." I was sure I would break apart soon if he didn't.

"Sorry, my lady, you've made me lose my head. I'm doing a piss-poor job of pleasuring you."

"No, you're not. I—" He didn't let me finish my protest and kissed me so fiercely I thought my lips would bruise. The almost-pain of it only intensified the crackling of the magic rushing through my body. Leb sucked my bottom lip into his mouth and pulled it between his teeth.

"I'm going to do the same to the lips between your legs too." His shyness from before was gone now and the twinkle I already loved was back in his eyes. He kissed his way down my throat, between my breasts, across my stomach, until he got to the red panties I'd worn beneath my dress.

"I didn't know any small garment could be so fine." Leb ran his palm across my lower belly, slipping his thumb under the elastic waistband, then pulled them down on one side, then caressed across the same path, pushing them lower until they were bunched at my hips.

"I didn't know taking them off could be so infuriating." I lifted my bum, begging him with my actions to take the damn things off already.

He laughed, not his normal chuckle, but a big, hearty, joyful laugh. "My apologies, I'll fix that right now."

With one flick of his thumb, he tore the fabric, slipped it out from under me and flicked it over his shoulder. "Better?"

"Yes, but I do hope the gingerbread warrior women have something I can wear tomorrow." I hadn't thought that the lead up to having sex could be fun, but I suppose I shouldn't have expected anything else with this big teddy bear of a man.

I was looking forward to more of this flirtatious foreplay. Why was it only me and Leb in this big old bed, though? They kept saying it would be all of us. "I feel slightly awkward asking this, but are the rest of you going to join in? I want to be able to bond with you all."

Zucker and Tau stepped forward and flanked either side of the bed. Tau rested his hip against the soft mattress and touched my cheek. "Until we find our land's lost pieces of the crowns, we cannot fully consummate our bond with you."

"Oh." Disappointing. I thought this would be one big love fest and all the bonds between us would be sealed with the magic I felt so strongly.

"But if you wish for us to be here, we can still bring you pleasure, amplifying your bond with Leb." Zucker traced the shell of my ear and licked his lips.

I glanced up at Leb and he gave me a nod. "It is the Viking way for one woman to be pleasured by many men. I would have nothing else for my *stjarna*."

The magic whispered in my mind that he'd just called me his star. The endearment warmed my heart and felt so right.

"Nuss? What about you?" It took a minute for me to find him. He'd tucked himself into a dark corner of the room.

"I will bear witness if you wish, sweet Clara, but I ask you to forgive me for not participating. It is not something I can do until we find the Snowflake crown." The fist of his unbound arm clenched and opened at his side and the magic between us pulsed just as hard as it did with Zucker and Tau.

I reached my hand out to him and beckoned him to me. He put his palm against mine and I wrapped my fingers around his. "Then tomorrow we must find it."

YOUR LOVE IS BETTER THAN COOKIES

CLARAMARIE

I understood what I had to do now.

If I wanted to bond completely with each of these men who'd come dancing into my life and stealing my heart, I had to find all the pieces of the broken seven crowns. That's why I was here. They might think it was to defeat this corrupt Mouse Queen, but I still wasn't convinced the Vivandiere wouldn't show up and do that herself.

No, I needed the crowns to be able to restore the magic of love to the realm, and I would only be able to do that by discovering it for myself. That's how I would help defeat the evil that had seeped into the Winter Realm. Not by fighting, not by leading an army, but by spreading the magic of love.

I realized now that when Mother Gingerbread gave me the piece of the broken crown from their Kingdom which she and her bonded partners had carefully guarded, she was blessing me with her son's hand.

This bonding was just the same as a marriage as far as I

could tell, but somehow so much more. Marriage in the human world was a contract, and mine in particular was going to be nothing more than a business deal made to bail my brother out of the poor decisions he'd made. Love had nothing to do with it. Only fear, obligation, and desperation.

This bonding with Leb, and soon with Zucker, Tau, and Nuss meant so much more than saying some vows and getting a piece of paper that said I belonged to another man.

This was a joining of our spirits and I honestly believed that without love, it wouldn't feel quite so powerful. Yes, I might be joining with them so they could be my consorts, but in this moment, I didn't care about that even a little bit. I only knew that I wanted to be vulnerable, and intimate, and closer to these men than I ever had been to anyone in my other life.

"Please stay, Nuss. I understand we can't yet be together, but I want you here." I squeezed his hand and hoped it wasn't too much to ask.

"As you wish, Princess." He slid his hand from mine and stepped back into the shadows where he sat in a lone chair in the corner.

I vowed to someday find out why he wanted to be alone when he didn't have to be. For now, I would give him what he needed, hoping later I could heal his heart.

Zucker pressed his lips to my ear and whispered, "I can feel your mind working. He's a tough nut to crack. We've all tried over the years. You know what? I'll wager watching you come for us, and again as you ride Leb's cock, sealing the bond, will do wonders to thaw that icy snowflake he calls a heart."

He swirled his tongue over my earlobe and then down to the sensitive spot just below my ear. If this would help heal my Nutcracker once again, I was all for it. I wrapped my arm around Zucker's head and held him close to me, reveling in the sensations his kisses were sending through me.

"I want to kiss you everywhere tonight," Tau said. "We'll

make your body sing and prepare you to take Leb's giant of a cock into your body."

Leb raised an eyebrow and grinned but didn't say anything. That more than anything else told me that Tau wasn't exaggerating about the size of Leb's penis. Oh boy. Instead of touching me, Tau pulled Leb's trousers down and I finally got a good look at every inch of Leb's body for myself.

That wasn't a cock. That was a whole damn Christmas tree, decorative ornaments and all. "Are those piercings?"

Leb stroked his hand up his cock from the base to the tip, dancing his fingers over the small barbell underneath and the four shiny metal balls that encircled the head of his shaft. What would those feel like in my hands, in my pussy?

"I promise, my Princess, these are for your pleasure. It's all for you." Tau took my hand and placed it over the head of Leb's cock, showing me how to play with his piercings and making them a whole lot less intimidating. Beads of Leb's seed leaked from the head and my pussy clenched, heating, and my own moisture flowed in response to his. Tau dragged my hand down to the second piercing underneath and Leb groaned in a way that I wanted to hear over and over.

Leb put his hand over both of ours and stilled our stroking with a hard squeeze. "Fuck me. I warn you, if you keep doing that, I'm going to spill my seed on her belly instead of in her cunt."

"Is it bad that I'd like to see that?" It didn't feel wrong, but I knew extraordinarily little about what I should and shouldn't do or think when it came to sex.

Tau, Zucker, and Leb all groaned, and not in the you're-such-a-fool way, but in a tone that made me realize I'd definitely said the right thing. That emboldened me, making me feel as if I could do no wrong now. That was something new in my life and exciting to me.

I wasn't entirely sure what to do with this feeling, but I had one idea. I looked at Tau, and then to Zucker. "I know we can't bond yet, but I want a connection with you. Could you, or rather could I, stroke you like we were just doing to Leb and make you come... for me?"

"Sweet princess," Zucker crooned, "the bonding is about pleasuring you, not us. When you and Leb come together, your bodies joined, it will link your spirits, and your magic will build."

The magic wasn't as important to me in this moment as the link I wanted with each of them. "But I want it to be about both of us, all of us." I glanced over to Nuss who was still hiding at the other side of the room. "Including you."

"I say give the lady what she wants." Leb smiled and moved my hand slowly over his shaft again.

Nuss's voice directed us from out of the darkness. "Her magic is awakening her mind and body. If she wants to see you come for her, that wish is coming from a hundred years of the alchemy within her being suppressed. Give her this, even though it's not what we've been taught to do. She knows herself better than we do."

"What about you?" I prodded at the boundary Nuss had set. I couldn't help it. "Will you give me what I want as well?"

We stared at each other in silence for a moment. I could practically feel the others holding their breath to see what Nuss would say or do. I could tell he wasn't going to join us, but I could feel the magic sparking between us. How could he resist it? I couldn't. I wanted him, I wanted them all in a way that made me pussy quiver with anticipation.

"Very well. I will give you what I can." Nuss stood and shucked off his jacket and the remaining tatters of his shirt, giving me a glimpse of the muscles in his chest and abs.

All four of my protectors were each perfect specimens of gorgeous men in their own ways. Their bodies were vastly different in shape and size, and it honestly made me think that my body, so different from theirs with my soft and plump curves, was the exact right match for each of them.

It flashed into my mind what the dark Mouse Prince would look like naked, his cock hard and his body hovering over me.

Nuss unbuckled his trousers and let them slip down to his hips. His cock jutted out of the opening, and he wrapped his hand around it. "This is as much as I can give you until we find the Snowflake crown. Then, everything I am is yours."

He sat back down in the chair, careful not to jostle his bandaged arm, and leaned back, his cock still gripped tight in his palm. If he wasn't going to join us, then... oh. Oh. He was going to stroke himself while watching us. All the little hairs on my arms, legs, and even my abdomen stood up as if reaching up and waving to him to look at them.

I hadn't thought anything except him joining us in the bed would be enough for me, but having him watch us was making me want the other three even more. I couldn't wait to put on a deliciously dirty performance for him.

Zucker stripped his shirt off over his head and dropped his trousers to the floor in the blink of an eye. "You are a magic miracle worker, my sweet, to be able to get our captain to participate. Let's give him a show, shall we?"

"Fuck my flowers, I never thought I'd see the day a snowflake would bend. This is an opportunity we can't pass up. You are truly magical, Princess." Tau pulled his hand from Leb's and mine, waggled his eyebrows at me, and climbed up onto the bed.

While the others had shucked off their clothes quickly, Tau undid the buttons on his shirt slowly, taunting me by giving me only peeks at his skin. Leb laughed and said, "If you're going to tease her, I am too."

He slid my hand from him and scooted down the bed until his face was level with my thighs. "You have no idea how long I've been waiting to do this, Clara."

With his big hands he pushed my thighs apart, lowered his head, and bit the sensitive inside, halfway between my knees and my pussy. I squealed, and tried to wiggle away, but he held me down and licked over the little sore spot. *Ooh*. The contrast in sensations make my brain glitch out.

He did it again, higher up my thigh, and I spread my legs even wider for him. With each little bite and then the soft caress of his lips or tongue immediately after, my core wound tighter. I wanted him to move even higher to see what it would feel like for him to do the same thing to my pussy lips, even to my clit.

As if I'd spoken my desire out loud, Leb did exactly what I wanted. A quick bite, at the very top of my mound, mere inches from my clit. He licked over the pain and then all the way down one side and back up the other. He nudged my pussy open with his jaw and the scratches of his beard added another layer to the sensations.

I reached my hands down to grab his hair and pull his mouth to my clit. I needed his mouth on me there or I would wind up so tight that I'd never come uncoiled. Then strong hands, one on each side of me, grabbed my hands and pushed them up and over my head.

This time, I was the one groaning.

"Whatever you're doing, Leb, keep doing it. Our princess is blissing the fuck out. Her magic is literally dancing across her skin." Zucker's voice sounded very far away, and I realized I'd closed my eyes. When I opened them to look for him, I saw he was stretched out next to me on the bed, one hand holding my wrist over my head, staring at me, and biting his lip. "I can't wait to get my own tongue between your legs, or even better, having you sit on my face while I fuck you with my mouth."

I was about to protest such an insane idea as me sitting on his face, but that was exactly the moment when Leb closed his teeth around my clit and flicked his tongue over my trapped sensitive nub. It happened so fast that my words came out as a cry instead. My back bowed and I struggled to close my legs around Leb's head. He held me down, keeping my legs spread wide apart.

"That's it, my flower, let go and come for him." Tau stroked his fingers over my breast and circled my nipple. "Or do you need just one more push to go over the edge?"

"Please—" I couldn't get more than that one word out.

At the same time, Zucker and Tau lowered their mouths to my chest, and each took a nipple into their mouths. Zucker sucked rhythmically while Tau swirled his tongue in circles. Sparkles of magic flickered up from my pussy to my chest and I exploded with a gasp. A thrill like nothing I had ever experienced before poured through me and stole my breath away as my clit and nipples thrummed out a pleasure beat.

Leb popped his head up from between my legs and licked his lips. "Your orgasm is the most delicious thing I've ever tasted. Now that your body's had a sample of these delights, it's time to make your cunt ready for my cock."

He slid one big, thick finger inside my pussy, and I felt every inch pushing against my inner walls. He pumped a few times, watching my face closely. Then he pushed in a second finger, and I groaned as he stretched me. "Fuck, you're tight, and I don't ever want to hurt you. Maybe we should wait until we've found more crowns and you've had the others first."

I shook my head and tugged at my arms. I wanted to pull Leb to me and show him how much I needed this, needed our bodies to be joined. The two Fae Princes stopped their ministrations on my breasts and lifted their faces to me, still holding me tight to the bed.

Zucker jerked his chin at Leb. "Let her ride you, our gentle giant, then she can take what she needs in her own time. We'll make sure she's pleasured."

Leb nodded and looked down at me. "Someday, I promise I

will fuck you so hard you can't walk for a week, but this is not that day. Come, take as much of my cock as you can."

The Fae princes lifted me up from the bed and Leb switched places with me. They helped me crawl over him and I had to spread my legs even farther apart to straddle his girth. I caught a glimpse of Nuss out of the corner of my eye. He glared at us, almost like he was mad, but I didn't feel angry energy from him, only quiet desperation. His hand was still wrapped around his cock, and he was stroking it up and down, slowly, evenly, almost mechanically.

I wanted so much to go to him, help him, and make it pleasurable, but he narrowed his eyes and frowned at me, giving me the slightest shake of his head. Fine. I remembered my promise to myself to give him a show, and that's what I was going to do.

"Lean forward, sweetheart, and put your hands on Leb's chest. I'll guide the tip of his cock into you, then you sit back and take as much as you want and need." Zucker slipped behind me and between Leb's legs and Tau helped me get into position. Leb put a hand on either side of my hips, supporting me in a way that made me feel completely safe.

"She's fucking dripping wet and ready for you, Leb." Zucker swiped his fingers across my pussy and pushed one, then two, then three inside. He pumped them slowly, opening them like a flower inside of me, stretching me out. "There you go, relax and open for me."

I was trying to relax, but I was giddy with the anticipation of truly bonding with Leb. I bit my lip and closed my eyes to concentrate on what Zucker asked of me, but then Tau jerked up my chin and said, "Look Leb in the eye as you take his cock into your body. Let your magic flow through you to him."

He nodded to Zucker, who withdrew his fingers and almost instantly replaced them with something much, much bigger. "That's it, my sweet. Your cunt looks fucking beautiful taking his monster cock. That's it, let him in."

Leb's hands on my hips trembled and a sheen of sweat formed on his upper lip and brow. "Fuck, fuck, she's so fucking tight, it feels so good. I'm dying to thrust into you, love."

"Not yet, big guy, easy, let her take what she can. Do you feel that, Clara? Your bond is almost complete. Sit back now and push his cock into your body."

Once again there was that bite of pain that only increased the sensations of the pleasure. "You're stretching me and feel so much bigger inside of me."

Tau helped to push me into an upright sitting position, and I sank further down onto Leb's cock until I was so full, I thought I would burst. I laid my head back and closed my eyes, holding my breath for just a moment while my body adjusted. When I could breathe again, I looked down at Leb and took him even deeper.

"Holy fuck. Lads, I'm about ten seconds from coming. Help her come again so we can complete the bonding." His voice was strained, and his arms were shaking.

"Our pleasure." Zucker moved back to the side and he and Tau slid their hands between my legs to find my clit. As one slid his fingers up one side of the little nub, the other went in the opposite direction.

My pussy clenched and I felt the next orgasm building. "Wait, I want Zucker and Tau to be pleasured too."

Tau laughed. "Trust me, darling, we are in ecstasy."

"No. I want to pleasure you. Me."

"As you wish, my lady." Tau directed my hand to his cock, and as he slid his fingers through my pussy, he moved my hand up and down his shaft.

"Gods, that's a fucking beautiful sight." Zucker followed suit and did the same with my other hand. He leaned across Leb's body and met Tau in the middle where they kissed, their tongues dancing together before my eyes.

Yes. This is what I wanted.

I stroked their cocks as they made out in front of me, and slowly, carefully moved my hips to take more of Leb. "If you're ready, lass. Let me."

He shifted his hips, withdrawing from me slightly and then thrust back in. The metal balls in his cock slid across a spot deep inside of me that had my inner muscles singing. He did it again, and again, until we all were in perfect rhythm.

I glanced over at Nuss, and his eyes were almost black. Snowflakes danced in the air around him, and he jerked his hand back and forth matching stroke for stroke my hands on the Fae princes, and Leb's thrusts in and out of my pussy.

I let go then, knowing all four of my men were feeling the same pleasure I was, that they felt as loved as I did in this moment. My own spirit rose up and out of my body, like a Christmas star, pulsing and then shattering, along with my own body. The orgasm crashed over me, and magic rained down on all of us.

Leb grunted and his hips jerked, his hot seed spilling into me. Zucker and Tau's fingers intertwined between my legs, and they groaned into each other's mouths. They both came, Zucker pushing his cock forward so his cum spurted onto both my hand and Tau's legs.

Tau's body tensed, as if he wasn't ready to let his orgasm wash over all of us. His cock was dripping with his seed, but he hadn't yet released. I swirled my thumb over the head and pressed my lips to his ear. "You're mine now, Tau. Forever. Let go and come for me."

He moaned and came in my hand, finally giving in and releasing into the magic and spirit flowing around us. The only one left was my protector, my staunch soldier, my Nuss. I found his eyes once again, and as if he had been waiting for me to watch him instead of him watching us, he gave his cock one more hard stroke and shot his seed all over his hand and belly.

In the nirvana we all drifted through after the climax of the bonding, the stories Drosselmeyer had told me flittered through my mind like a disjointed movie. His characters—the Nutcracker, the Sugar Plum Fae, the Dew Drop Fae, the Gingerbread Viking, the Mouse Prince, and the Vivandiere—went on adventures where they explored the lands of the Winter Realm and found many treasures along the way. Treasures that they didn't collect or take home as plunder, but that they left behind for others to discover too.

Those treasures were the seven crowns, and they belonged to me.

PRELUDE TO A STOLEN KISS

KONIG

I fisted the scrap of red silk fabric I'd torn from Princess Clara's dress and pressed it to my nose to deluge my senses with her soft vanilla and whiskey scent. Just the smell of her had my cock hard and my seed leaking from the tip.

Her magic crackled everywhere through the air and was contained by the mountains surrounding the idyllic little Gingerbread village. There wasn't a house in the stronghold that was unaffected by the power of her sexual awakening. From my hiding spot, in the rocks and scrub on the slope behind the longhouse, I could see into at least ten windows, and each revealed men and their woman in the throes of passion. The houses I couldn't see into had the scents and sounds of sex emanating from them.

I couldn't blame any of them. Princess Clara and her magic were intoxicating. I was drunk on her myself. It was the only explanation for why I was sitting here in the snow, my cock out, and my army on hold. We could have invaded hours ago. The Vikings weren't as well hidden as they thought. It only took one report from a dying mouse to discover the rebels of the Nutcracker Guard had retreated to the arms of Mother Gingerbread.

Yet here I sat, basking in her magic if not her presence, ignoring the directive of my queen, because I was jacking off.

I knew full well I was sabotaging myself, my army, and my queen, but I still wrapped that slip of silk around my cock and fucked my own hand, imaging it was her mouth, her cunt, her ass. When the second wave of her magic, so much stronger than the first, hit me, I grunted, not ready to orgasm just yet.

Then she demanded that I come for her.

Her soft and gentle spirit grabbed mine by the throat and commanded that I taste her magic, drink her in. I felt the spirits of Leb, Zucker, Tau, and even chaste Nuss, dancing and joining with hers, fulfilling their destinies. Leb's bond with her would be consummated and his connection with her forever unbreakable.

I couldn't resist her claim on my soul and shot my seed into the snow, letting her magic wash over me just for a brief moment as I climaxed with the rest of them.

For me there would be no after sex snuggles or cuddles, no sweet nothings whispered to each other, no promises made for a long life of love together.

Because my destiny was fucked the day the Mouse Queen found our kingdom's crown. My life was no longer my own, my friends were gone, and my dreams were dashed by one heartbreaking curse. I belonged to the Queen now and even Princess Clara of the Land of Spirit and Magic couldn't save my forsaken soul.

Perhaps I could save hers.

This battle to usurp the Queen was lost before it even began. The Nutcracker Guard and the other rebels simply didn't know it. If, however, I could stop the princess from finding the other crowns, I could get her to give up on this quest and send her packing back to the human realm where she belonged before this civil unrest destroyed everything.

She would be miserable, but she would be alive.

I'd made a mistake when I allowed her to slip through my hands once before. I wouldn't make it again, though her strengthened bond with Leb would make my job more difficult and my intentions harder to hide now.

Tomorrow, they would start their hunt for one of the four remaining crowns. Probably one of the Fae Kingdom's, if I had to guess. Only Clara would have the ability and knowledge to find it.

I couldn't let that happen. I either had to steal the crown out from under her nose, or separate her from the rest of the guard. A bond with one Christmas prince I could keep from the Queen, but not two. She would make my life and that of my people hell if she even suspected the princess was gaining power.

The scratching and squeaks of a mouse coming through the rocks and snow pulled me from my thoughts. I tucked myself back into my pants and slipped the red silk through my belt loop. The animal climbed up on the nearest rock, bearing a note tied around his belly.

I slid the paper from the string and tucked him into the warm pocket of my shirt underneath my jacket. The wax seal on the outside bore the crest of the queen. I flicked the seal into the snow and unrolled the paper.

Our new friend, Friedrich, would like to be commissioned as Lieutenant in my army, and receive the benefits of the position.

As I believe you've recently lost one of yours, he would be a good replacement.

~ Your Queen

While the compulsion of her spell over me swirled upon the

paper, she knew as well as I did that without a direct command, I didn't have to obey. Nothing in the note actually charged me with any obligation. She was merely placating this stupid, greedy boy.

Born under the Christmas star, he and Clara could have ruled the Winter Realm as a brother-sister king and queen. That was not to be, though, because I knew his type. He wanted all or nothing. Nothing for anyone else, anyway. He would let the kingdom fall into utter ruin before sharing the power of the throne.

That was even more dangerous than the machinations of the Mouse Queen. At least the queen had seized power in an angry act of rebellion against oppression. She just didn't see past the end of her own nose. She could have freed everyone, but instead fell prey to the same lust and abuse of power as the snowflakes.

And then, instead of using her influence to make life better in the realm, she'd decided to make it harder for everyone but her. Her new pet human would do even worse.

I pounded my fist into the snow. Enough was enough. I had only eleven more days of Christmas and every plan I'd had to somehow get the princess on my side was squashed in the snow like the guts of so many slain mice.

If I couldn't win her over, I would steal her away and make her see. It was the right thing to do, even if it turned my stomach. I knew it back at the battle in the Christmas Tree Forest. Instead, I let her fear and beauty sway me into hoping there was another way.

There wasn't.

She would be mine, even if I had to kill each and every member of the Nutcracker Guard to make it so. It wasn't like my heart could break more completely than it already had. Murdering the men I'd pledged my loyalty to, and then died inside when they broke that honor into dirty little pieces, would be the final blow I needed to give up any hope I was anything other than an instrument of the Queen's.

I hunkered down and waited until the morning's light roused the princess and her guards from their love-drunk stupor of the previous night. Mother Gingerbread was a master strategist and had everything they needed prepared for their journey, including three sets of decoys to throw my army off the trail.

Each decoy had two lithe warriors that looked like the Fae, a burly Viking, and a leader dressed in the Nutcracker uniform. Where they'd gotten red silk for each of the women in the shill groups, I didn't know, until I saw the real princess walk out of the longhouse in a cut-down version of her dress.

She fucking glowed like the Christmas star.

Leb wrapped a great fur coat around her, hiding every bit of her bright dress and her luscious skin. Their ruse might work on my lieutenants who lay in wait at the base of the mountain, but they could never again hide Princess Clara from me.

I coaxed the little mouse from my pocket where he had spent the night and sent him back down with a message for my army: my trackers should take a patrol and follow the woman in the red dress and her men, but weren't to attack, only report back to me which land they were traveling to. They didn't need to know the intricacies of my plans.

The four bands of travelers mounted their horses and disappeared into the secret tunnels carved into the rocky mountainside that served to keep the stronghold of the Gingerbread kingdom safe from my army.

I shifted into my animal form and snuck into the tunnels behind them. The Vikings were smarter than I thought and had covered themselves in spices so pungent that they overwhelmed any other scents. Had any of my other trackers been trailing them, they wouldn't be able to differentiate between the real princess and the others, even with their sensitive noses.

My eyes watered at the intensity of the ginger soaking into every cell in my body. I'd have to warn the others to keep their distance. Even with their disguises and their covered scents, though, I would know Clara anywhere. Just as her consorts did.

Once they were all safely away, I would send the attack back through those tunnels and up and over the mountains to rain down vengeance for the deaths of so many that the Gingerbread Vikings had claimed in this war.

They were the last land to be conquered by the Queen. They would be the hardest to get to fall in line. Not like the Land of Spirit and Magic, which had seemingly capitulated so easily. The Queen assumed they'd submitted to her will, until she found out they'd hidden the prince and princess.

She'd taught the other lands a lesson when she destroyed Spirit and Magic. All these years later and still no one ventured anywhere close to their borders.

Except me.

I followed the true princess and stayed focused, looking for any opportunity to snatch her from them, even if that meant killing them. I would likely have a good ten days before I had to report in to the Mouse Queen. Ten days to save my people. Ten days to save myself.

In that time, I either had to seduce the princess, or force her to see the reality of what was really happening in the Winter Realm. Even if that meant that I had to destroy her.

THE CLIFFS OF THE GINGERBREAD KINGDOM

CLARAMARIE

My life in the human realm was quickly fading from my mind. There, I had no purpose other than to be a doormat walked all over by society, my friends, my family, even my fiancé.

I regretted leaving my father behind, but it wasn't as if he'd even realize I had left. Drosselmeyer would ensure he was taken care of, leaving me free to fulfill the destiny I was so clearly meant for here in the Winter Realm.

For the first time since I was a young girl and had taken my first ballet class, I found myself looking forward to whatever would happen next. The adventures of the Vivandiere and her soldiers were still fresh in my mind, and we had only to follow the stories to find the missing pieces of the fabled seven crowns.

The tale of the Sugar Plum crown in the Land of Sweets was the one I remembered the best, so we were headed to Zucker's family first. I was giddy with the anticipation of finding their crown and consummating the bond with Zucker next. He seemed to know my body better than I did. I loved knowing that when he and I bonded, it would bring him and Tau closer together too. They rode side by side, behind Leb and I, guarding the rear.

Nuss was leading the way, still quiet today, watchful, on guard. The new sword Mother Gingerbread had made for him overnight sparkled in the morning sun, dangling from his belt. Every time he reached for the hilt, I saw how frustrated he was by not being able to use his other arm, having to switch between his weapon and the reins of the horse.

"If you keep those thoughts to yourself, churning in your head, lass, smoke will start coming out of your ears. Share your burden with me. Please." Leb gave me a squeeze, pulling my body even closer to his.

Since I knew little to nothing about horses, I'd chosen to ride with him again. I enjoyed his warmth against me, but worried about the hardness of his cock. It had been rubbing against me for the past hour as we rode down the mountain. How long could he possibly endure that?

Perhaps we'd have to stop and take care of it. "I'm just wondering how long I have to wait before we make camp and can take care of your little problem poking me in the butt."

"Oh, it isn't little. You know that well enough." He gave me a fond little pinch for my troubles. "But there's something else bothering ya."

There was, but I couldn't quite put my finger on it. Perhaps the odd feeling that we were being watched, but that wasn't exactly it. I didn't get the sense of eyes on us, more like a dark presence following and surrounding us.

At first, I thought it had to be the dark warrior, Konig, the Mouse Prince, even though I refused to believe he meant me or any of us real harm. He could have easily killed or captured us all back in the Christmas Tree Forest yesterday, but he hadn't.

He'd saved me from his own army, kissed me like he meant it, and then told me to run. I hadn't yet relayed that part of the story to the others. There simply hadn't been time, what with all the bonding we'd been engaged in. I felt their distrust of Konig, though. It felt like a thousand paper cuts on my heart.

Healing that was on my to do list. One step at a time.

No, it wasn't Konig that was making me uncomfortable. There was something or someone else. Perhaps the Mouse Queen herself?

I wasn't ready to face her yet. I still had to use my magic to reawaken the spirits of the people in the Winter Realm. Then the Vivandiere could reveal herself and rejoin the story. She was the one who would usurp the Mouse Queen.

Not me.

In my secret heart of hearts, I hoped and prayed that the Vivandiere was my mother. That she too had gotten sucked back through the Christmas tree portal and into the Winter Realm. I pictured her waiting for me, and when the time was right, when I'd restored the Land of Spirit and Magic, ascending to her rightful throne once again and leading the rebellion against the Mouse Queen to victory.

So much else in my life up to now had been a lie, why not her death too?

"I'm sorry. I don't know what it is. I have this uncomfortable feeling that something awful is about to burst our happiness. It's probably only that I've never felt so happy and fulfilled before, so I'm waiting for something bad to happen."

"Ah. Don't worry, we'll always be here by your side, fighting any battles, both military and mental, that come your way. I won't say our road ahead will be easy, but I do promise to fuck the worries right out of you anytime you need."

I laughed, because Leb wasn't joking, even the littlest bit. He was sweet, and sexy, and protective, and horny all at the time. I was grateful he was the first one I got to bond with because his fierce faith in me, Zucker, Tau, and Nuss was the perfect way to start this journey of love.

Leb's horses snorted and kicked up, dancing back, balking at something in our path. "Whoa, whoa. Hold on, lass."

Another horse jumped into our path from behind an outcropping of rocks, and my heart that had been flying so high crashed like a shattering Christmas bulb into the bottom of my stomach.

"Hello, little sister. I always knew you were a whore."

Dear Reader~

ClaraMarie and her Nutcracker Guards' adventures in the Winter Realm are just beginning.

To continue their story, join my Curvy Connection newsletter to get a bonus chapter and then continue on book two - Stolen.

STOLEN

CLAIMED BY THE SEVEN REALMS - BOOK TWO

*For everyone who doesn't dance because they think they're too fat.
You're perfect the way you are.
Dance.
And fuck the haters.
(Well, not literally. That's a different kind of romance. *wink)*

To dance is to be out of yourself. Larger, more beautiful, more powerful... This is power, it is glory on Earth and it is yours for the taking.

— AGNES DEMILLE

STEEL IN THE WINTER REALM

CLARA

*I*n one breath I went from comfort and joy to death and despair. Honestly, that seemed pretty on pointe for life in the Winter Realm. One minute, I was filled with the magic of discovering this whole new world, falling in love, finding my mission in life, and getting the best orgasms from four of the hottest men to ever be born under the Christmas star, and the next someone was trying to kill is.

Yesterday felt about a million years away. I think time might move differently here in the realm than in the human world. Only a day had passed since Nuss dragged me through the portal between our worlds in our Stahlbaum family Christmas tree as we were chased by mice. But so much had happened since and I wouldn't trade even a second of it.

Well, maybe a couple of the seconds when I was being eaten alive by those horrid mice. But the rest? Good times, good times.

I gasped because, a horse jumped into our path from behind

an outcropping of rocks, and my heart, that had been flying, sunk like a crashing Christmas bulb into the bottom of my stomach. There was one particular person in my life who liked to ruin anything I had that was even slightly nice. Of course, he would try to ruin this for me too.

"Hello, little sister." Fritz looked from my Viking, behind me on our horse, to Nuss, and back to Zucker and Tau. His mount side-stepped and jostled about as if it was uncomfortable, but my brother didn't seem bothered. "I always knew you were a whore."

He curled his lip the same way I'd seen him do when he had to help look after father. "You should have married Herr Drosselmeyer when you had the chance, if only to save the family's reputation."

Older brothers were the worst. Mine especially.

Here I was, excited about the adventures ahead of me, filled with love and magic, then Fritz had to come along and try to break my toys. A couple of days ago, his words would have burned into me and hurt. I may have only been in the Winter Realm a brief time, but this world, and the men I'd connected to in it, were more my family than Fritz ever was.

Family was what I was making here, not the blood bond Fritz and I shared. "What are you doing here, Friedrich?"

He hated when I called him that. It was an old Stahlbaum family name and he wanted to be more modern and sophisticated than that.

"I've been sent to bring you home. Cleaning up your little messes, just like always." Fritz flicked his hands over his pants, as if wiping away some kind of dirt. He was trying his best to appear like this conversation was boring and beneath him. That was always his superpower back home. Made everyone else around him feel little and stupid.

"You will watch your mouth when speaking to the princess."

Leb's voice boomed, and I got more than a thrill from knowing he had my back, figuratively and literally.

Fritz's eyes snapped to evaluate Leb and I could practically see the calculations he was doing in his head to assess the threat. "You have no say in this, peasant. I am head of the Stahlbaum household and ClaraMarie is my responsibility."

Ooh. Someone who hadn't known what a scared little shit Fritz was might have missed the way he sunk back in his saddle before he struck back. But I saw. With each jab in this battle of wits between us, my vision grew sharper, and my strategy whirred. Both were new sensations in my dealings with my brother. He knew he was outnumbered and out manned. This was a rare turn of the tables.

Welcome to my world, big brother.

Nuss looked to me, communicating with a simple look that I was in charge here. He waited until I nodded, then put himself between us and Fritz. "But we aren't in the human realm anymore, and any authority you thought you had over our Clara ended the moment you came through the Christmas tree portal."

Fritz's hand hovered over the scabbard at his side. When had he learned to ride or use a sword? He must not be greatly confident in his skills, because if he was, he would have drawn. It was unusual to see him unnerved. I was happy to take advantage of it.

The men were making it clear, I was the general in our army, and that gave me a rush just the same as when my magic had risen up last night.

I gave Nuss my thanks with a soft blink of my eyes, and he backed his horse up a few steps. There was something new inside of me and I was guessing it had something to do with my bond with Leb last night and the fact that he came from a race of warriors in a matriarchal society. With every move one of my men made, I felt more empowered, not less. That gave me the courage to call Fritz out on the real betrayal. "Not to mention that you joined the wrong side of this fight when you got cozy with the Mouse Queen."

The entire mountain went silent. I gave Fritz the smiling smirk he deserved. "Didn't know I found out your dirty, little secret, did you?"

Leb snickered behind me, and I had to admit that having my guard around me gave me that extra bit of security I needed to stand my ground and even up the ante. I was a little surprised none of them had gone at him yet. I wasn't used to men both defending and deferring to me. It was something I could get used to though.

Fritz didn't like that I had the upper hand and that could go very badly if we weren't careful. While my brother was a dickhead and was in league with the wrong side, I also didn't want to see him killed.

"I'm not keeping any secrets, unlike you, little sister." His sneer was defensive this time. "I suggest you surrender and come with me quietly, so you don't cause any more trouble."

Tau and Zucker sidled up beside me and Leb, making a nice wall of muscle. I sat up even straighter. "You've got that backwards. You're the one who'll be coming with us so that you don't cause any more trouble. If you hadn't noticed, here in the Winter Realm, we're equals, and you're outnumbered."

The tingle of the magic I'd discovered inside of me last night, flowed along my skin. I swear, yesterday I didn't have this same confidence. There was more to how I was feeling and what was happening than I'd thought before. Bonding with Leb must have given me a little of his Viking spirit, because I was ready to take Fritz on head-to-head.

Learning some self-defense and even some offense was quickly rising up my priority list. I didn't want to get stuck throwing snowballs again, and I sure would like to see Fritz flat on his back in the snow from a good swift kick to the knees. Or the family jewels. My magic went all zip and zing thinking about it, and Leb wrapped his hand around my waist, then leaned forward and whispered in my ear. "I can feel your magic rearing to get out and take this crumble of a man down. But save it, lass, for the journey ahead. I'm more than happy to chop his head off for you."

Ooh. Why did Leb's bloodthirsty threat turn me on? "That sounds like fun, but alas I cannot condone killing my own kin, even if he is a royal ass. I'm having a bit of fun poking at him though. I don't normally get to in the human realm."

"Then have at. He needs a good blood-eagle to the soul." I could hear the contempt for Fritz in every one of Leb's words.

Now it was going to get fun. For me anyway. Not so much for Fritz. "Here's what going to happen, brother. You're going to ride down the mountain with us, and you're not going to say a word the whole way. When we get back to the Christmas Tree Forest you can either go home through the portal, and mind your own business, or you can come with us to the next land and maybe learn how you've chosen the wrong side."

Nuss drew his sword, Tau notched an arrow, Zucker twirled a dagger in his hand, and Leb laughed. It was the last that scared Fritz the most. He hated to be laughed at.

"You have no idea who I am here in your precious Winter Realm." He directed his ire at Leb, but I full-well knew that was a proxy for me.

I did wonder how long or how often he'd been here. Nuss implied the portal only opened to come here at midnight on Christmas morning, but that didn't explain how he'd gotten into the human realm before it opened. That was a question for later. "Doesn't matter, because I know who I am here."

I wasn't his doormat any longer. I had a mission to spread love, find those broken pieces of the seven crowns, and help my true people prepare to fight alongside the Vivandiere to defeat the Mouse Queen. Who, apparently, was Fritz's new special friend.

Gross.

Since he was my brother, I felt responsible for making sure he didn't make things worse here like he did at home. "We've got places to go, and I don't have time for your shenanigans. Fall in line. Now."

Ooh. I sounded so warrior woman.

"Now can I chop off his head with my axe, lass?" I felt Leb reaching for the axe on his back.

Fritz glared at me, dragging me into an old-fashioned stare down to see who would blink first. "I'm getting closer to saying yes."

"In the meantime, might I suggest we tie him up and make him walk?" Nuss nodded to Zucker and Tau and faster than I could say Christmas tree, the three of them had him surrounded, off his horse, hogtied, and gagged.

"Whoa." Seeing them so easily take Fritz down was exhilarating. "I was being a word warrior there for a minute, but you guys are like a coordinated troop of soldiers."

"Sweetheart," Zucker patted my thigh. "The warrior magic of the Gingerbread Kingdom was flowing through you straight to us. We were merely tapping into your power."

Fritz struggled and rolled around, but it did nothing except get him a face full of snow. Ha.

I turned in the saddle just enough to be able to see Leb better. "When we bonded, I thought we were awakening my magic, but you were giving me some of yours, weren't you?"

"I was in such a hurry to fuck you, we didn't even think about how little you know about how life in the realm works. But you've got the gist of it."

Fritz made some talking sounds that absolutely were slurs at me. I gave him the stink eye and Nuss stepped on his back, smashing him deeper into the snow. "This is part of why the four of us decided to stop competing against each other for who would be your consort."

"Only part?" I'd meant that to be a little joke knowing that they were each as anxious as I was to find the other pieces of the crown that belong to their lands so we could consummate our bonds.

Nuss's eyes went dark, and I got the warm fuzzies in my lower belly. That was the same look as when he was watching us from his throne in the corner of the room. It took me a really long minute to tear my eyes... and thoughts away.

Tau looked between us and grinned. "Yes, my flower, only part. But we did hope that combining what's in our souls with your magic would strengthen you, and thus all of the lands."

Zucker snickered. "Yeah, that's the part I was thinking about last night. Not the part where your—"

"Zzz. Pssst. Shh. That's enough of that kind of talk in front of my brother." I pretended to smooth my hair just to cover the way I knew my cheeks were lighting like bright red balloons. It wasn't that I was embarrassed or shameful about what we'd done. Just that it was meant to be between us.

And well, yes. I could do without Fritz's judgmental glares.

Zucker gave me a long, heated look and shoved Fritz's face deeper into the snow. "I'll hold my tongue now, if you'll hold it in your cunt later."

"Ahem. Yes, umm. Let's be on our way. Can we drop him off in the Christmas Tree Forest and shove him through the portal before our next destination?"

Nuss grabbed the back of Fritz's jacket and pulled him up to his knees. "I think we'd better bring him back up the mountain to Mother Gingerbread. She'll get a good kick out of interrogating him, and we might learn how the Mouse Queen got to him."

"I'll never talk." Fritz spit snow from his mouth, sputtering at being manhandled. "Your mommy doesn't scare me."

Leb laughed that big hearty chuckle. "You should be ready to pee your pants, small boy. She scares the rest of us. But if you aren't that attached to your bollocks, feel free to tell her that yourself."

"I will." Fritz squirmed in Nuss's hold but didn't get anywhere.

"Let's bring him to the Land of Sweets. A good vat of boiling sugar poured over his cock should get him talking."

I looked at Tau and Nuss, both of whom shrugged. Tau shook his head. "My people can't do much more than whip him with some violets. Maybe the Snowflake nuns can guilt it out of him."

"Okay, Land of Sweets it is then." Nuss shoved Fritz toward his horse and tied him to the reins so that he'd have to walk behind.

Hmm. There was a story there and I wanted to hear it before we got to Nuss's land of Snowflakes. I hadn't even realized the Winter Realm had religion. I'm not sure why I assumed it didn't, really. Organized religion often came with the trappings of purity culture. That had to have something to do with why he didn't join in with us last night.

Could it be possible that my handsome and sexy Captain of the Nutcracker guard was a virgin?

"Come on now." Leb gave our horse a nudge with his feet. "Let's get a move on. It's already the second day of Christmas and we've got more crowns to find."

I had two already. The one from the Land of Spirit and Magic that my mother left me. Ha, take that Fritz. And the one from the Gingerbread Kingdom. But I only had three more princes to bond with.

Although I'd kissed another.

WHERE IS THE VIVANDIERE?

CLARA

I glanced up along the path we'd come down and scowled. Nothing moved, yet something was out there. I don't know how I knew, but I felt the presence of the Dark Warrior, Konig, the Mouse Prince of the Land of Animals. Was he following us, watching? Had he watched us last night?

A messenger angel streaked down the mountain toward us and Nuss caught her on the elbow of his still broken arm. He flicked open the roll of paper and flashed us a warning look. "They've started their attack, Leb."

"Shite. Get that dickhead back on that horse and let's go. The mountain's defenses are set to trigger an avalanche. Let's go, go, go." Leb snapped his reigns and took the lead down the rocky path.

"An avalanche? Sweet baby Jesus." I quickly checked that everyone was with us. I'd already been through losing them in the last battle. I didn't want to go through that again.

Nuss tossed Fritz up across the back of the horse like a

trussed-up animal, and all three of them jumped onto their own rides. Leb gave us a hee-ya command and the six of us went barreling down the tiny path at a breakneck speed.

The mountain behind us rumbled and the spikes of anticipation already pumping from my heart screaming at me to run, went into flat out we're-all-going-to-die mode. A mountain of snow and rock and trees were in pursuit and catching up fast.

"Nuss, we aren't going to make it. You got a plan?" Leb shouted, and I hoped someone had an idea. The snow was already flying around us and while Leb could probably survive an apocalypse, the rest of us were vulnerable.

"Fuck it. This was supposed to be a last resort." He pushed his horse to put on a burst of speed and rode up next to me. He kicked one leg over the horse, standing in one stirrup, hanging onto the reins with one arm like a fancy Lipizzaner rider doing tricks.

What the hell was he doing? Leb held me tight around the waist, as Nuss leaned in and, going at lightning speed across jagged terrain with a fucking avalanche bearing down on us, he kissed me. Not just any kiss, either. Nuss sucked my bottom lip into his mouth and bit me.

I don't know how, but when he did that, he took some magic from me. The tingles of my newfound powers shimmered through my vision like snowflakes, over to Nuss. I yanked my mouth away and touched my lips. My fingers came away with a touch of blood.

Granted it would be hard to be gentle while galloping through an avalanche, but he'd done that on purpose. There had to be a reason. Nuss would never hurt me. What was going on?

He licked his own lips and then flipped backwards on his horse, pulled out his sword and aimed it at the snow.

What in the holy Christmas Star was going on? The snow coming toward us split, like a forked tongue, but only enough to save us for the next few minutes.

"Damn it. It isn't enough." Nuss cursed and pointed toward Zucker and Tau. "You keep her safe, you hear me. Even without the Land of Snowflakes' power, she will still be strong enough to overcome the Mouse Queen."

Oh, no. I didn't like where that was going. "Don't you even think about sacrificing yourself for me again. I need you, I need all of you here with me."

Nuss ignored me and jumped up on his horse's back, much wobblier than I liked. His balance was off without the use of both of his arms. I shouted to Zucker and Nuss. "Help him. Don't let him fall."

They both sped up and put themselves on either side of Nuss's horse so even if he fell, they could catch him. Their support didn't help even a little. Nuss jumped from his horse to the one carrying Fritz laid out across its back. If he was going to save Fritz over himself, I was going to find a way to bring him back to life and then kill him.

But Nuss used his sword to nick the back of my brother's neck. Fritz squealed and I wanted to scream at him to shut up. The same shimmers of magic that had flowed from me went up and along Nuss's sword. He once again pointed the tip at the snow and this time, it rumbled and tumbled and changed its path completely. The mass of it went around us, leaving the trail in front of us mostly debris free and safe.

It only took us a few more minutes to make it down to the edge of the Christmas Tree Forest, where we could stop and look back at the destruction we'd avoided. I slipped down out of Leb's lap, and marched over to Nuss, yanking him down by the pantleg. "What the hell was that?"

Nuss hopped down and stepped away from me, looking down into the snow. "I told you it was a last resort."

Zucker and Tau joined us, boxing Nuss in. Zucker poked him in the chest. "You drained magic from the Prince and

Princess of the Land of Spirit and Magic to use for yourself. How, why?"

Nuss sighed and looked out over the crags of snow and rocks that could have killed us. "It is a secret long held by the Land of Snowflakes. You all see now why I've been so adamant that we do everything in our power to keep her safe."

He pointed to me, and I both wanted to kiss him again and slap him at the same time. Why was he keeping so many secrets from me?

Nuss continued on. "Had I known Fritz was here in the Winter Realm we would have had to rescue him too. The Mouse Queen can never get a hold of either of them. We'll be lucky if she doesn't already have some of his magic."

"Is this why you didn't want to touch me last night?" My bottom lip was still swollen from his harsh kiss, but it hurt less than where my thoughts were going.

Nuss swallowed hard and then knelt at my feet. He took my hand in his and gave it a soft kiss. "No, my lady. I want nothing more than to bond with you. But we must first find the crowns."

That meant we were headed straight to the Land of Snowflakes next because Nuss and I had some things to work out in and out of the bed. The siphoning my magic thing was high on the list. "What was that you said about me not needing the Land of Snowflakes power? Don't I need all the Lands?"

The four men looked at each other and did that silent communication thing that comes from knowing each other so well. Nuss answered for them all. "We don't know. It's not like the Winter Realm has ever lost an entire land and its royal family and been taken over by a power-hungry animal before. We hoped that by all of us bonding with you, we could grow your magic exponentially."

I'd assumed just Fritz and I were lost, not the whole land of Spirit and Magic that we'd been born to. Something niggled in my memory. "Drosselmeyer's stories must have mentioned something about this. Fritz, do you remember the stories of the Vivandiere and the seven crowns of the Winter Realm?"

Fritz wiggled around like a giant floppy fish, but Nuss had thoroughly tied him to the saddle, and he wasn't going anywhere. "Why would I? That was baby stuff."

"God, Fritz, don't be a dummy." I threw my hands up and rolled my eyes at him even though he couldn't see me. "Clearly it was all real."

"The realm might be real, but do you see a soldier woman traipsing around here? And if the Mouse Queen is so awful why hasn't the Vivandiere fought back herself?" Fritz's voice was beginning to grate on my nerves, as was his attitude.

But he had a point. Where was the Vivandiere? I turned to the men. "Are there legends or stories about what happened to her?"

"Who are you talking about, lass?" Leb was the last person I'd expect to keep secrets from me, so his question struck me as weird.

These were stories about their lands, they happened in their realm. I only knew them second-hand and had heard them as a child. "The soldier woman who hid all the pieces of the seven crowns from the wizard."

Nuss remained much too quiet and when we got to his land, he and I were having more than one conversation. I wasn't bonding with someone who didn't trust me.

"What about you two? Do the Fae lands keep secrets too?" I didn't think Zucker had held anything back from me. He'd been enthusiastic about everything from the first kiss.

"Subterfuge isn't the Sweet Fae way. But I don't know of a soldier woman called a Vivandiere. Tau?"

"I've got nothing. But perhaps the stories predate us. If that's so, the Fae Queens might know. They've both lived an exceptionally long time."

I'd been going on the assumption that I could find the pieces of the seven crowns because I knew all the stories of how and where they'd been hidden. But what if none of the stories were even real?

"How old are the Fae Queens?" Surely, they would remember. Or if they didn't, we'd find out just how much trouble we were in.

"Hundreds of your human years," Zucker said.

What? Hundreds? Let me get this straight in my head. Fritz and I were born on the same day as all the men, so they were the same age as we were. Which was strange. They all seemed much older than me. But that must be because they had so much more life experience than I did.

Drosselmeyer was at least twice as old as I was, probably three times. I didn't really know. He told Fritz and I the stories when we were young, but as if they happened in his lifetime. The Fae Queens were probably the same age or even younger than Drosselmeyer if they had sons my age. Mother Gingerbread didn't seem that old.

It couldn't be right that the stories were so old that they hadn't heard them or that my men were a hundred or more years older than I was. "I have a strange question. But does time move the same in the human realm as it does here?"

Tau shook his head. "No, vastly different and I'm sure that's been strange for you and Fritz to be caught in the middle of that. Sometimes, like now during the twelve days of Christmas, we move much faster than the humans. One day here is like two hours there."

I've been in the Winter Realm a day, and only a few hours have passed at home? I'd be surprised if anyone even noticed I was gone. "At other times this world must pass the time slower because I think you all are older than I am, even though we're supposedly born on the same day."

Tau nodded confirming my suspicion. "Correct. But very

few residents of the realm are privy to information about the human world. Mostly only royalty."

I slapped my hand over my mouth to cover my sudden gasp. Because the men weren't the only ones who seemed to have a few years on me. I marched over to Fritz and slugged him in the tied-up arm. "You've been here before, a bunch of times, haven't you?"

"Ouch. Now who's the dummy, little sister?" Fritz squirmed around and glared at me.

"Oh, you still are. I can't believe you didn't tell me." I hit him again for good measure. Had to be the bit of warrior magic from the Gingerbread Kingdom in me feeling violent. If I didn't think he'd have valuable knowledge that we could use, I'd shove him off this horse right now and tie him to a Christmas tree. My friends the pixies would feed him, so he wouldn't die.

"Oh shoot, we left Trost and Freunde in the Gingerbread Kingdom. Will they be okay with Mother Gingerbread?"

The pockets of my coat fluttered about and out popped my pixie friends. They buzzed around my face, flailing their arms, and making all kinds of sounds as if telling me all about their own adventure surviving the last hour in my pockets.

I laughed and held out my hands for them to land on. "When did you two hide in there and why didn't you come out before now?"

"They come when you call them, lass." Leb patted Trost on the head. "Those are your Marzipan pixies. They've formed their own sort of bond with you."

"Mine? Like I own them?" They weren't pets, more like small people. "I don't like the thought of that. I don't want to own a person."

"No, no, yours in the same way we belong to you. It's your Spirit and Magic that have them being loyal to you. They're as free as any other being in the Winter Realm to come and go as they please. Their pleasure is to serve you."

Aww. That had me feeling all gushy and mushy inside. "That I can do."

Zucker gave Trost a little twirl and they giggled. Then Freunde jumped onto my finger and swung back and forth like they were doing gymnastics. "Thank you for your friendship, little ones. I promise to cherish it always."

"You are such a sap, ClaraMarie. They're fricking servant fairies. You don't have to say thank you."

How was I even related to this schmoe? "Somebody punch him for me."

Both Zucker and Tau did exactly as I asked, and I enjoyed every one of Fritz's groans. "Thank you."

"Lass, we need to get a move on. The Mouse Queen's army will likely soon figure out you're not in the stronghold. I'd rather we had you safe in another Land where we have support before that happens."

Now to decide whether to go to the Fae Queens to find out about the Vivandiere stories or to the Land of Snowflakes to dig into Nuss's secrets. But if I had to find the Snowflake crown and the stories weren't true, it didn't do us any good to go there. I didn't like either choice.

BIG ROCK CANDY MOUNTAIN

ZUCKER

A black line of mice snaked its way down the side of the mountain. I thought we'd have more time, but Konig was a crafty bastard at best and a ruthless general at worst. We were getting his worst today. I pulled one of my daggers from the sheath and pointed it up the quagmire of snow. "Nuss, can you do your magic trick again to bring another avalanche down on them?"

"Not without hurting Clara or the Prince."

Tau drew his bow and let off three arrows in one shot. They flew straight and far and struck the head of the column of mouse soldiers. "If we hurry, we can get to the edge of the Sweet Fae lands. We can hide in the border's glamour."

"I don't know what that means, but if it means not being eaten alive by mice again, I'm in." Princess Clara ran back toward her horse and Leb had to sprint to keep up with her. We took off in a dead run for the border of the Gingerbread Kingdom and the Land of Sweets. But we would be exposed until we hit the Fae magic that the uninitiated got lost in. Konig would have a tough time getting through, but he'd know exactly where we went.

I directed us toward the nearby line of trees. "If we skirt the edge of the Christmas Tree Forest the army won't attack the pixies and won't know which land we've headed for."

Clara looked horrified at the idea. "You're sure? Won't or can't."

Nuss glanced behind us and gave his horse a nudge to put on some speed. "No one has issue with the Land of Comfort and Joy. They are, and have always been, neutral and the Christmas Tree Forest neutral ground."

"How many wars have you guys had?" The Princess was getting a fast initiation into the politics of the Winter Realm.

"A few." Most were long since forgotten, but not the schism between the Fae lands. That caused generations of discord between our people. I never thought I'd get to introduce Tau to my family. Clara was making that possible. Probably.

I had to keep the hope alive that her presence would keep him safe from any angry Sweet Fae who had long memories and weren't quick to forgive the past. Like my mother.

We slipped into the cover of the forest and made a quick turn toward the border with my homeland.

The magic of anticipation danced across my skin and into my blood. We were headed to the Land of Sweets, and I'd been gone for far too long. I could hardly wait to show off the Prince and Princess of my heart. My mother always said I fell in love too fast. She wasn't entirely correct. Lust, sure, but love?

No. I'd only ever been in love with one person until Princess Clara. But to the Queen of Sweets' point, I'd fallen in love with both her and Tau at first sight. Tau had taken me far too long to seduce. But sweet Clara was as sensual as any Sugar Fae, and half the anticipation running through me was hers.

The rest was from a preternatural sense that I'd developed

over the years. We were finally going to find the broken piece of the seven crowns that represented the Land of the Sweets. I'd already had a taste of Clara's magic last night and knew it would be all the more sweeter once I could bond with her.

The only thing that would make it even better was if Tau and I could bond with her together. Then, perhaps I'd find out what he was holding back from me. He wanted love. I loved him. But he wasn't wrong when he said it would fill in something missing when Clara was between us.

The tingle of the glamour whooshed over me as I led our band out of the forest and into the snowy hills of the Land of Sweets. The Fae guard would feel our arrival and descend upon us soon. I stopped and waited for the rest to come through and put myself on one side of Tau. I gave him a look of concern and he nodded, gravely understanding the threat he was under just by being here with us.

He pulled his quiver with his bow and arrows from his chest and buckled it to the saddle behind him to show himself to be unarmed. Leb slowed his stallion so that he and Clara rode to the other side of Tau. Nuss moved in front making a shield around Tau.

They all remembered our first days together in the Guard, when Tau and I were at each other's throats. Hate sex was almost as good as bonding. But that was back when I was the one who didn't entirely believe we'd ever find the missing princess.

"Halt in the name of Queen SugarPlum." A Sweet Fae guard shouted from his hiding place in the glamour. We all slowed our horses and I held up my hands and nodded at the others to do the same. Sweet Fae guards were lethal assassins who wouldn't hesitate to kill unwelcomed visitors.

"I know I've been gone a long time, but surely you recognize your own Prince." I let my silver hair down from the tie keeping it out of my face as we rode and let my Fae aura shine. The purple light spread into the glamour, revealing six Sweet Fae guards with their swords trained on us.

"Prince Zucker? Is it truly you?" They descended on us and had their blades at the throats of Nuss, Tau, and Leb in an instant. "Who are these strangers with you? Have you been coerced into letting them into our lands? Say the word and we will free you and your lovely captive companion."

"Hey, I could be a threat too, you know. How do you know I'm not some—"

I cut Clara off before she could get us all into more trouble. "Ladies, gentleman, allow me to introduce you to Princess Clara from the Land of Spirit and Magic."

They collectively gasped and I had to hold in a chuckle. Mostly because I understood exactly how they felt. I was still flabbergasted she was here, even more so that she was soon to be my spirit mate.

Clara waved and made eyes at them all. "Hi. Nice to meet you. Please take your swords off my, umm, friends' throats."

The ones by Nuss and Leb stepped back, but the one with her sword to Tau, glowered. "Surely you don't claim this Flower Fae."

I was about to say something, but Clara reached out her hand and put two fingers on the Fae Guard's blade. She pushed the tip down and away. "I do. We aren't yet bonded, but he is mine, just the same as Zucker, Nuss, and Leb are. Kindly, back the fuck off."

Oh, sweet Christmas star, her newfound warrior magic was going to be the death of us. But damn, I found her dirty mouth hot and couldn't wait until she let me slide my cock between her lips.

To my absolute surprise, the Fae guard dropped her sword and gave Clara a small bow. "Yes, my lady. If you're sure."

"I'm sure. But I do appreciate your fierce determination to protect me and your prince. I'm rather found of him too."

Clara gave the guard a wink, entirely charming every Fae here.

If Tau and I didn't already have a claim on her, she'd have no end of lovers wanting to warm her bed while she was here in the land of the Sweets. I was even sure I saw a bit of pink on the cheeks of the guard Clara had engaged with, and I'd never known a tough Fae guard like her to blush.

"Please follow us, my lady, my liege." The guards formed a phalanx both in front and behind us. They may have ceded to Clara, but they didn't entirely trust Tau.

I hated how stiff he now sat in his seat, and wanted nothing more than to wrap an arm around him and pepper him with kisses. I needed the assurance he was okay probably more than he needed it from me. Regardless, tonight I was getting him into my bed. Even better if Clara was between us.

"Zucker, what is that?" Clara pointed to a candy cane vine fluttering with peppermint butterflies. Then she pointed to a candy floss bush, and then over to a maple sugar tree.

Her delicious innocence at experiencing the wonders of the Winter Realm had every instinct to protect her from the harsh realities of our world bubbling up like hot caramel. "Welcome to the Land of Sweets. We're the main provider of foodstuffs for the realm because of our rich natural resources."

I plucked a sugary leaf from the maple tree and held it up to her lips. Her tongue poked out giving the point a taste, and my cock went from my usual ready at any moment half-mast to ready to throw her to the ground and fuck her in the snow instantly.

"Mmm. That's yummy. But do you all only eat sweets? I think my teeth are going to rot out of my head."

Tau laughed. "I think you'll find most of the Sweet Fae are sugar addicts."

His joviality was cut short by the blockade in front of the gates to SugarPlum castle. The Sweet Fae Queen in all her glory, surrounded by a whole host of guards, weapons pointed at us, stood directly in front of the only entrance to the gates around the castle and its grounds.

"No friend of the Sweet Fae would bring such rabble into my house. What are your intentions?" The magic of her charm and raw sexuality wafted through the air, wrapping itself around everyone, including the guards until they were all so enamored with her that their tongues hung out. I alone was immune.

"Hello, mother. Pull your allure back a bit, will you? I'd like to introduce you to the Princess of Spirit and Magic." I motioned to Clara and noted that she too was unaffected by my mother's charms. Interesting.

The Queen raised an eyebrow and did her best to look even more intimidating than she already was. Clara blinked a few times and smiled back. An entire lifetime's worth of emotions flickered through my mother's eyes as she measured up the princess.

I had absolutely no idea which way she would decide. My mother hadn't ever put much credence into the Christmas Star prophecy and never understood why I wanted to join the Nutcracker guard in the first place. She'd be content for the Mouse Queen to run amok throughout the rest of the lands as long as they still bought our sweets and stayed out of our lands.

I wanted more for the Fae.

That same tingle of anticipation danced across my skin and psyche as I held my breath waiting for the assessment of the one woman, besides Clara, that I'd ever given a damn about. If my mother decided she didn't want to have anything to do with Clara, we'd have a challenging time searching for the broken crown of the Sweet Fae. But with her blessing would come all the strength of her army behind our mission.

"I like her, you may enter." She gave a little flick of her fingers and the sex magic snapped back, releasing everyone from her spell. She scowled at the guards closest to her and shooed them away. "Go, get, go, you silly Sweets. We've got a celebration to plan to welcome home my son."

I didn't miss that she left off the part of welcoming my friends. She may have approved of Clara, but it would take more than a smile to get Tau into her good favor. I'd rather not have to choose between the two of them, but I would, and Tau would win every day all day, twice on Sundays.

We dismounted and I took Clara's hand to lead her though the gates. I reached for Tau's as well, but he shook his head and fell in line behind us.

Clara worried her lip between her teeth. "I don't think your mother liked me very much."

"It's me she doesn't like, Princess," Tau said very matter of factly. "But I can live with that as long as you have my heart and I yours."

Wait, was that line meant for me or Clara? Damn it. I didn't care what anyone in the Land of Sweets thought, not even my mother. I whipped around, putting Clara between the two of us, and grabbed the back of Tau's neck to pull him close. I gave him a hot and hard kiss. I'd put Clara between us to keep her protected and so she wouldn't think she wasn't a part of this but wanted to grind my hard cock against Tau too. I needed him to know it was more than my body he had claim to.

Tau broke the kiss before me, but he wasn't unaffected. "I know."

"Just so we're clear." I searched his eyes, willing him to understand exactly how important he and his heart were to me.

Clara eyes were as wide as dessert bowls and her breathing was soft, but fast. Her magic surged up between the three of us and made the embrace feel like a warm hug that could turn into something so much more. As soon as we found that crown it would. Nobody said I couldn't fuck the sugar out of both of them while we were looking for it.

"I'm fairly sure everyone here gets it now. But can we move along? My arse is sore from riding all day and your Queen said something about a party, where I hope you've got some of that famous Sugar Plum cider, but any old ale will do." We three looked over at Leb, who had pulled his axe out and was tapping the broadside of it against his hand.

Uh-oh. Nuss stepped in front of us and pulled his sword out as well. He jerked his chin toward the gathering crowd of Sweet Fae, most of whom had menacing scowls on their faces.

My mother turned around, looked at the three of us in our embrace and at the fae staring at us disapprovingly. She rolled her eyes, shook her head, lifted her layers of flowing skirts so they weren't in her way and marched back down the walkway to us.

Oh, fuck. Here we go. I knew there'd be backlash to my actions. I thought I was prepared. I squeezed my lovers in my arms and then turned to face her. She got within two inches of me, stopped, looked me dead in the eye and that's when I knew.

She might be a fierce Sweet Fae warrior who was feared by most everyone in the Land, but she, above all, believed in the magic of love. In a move I never thought I'd see the Sugar Plum Queen make, she put her hand on Tau's cheek and patted it. Then she repeated our words. "Just so we're clear. I know too."

Then she clapped her hands to get the onlookers attention, as if she didn't already have it, and let her voice and her allure project through them all. "You all are much better looking with smiles on your faces rather than scowls. Change those faces or feel my wrath."

The Queen of the Sweet Fae whipped right back around and continued her march toward the castle, while we all stared after her.

"Man, I wouldn't want to be on your mother's bad side," Clara said.

I'd worried for a long time that I wouldn't ever be in my

mother's good graces, that she wouldn't accept me because of who I loved. I hadn't been home in far too long because of this mission and my fervent relationship with Tau. The relief of knowing the Queen was my true ally flowed through my heart like a river of the sweetest plum syrup. "No, nor me. But I would for the two of you."

"Hey, what are we?" Leb waved his hand between himself and Nuss. "Chopped nuts?"

I had a quick remark about something I'd like to do to Nuss's nuts, but held it in. It had become hard for any of us to express how we felt about the others in our brotherhood since Koenig's betrayal.

Instead of saying something smart I gave Nuss an eyebrow waggle and he returned it with his usual eyeroll. He clapped Leb on the arm. "Yes, my Viking friend, that is exactly what we are."

I did love them both, but not in the same way as I did Tau and Clara. They knew and understood that, or at least I thought they did.

Perhaps once we were all bonded with the princess it would be easier for me to express what was in my heart. Just the act of thinking that had me wondering if that was Tau's reticence too.

The sooner we could find the Sweet Fae and the Flower Fae crowns the better. First, we had to attend this welcoming party and hopefully survive long enough to convince the rest of the Sugar Plum court and our people to open their hearts as my mother had. Not everyone would fall in line just because she told them too.

Our guards kept close as we walked the rest of the way to the castle. When we reached the gates, I directed the guards to take Prince Friedrich to a secured area. I wished we had a dungeon to throw him in, but locked rooms would have to do until we could figure out what to do with him.

Trumpets sounded and Clara gasped as we walked forward

into the castle's courtyard, decorated in colorful banners abuzz with Marzipan pixies. Never let it be said that the Fae were ever unprepared for a party. The courtyard was already filling with revelers, piles of food, and every Sweet Fae's favorite, a dance floor.

Clara's pixies appeared from the depths of her furry cloak and buzzed around her head. She laughed and held out her hand for them to land on. "I think they're asking if they can go play with their friends."

"That's about the gist of it. Marzipan pixies go crazy for a party. They love very little more."

"Off you go then. See you soon, you two." Her pixies flitted away, and each brought back a treat for Clara to try. Freunde brought a mug of rich, dark coffee, and Trost brought some sugared fruits. "Oh, you didn't have to bring these to me, but thank you so much."

Those pixies loved when she was so open with her gratitude. Most of us took them for granted, and I'd have to try harder to be more gracious of our little friends and the way they loved to feel helpful.

Clara tried each of the treats the pixies brought over, and we made our way into the party. When we got to the dance floor, she stopped and stared. There was a longing in her eyes that had my insides clenching.

"I hope you know how to dance, Princess." I pointed out the dance floor and the merrymakers already doing a few steps around the edges.

Clara stopped and stared. "Dance? You want me to dance?"

"I want to dance with you, love." I could hardly wait to hold her in my arms and let the magic inside of her free.

DANCE OF THE SUGAR PLUM FAIRY

CLARA

For the two whole days that I had been in the Winter Realm, all I had experienced was war. I wasn't even sure if anyone in this place knew how to do anything but fight. Well, and have super amazing sex. Maybe it was because the first people that we visited were the gingerbread Vikings and they were clearly built for battle.

The Sweet Fae we'd met so far looked more ready to eat my face off than throw a party, but that's exactly what was happening. It took me months of planning, calling caterers, getting in a tree and a professional decorator, cleaning the main floor of the house, sending out invitations, and a million other preparations to throw our annual Christmas Eve party. The Sugar Plum Queen put this feast, with an entire symphony and dancing together in, what, like thirty minutes?

"Come, Princess of Spirit and Magic and let me look at you." The Queen pulled my hand away from Zucker's and had me doing a little twirl for her. "You are quite beautiful, I can see why my Zucker is taken with you. But your dress is a bit in tatters. That just won't do."

She clapped her hands, and a dozen ballerinas in every color, shape, and size, dressed in fluffy pink tutus surrounded me in an instant forming a wall around us. They fussed over me, with someone pinning up my hair, another patting my face with powder, and a half dozen of them with hands flying over my dress and fabric whooshing around me. I almost felt as if I was caught up in a bippity-boppity-boo of a fairy godmother.

I honestly never even felt my dress come off, and I was never naked, but within a few moments and a lot of squeals, I was in a similar outfit to the women around me. Except the bodice of mine was encrusted with sparkling jewels, and the skirt was covered in an intricate hand-embroidered design. I even had pointe-shoe-like slippers on, with ribbons beautifully wrapped around my ankles. They were pretty, but there was no way I'd be able to walk around in them all night.

The Sugar Plum Queen tipped her head to one side. "Go on, try them out."

My toes weren't taped, I didn't have my little lambswool half socks to cushion, and I'd be tumbling over in pain within a millisecond, but I did as she asked. The Queen wasn't someone to say no to. I took a couple of steps, and it was as if these were my own pointe shoes from my bag at home. The elastic and ribbons were cut to the exact right length and everything.

I popped up onto the points and tip tapped a few steps. Someone had already banged the toes out, so they weren't overly loud and there was just the right amount of support in the box. I couldn't believe how comfortable they were. It was like dancing on clouds, or puffs of cotton candy.

This was the most fun dancing I'd ever had and I'd only taken a few steps. I did an extra twirl and landed right in Zucker's arms. "You're a fucking gorgeous dancer, Princess. Shall we?"

Oh goodness. Tittering about was fun, but to do a real dance with a danseur? I'd never. No one ever wanted to be partnered up with me.

The other ballerinas clapped and took up positions all around the edge of the dance floor, ready to support the leading role I'd apparently just been cast in. I glanced over at the Queen, and she gave me a nod of encouragement.

What in the world would have happened if I hadn't been trained in dance? It was clearly a part of their culture and expected of me. God, I hoped I didn't make a fool out of myself.

I dragged my feet. "I look ridiculous in this costume. I'm like a parade float."

"I don't know what a parade float is, but I assure you that ridiculous is not what you are. I, on the other hand, have a ridiculously hard cock just thinking about getting to dance with you, and if you'll notice so does every Sugar Fae man here."

I glanced around the gathering of Zucker's people, and he was right. Every man had a bulge in the front of their pants, and some were even stroking themselves. A few were partnered up with other men or women and they were, umm, enjoying each other's bodies too.

"This isn't a giant sex party or something, is it?" I was just getting used to the idea of bonding through sex with more than one man. I wasn't doing it in front of a crowd.

The other thing I noticed this time around was that none of the women here had the tall, ultra-thin body of a ballerina. Yet, they all looked like beautiful dancers to me.

Most of them had bodies similar in shape to mine. Thick thighs, a belly, a big round bottom, and actual breasts that filled out the front of their costumes. Was this why I was curvy yet still felt drawn to dance? Even the Queen was lush and round, just like Mother Gingerbread had been.

I couldn't quite fathom that kind of dissonance from the

world I grew up in that told me that a larger body wasn't meant to be a ballerina or a soldier.

"Later tonight, I'll explain in more detail the intricacies of the Fae's sexual culture. We are much freer with the pleasures of the flesh than say the Land of Snowflakes, and apparently the human realm." He winked at me, and took a place beside me, holding out a hand to begin the dance. "But don't worry, this isn't an orgy. Those are only for special occasions."

"You're a tease." Which I was starting to like very much.

"Anticipation is half the fun, my lady." Instead of starting us in a traditional stance, he pulled me to him, and wrapped one hand around my waist and held my other up as if we were going to waltz instead of perform a Grande pas de duex. "Ready?"

"Zucker," I didn't want to screw up what seemed like an important moment. "I don't know the choreography. I can't just go out here and dance."

He ignored my protest and led me to center stage. "The dance will come from your spirit, pretty princess. Every Winter Realm borne has that inside of them. I promise you'll know what to do."

Zucker bent his head and pressed his mouth to mine, parted my lips with his tongue and the magic inside of me sparkled to life. I heard oohs and ahhs from the audience directed at us but was too caught up in this kiss to care. I lifted myself up onto my toes, deepening the kiss and putting my hand on Zucker's shoulder, ready to let the magic flow through me and into the steps of the dance.

There were more joyful exclamations and clapping, and when I opened my eyes, swirls of colorful snowflakes spun around us, showing me exactly how and where to take my steps. It was just as Zucker had said. My spirit was guiding me, and I knew what to do without even having to learn someone else's choreography or practice any routine.

The tinkling celeste music binked and bopped as if timed to my little bourrée steps. Do do do, do, do, do, doodle-loodle-loo. Zucker followed along as my cavalier and we floated to one side of the stage, me up on my toes on pointe, and back down again. My hands and fingers flowed, chasing the streams of magic, on their spinning path. I reached for them, performing my absolute best arabesques, kicking my leg gracefully up into the air. I'd studied dance for so long and knew the names and mechanics for each and every move, but in this moment none of that mattered. It was only the music and the story I was telling through the motions of each lift of my foot, each flick of my wrist.

These moves made me feel more beautiful than ever. More so than the time I'd tried on my wedding dress. How far away that seemed now. I was in a different place and time, and while I'd felt like a fairy princess that day, it was nothing compared to dancing for the gathered crowd of Sweet Fae.

All eyes were on me, and I wasn't the least bit uncomfortable with them all watching. It was as if this was the one role I was ever meant to be cast in. The reason I'd never fit any other part. This one was here waiting for me.

I followed the magic around in a long oval piqué manège, stepping and spinning, running my hands through the sparkles, darting over mystical obstacles with quick, fast coupé jeté jumps. While the dance was exhilarating, my energy was starting to flag. But I could see the finale of where the swirls of magic were leading me, so I pushed until I was almost there. Zucker bounded his way to where I would end the dance, and Tau leaped in next to him. I gave a final Chasse up, where they both lifted me into the air, one under each shoulder, holding me above the crowd and spun me in a grand finale.

When they brought me back down to earth from my flight among the angels, I was breathing hard and feeling the glow of the most thrilling moment of my life. The Fae around us clapped and cheered. Even Nuss and Leb were applauding and staring at me like I was their absolute pride and joy.

"Princess, this performance won't be forgotten by the Sugar Plum Court for an awfully long time. What a way to demonstrate the way to the lost broken piece of the crown here in the Land of Sweets."

We all took bows which gave me a moment to consider what Zucker had just said. We turned and bowed to the other side of the stage, and I still wasn't sure what he meant.

"I'm not sure what you mean. I was just following the magic, like you said. My spirit guided me through the steps."

"I suppose from inside of the dance, you couldn't see the magical glamours around you, but the rest of us could." Tau wiped a bead of sweat from my upper lip and stared down at my mouth. "It's why I had to join at the end."

The Fae around us hadn't stopped cheering and were gathering around us on the stage. Nuss and Leb pushed their way through the throng of people to get to us. The four of them boxed me in and took a step forward to lead me off the dance floor.

"Wait." I held up my hands and didn't move an inch. "What are you two on about? What did you see that I didn't?" I thought I was just following the spirit and the magic like Zucker said I would. Now they tell me there was some kind of show going on around me?

Tau had been watching from the sidelines until the very end of the performance. "Your dance and the projections of the glamour showed you following a path from the Sugar Plum castle through the Fae lands and finding a crown."

Zucker nodded and smiled down at me sending a whole rush of butterflies whizzing from my belly and between my legs. He was as excited as the rest of his people, and I was caught up in it. "That's why everyone is cheering. You've revealed where the broken piece of the Sweet Fae crown is and now we can retrieve it."

Tau looked between the two of us. There was something more and I could almost feel his trepidation coursing out of him. I put my hand on his arm and he calmed a little. A zip of the excitement from Zucker went through me and met the zing of Tau's worry, melding the two of them together into something calmer.

They both took a deep breath and met each other's eyes, and I was swept up into a different kind of magic flowing between the three of us. Tau cleared his throat and broke the spell. No, not broke it, the zips and zings of this connection was stronger than ever, and it had my chest fluttering. But Tau was worried about something. "Your path showed you going all the way to the border between the Land of Sweets and the Land of Flowers."

"Yes," Zucker said, agreeing, but with a note of confusion in his voice. "Do you not want us to journey that close to Flower Fae lands? If my family can accept you, is there not hope that yours will welcome me too?"

Tau gave the slightest shake of his head. "I wish I could say that they would. I was raised to hate you and everything about the Sweet Fae. You know how long it took me to give in to the attraction between us."

I waited for Zucker to scowl or darkness to cloud his eyes. Instead, he grinned that cocky smile that made me giddy and more than ready to find the crown and bond with him. "Then I'll just have to seduce the rest of your Land the same as I did you and make them all fall in love with me."

Tau rolled his eyes and shook his head, but he smiled too. That was apparently the right thing for Zucker to say. Love was high on Tau's priority list and my own heart went melty because of that. No one back home had ever thought falling in love was important, especially not for me.

The Winter Realm was giving me the chance to fall in love not just with one man, or even four or five, but also with myself.

I took both Tau and Zucker's hands in mine and brought them together over my heart. "If the Flower Fae have learned to hate, we'll be the ones to show them how much more powerful love is."

The Sugar Plum Queen pushed her way into our circle and grabbed my hand from the two of them. "If anyone can do it, it's the Court of Spirit and Magic, but you'd better hurry. We just caught a mouse at the border trying to get in."

Where the hell was the Vivandiere when we needed her?

SUGAR, FLOWER, SOLDIER, SPY

TAU

Konig was fucking relentless. Granted, since the prize was princess Clara, we all were. I'd do anything for the magic of her love.

My own people had almost turned their backs on me when I joined the Nutcracker guard. The only way I had convinced the DewDrop court that I needed to serve alongside the other lands was when the Mouse Queen had let her rodent army loose on our fields. The devastation had nearly caused civil war within our own land.

Not everyone had such fear and loathing of the other, especially when we didn't have enough food to feed every man, woman, and child, but the Sweet Fae did.

But the ones who did hate, who didn't want to take any help, would be the ones guarding the border. "If the cave we saw Clara enter in the dance is where I think it is…"

I wasn't ready to say it out loud. I didn't want to get everyone's hopes up that we could possibly find two pieces of broken crowns at the same time. because finding both the Sweet Fae and the Flower Fae crowns would mean our two peoples had been fighting for the wrong reasons since the beginning.

I redirected my attention on Clara. Her emotions were all of wonder and hope, and I needed them to feed my spirit. There were so many intense emotions pushing at my consciousness and it was hard to tell the difference between those of the people around me and my own. It had been a long time since any of us had been at such a large gathering of people.

Since the beginning of the rebellion, it had mostly just been the four of us, recruiting more residents of the winter realm to the underground resistance, and fighting back in small groups. The sooner we left on this quest for the Sweet Fae crown the better. "You won't be able to enter the cave we saw in your dance without both of us."

Zucker crossed his arms and nodded gravely. I irritatingly found old prejudices against the Sugar Plum Court bubbling up inside. If he was familiar with where this cave was, and so was I, we both had more knowledge of each other's lands than the average Fae. Which likely meant that Zucker had spied in my land in his youth, just as I had in Sweet Fae lands.

Why was I the one being suspicious, and he only thinking of our mission? I'd blame that on the swirl of emotions all around us. Not the ones buzzing around inside my own chest.

"Okay." She waved her hand between the four of us. "I sort of thought we'd all go there together anyway."

Nuss narrowed his eyes and shook his head. "I hoped we'd at least have one night of peace here. I'll go on the offensive and keep Konig distracted while the rest of you go find that broken piece of the crown."

Leb grabbed the back of Nuss's shirt to stop him from moving. "Oh no you don't. You're not getting out of being there when Zucker and Clara bond. Good try."

Clara bit her lip, trying to keep the hurt in her heart from showing on her face. It didn't work. Nuss took one look at her and went from determined to horrified.

"No, I... Clara, I swear to you, I'm only trying to protect you."

While we were all training to find and protect her, we should have given Nuss some lessons in protecting her heart too. Or fucking being around a woman at all. When the hell had he gotten so damn awkward?

"Then come help me retrieve this crown. I promise I won't make you join the bonding. I don't ever want you to do something you're not ready to."

All right. Now I wanted to kick Nuss's ass. What I was going to do was make sure he was watching every single minute of the consummation of the bond between Clara and Zucker, and then the same when she and I bonded too. I admit I was mad at him for not joining us in bringing her pleasure. Stupid Snowflake and his stupid religion.

But maybe the dumbass had actually learned a lesson. He stepped up to Clara, lifted her chin and stared into her eyes with so much want and need pouring off him, I could practically taste it. He licked his lips and I swear he was going to kiss her. But of course, he controlled himself. "I think that's what I'm supposed to be saying to you."

The Sugar Plum Queen cleared her throat, but it took Nuss and Clara a moment to break their gazes from each other. "While I'm the last fairy to tell you to get a room, perhaps you could restrain yourselves until we can get you out of the castle and on your quest to find the crown?"

If we didn't get him naked during the next couple of bonding's I'd be surprised. Even the stoic Nutcracker Captain could only hold out for so long. Nuss still didn't step away, and I was about to shove the two of them together just to relieve the tension.

"I swear to the Christmas star, we should have gone to the Land of Snowflakes for your piece of the broken crown. But since we didn't, you're going to have to keep your dick hard a little longer. Now, let's get—"

A burst of emotion, a craving deep need, hit my psyche like a punch to the gut, taking me almost to my knees, and stealing my breath with its intensity.

Zucker grabbed me under the arm to steady me. "What is it?"

"The mouse army..." my voice creaked out, "they're inside the barrier to the Sweet Fae lands, and Konig is with them."

Clara's face paled and then her cheeks lit up like pink petunias. She was trying hard to bank her feelings. Toward Konig.

She was fucking attracted to him.

I'd never wanted to forsake the empathic gift I had before. I'd worked for years to hone the small amount of magic that came with being Fae, but in this moment, I wish I didn't know how she felt at all. Clara didn't know him like the rest of us. She only saw him as the dashing captain of the opposing army.

The rest of the guard were more focused on me, and I wouldn't give up her secret just yet. Once she and I were bonded and her magic amplified my gifts for her use, she would see the Mouse Prince for what he really was. A traitor.

The sooner we got her away from him, the better. "Zucker, your majesty, you're not going to like that I know this, but I promise when it's all over we'll figure how to deal with what I'm about to say."

The Queen gave me one raised eyebrow. "Go on."

If we were in the Land of Flowers, and I was Zucker... no, I couldn't think like that. The Sugar Plum Queen had accepted me. It was another step toward peace between our people. Clara's spirit and magic would be the leap forward we needed. A leap we wouldn't be able to make if we couldn't get out of the castle and find that crown. "I apologize in advance, your majesty. You should close the castle up tight, draw up the bridge and make this the fortress I know it to be."

Zucker shook his head as if what I was saying was no big deal. "Everyone knows Sugar Plum castle is ready for battle."

Yeah, but few knew this next part. I lowered my voice so only the six of us would hear. "And we should escape into the peppermint caves through your network of tunnels beneath the castle."

The queen closed her eyes and took a long breath. "I could make you forget you ever knew that, but I won't if you promise to bring me the sugared head of the Mouse Queen."

None should ever make the mistake of forgetting the Sugar Plum Queen was primarily a warrior queen. Clara stared hard at Zucker's mother and tipped her head in that cute thinking thing that she did. "You aren't by any chance the Vivandiere, are you?"

The queen eyed Clara with a new appreciation. "Who told you about her?"

"A story-teller from the human realm." That's all she said. The curiosity of all the rest of us was palpable in the air around us.

The queen looked over her shoulder as if she was worried someone else might be listening. "I am not the Vivandiere, but I will tell you this. The stories are all true."

"I knew it." These were the answers Clara had been seeking and we didn't have any more time. "Where is she now? Why isn't she here to help fight against the Mouse Queen?"

I sucked in a sharp breath as another wave of Konig's emotions struck me. He wasn't just here to for a battle, he was here for Clara. "We have to go, now."

Leb picked Clara up and pushed his way through the crowd toward the towers of the castle, opening a way for the rest of us to follow. "One of these days we are going to quit running and bring the fight to that bastard."

"We will," Nuss held out his arms to hold back the revelers

that knew nothing of the approaching army. "Once we have the crowns and can rightfully take back the throne."

Zucker went next. "Shit. Mother, I've had the guards put the Prince of Spirit and Magic in the south rooms. He's in league with the Mouse Queen. See what you can find out from him about—"

"Holy sugary snowflakes. Go, already. I'll take care of the stinking traitorous prince."

I wasn't sure if she meant Friedrich or the Mouse Prince. Both, if we were lucky.

I sprinted ahead of Leb and into the first tower. While I'd only ever been in the tunnels and caves outside the castle, the schematics of the building itself were seared into my mind. Zucker joined me and opened a big wooden door before I had to reveal exactly how much I knew about his home. Someday I would have to come clean.

The room he led us into looked like a very average sitting room, with a whole host of plush chairs, antique tables, and tapestries all decorated in sweets, desserts, and sugary treat motifs. I'd laugh, but the DewDrop castle was just as decked out with flowers and other flora.

Zucker grabbed the edge of a wall-length tapestry and pulled the bottom half away from the wall. If I didn't know there was a hidden door there, I never would have guessed. The whole thing was expertly painted to look like the stones around it. "None of you ever saw this."

He pushed against the stones and they sunk back, then popped open, revealing the secret passageway. Just inside was a cache of weapons which I was thankful for, because it included a quiver with arrows and a bow. I slipped the quiver over my shoulder and tested the tip of an arrow. Sharp. Good, because we might need them.

"Oh, my giddy aunt. This is all very cloak and dagger fabulous." Clara ducked under Zucker's arm and into the darkness.

I followed next and took her hand. I let the flower power inside of me that gave me a sparkling green aura push up and out of me, and the hallway lit up enough for us to see our way forward. Leb and Nuss followed me and soon Zucker's purple aura added its light from behind. The passageway sloped down in long spirals until we were well below the castle grounds. We stopped at the bottom, where the tunnels split off into six different directions.

"How do you know where to go from here?" Clara asked, looking around the darkness.

Zucker came forward and pointed to some symbols carved into the walls. "Each tunnel takes us toward one of the other Lands. The axe for the Gingerbread Kingdom, the snowflake for the Land of Snowflakes and so on. We'll go this way."

He pointed down the tunnel marked with the flower. Clara hesitated and stared at the other arches in the stone. She pointed to a spot that had been scratched over, obliterating the symbol beneath. The tunnel went even more silent as we all swallowed our next breaths.

"Is it someplace bad?" Clara whispered.

I pulled one of the arrows from the quiver on my back and forfeited the sharp arrowhead. I scratched the symbol that had represented the Land of Spirit and Magic, an elongated eight-pointed star with a wisp flowing behind it, that now reminded me of the way our princess looked when she danced, curvy and elegant. When I was finished, Clara stepped closer and ran her fingers over the mark.

"This is for the Land of Spirit and Magic, isn't it?"

I nodded.

"No one goes there anymore?"

"There isn't anywhere to go. Your Kingdom was destroyed long ago."

"No." She shook her head and tipped it to the side looking

down the dark hallway. "I don't think that's right. There is definitely something still there. I can feel it, right here."

Clara took my hand and placed it against her chest. Magic, just like that which we felt last night during the consummation of her bonding with Leb, tingled across my knuckles. She reached her other arm out toward the rest of the guard. "Each of you, give me your hands."

One by one they put their hands on top of and beside mine. Swirls of magic lifted off her skin and lit up the darkness even brighter than either of our Fae auras. Leb groaned and Nuss closed his eyes. Zucker looked at me and I could read the heat in them.

"We have to go there." Clara took a step forward, breaking our contact with her. The spell faded, and the tunnel went pitch black once again.

Clara gulped back a sob and turned, throwing herself into me and Zucker. Her sadness tasted like wolfsbane, it was so strong and pungent. "I promise, my lady. We four will do everything in our power to help you reclaim your land. But the first step to that is finding the broken crowns."

THE MOUSE CROWN

KONIG

The Nutcrackers thought they could escape me, but the longer I was near her, the connection between Princess Clara and I grew tighter. I'd been able to use my shifter senses to track her, but the moment I kissed her in the Christmas Tree Forest, I didn't need those anymore. It was as if there was a magical tether between us.

That connection had grown taught when they'd escaped into the Sweet Fae lands. I'd set my ambush at the border of the Land of Snowflakes, assuming that's where Nuss would want to take her next. How the fool had simply sat there and watched when the others had joined in the bonding was nothing less than I expected. But I knew what his people had riding on him finding their crown and their subsequent bonding.

I should have set up a contingency plan for the fae borders. They were smart to use the glamour there to deter my army. But Zucker and Tau weren't the only ones with good spy craft. My spies were practically undetectable when they were in mouse form and had discovered the ancient tunnel system beneath SugarPlum castle used as escape routes long ago. I kept that information to myself for when I needed it.

This was exactly where I'd lay my trap. It didn't take much to figure out that this is where they'd go when my army attacked the castle where they celebrated their escape from me.

There was more than one way to catch a princess. I'd much rather have her come to me willingly. That would be much more devastating for the rest of the Guard.

I shifted into my mouse form and pushed my way through the fae glamour. No one took notice of a single mouse scurrying around a party filled with people and food. I watched in awe as Clara danced. Her magic was so much more than any of the rest of them understood. Being here in her presence loosened the binds of not being close to her that felt wrapped around my chest when I couldn't be near her.

All the more reason I needed her to see the atrocities this war had wrought on the Land of Animals. She could never be bound to me in the same way she was to Leb, but that didn't mean I didn't have my ways of making her do what was right.

Before her performance was even finished, I called to the mouse army to begin the attack on the SugarPlum court. Then I scurried into the castle, counting on Zucker and Tau to use the tunnels to escape. There would be no other option.

Ah, here they were now. Into the tunnels they went, not for a moment noticing me hiding in the shadows and debris following along. I relished being so close to the princess while I could. Her magic warmed even my cold spirit.

I'd have to be very careful not to fall in love with her. She was a means to an end. That didn't mean I wouldn't enjoy fucking her until she fell in love with me.

The party paused at the junction where the tunnels split off toward the other lands. My army was ready to shift to any of the exits. Except of course the one that led to the land of Spirit and Magic. No one went that way. I waited, holding my breath when Clara had stared down the tunnel toward her lost kingdom. She was drawn to her land just as I knew she would be. I could feel the need rolling through her.

Excellent. I knew exactly what to do with her once I stole her away.

They finally moved down the tunnel leading to the Land of the Flowers. If I hurried, I could not only capture the princess, but I could exact my revenge on the others at the same time. It would be a delicious victory. Far enough away that they wouldn't notice, I shifted again into the form of man and called on my animal speed to get to the cave where the tunnel let out above ground again.

I opened my senses as wide and far as I could, sensing the animals in the area. Some horses would do, but I didn't feel any nearby at all. There were birds, wild boar who were skittish from being hunted, and a den of gentle foxes. I asked them all if they knew where there were any fellow beasts that would carry a band of weary travelers, and they all told me the same thing.

No large animals were to be found in the fae lands. They'd all been hunted for food. I damned my mother for her lazy short-sightedness. The troubles she'd stirred between the fae had the people starving each other out. Hungry fae, even Sweet and Flower would hunt to feed their families.

No docile animal was safe. The bastards. I supposed my people were lucky the fae hadn't come hunting in the Land of Animals.

I stretched my senses even farther and found a small herd of reindeer at the edge of the Christmas Tree Forest. *I promise no harm will come to you here if you offer your aid to my friends. They are on a great quest and under the protection of my army. That protection will extend to you. I give you my word.*

Only part of that was a lie. I wouldn't let harm come to them. I mentally sent orders to my mice to escort the herd here and gnaw out the eyes of anyone who even looked at them hungrily.

But reindeer weren't suited for riding. What we needed was a sleigh. It wasn't likely I'd find one out here in the Sugar Fae wilderness. Perhaps I could fashion a basic sledge. Even as fast as I ran, it was unlikely the princess and her Guard were more than an hour or so behind me.

I needed more help. This time I reached toward the icy rivers of the bordering Flower Fae lands. I knew just who to call upon. It didn't take me long to find a family of beavers not far away. *Friends, can you help me. I need wood and your best teeth for carving.*

The mental image of the sleigh I wanted excited the elder of their family and he then sent the call for help to others of their kind. Within minutes a whirlwind of woodpeckers, squirrels, chipmunks, and finally the beavers, gathered around a thick deep brown tree. It smelled of chocolate, but the beavers assured me it was true wood. It seemed many of the plants in the borderlands were hybrids of sugar and nature.

I set them at their task, knowing their industriousness would be my saving grace. The greedy fae only gathered and consumed the resources around them, instead of trying to live as one with the land. Animal's culture could only add to their bounty, but they refused to see even shifters as little more than stupid servants or pets.

There was one more task to set my trap. My heart beat against my chest faster in anticipation, even though this was going to fucking hurt. If I hadn't been a weak fool, I would have already used the spell.

My weakness wasn't of the flesh, but of the heart. No matter the betrayal, deep inside, I still believed that the rebellion could defeat the Mouse Queen. I was stupid. They couldn't.

I had to let that dream go.

At the entrance to the cave, I found an arrowhead left from

some Flower Fae spy and grabbed it up. It would make a perfect carving tool of my own. In six places, the points of the Christmas Star, I carved the symbol for the Land of Animals into the stone. It was the same mark I wore on my own heart. The one my mother had carved into me the day she discovered I'd joined the Nutcracker Guard in their rebellion.

When the final emblem was carved, I tossed the dulled arrowhead aside, and drew my sword from the scabbard. Before I could think too much about the pain I was about to inflict on myself, I grabbed the tip of the blade in my fist and drove it into my chest.

Fucking hell that hurt. The cold blade burned as it sliced through my skin and muscle. My enhanced shifter healing wouldn't take long to heal me, but that didn't mean I liked the pain in the first place. I pushed the blade in even further until it slipped past my sternum on the right and pierced my heart.

I dropped to my knees and had to grit my teeth not to cry out. Finally, the blade hit the metal of the crown inside and repelled it back out of the wound. The magic of the Land of Animals seeped from my chest along with my blood. I needed that magic, yes, but what I needed more was the curse mixed with it that compelled me to follow the Mouse Queen's commands.

I swiped my fingers through the blood and scrabbled to my feet, lumbering over to the marks I'd carved on the walls. The blood I smeared across the carvings seeped in, sealing the magic and the curse in with it. The moment the crowns she wore on the chain around her neck reached out to find the crown they thought was buried in the stone, just a touch of the curse I carried would be Clara's as well.

She would be compelled to follow my commands.

I spoke the words aloud, groaning them out. "The sleigh is safe, and it will save you time. Use it to find the Sweet Fae crown. Then bring it to me."

My curse was set into motion. I stumbled back out into the light and over to where my animal friends were working. They'd done so much better than I ever could have imagined myself. The reindeer had arrived and the mice with them had used the local grass to tightly weave cushions, blankets, and even a full set of reins.

Thank you, my friends. We will be ever grateful, and I am in your service. With that I sent them all back to their homes and found a place among the rocks to hide and wait for Clara and the Nutcrackers.

Tonight, she would be mine.

A STOLEN PRINCESS

CLARA

The pull to walk down the dark passage, toward the place that I was born, yanked at my heart. I didn't remember anything about it. I didn't even realize until this moment that I had even been there before. Up until this very moment, I'd been under the assumption this was my first time in the Winter Realm.

That wasn't correct. This place was my home and something long ago had happened to steal me away from it.

I wanted to know when, why, how, and who'd done this to me. Right off the top of my head, I could think of three people who might know and none of them were standing here with me. Sure, my men probably had some insights and perhaps there were even stories, but they'd been babies too when it had all happened. They'd called me a lost princess, but I wasn't.

I was stolen.

As much as I wanted answers and to see what remained of my birthplace, Tau was right. The best way to get all the answers I wanted to the litany of questions that kept coming up each day I spent here, was to find those crowns.

I touched the symbol Tau had carved into the stone and engraved it on my heart. Somewhere deep inside, a new bit of magic unlocked and I could feel the spirit and magic inside of Leb, Nuss, Zucker, and Tau mixing with mine.

And one other.

We'd been running from the dark warrior, the Mouse Prince Konig, since my arrival, but I felt him in my heart just as I did the others. Someday soon, I needed to run toward him, not away.

In the sparkle of magic where I could feel their spirits, there was love, loyalty, determination, and a deep sense of responsibility. But there was also a sense of loss and betrayal. Those were old wounds, and they weren't healed.

I took one last look into the dark and then stepped over to the passageway marked with the flower. "How far is it?"

Zucker moved into the tunnel, illuminating it with his beautiful purple inner light. "The tunnels all connect to one of the many sugar caves dotting our land. Each are about an hour's walk from the castle.

I had the stamina of a dancer who'd trained hard for years. Just because I had thick thighs, didn't mean I couldn't run. "If we hustle, we could probably make it, what, twenty minutes?"

The need to get this quest to fruition banged against the inside of my chest. Not only because of my want of the truth of what happened to me, but because with each passing moment, the craving to bond with each of my Nutcracker guards grew stronger. I could literally feel the magic in my spirit awakening, stretching, and wanting to reclaim everything I'd missed experiencing here in the Winter Realm. Falling in love, bonding, and consummating that bond were all at the top of my list.

I hoped these ballet slippers held up longer than a couple of performances, because running in them would be as hard on them as the leading role in Swan Lake. I started off down the tunnel at a good jog. The men all followed along, and the further we went, the more distinctly I got the feeling I'd been here before.

"Princess, slow down here." Zucker matched my pace and drew his daggers from his belt. "The incline will go up in a moment and we will rise into the cave. There could be any number of enemies waiting for us there."

I was ready for a breather anyway. "Is this the cave you all saw in my dance?"

Tau shook his head. "No, we still need to journey to the border. We could camp in the cave tonight, but I'd rather we continue on now before anyone has a chance to catch up to us. We have the advantage right now since only the Sweet Fae at the party have seen the dance. But news will spread fast."

"I want to keep going. The sooner we find the crown, the better."

Leb drew his axe. "Let me go first. I am enemy only to the mouse army. If there are Flower Fae waiting for us, I'll just knock them down with a stiff blow of Kuchenir."

"Did you name you axe?" Zucker huffed out a laugh.

"Yes. Of course." Leb patted the axe against his huge fist. "You should always give your best weapon a name of reverence. Have I taught you nothing?"

We all stepped aside and let Leb pass, but I looked over at Zucker and Tau. "I want a history of the Fae and their problems later. I thought we'd been helping an already united people against the Mouse Queen, but it seems like you all fight more than Fritz and I do."

Nuss snorted and I pointed at him. "Don't think you're getting away without letting me see into the ooey gooey center of Snowflake culture and whatever happened between you and the Mouse Prince."

If the five of us were going to be bonded, they had to be a whole lot more open with me and that was starting tonight.

I followed Leb up the slope at a few paces behind because if anyone could just shove some attackers aside, it was my Gingerbread Viking. I imagined most any assassin would pee their pants at the thought of going up against him.

Zucker had said these were sugar caves and I'd imagined they'd be filled with crystals of sugar sort of like the salt caves back home. The miners in the salt mines of Salzburg had carved intricate designs and even statues into the stone and salt. We found the cave empty except for the dazzling crystals. Perhaps that was a small, but nice bit of human culture to add to all the amazing things I'd learned about in the Winter Realm.

"Let's keep moving, I can practically feel the crown calling to me." I hurried forward through the cave, heading toward the new bit of light from the outside.

It wasn't long before moonlight joined the auras of Zucker and Tau. Leb took the lead again and was the first out of the cavern. After so much darkness, even with the purple and green light of my Fae men's inner lights, the reflection of the moon off the snow outside was glaring.

I looked away, and if I hadn't, I would have missed the symbol freshly carved into the rock at the very entrance to the cave. I'd seen the very same one at the intersection of the tunnels that represented the one that went toward the Land of Animals. A mouse wearing a crown.

Konig was here. Or he had been. Recently.

I quickly made myself look anywhere but the symbol. I absolutely knew that I should tell everyone what I'd seen. But I didn't.

"The coast is clear," Leb shouted from outside. "And someone has left us a present."

We rushed outside and found him standing, arms wide, in the back of a pale blue sleigh, decorated with an intricate snowflake motif, hooked up to eight reindeer. Nuss cracked a grin and walked over to the closest animal and patted it on the back, then ran his hand along its neck, expertly ducked under the rack of antlers, and adjusted the harness. "Now this is my kind of ride. Where did you come from, you beauties?"

The animal responded with a snort and a snuffle of Nuss's hand. "Oh, ho. I don't have any treats for you, but I promise to find you something sweet when we reach our destination."

Aww. I hadn't seen Nuss this animated since the first moment I met him under my Christmas tree. He had an adorably soft spot for animals and someday, I was going to get him a puppy just to see his reaction.

"These guys will get us where we need to go quickly." Nuss bounded back to us and jumped into the front and took the reins in his good hand. He looked at me, Zucker, and Tau with a hurry-up face.

"Are we not questioning whose sleigh this is or who left it for us? This is pretty damn suspicious." Zucker crossed his arms and Tau didn't move.

Nuss smiled and shook his head. "If they've been used nefariously, they'd know and be fidgety. I don't know how they got here, and we may be stealing someone's ride, but we are within walking distance of the castle and they can get there safely."

He was the last one I expected to be so trusting. I had a sneaking suspicion where these animals had come from.

"Princess," Nuss's voice was on the verge of pleading. He held out his hand to me. "Open your spirit to these animals. You may be able to sense something about them."

"I've never done something like that. You know more about my magic than I do. Can you help me?" I wasn't really looking forward to him cutting me like he had Fritz, but I also wanted to know if my guess was right. I touched my lips briefly thinking about the biting kiss he'd given me and then shook my head. No way. That had been in the moment, and he wouldn't do that again.

Nuss's entire countenance changed, and he was back to the wary man he'd been the past two days. He handed the reins back to Leb and climbed back down. In three quick strides, he was right in front of me. I held out my wrist thinking that would be the easiest place for him to nick my skin. He didn't even look down to my proffered hand. He hauled me into his arm, bent me back like I'd seen in the movies, and kissed the magic right out of me.

This was no chaste kiss, there was no reticence, but it also wasn't hurried and flurried like during the avalanche. Nuss kissed me with pure wanton need and lust, and I was here for it. My magic swirled between us, sparkling behind my eyelids, and tickling the edges of the connection between me and everyone else here.

Including Konig.

I gasped and Nuss broke away from me, although he didn't let me up. "What do you see, princess of my heart?"

I blinked up at him and not only saw Nuss, but a blue aura all around him. He stood me back up and the entire world around us had the same blue glow as he did. I quickly searched for Konig but couldn't see anyone else. I knew he was there, yet only my sense of his spirit told me so.

"I don't entirely understand what I'm seeing. It's like the magic from when we bonded, but it's everywhere, around every living thing." I blinked my eyes, thinking the blue haze might fade, but it continued so strong, it was if I could reach out and touch it.

"That's spirit, allowing you to see it." Nuss nodded toward the animals and then motioned to each of the men. "All living things have it, but only those who can control magic can see it."

Nuss's blue spirit glow sparkled with hundreds of tiny white lights, like falling snow. Except in a sort of cross over his heart, and his broken arm. They were both dark, as if in a shadow. Leb's spirit was dotted with oranges and golds and had a few darker areas around his hands. Tau's was lined in the same green of his aura, and he too had dark spots, but his were across his forehead. Zucker's spirit was laced with purple, and the darkness from him was right across his chest.

I think I was seeing wounds of their spirit. When I looked at the animals and plants around us, their spirits were solid and glowing bright with all the colors of the natural world. "I don't see any darkness around the reindeer at all. They seem happy and healthy if the pretty glow of their spirits is anything to go by."

"That's exactly as I thought. This sleigh hasn't been placed here nefariously, but perhaps by the Christmas Star herself to help us fulfill her quest." Nuss grabbed my hand and guided me up into the sleigh.

I waited until all five of us were seated before I finally let the truth out. I couldn't and wouldn't keep secrets from them and it had been a stupid decision to think I ever should. "I don't think it was the Christmas Star who left this for us. It was Konig."

All four of them stood back up and drew their weapons. They held them out, pointing in every which direction looking for an enemy. I sighed and rubbed my head.

"He's not here now. Or I didn't see him or his spirit anyway. I don't know the history between you all and him, but this is the second time he's helped us to get away from the Mouse Army, so I think we should trust him a little bit. Enough to take the sleigh and go get that piece of the broken crowns."

Not a one of them responded. They were all on high alert and protecting me apparently meant ignoring me all of a sudden.

The intensity of the glow of the spirit all around me was fading, except for one bright and golden glow just over the next hill. "The crown is waiting for us. I can see its spirit too."

Nope. Still nothing. I wasn't used to them ignoring me. Funny how I had been used to that from everyone in my old life in the human world, but not at all since I'd met the four of them. What happened to earlier today when I was the warrior general? I was only getting stronger, but suddenly, they were treating me like a fragile porcelain doll.

Fine. I'd take matters into my own hands. I picked up the reins that Nuss had dropped and gave them a little flick. A burst of my magic went through them, and the animals surged forward. The men all fell back into the seats as we took off across the snow and I giggled my butt off.

There was more than one way to end a conversation and remind them that I was stronger than they thought. I'm sure I'd hear all about it when we reached our destination, and they'd all be on high alert, but I just had this gut feeling deep inside that reuniting them with Konig was going to be important and would be good for them all.

That was the first time I'd accessed any of my magic on my own. I wasn't entirely sure how I'd done it, but when I needed it, there it was. If loving on my men was the best way to access it, I wasn't going to be sad about that even a little bit. I'd rather that than to have to sacrifice some blood. The idea of kissing and making love and sharing a bonding experience being the key to the magic settled in nicely in my psyche next to my mission to bring love back to the Winter Realm.

Everything I'd learned today made it even more clear that all the lands needed more love and a whole lot less hate. Hate was exhausting. No wonder they were all fighting all the time.

I looked around at each of my protectors to make sure they weren't too upset with me. They were. Nuss grumped and held out his hands for the reins. I was going to tell him that I had this, but then remembered the affection he'd had for the reindeer. I didn't need to prove I was a strong woman, not with him, not with any of them.

I placed the strips of leather into his hand and snugged up against him, threading my arm through his bandaged one. Someday I would learn how to use my magic to heal both his physical and spiritual wounds. Perhaps when he and I bonded.

The Land of Snowflakes was definitely next on my list. Leb, Zucker, and Tau kept their weapons at the ready, but we made quick time in the sleigh. It was almost as if the crown was pulling us to it, that it was waiting to be found.

In fact, as we got closer to the shining light of spirit at our destination there was much more waiting for us than just the Sweet Fae's broken piece of the seven crowns.

THE GROTTO OF LOVE

CLARA

Tau tapped Nuss on the shoulder as we got close to the cave where the broken piece of the Sweet Fae crown was hidden. He pointed to the enormous trees on the far side of the cave entrance. They reminded me of those long tree-lined walkways with branches draped in long flowy moss. But these ones had mounds of pink fluff hanging down from the canopy above, and the air was scented with both the woodsy scent of a forest and the sweetness of cotton candy.

Most of my spirit vision had faded, but I could still make out the green auras of at least half a dozen Flower Fae hiding in the branches. The men stiffened and I wasn't surprised that, as warriors, they'd spotted the ambush too. Tau spoke so only the four of us could hear him. "They won't shoot as long as I'm with you and they think I am unharmed. I suggest you allow me to go into the cave with you first, Princess."

"I know that I don't understand all the politics of what's

going on here, but I'd like to make a statement by walking in with both of you at my side."

Tau glanced to Zucker, and they did that communication with their eyes that only someone with their close connection can. Zucker nodded and the three of us got out of the sleigh. Leb and Nuss stayed, looking slightly awkward and not knowing what to do with themselves.

"I've changed my mind," I said. If I was going to make a statement, might as well go big. "I want all four of you with me, as a united front. Let your kinsman see that I play no favorites and hold no alliance or bond over any other. You are all important to me and I could do none of this without each one of you."

Leb gave me a big old grin and hopped out of the sleigh. "I'd kiss you, lass, if I wasn't sure I'd get an arrow in the back for it."

There was the tiniest bit of vulnerability in Leb's tone. I'd assumed he and I were solid now that we were bonded, but I needed to remember this relationship was just as new to the four of them as it was to me. They might have grown up on stories of our connection and pledged themselves to be my guard, my protectors, but none of us had had more than half a day where we weren't fighting or running to even get to know each other or express our feelings.

"I'd kiss you back, my ginger giant." I blew him a kiss anyway.

Nuss remained in the sleigh. "What about Konig and the mouse army?"

In my mind I included Konig as one of my men. I wasn't sure of his role in this battle between good and evil I'd dropped in on, but in my heart, I knew he was on my side. "If he shows up, we'll deal with that then."

I don't think Nuss liked that answer. I was starting to understand that he was the kind of guy that needed a plan, with a contingency plan, and probably a back-up plan for that. But the next few days were probably going to be pretty harried, and we were going to have to be adaptable. I wanted to wrap him up in a big hug and tell him this was going to work out.

I didn't know that it was, but I was going to believe it.

Nuss had been the stalwart captain all this time, my hero from minute one. His reticence was new to me. I wished I understood him better. Land of Snowflakes, I was coming for you next because I'll be damned if I'd allow him to feel anything less than as strong and powerful as the Nutcracker Captain I know he'd trained to be.

I walked back to the sleigh and took his hand. "Believe, captain. Believe in me, believe in us, believe in the magic. Everything will be okay."

A spark of my magic zipped from my hand to his and the soldier who'd come for me under the Christmas tree was back in his eyes. "You might be the only thing I believe in, Princess Clara."

He jumped from the sleigh and the two of us joined the rest of my guard. The four of them formed a box around me, Tau and Nuss in front, Zucker and Leb at my back. We moved forward as a unit and into the entrance of the cave.

It took a moment for my eyes to adjust, because it was both dark, and brilliantly lit from the spirit light of the broken crown... or should I say, crowns. I could see now that there were two lights, one lined in green, the other laced with purple. But they weren't two separate lights, all three colors were intertwined.

I blinked a few times, and the rest of the cave came into focus. Like the sugar cave we were in before, there were giant crystals all along the walls, but where those ones had been clear and white, these were every color of the rainbow. "Whoa, no wonder the Vivandiere chose this place to hide the crowns. The atmosphere around is befitting their magic."

"I've been to this cave before," Tau said, as much wonder in his voice as I felt. "It didn't look like this at all. Come on let's go in deeper to where the flowers grow."

"Underground flowers? How do they grow with no light?"

Tau laughed. "Wait until you see this. The sugar crystals reflect light down into the cavern below. Right where our two land's border there is an underground grotto, filled with the most beautiful flora and fauna."

"How many times have you been here?" Zucker asked Tau. There was a bit of edge to his voice that I hadn't heard between them before. I didn't like that. The sooner we found the crowns the better.

"Only once in my youth. It's forbidden for all but the royal DewDrop Court. And even then, only on incredibly special occasions. My father brought me the night before my archer's test. He said he wanted to show me what we fought for."

"If we had not met serving in the nutcracker guard, would you have fought me for this treasure?"

Tau froze in his tracks. He turned and grabbed the back of Zucker's neck in the same way I'd seen Zucker do to him. "I think once you'll see it, you'll understand. I've never been able to get this place out of my mind, and it is the reason, along with the prophecy and the princess, that I did join the nutcracker guard. Places like this shouldn't be only for the privileged. I want this to be for the whole realm."

The connection between the two of them zipped through me as well. This time the magic was not just all awe-inspiring, but sensual. Those zings went down my spine and settled between my legs. The love between them made me want them even more.

Leb leaned down and whispered in my ear. "You will be the stuff of my pure fantasies when you bond with the two of them. I can hardly wait."

I'd never been anyone's fantasy before. It seemed silly but those naughty words gave me even more confidence than Leb's warrior magic or feeling like a warrior woman myself. Perhaps because I could see myself commanding troops if I had to. Even under Fritz's thumb, I'd always done what I had to do to keep our family going.

I'd never seen myself as a sexual being. Not until last night when he and I consummated our bond. But that experience was so new and unique that I hadn't thought about what it would feel like to do it all over again with each of my men. Of course, I knew I'd bond with each of them, and consummating that bond meant sex, but I guess I hadn't actually thought about it in that way. I'd been so focused on showing their world how to love again, I forgot I was the one who would be falling in love.

Somehow... that also meant falling in love with myself. As a warrior woman, as a princess, as a dancer, and as a lover— a sexual being in my own right.

I felt the heat of a blush creep up my cheeks before I even said what I was thinking to Leb, but I said it anyway. "I can hardly wait for you to watch."

I refused to think I was weird for liking it when Nuss watched, and I would enjoy it just as much when Leb did too. Although now I was wondering what it would be like when none of them were watching, and we were all entangled together.

Leb kissed me on the top of my head and then gave me a swat on the butt, moving us along the path. The deeper we went into the cavern, the warmer it got. For being the Winter Realm, it was downright tropical in this cave. I pulled at the tight bodice on the ballerina's costume I still wore and longed for a tank top and shorts.

Tau and Zucker rushed ahead and the three of us simply followed the path that was indeed lit up by the reflection from crystal to crystal. Interestingly, the spirit light from the crowns didn't bounce off the chunks of sugar in the walls. It wasn't really light then, was it? Another kind of magic, I supposed.

While I'd learned so much about the magic inside of me, I

wondered if there would ever be anyone from the Land of Spirit and Magic who could teach me about my innate abilities like there had been someone for each of my men.

When I caught up to Zucker and Tau, they were standing together, hand in hand, looking out over an underground oasis. Colorful crystals hung not only from the walls, but from vines, trees, and flowers. Bees and butterflies flew from bud to bud, and the air sparkled with a hundred thousand fireflies.

I came up beside them and found what they were staring at. In the center of the pool, there was a small grassy island, and growing straight up from the center of it was an enormous dewdrop flower, with its pastel green and violet petals open wide. While the giant flower was spectacular, it was the fact that the stem was wrapped in a vine of candy canes. The two were so intertwined that every inch of the flower itself sparkled with fine sugar crystals. At the tip of each of the thin filaments of the stamen, instead of anther pod, I could swear was a sugar plum sweet.

I turned around and faced my two Fae princes and touched my palms to each of their cheeks. "That's where we'll find the broken pieces of the crowns, from both the Sweet and Flower Fae lands."

Leb clapped them both on the back. "As it should be, lads. Now let's go get it. Anyone know how to swim?"

Oh. Ha. I hadn't thought of that. I didn't suppose there was a whole lot of swimming in a land where everything was ice and snow. "I can."

I hated to get my clothes wet if we were going back out into the frosty winter. I guess I'd have to take them off. But I hadn't even put them on myself. I wasn't sure I could get out of them on my own. I undid the ribbons on the shoes and slipped them off, but I'd need help with everything else.

"Can you help me get out of this bodice? I don't want to swim in this outfit and get my clothes wet." Tau, Zucker, and

Leb all reached for me with a sparkle in their eyes, but Nuss batted their hands away.

"Allow me."

I scoffed at him. "I can undress myself, thank you very much."

"Let me do this, princess." Nuss's tone had gone back to the captain of the guard, man in charge, delicious kisser, and I melted.

He turned me so I faced the pool and had my back to all of them. I felt the bodice's lacings tug and then loosen bit by bit. It had never been tight and uncomfortable before, but now I found that I couldn't breathe. I waited for his fingers to touch my skin, to send that flash of magic to caress the connection between us. All I felt was Nuss's breath on the back of my neck. He was so close yet said nothing until the top was loose enough to take off.

"Lift your arms over your head." I did as he told me and the anticipation of having his fingers brush over me as he pulled it off was killing me.

Zucker and Tau stepped to my sides, and each grabbed the hem. They skimmed it up and off, leaving me naked from the waist up. I dropped my hands to cover my bare breasts and waited. Was Nuss finished with me so soon?

But no. My Fae Princes moved away and Nuss pressed himself to my back. He wrapped his arm around my waist and found the tiny ribbons securing the fluffy skirt at my waist. With a flick of his wrist, the ties were undone, and he pushed his hand down into the space between the material and my stomach.

I sucked in a long, deep gasp as his hand continued down much farther and he cupped my pussy. "Never think that I don't want to share in giving you pleasure. Everything I am and have is for you."

"But?" I could hear it coming in his intonation, so I pushed him to continue.

"You need to have time to bond with each member of your guard. I will give you that, because when it's my turn, when we have the Snowflake crown in hand, I'm not going to want to share this, share you."

I opened and closed my mouth, the words being blocked by the pure lust his declaration had bubbling up inside of me. I'd always thought I'd ever only be with one man. Now I couldn't imagine not being with all my men. So, I didn't understand why Nuss's possessiveness was sending tingles through my core. "But I thought you agreed to the kind of bonding the Gingerbread Kingdom has with their women."

He pressed his lips to my ear and stroked over the soft fabric covering my pussy. "I have, and I will share your magic, your love, and your body with each of my brethren, but when you and I consummate our bond, you will be mine and mine alone for that one brief moment."

Before I could respond to his words, he shoved the skirt down my legs to pool at my feet. He followed it down, coming around and kneeling in front of me. "Leb, come and get her skirt."

Leb came over and waggled his eyebrows at me but didn't say a word. I'd needed him to break this tension, and he left me to the wolves, or rather the puppy who'd turned into a wolf before me.

Nuss took my hand and set it against one hip, then placed his own on the other. "Push the tights down for me."

He wasn't asking, and I was sure as sugar complying. The tights and soft panties underneath inched down my thighs, a little on my side, a bit on his, until they were at my knees and my pussy was bared to him. He stared at me and licked his lips, and I felt the wetness build between my legs. Would he taste me, right here, right now, in front of the others?

With a final nudge, the tights and panties dropped past my knees, and I stepped out of them. Nuss plucked the panties out of the pile and stuck them into the pocket of his jacket. "When you consummate your bonds tonight, I'll be watching again, and stroking my cock with these."

Whoo, man. I swallowed and pulled my bottom lip between my teeth. He had me more than ready. And I'd thought Zucker was the master of sensuality and anticipation.

Nuss stood and stepped aside. Zucker and Tau came up and escorted me down the short slope until the water of the grotto's pool tickled my toes. I dipped one foot in, and it felt funny until I realized the water was exactly the same temperature as my body.

"You're sure you're safe swimming to the flower's island?" Tau let go of my fingers as I walked in deeper.

"I'm sure. Unless there are any marshmallow crocodiles or strawberry stinging jelly-fish."

I probably shouldn't have said that.

LOVE IS LOVE IS LOVE

ZUCKER

I'd never known real fear until I watched Clara glide silently through the water in this strange underground grotto. To watch her strong athletic movements propel her so easily from this sugar crystal shoreline and across the invisible border between the Land of Sweets and the Land of Flowers had my own heart pounding.

I was normally an enthusiastic fan of the trembling of my very cells in anticipation but seeing her go to a place that I couldn't, had me fidgety and feeling helpless. I paced at the water's edge. What the fuck were we going to do if something went wrong while she was in the water? Go out there and drown ourselves?

I was ready to crawl out of my skin, much less my clothes. "Tau, the Land of Flowers is filled with rivers and lakes, surely you've learned to swim in them."

He shook his head. His arms wrapped around him and projected just how nervous he was too. Likely feeding off my emotions. "They're freezing. More than a moment in them and its death. I've never seen a body of water this warm."

"The lake in the Land of Spirit and Magic is warm," Nuss said like that wasn't the news of the century.

"How do you know that?" Leb asked. He was the calmest of us all. Perhaps because he was bonded with Clara and saw her as a powerful warrior woman like all the Gingerbread Vikings.

The Land of Snowflakes bordered what used to be Princess Clara's land, but there was nothing more there now than a darkness that would steal anyone's spirit who even approached it. Or so we'd all heard.

Nuss sighed.

"Don't keep secrets from us now, captain asshole." Leb smacked him on the back hard enough to make him stumble forward to the water's edge.

Nuss caught himself just before his boots hit the water. "There's a lot about the Snowflake Court and the Church of the Christmas Star that you don't know."

I thought we were a tight unit. We'd all made a commitment to each other and to Clara. This was all too much like when Konig betrayed us. We'd never been the same since, but we'd made it work. "Like how you're able access Clara and Friedrich's magic?"

"Yes."

"Why are we only finding out about this now?" This nervous energy inside me had to get out and if I couldn't use it to keep Clara safe, I was just as happy picking a fight.

Until Clara screamed.

Luckily my training as an elite Nutcracker guard meant I knew how to fight even when my own heart wasn't beating in my chest. I walked straight into the water, but Leb grabbed me from behind and dragged me back to shore. "Look, she's alright."

Clara bobbed in the water and held her arm up, holding

some kind of green stringy plant. "Sorry. I'm okay. It's just that this brushed up against my legs. Umm, it's seaweed, I guess? It smells like green apple saltwater taffy."

She took a small nibble out of it and nodded. "Yep. This is such a strange place."

Her laughter was the only thing that restarted my blood pumping through my veins. Tau put his hand on my shoulder and squeezed. "First thing after this war is over, we're all learning to swim."

It wasn't another moment before Clara reached the island and climbed up on its shores. As she approached the flower, hundreds of smaller buds bloomed at her feet, forming a path around her. She was a nature goddess come to life before our eyes.

"I found them." She reached up to the large candy cane and dewdrop blossom, and I swear it bent to her. The most powerful scent of violets, plums, and peppermint wafted to us, and it acted like an aphrodisiac. My cock went instantly hard, and Tau moaned beside me.

Which piece of the broken crown has she found? I wanted so badly for it to be the Land of Sweets so I could claim her body for my own. But equally needed it to be the Land of Flowers so I could see her and Tau together.

Clara reached up and plucked something from the center of the flower and held it to her chest. Magic like I'd never felt before exploded into the grotto and both Tau and I were yanked from the shore and dragged across the water to the island. We tumbled into the soft flowers around her, and she let out an excited laugh.

"Look." She held out the item she plucked from the flower and in her hand were two broken pieces of the seven crowns. The Flower Fae crown with its green and bendy vines that had grown around the purple, sparkling, sugary crown of the Sweet Fae.

"No wonder you two are so close. The spirits of your people are so intertwined, they can't be separated." She knelt in the flowers in front of us and bent her head. "Help me take the necklace off so I can join them with the other two."

I unclipped the fastening on the chain and the crowns from the Land of Spirit and Magic she'd brought with her from the human realm, and the one Mother Gingerbread had given her from the Gingerbread Kingdom fell into her waiting hands.

She slipped the chain through the vines of the Flower Fae crown right where it met the stylized Sugar Plum of the Sweet Fae crown. Then she put the necklace back on letting all four crowns dangle between her breasts. Her eyes rolled back in her head, and she let out a sighed whimper that had both Tau and I rushing to take off our clothes.

"I need you both, right now." A flush rose up Clara's breasts and her eyes went dark with lust. "Is this the effect of finding the crowns?"

Clara reached for my shirt and tried to pull it over my head, but it was a struggle since I was doing the same to Tau.

"Only you and Leb can answer that," I said and just ripped Tau's shirt open.

Leb's laugh boomed across the water. He cupped his hands and shouted to us, "Yes, it is."

Tau pushed Clara's hands away and tore my shirt open as well. "I've never felt so frantic to be with anyone like this in my life. I need to be with you both, and it feels like I'll die if I don't."

Clara was already naked, and I ran my hands down her arms and across her chest, teasing her with my touch, while avoiding her breasts. She leaned forward into me, and her hard little nipples pushed against my flesh, sending a shockwave of magic through me that turned to pure sexuality.

Tau pushed himself up against her back, so she was between us and grabbed her hands, directing them down to unbuckle my belt. They worked together and I did my best to distract them both with kisses and nips to Clara's throat, ear, and finally her lips.

I kissed her like I'd never get enough of her. There was so much more to this kiss than any I'd stolen from her before. It was as if I'd never experienced touching my mouth and tongue to someone else's before. The flavor of her exploded across my tastebuds and every emotion, want, and need I had was amplified times a thousand.

"Stars, I can literally feel what you're each experiencing as if I'm the one kissing her and you at the same time." Tau's voice filtered in low and husky and needy.

Their fingers finally released the fastenings to my pants, and I couldn't get them over my hips fast enough. I wanted both their hands on me now. I felt Tau's fist wrap around my cock first and then he guided Clara's softer hand to do the same just above his. Together they stroked up so slowly, I was sure to perish before her fingers squeezed the head and then went back down again before I was ready.

"He's this hard for you, sweet flower. You're going to love having this big cock inside of you, Zucker pounding into your cunt, making you cry out his name."

Clara groaned and shivered with each of my kisses. "Yes, I want that."

I dragged myself away from their touch. My need for them both was greater than any arousal I'd ever felt, but I was no inexperienced selfish lover. They too would know pleasure at my hands. Frantic, frenzied fucking was fun, sure. Consummating a bond with one's true mate should be more sacred than this.

I had to be the one to control the scene and give them both a delirious number of orgasms if I was to prove myself as deserving of being their partner in love and life. "If you keep stroking me like that, we won't get to the pounding part."

Tau and I had been lucky enough to be a part of her first

sexual experience bonding with Leb. We needed to make this one just as special for her. I also recognized this was a unique experience for me and Tau. We always knew we'd each be bonding with the princess, but he'd been right when he'd said it would bring us closer together.

Our lives were as intertwined as the crowns Clara had found, now our spirits could be too. I had to hope this was the missing piece he'd felt between us. That tonight as we bonded with Clara, that our own bond would be consummated as well. Because I was nothing without him.

Suddenly, I knew how to make this bonding perfect and right for all three of us. To make it work, we needed Clara's body to be supple, relaxed, and her cunt as wet as possible. Stars, I was going to love getting her body ready, and pushing Tau's to the edge.

"Stay on your knees, sweet princess, but spread your legs nice and wide. Tau and I are going to make you come so you're wet and ready to take our cocks. Together."

That delicious pink flush raced up her chest to her throat and cheeks. "Both of you at the same time?"

Behind her Tau's eyes went dark and sparkling. My sexual prowess and his empathic gift were saturated in Clara's magic, and I had no doubt he got every single mental image I had of the two of us taking her simultaneously. He helped steady her as I pushed her legs open and then quickly shucked his own pants.

He was normally much better with words than I was, but there was something in the way his muscles were tensed, and his breathing already rapid that told me he was feeling overwhelmed. We certainly hadn't expected to find the Flower Fae crown tonight. None of us thought all three of us would be consummating our bonds on only this second day of Christmas.

This was so damn important to him. More than I'd ever

understood before. There was one gift that I could give to him in our joint bonding with Clara.

"Yes, at the same time." But Tau was going to take her body, slide his cock into her cunt, first. It would mean everything to him to have that one moment where she belonged only to him. It wasn't as important to me as having them both be mine.

I laid flat on my back and shimmied to put my face between her spread legs. It certainly wasn't going to take much to get her ready. Her thighs were already glistening wet. I licked the inside of one thigh and then the other. I could taste the sweetness of the sugary water she'd had to swim though to get here on her skin. "Lean forward, down on your hands and knees. I'm going to suck on your luscious clit while Tau stretches your cunt with his fingers to prepare you for our cocks."

I didn't wait for her to get herself settled before I dragged her hips down and ran my tongue up through her pussy lips. She was as sweet as anything I'd ever put in my mouth before. Clara sank down onto my face and I loved that she wasn't shy about taking her pleasure from me.

I gave her a good couple of flicks of her clit before I sucked it into my mouth.

"Oh my God," she moaned and more of her juices coated my lips and jaw. She was so close already, and I was just getting started. Her little bud fluttered in my mouth. If she came so quickly, I was going to start counting how many times she climaxed just to see how many we could ring out of her.

While my face was buried in her luscious cunt, I felt Tau crawl over me, straddling my chest and he came up behind Clara. "Bend down, as you're told, sweet flower, or you'll get a spanking instead of my fingers in your cunt."

That had her getting even more wet. As Leb had proven last night, she was turned on by a little bite of pain with her pleasure. I'd remember that for later.

Apparently, Tau hadn't forgotten and as he bent Clara over

me, he gave her a slap to the ass anyway. She gasped and I kept lapping and suckling at her quivering cunt. I pulled away for just a moment. "She likes that, Tau. Do it again."

I didn't wait for him to do it before I dived back in, because if a spanking was going to get her to come, I wanted every bit of that magic in my mouth.

Tau spanked her three times and then pushed two of his fingers into her cunt. I gave them a quick lick to let him know what was in store for later.

"Oh, oh. How do your fingers feel just as big as Leb's whole cock inside of me?" Her head dropped and her hair flicked over my waist, the strands tickling my own member.

As if I wasn't already hard as a fucking candy cane, my cock stood up straighter, got even stiffer, and the first drops of my seed leaked from the tip knowing her mouth was this close. My hips jerked of their own accord just wanting to feel the warmth of her breath.

"You're so fucking tight. Relax sweet flower, or we'll never be able to get inside of you." Tau's fingers went in and out of her slick cunt and I lapped at them both.

The only thing better than this would be if it was his cock sliding across my tongue and into her cunt. To my dismay, Tau withdrew and yanked Clara upright. I continued to eat her sweet pussy and waited for whatever it was he was preparing to do. I trusted him completely with her body and mine.

Tau whispered something to Clara, and he must have said exactly the right thing to her because her legs clenched tighter around my head and her thighs trembled. Come on baby, let me taste that orgasm.

She bent back over me, and I thought I was prepared for anything and everything. Nothing in this realm or the next had me ready to feel Clara's mouth wrap around my cock head and suckle while Tau's dick slid into her cunt right in front of my eyes.

The magic between the three of us connected in a way it hadn't before as if a missing piece of a puzzle had just locked into place and that puzzle was a map of love, life, and the answer to all the mysteries of the universe all in one.

Not only could I feel their bodies, but I sensed how they each felt as I touched them. The sensation of me licking Clara's clit mixed with the sensations of Tau's cock pumping in and out of her, and the utter bliss of her tongue swirling around the sensitive underside of my cock head. I was living the reality of every touch, taste, sight, smell, and sound they experienced along with my own.

It was more than I'd ever imagined, and I would never get enough.

ROMANCE IS THE LANGUAGE OF BELONGING

TAU

I'd been searching my whole life for a connection that I was never sure I'd find. The first time Zucker kissed me, I felt so close to touching that thing I needed, I'd almost come in my pants. The first time he fucked me, I was sure we'd find it together.

But there was always something missing, a bit of magic just out of reach. I loved Zucker like I'd never loved anyone, more than I even thought possible, and I hated that it wasn't enough.

At first, as we trained, and then discovered the other Princes born under the Christmas star, then formed an alliance among ourselves to find the lost princess, I told myself it didn't matter. But the nearer we got to finding a way through the Christmas Tree portal, the more anxious I felt.

No matter how many times Zucker and I fucked each other, I was never fully satisfied. I hid that fact from him because I didn't want him to be hurt. My own spirit was battered and bruised even thinking that he might ever discover my secret.

The night she came to us, I finally knew. She was the missing piece. That must be it. I was destined to love the Princess of Spirit and Magic, and here she was right in front of me. Loving her didn't mean my feelings for Zucker were any less than before, in fact, I was sure it would only make them stronger.

I had no idea that bonding with her would change everything. I'd thought it would make a new connection, deepen the one I had with Zucker, and even bring me closer to the other Nutcrackers. All I ever wanted was to feel like I belonged to a something bigger than the small, narrow-minded, hateful world of most Flower Fae.

I wanted to belong to my brothers in arms and to the princess, and them to me.

I had a feeling that something special would happen when the three of us were truly joined. I whispered instructions on how to take Zucker into her mouth and use her tongue to make him feel good. I felt the first zip of magic when she did as I told her. The moment I pushed my cock into Clara's tight cunt and the three of us were entwined in a circle of love, life, sex, and bonding, her magic exploded through us and the nirvana running from the two of them to me and back was exhilarating.

Not only was I experiencing everything they did, I could also sense Leb and Nuss. It was as if their two hands were also stroking over my cock along with the tight inner muscles of Clara's pussy.

I glanced over to the shoreline and both Leb and Nuss had their trousers open and their dicks in their hands. I wondered if they could feel this connection too or was it only me and Zucker while we were physically connected Clara.

Perhaps we'd find out when Nuss finally nutted up and joined us in pleasuring our princess.

Clara had been well and truly fucked last night by Leb, so as much as I wanted to fuck her fast and hard, I held myself back, sliding in and out of her wet pussy with a steady rhythm, not pushing her too hard. Zucker wasn't holding back in the least.

He loved having his head between soft, luscious thighs, almost as much as he loved licking a dick. There was power in being able to make someone come that way, and it fueled the innate sexual gift that the Sweet Fae possessed. His power of allure was always strongest after making someone come for him.

I would know.

Clara's inner muscles tightened like a fist opening and squeezing around my cock. With each bob of her head, each of my thrusts into her, and stroke of Leb and Nuss's hand, she was closer and closer to tipping into her first orgasm. It was going to be almost impossible not to come when she did, but I would somehow manage.

I didn't want to spill my seed until Zucker and I were inside of her together. Our essences mixing together in her cunt, and maybe even her womb. I would swoon over a baby with his purple eyes, her blonde hair, and my green aura. That would be magic indeed.

She moaned deep and lifted her head, arching her back. "It's too much, I can't hold on. Ohh, yes."

Her pussy fluttered around my cock, and I shoved in deep, wanting to give her something to come around and not wanting to miss a moment of her orgasm.

Zucker popped his head out from between her legs and grabbed his cock, pumping it fast and hard. "Holy fuck, I can feel her coming as if it's my own climax. Fuck, fuck, Clara, fuck."

He spurted onto his belly and his climax added another layer to the pure bliss surrounding us in its lust-filled haze of magic.

I clenched my own teeth so hard I tasted blood. I'd sacrifice that so as not to come yet. I grabbed the base of my cock and squeezed hard to hold the impending orgasm back. That was a trick he'd taught me when neither of us could get enough of each other's bodies, so we'd wanted to fuck all night. Sweet Fae could come over and over, but I had my limits.

Clara collapsed over Zucker's body, and I slipped from her pussy. The magical connection to everyone's emotions and physical feelings didn't simply break when our bodies were no longer joined. It was more like a slow drain with the connection only fading little by little. Leb and Nuss hadn't come yet, and I could still feel both stroking, getting closer to orgasm themselves.

Wait. Holy fuck, it was three. There were three hands stroking. I distinctly felt a third.

I shot a quick look down to see if Zucker had his hand on his cock again, but both of his were caressing Clara's plump ass. Who else was here in this quiet secluded sanctuary invading our bond?

Just as I was about to sound the alarm, the feeling faded and no matter how far out I tried to reach with my empathic senses juiced up on Clara's magic, I found no other consciousness other than the small creatures who inhabited the grotto.

No one else seemed even the least bit concerned, including Zucker and Clara, whom I knew were feeling everything I was. I must have been mistaken or imagined it with all the intensity of everyone else's experience hitting me at the same time. The last of the magical swirls of our connection finally faded.

I dropped to the ground to join the two of them. "You'd better get your second wind. We're just getting started."

Clara giggled and the sounds was just as magical as her moans during orgasm. I grabbed her and rolled her, so she was on top of me, straddling my waist. I placed her just so and pushed my cock between her folds, rubbing my head across her sensitive clit.

She gasped and threw her head back, rocking her hips and

rubbing herself along the length of my hard dick. "You're both still hard, but Tau, did you not reach your climax?"

The pressure of her body pressing down on me as I slid through her pussy lips was as good as pumping into her wet channel. Only this was even better because she was in charge, she was pleasuring herself with my body. "I'm waiting to be inside of you with Zucker."

She looked down at me with those bright sparkling eyes and bit her lip. "I... don't see how you'll both fit."

Zucker rolled to his knees and crawled behind Clara, pushing his way between my knees. He wrapped his arms around Clara and cupped her lovely round tits in his hands. "It will be achingly tight, sweet one, but that's why Tau fucked you, and we made you come first. To open your body and relax your channel."

He bumped his hips against Clara's forcing her to slide her pussy across my dick again and again. I concentrated hard on counting each and every strand of hair on her head to keep my body in check. Zucker knew exactly what he was doing to me. His favorite game to play was to see how far he could push me before I came for him. It was even more fun with Clara between us.

"I want to seal the bond between us, and you two are going to make me spill my seed before I'm ready. Take me into your body again, my flower. I need you both, now." I grabbed her hips and stopped their slow torture.

Zucker smiled and buried it in the crook of her neck. He whispered to her, but loud enough for me to hear what he said. "I was hoping you'd suck on Tau's cock and taste yourself on him, but I can see he wouldn't last a second in your talented mouth."

Clara batted her eyelashes at me, and stars in the sky, I was in trouble if these two were in league with each other to fuck the living nature out of me. She covered my hands with her own. "If the fates allow, we'll have plenty of time for all of you to teach me every single thing you'd each like best for me to do with your bodies. But I too want to complete the bond. We were so close to something new and special before, that I think together, we can make magic."

Make magic, make love, make life.

Zucker nodded in a way that was much more serious than two minutes before. "You already are magic, sweetness. I don't mean the inherent power you have, but the beautiful person you are, with your strength, your grace, your charm, and your stalwart heart in the face of all that is so new and different for you. That's the magic here."

Wow. I'd never heard him talk like this. I sat up and took his hand. I wanted to kiss him but didn't want to remove Clara to do that. I gave his arm a tug and made him come to me. "I think that's supposed to be my line."

I pressed my lips to his and pushed my tongue along the seam of his mouth. He let me in, taking my tongue, giving what he knew I wanted. That was what we'd always done, give and take, take and give. With Clara though, we were something more. We could become one.

He broke the kiss before I was ready, but he never was a patient one. He was right to do it. I didn't want Clara feeling left out. When I looked at her, the sparkling in her eyes was tenfold and she licked her own lips. "I love the way you love each other and I'm grateful I get to be a part of it with you."

Her heartfelt words meant so much to me, I couldn't even speak. Any words about how I was the one thankful that she was here with us were lost in my emotions. Zucker did what he does best and showed us both.

"Clara, raise up on your knees a bit. I want to put Tau's cock into your hot cunt once again." Zucker was the one who gave her ripe ass a slap this time, and I thoroughly enjoyed the little oh her lips made and the blush on her cheeks. He reached between the two of us and found my cock, gave it a few hard strokes just to fucking tease me, and swiped my head up and down her slit, driving both me and Clara crazy.

Clara broke first. "Zucker if you keep it up, I will forgo all my lessons in using my mouth on you and Tau and ask Leb and Nuss to let me pleasure them instead."

Zucker laughed. "Ah, but my sweet princess, I would enjoy watching you suck their cocks too. Especially if I was fucking either of them or you while you do it."

He punctuated his threat by spearing my cock into her waiting pussy but shoving two of his fingers in along with and scissoring them back and forth. Both Clara and I moaned. "And that, my loves, is just a taste of what's to come."

The same magic connecting the three of us began its delightful build up. I could already feel the zips and zings of sensation spurring Clara's arousal. Zucker and I had shared a bed with many a fae, but we'd never fucked a woman this way before. I wasn't sure if it was his anticipation or mine that had my heart fluttering in my chest.

I pulled Clara down for a kiss and took her mouth soft and slow. She was so incredibly precious to me and for the first time since I'd met Zucker, I was the one without words and needed to use my body to show her how I felt. Our tongues danced, and even though I was supposed to be waiting for Zucker to slide his cock in, I couldn't help but thrust into her soft, wet pussy.

I ate up her little whimpers and decided I wanted to be kissing her when she came this time too. I'd take everything she had and keep it safe for as long as I could. Hopefully forever.

Zucker put a hand on my thigh and stilled my fucking. Clara and I both felt his cock head notch at her entrance. "Hold steady, you two. I'm going to push in nice and slow to let Clara's cunt get used to the stretch."

I pushed my hands into her hair and held her tight to me.

Zucker pushed barely an inch in and the connection between all three of us skyrocketed to an even stronger level than before. The touch of pain Clara suffered as her channel stretched wider with two cocks inside of her, pushed her pleasure at the same time.

Having Zucker's cock slide along mine in such a tight space was like nothing I'd ever experienced. We'd been inside of each other before, we'd jacked the other off together, I'd sucked his cock while he sucked mine until we both came. None of it compared to this.

"That's it, sweetness, you can take us. I'm almost there. Fuck this is like a magical fucking fantasy." Zucker sank in as deep as he could go, and Clara's magic exploded around us. Blue and white and gold and red wisps sparkled through the air and perceptively wrapped us in a bubble of joy and wonder.

Our sensations were tripled again, no, even more. We were in each other's minds, bodies, but we had Leb and Nuss with us once again too. And that mysterious sixth consciousness, filling us all with more emotions of need and lust.

Because we were all so intertwined, when I moved, so did Zucker. Our cocks pressed into each other, sliding back and forth inside the squeeze of Clara's incredibly tight pussy. She groaned into my mouth, and I swallowed her every sound, returning it with a growl from deep within my spirit.

Nothing existed except our minds, our sensations, our bodies. We were one, all of us, and I finally belonged to someone so completely. More than just someone, five spirits tangled with my own and we would never be separated ever again.

I gently rocked my hips and let Zucker take over. He meted out a steady rhythm, driving us closer and closer to that precipice of bliss. Faster and faster, he fucked us until the sweat beaded on his upper lip and he had to make us come or the pleasure rippling in shockwaves around us would become unbearable.

"Just a little more, sweetness, you're almost there. Come on, let go, be mine, be ours." Zucker pleaded for Clara to come, for us both to give in to his relentless fucking and explode.

What he didn't understand was that as tightly wound together as we all were, we couldn't come until he too let go. Only for him would I have broken my kiss with Clara. For him, I did, promising to taste her cries many more times in the future.

I caught Zucker's eyes with mine and though I was breathing hard, and could barely catch a breath to speak, I found the words he needed, finally able to say them and truly mean them. "I love you, Zucker Pflaume-Fee. I belong to you, in this circle of spirit and magic with our one true bonded mate. Let go and give yourself to us in return."

He knew the words before I even said them, and Clara echoed them in our minds. The first tight chord of her orgasm burst and Zucker followed her, letting himself love and be loved in return. His hot seed spilled into her first, and my cock and balls tightened, and I shot into her too.

When Zucker slowed then stilled his thrusts, I slowly continued, mixing our essence inside of our princess, and pushing it deep, hoping for new life. Even though it was unlikely until she was bonded with us all, I wanted her womb filled with both me and Zucker.

The three of us didn't move for a long time. We panted, and let our hearts race, slowing in their own time, still locked together in body and spirit. Zucker gave out a long exhale and then palmed the back of Clara's neck just as he had to me a million times. "I didn't know what love was until I was in your minds. I am not worthy, but I will strive to be every day."

She kissed me softly on the side of the mouth and we all felt it. Then she whispered. "You are worthy of love. Never let anyone tell you otherwise. I spent a lifetime letting others make me feel less than, and you've helped me understand that love doesn't work that way."

Zucker and I slid out of her body, and we reveled in the magical afterglow. Unlike before, Clara's mind and body hummed in a new way. Instead of the slow fade like before, she closed her eyes and pulled her Spirit and Magic back into herself while leaving us with a piece of our spirits filled in with a part of hers.

The bond with both of us was now complete, and her magic could use and amplify our gifts. In two short days, she was the most powerful magician in the Winter Realm. She had yet to find the Snowflake crown and consummate her bond with Nuss, so there was more power ready and waiting for her to yield.

She stood and gave Zucker the same kiss and then looked out across the grotto. "All five of you are worthy of my love."

But there were only four of us.

Until Konig walked into the grotto.

I'VE GOT YOU, UNDER MY SPELL

CLARA

When I lived in the human world, I don't think I ever truly knew what it felt like to be loved. So much of society told me, that because of what I looked like, I wasn't worthy of romantic love.

Oh, I fell in love at the drop of a snowflake. There was always some boy at school, the guy who worked at the bookshop, some friend of my brother's. I didn't know how to not be in love. School girl crushes that ruled my every emotion.

As the years passed and my friends and the other girls I went to school and dance classes with found boyfriends and I didn't, the fearful realization sank in and entrenched itself. I would never get to experience for myself the rush of joy they so clearly felt when they were with their beloveds.

I didn't understand then the difference between unrequited love and the real thing. Because being loved in return was... magic.

I didn't understand that I couldn't find the right one for me because I wasn't in the right world.

I really didn't understand was that I wasn't destined to love and be loved by just one man—another tenant of the broken human society that told me I was wrong. Why did that world have to make love finite when it was so much grander?

Standing here in this special place where love was set to grow, I once again embraced my mission to show the Winter Realm how to love again. I was learning lessons in how to do it myself, but I was confident that once I'd fallen in love with, and bonded with, each of my true loves, that I could share that with the rest of the people here.

War and hate had no place in such a beautiful land.

I could help end that.

And I was going to start right now.

Consummating my bond with Zucker and Tau was so perfect and beautiful, because not only did they love me, they loved each other. Their natural gifts of sensuality and empathy burst to life for all three of us, connected by my magic, and I couldn't have asked for a better present.

I could hardly wait until I got to join with all of them at the same time. Each were so important to me in their own ways, but together we would be unstoppable. If any troop were to make this world ready for the return of the Vivandiere and the defeat of the Mouse Queen, it would be the six of us.

Yes. Six.

Leb gave me the courage to be a fierce warrior like him.

Tau helped me connect to my own buried fears and emotions and see that being together was better than isolation.

Zucker showed me that the only thing keeping me from being a strong, sexual woman was my own lack of self-confidence.

Nuss would be my forever protector, and soon I would learn the lesson he had for me. Even with Tau's empathic connection, he was still guarding himself from me. But of them all, he knew and understood me the best. He was the one who had first-hand knowledge of how to access my magic. For that I would be ever grateful.

But it was Konig that I needed to bring back into the fold. While I didn't know or understand what happened to make him their enemy, I could sense the deep betrayal felt on both sides. I should wait until I'd bonded with Nuss, to try my first bid at repairing old wounds with love. But then I'd miss the opportunity to heal them sooner rather than later.

Konig was here now. He'd been with us half the night. If he was going to attack and hurt or kill anyone, it would have been easiest when we were otherwise busy. But he wasn't here to do that. He wanted in. To our lives and our hearts.

Because his was broken.

I was going to fix it.

Konig dropped down from his hiding place, where he'd watched the three of us consummate our bond and had joined in spilling his own seed just as Leb and Nuss had over on the shore. I felt him the instant I connected with Tau. But I'd known all along he was with us.

"Hello, princess. Have a good fucking?" Konig strode toward me as if on an afternoon stroll and he saw a pretty flower he wanted to pluck.

I opened my arms to him but Tau and Zucker jumped in front of me. Zucker had grabbed his daggers from his clothes, and he held them out pointing at Konig's head. "Stop right there, bastard. This is no place for a rat."

"Maybe not, but I think the mouse army would enjoy this warm oasis." Konig snapped his fingers and hundreds of mice swarmed up from around his feet, dropped from the ceiling, and popped out of every plant and flower.

"Konig, stop. We don't have to fight." I didn't yell, I didn't scream, I didn't even cringe at the sight of all the tiny animals.

They were a part of him, and his own special gift, and I was no longer afraid.

"Oh, but I'm afraid we do. You see, I am bound to follow the Mouse Queen's orders and she wants me to bring you to her." He spat when he talked of the queen.

The mice swirled around my feet, but never touched me. Zucker and Tau weren't so lucky. I don't know how, but the mice wrapped the two of them up in what had to be miles and miles of grass and vines so that they couldn't even move. The bindings covered their mouths and though they grunted and tried to shout, their words were distorted and muffled.

I grabbed and scratched at the cords, ripping and tearing, but there was always another and another mouse to replace anything I tore away. Tau shook his head at me and the uselessness of trying to free them surged into my gut. I gave up and turned back to Konig ready to beg him to let them go. But when I saw the pain buried in his eyes, I changed plans.

"Then I unbind you. You don't belong to her, but you and I do belong to each other." I'd felt the link between us the first time I saw him. He felt it too.

Konig's eyes went dark and his whole face matched. "If only it was that simple. Even you with your Spirit and Magic cannot break this curse."

He strode toward me and for the first time, I was afraid of him. Had I been so mistaken? I was sure love would conquer all. But it wasn't even showing up for the fight. An angry, grim Konig advanced on me.

The temperature in the grotto dropped and the moisture in the air froze. Millions of snowflakes formed before my very eyes. A huge crack sounded, and I whirled around to look toward the source at the shore. Nuss had his sword shoved into the water's edge and a thick layer of ice ran across the warm lake toward the island.

The power of the Land of Snowflakes at work.

Leb had somehow called down a reindeer from outside and was riding on the back of one like knight in shining armor coming to my rescue. His axe was over his head, and it looked as though he was going to hurl it at Konig.

This was all going so, so wrong.

I threw myself in front of Konig, my arms sprawled wide in defense, and Leb roared out at me. "Clara, don't, move."

Konig grabbed me around the waist, pulling my bum tight against his front. He lowered his face, scraping his scuff against my skin, and kissed my neck. "Yes, do as your Viking says. Don't move, or they'll all suffer. My army are here only to capture you, but they can be set to kill just as easily."

I froze as still as the air and ice. "I can't let you injure them, because I see you, my Mouse Prince, it would be the same as hurting me or yourself."

He scowled at me and snapped his fingers once again. The mice spewed forth from the island across the newly formed ice, building a bridge with their bodies up and over it. Konig shoved me toward the living bodies bridge. I shoved him right back. "What are you doing? This isn't right. We can defeat the mouse queen together."

"With your little band of rebels, princess? They've lied to you, just as they did to me. They only want what is best for themselves and their lands. You'll soon see." He grabbed one of Zucker's fallen daggers and pointed it at me this time. "Now, move."

Leb was almost here and Nuss was right behind him, sliding across the ice like he was on skates. I needed to stall for just a little bit of time. If the four of them could band together, we could capture Konig and make him see the light. "Can't I please get my clothes? I'm so cold."

"No, no. I'm thoroughly enjoying watching your tits and ass jiggle," Konig gave me a shove and I was forced to step onto the first writhing stair of the bridge made of mice. "Although not as much as I'll relish it when I'm fucking you and you're calling only my name as you come on my cock, just as you for did Leb and Zucker and Tau."

I refused to think of his words as a threat. Mostly because I did want him to claim me in the same way the others had.

Leb leaped from the reindeer onto the island and Nuss was coming up under the bridge. I just needed to keep him talking a little longer. "You won't be able to do that if you give me to the Mouse Queen."

Konig spun and threw the dagger, not at Leb, but at Zucker. Leb dove in front of the blade, taking it in the shoulder to save his friend. Konig took advantage of that and rushed me, grabbing me by the arm and hauling me further up the bridge. "I'll turn you in to her, but not until I'm obligated to on the twelfth day of Christmas. Until then you're mine and I'll do with you what I like."

"Princess, jump. I'll catch you." Nuss was directly below us and he held his good arm aloft toward me.

I had no doubt even with just one working arm he would catch me, but I couldn't let Konig escape, even if it meant I didn't. He was supposed to be with us, not working against me and his brethren. I ripped my elbow from Konig's grip, but not to run away. I had to pray that the others would understand what I did next and didn't think I was betraying them.

I did what I hoped was the last thing the dark warrior before me would expect. I pushed my hands into his hair and pressed my lips to his, kissing him with everything I had.

To my relief, he responded by wrapping an arm around my waist and the other across my back and kissed me back. This wasn't like the quick kiss he'd stolen from me in the Christmas Tree Forest. This was passionate, and needy, and my magic responded to something so much more than lust from him.

I could taste, and feel, and sense the love hidden deep in his heart. It was there, it was for me, and I was going to save him by bringing it out. My magic swirled up and I called on the gifts from the others to help me.

I poured all my newfound sensuality into this kiss, and felt his emotions respond in kind. His heart was walled up so tight, yet inside that wall was a warrior's spirit fighting for what he thought was righteous. If he was bad or evil, he wouldn't care, but above all, that's the gift I felt in him, that I connected to with my magic.

He cared so deeply, it physically hurt.

The intensity of Konig's emotions being bared to me overwhelmed my senses. Suddenly, I felt like I was tumbling, caught up in a maelstrom of magic and lust. Oh, oh God, I was falling. The mouse bridge beneath our feet was collapsing, and we were caught up in a literal tornado of mice, swirling around us and carrying us across the ice and then up the tunnel to the cave entrance.

We emerged back out into the snow and freezing temperatures, just as the sun was setting. We'd been down in the grotto the entire day, secluded in our little world of love and bonding. The harsh reality of my situation hit me as a cold slap in the face.

"You can't control me with the promise of your body. You already belong to me, at least for the next few days. I'll take you when and how I like, and you'll be begging me for more, not the other way around." He marched me over to the waiting sleigh, minus one reindeer.

"You know that's not what I was trying to do."

I wasn't going to save Konig by convincing him to open his heart and rejoin the fold of the princes born under the Christmas Star. He was taking me away from them. I shivered, only partially from being bare to this snowy world. I'd really screwed up and had no one to blame but myself.

I wasn't going to cry or beg or play the victim. The warrior magic in me wouldn't allow that, even if old human Clara was already doing all three of those inside. I wrapped my arms around myself, straightened my spine, and held my chin up high.

What I was going to do was fix the problem I'd just made. The way I'd been trying to reach him so far was all wrong. Appealing to the good in him would have to wait until I'd chipped away some of the layers he had built around his heart. How to get him to see reason wasn't entirely clear to me. I needed some of Nuss's good old know how and understanding of my magic.

Then like I'd conjured him up, Nuss was here. The mouse tornado deposited him and the missing reindeer next to the sleigh. Except it wasn't my magic that brought him here tied up and gagged.

"Get in before you freeze to death. I don't fuck dead princesses." Konig secured the reindeer back into its harness and pointed to the seat of the sleigh. "Your dress and some warm blankets are in the bench. Get dressed and ready to go."

He grabbed Nuss and pushed him up against the side of the vehicle. Nuss did his best to put up a fight, but the bindings didn't allow him to do much than wiggle like a worm. It didn't take him more than a minute to maneuver Nuss into the floor of the back seat. The whole time I stood there looking like a fool with my stomach falling so hard and fast it was a worse feeling than being in the avalanche.

I'd led us right into his scheme by coercing the men to take this sleigh. It had come from Konig, and it was all a set up for this. "What are you going to do to Nuss? You don't need him, leave him be. Just take me."

Konig rounded on me, and that dark look was back on his face. My heart skipped one beat, then two, as I froze, my fight or flight instincts completely scared into submission. "You have no idea what I need. If you did, you would have come with me three days ago. Nuss knows that and I'm sure he's spun quite the tale of his chivalry and courage while painting me out to be the mud that dirties his boots."

It was hard to force my voice out in the face of Konig's anger, but I managed a whisper. "He hasn't, I swear it."

"Don't lie to me to save him. Of course he has. There was a time I thought a Snowflake could have good in them, but he proved me wrong. Now get the fuck in the sleigh before I tie you up. Unless that's what you like, pretty princess."

I still couldn't move.

He eyed me up and down and his eyes flickered over my bum that was red from more than just the cold. "I already know you like to be watched, you like a little pain with your pleasure, and you enjoyed that spanking you got. I'm willing to bet you're getting wet right now thinking of me binding your wrists over your head and making you kneel on the floor for me."

Nuss made a series of noises that I was quite sure were threats to Konig's life, but he couldn't do anything for me now. Because Konig was right. I did want him to take control.

I wanted him to tell me exactly what to do to pleasure him, and how to do it, and when, and where. None of the same thoughts had even crossed my mind when I was with Leb, or Zucker, or Tau.

My magic rose up and sparkles of blue swirled around the two of us. It drew Konig to me and he shoved his hand into my hair and gripping a clump of it tight, tipping my head back so I could do nothing but look up at him. The second he touched me again, I understood what his gift was.

He had the power to command.

OF MICE AND MAGIC

KONIG

She was mine.

The fabled lost princess of the Land of Spirit and Magic, born under the Christmas Star along with me and six other princes, had finally returned to the Winter Realm, and she belonged to me.

At least for the next eight days. The Mouse Queen would have my head when and if she found out that I had the princess and hadn't immediately brought her to the castle, but that was her own damn fault for not being more specific.

I may have to obey her commands, but only in the extremely specific way that the curse demanded. The queen hadn't specified when I had to bring Clara to her, only that I had until the twelfth day of Christmas. That gave me plenty of time.

Surely if she could fall in love with the rest of the Nutcracker guard in two days, I could get her to fall in love with me in a week and see exactly how they had all betrayed the meek of the realm instead of protecting them.

If she didn't see how the other lands had mistreated my people, than she was just as corrupt as the rest of them. I wasn't yet ready to accept that such pure Spirit and Magic could look the other way at the atrocities wrought on the inhabitants of the Land of Animals, but I'd been wrong about those I believed in before.

Clara looked at me like she was both scared and turned-on at the same time. Perhaps she was. For being a naive virgin when she'd entered the Winter Realm, she'd grabbed onto her sexual desires like a fiercer warrior than I could have foreseen.

She was so much more than any of us expected.

"Don't make me tell you again to get dressed and sit down, or so much more than that spanking you so desire is what will be waiting for you when we get to our destination." She had to be fucking freezing and yet she still stood her ground.

"I... don't want you to spank me." We both knew she did. Her pink ass had color in it not from the cold but from Tau and Zucker's hands.

Stars above she was fucking magnificent standing here in her naked glory, defenseless and yet still fighting. She was the champion my people needed on their side.

"Yes, you do. And I will do that and so much more to pleasure you, princess." As would the good prince of the Snowflakes. He just didn't know it yet.

Out of us all, he thought he knew the most about how her magic worked. Nuss was sure only he could control Clara and bend her magic to his will. The Snowflake court and their all-knowing church decided they were the gatekeepers of all the knowledge left over after the destruction of the Land of Spirit and Magic. But what they didn't know was that the behind those forbidden walls, was not simply eviscerated grounds destroyed in the battle between good and evil. The Steel Tree Castle still stood, and within its ruins was all I needed to learn.

A beautiful blush rose up her chest and cheeks. Wasn't I

going to have fun bringing that out in her over and over? But along with that flush came a defiance that made me want her all the more. "You can't tell me what I do and do not want."

She clasped her fists at her side and the magic swirling around us turned into a snow flurry, obscuring her from my view for just a moment. She forgot, or perhaps didn't understand, that the beast in me didn't need sight to track her every move. My other senses served me just as well.

When she tried to make a run for the Flower Fae border, I was ready.

"Hey, hey, you flower people assassins up there, help me." She shouted toward the trees where the guards had their arrows trained on us.

The only thing those Flower Fae were going to shoot at were Sweet Fae trying to cross the border. They hadn't even flinched at the mouse army surrounding this cave entrance since it was on the Land of Sweet's side. Probably happy I was invading the Sugar Plum Court.

I heard their bow strings stretch at the ready. Shit. Had they figured out what an advantage it would be to have the princess in their land? They had seen Tau enter the cave with her and yet not return. I had no doubt they had their spies headed into the cave from the Land of Flowers side now and that meant a rescue mission for at least Leb and Tau.

Enough. I wasn't losing the small advantage I had over the Nutcrackers.

I captured the princess, and this time didn't give her a choice. I threw her over my shoulder and held her arms and feet in a soldier's carry. No amount of squirming would allow her to escape me.

"I don't want to hurt you, my lady, but I will if I have to." In the service of my people, I would sacrifice her strong will and her comfort.

In hauling her back to the sleigh, I caught Nuss's glare. He would hate me even more in the coming days. That was nothing new. He thrashed against his bindings and made a series of sounds that were likely cursing my name.

I was already cursed. His wouldn't hurt me any more than the Queen's.

For a half second, I considered throwing her in the back seat with him, just to show her that she had no power in this situation. She might have some access to her magic, but without her bond to the Snowflake Prince, she wouldn't be able to use it to her full ability yet.

The draw to have her by my side as we raced to the castle was more than I could resist, even if she'd be a pain in my ass the whole way. I dropped her onto the seat, loathe to let her skin escape my touch. Once we got to our destination, I'd keep the rooms nice and warm so I could keep her naked the whole time. But until then, I wouldn't have her freeze to death.

"We don't have time for you to dress now." I yanked the pile of soft woven blankets out and tossed them onto her lap. "Wrap yourself in these from head to toe, and if you move even and inch from that bench, I'll strap you down for the duration of our ride with my belt."

She did something I didn't expect even a little bit in response. She stuck her tongue out at me. Such adorable defiance.

"I can think of a lot better things I'd like you to do with your tongue, but they'll have to wait." I sat next to her and took up the reigns, thought I didn't need them. With nothing more than a push of my thoughts, I sent the reindeer the mental map of our route to the Christmas Tree Forest and then across to the border of the Land of Spirit and Magic. We'd skirt along the far side where the once thriving jewel of the Winter Realm met the wild Land of Animals.

They took off like an arrow, and the princess squeaked beside me. She glanced back toward the cave, but no one was coming to rescue her. My army would keep the other Nutcrackers busy until we were far away.

I didn't count on the Flower Fae to take any notice of us. In fact, I'd assumed the opposite. The first arrows landed hard into the side of the sleigh. Those were only warning shots because their assassins didn't miss.

"Get down, and stay down, princess. We've just been marked as enemies of the DewDrop Court." We'd have to risk going deeper into Sweet Fae territory if we were going to avoid getting shot. I could take an arrow or two, but I didn't want the reindeer hurt.

"Oh my God, why are they shooting at us? I'm on their side." She ducked as another volley slammed into the path ahead of us to tear up the runners and knock us off course. My nimble reindeer avoided them easily, but I feared the next round would be aimed at them.

The countryside was hilly and riddled with caves where the sugar was mined. Only one led back to the tunnels under the castle. I'd snuck through before but didn't dare risk that again. It was the Christmas Tree Forest or bust. I steered the sleigh into the candy cane trees to obscure the line of sight for anyone shooting at us and spurred the team to go faster than ever before. We were practically flying already, but they found a little more speed for me.

They too understood our cargo and what was at stake.

"No one but Flower Fae are on their side. They hate everyone, including you and me, and your snowflake pal." If Tau was discovered injured, there was already a death sentence on my head. Still only warning shot arrows came at us. We were far enough from the border between the two fae lands now that they shouldn't be able to reach us. Unless this incident broke the current treaty and the Flower Fae had just invaded.

I mentally checked in with the mice I'd left behind in the grotto. Sure enough, they were swarming around Flower Fae who'd snuck in from the entrance on their side of the border to rescue Tau. The DewDrop Court up until now spent most of their military resources on their long-standing civil war with the Sweet Fae.

The Mouse Queen would not like that I'd stirred that nest of stinging nettles. That was something I'd deal with later. Hopefully much, much later, with Clara by my side.

Unless I did something drastic right here, right now, we were never going to make it to the Steel Tree Castle, much less the Christmas tree forest. "Princess, it's time to share some of that magic of yours with me."

She stared at me wide-eyed and worried. From the fear written there, she knew her blood could give someone access to her magic. Not even the Mouse Queen knew that. I shouldn't either. But I knew a lot of things I wasn't supposed to.

I'd bet the Prince of Snowflakes and his damn Church of the Christmas star did. If he'd fucking hurt her, I was going to kill him. Slowly.

Fuck. I knew that avalanche was too big to only have been triggered by the Gingerbread Vikings' booby trap on the mountain. Nuss had access to both the prince and princess that day. He'd probably been drunk on having access to all that power to destroy me.

"I'm not going to hurt you, Clara. But those assassins will." I pushed the blanket around her shoulders back just enough to grab onto those soft blonde curls and twist them around my fist. "Open your heart to me as you have the Nutcracker Guard, and I can save us from a painful death."

The kisses I'd stolen from her before were about lust and power, not a connection. She needed a bond to let her magic flow. Now was a shitty time to ask for that, but I was running out of options.

"Kidnapping me is not the way to win my heart, Konig." There was steel in her words, just as in her spine. She truly was a Stahlbaum. Once again, she surprised the shit out of me, for when I'd determined to kiss her and steal any bit of magic that rose up, Clara leaned in and brushed her lips over mine. Then she whispered, "So I guess I'll have to win yours."

She wrapped her arms around my shoulders and kissed me, pouring her magic into my very spirit. My skin tingled from the inside out, my cock went so hard I thought I might come in my pants, and the world around us became so still and perfect that it was like a painting hanging on the wall of a castle.

I could kiss her forever.

Or I could save our lives.

For one more second, I let the magic seep into my cells, felt it take over as far as I could allow it, and then I broke our kiss. With all the force I could muster, I pushed the magic out, along with my mental command to the team pulling the sleigh. "Let's see if reindeer really know how to fly."

I gave a snap to the reins and the world around us slowed like a frozen night. The reindeers' hooves pounded along the ground and then into the air. Their breath freezing on each exhale puffed in the sky, higher and higher, and the sleigh slipped off the ice as if it weighed nothing at all.

"How are you doing this?" Clara looked down to the ground falling away below us and gripped the side of the sleigh with both her hands.

"I'm not. You are. I only told the animals what do to with the magic at their disposal." Clara stared back at me with all the sweet naivety of someone who hasn't been hurt by betrayal and war. It would be so easy to love her.

If only everything in my life was different, I would do exactly that. But no amount of magic could break the curse on my heart, and so I'd have to live with hoping she could at least break the curse on our land and my people.

Nuss floundered around in the back seat and made way too

much noise. "Careful there, captain, or you'll end up a falling snowflake."

"Where are you taking us?"

I wished we could fly straight to the Land of Spirit and Magic, but there was only one way through the magical barrier placed around the eviscerated land and it wasn't by air. "We'll land in the Christmas Tree Forest, then you'll have to trust me. You'll want to see what I have to show you."

"Just tell me."

"To even speak the words aloud is forbidden." The queen had told me never to call that place by its name, and I could do nothing but obey.

"You're taking me home, aren't you?" Her spirit twirled in her bright blue eyes like a ballerina.

Somehow, I knew she didn't mean to the human world. She understood now who she was, and that would make it all the harder for her to see how her land had been destroyed by greed and fear. "Yes."

I turned away from her and scowled out at the final rays of the sun setting behind the Gingerbread mountains. I was letting myself be too soft with her. This was a harsh world she'd come back to, and kindness and love were the last thing on my agenda.

I needed her to fight for the throne, and to save my people from the tyranny of the Mouse Queen. Falling in love with her was the last thing either of us needed. The Nutcracker Guard thought bonding with her as consorts was the way to get her on their sides.

She didn't need to be loved or love in return, she simply needed a crown and a good fucking. With the four dangling around her neck and the one I'd stolen, she'd be the most powerful princess of the Land of Spirit and Magic this realm had ever seen.

Seven crowns would be better, but five would have to do.

We were just coming over the edge of the Christmas Tree Forest and Clara pointed down. "Look, is... is that Fritz running through the snow?"

I always knew some of the Queen's loyal mice were in my army. They'd pledged fealty to her under coercion just as I had. When I'd sent the mouse army to attack the SugarPlum Court, I knew some were on a special assignment to find the queen's pet and return him.

While they were loyal to her, they were still under my command, and I could see and feel their thoughts. Even if I couldn't control them, she couldn't hide their mission from me.

Clara pointed again. "It is him, and he's got my marzipan pixies in a cage. We have to stop him."

A day ago, the queen couldn't care less about this wayward prince. He'd proven to be nothing but a spoiled brat with no magical talent hidden within. Nothing like Clara's natural ability. But still, he was of the Steel Tree Court and his blood was just as hers. Powerful to someone who knew how to wield it.

If she wanted him back now, well, I didn't want to consider the consequences. If we stopped and tried to get him, I would have to fight my own army. If we didn't, it became a race to see who could learn to utilize the lost magic.

I wouldn't hurt any of my own people. Ever. I was simply going to have to bet that I had a better shot at accessing Clara's magic with the broken pieces of the crown and the connection I would forge with her. If that didn't work, I'd convince her by letting her see the dire circumstances of the Land of Animals firsthand.

"No, your pixies will have to be one more sacrifice in this war. We can't let your brother even see us."

"What? No. We have to save them." Clara struggled to move away from me, but I wasn't letting her anywhere near the edge of the sleigh where she could fall.

I wrapped my arm around her and let her squirm and even

punch me in the chest. None of that hurt me. The tears pooling at her lashes tore me to pieces. I'd survived worse.

"They're my friends. I have to help them."

I directed the reindeer to turn away from Fritz's path toward the Land of Animals. We could circle the outer edge of the forest to get to the place we could slip into her land. Until then I'd have to mouse up and ignore her tears. "You'll help them and everyone else in this forsaken realm when you usurp the Mouse Queen."

Clara looked up at me and those tears fell, forming icicle trails on her cheeks. "You've got the wrong girl."

THE LAND OF SPIRIT, MAGIC, AND DESTRUCTION

CLARA

*K*onig was nothing that I'd thought he would be.

Dark and handsome, sure. Lustful and made my belly go all a flutter. Yep.

An asshole who would hurt those closest to me or let them be harmed. That I hadn't seen coming.

Which was really stupid of me. He'd been trying to kidnap me from the moment we met. Him with a sword in his hand and doing his best to kill my protector. What in the hell was wrong with me? I couldn't believe I'd been so stupid and so incredibly wrong about him.

Or that I'd thought I could save him.

All he cared about was usurping the Mouse Queen. Why couldn't any of them see that I couldn't do that. I wasn't the Vivandiere. They needed a real warrior, a woman who could lead them in battle.

All I knew how to do was dance and my newly acquired

wanton skill of having sex with men I'd met only a few days ago. Maybe Fritz was right, and I was just a whore.

No. Nope. Absolutely not. It didn't matter that I hadn't known Leb, Zucker, or Tau for exceedingly long, we were destined to be together. I had a deep and meaningful connection with each of them. We were in love.

L.

O.

V.

E.

Love. That's how I was going to help the Winter Realm. I knew that all the way to my spirit and back.

I was hurting right now because Konig hadn't fallen in line with my plans like a good little boy. What had I expected? That one kiss from me would cure all his darkness?

Sort of. Yeah.

I'd also thought that the Land of Sweets and the Land of Flowers sounded like nice places filled with nice people. Not spies, intrigue, and poisoned arrows.

God, I hoped Leb, Zucker, and Tau were alright. I could survive anything if they were alive. At least I had Nuss. It was entirely my fault we were in this situation, but I wasn't above telling him I was sorry. He'd gone awfully quiet back there. I hoped he was working on an escape plan.

"Hold on to something. I've never landed a flying sleigh pulled by eight reindeer before." The ground rose closer and closer, and I considered jumping at the last minute and mad dashing off to find Fritz... and beat him senseless with the cage after I freed my pixies. What did he want with them anyway?

There was the small matter of my not having any clothes or shoes for one. The blankets Konig gave me were fine while we were sitting in the sleigh, but no doubt I'd leave them strewn along the snow the second I tried to run from him.

Not to mention, I'd seen him move. He was faster than a

flea. I'd get all of ten steps before he caught up to me, and then I knew there would be hell to pay.

In spankings.

Dammit. I shouldn't still be turned on by him. I was blaming Zucker's sex magic for that.

Sigh. No, I was not. I had a connection with Konig, just like I did with the others. No matter how wrong it might be, I already had feelings for him that I couldn't deny.

That meant to me that he couldn't be all bad. I just needed to be more careful about what I let him get away with from now on.

The sleigh bumped down into the snow and the reindeer didn't miss a beat. They just kept on running, dragging us along behind them. The trees in this part of the forest were even more dense and getting thicker by the moment.

A branch smacked me in the face. "Ouch. Can't we slow down?"

"No, we're getting close." Konig growled and focused entirely on the path ahead. The sun had finally fully set, and the forest was dark. Darker than where I'd first landed with Nuss. None of the trees here were lit up and there certainly weren't any marzipan pixies to make the place joyful.

I peered into the darkness, trying to see anything. I felt it before I saw it. Tingles of magic danced across my skin and the little red crown charm my mother had left me lit up, glowing from within.

But there was something wrong. The sparks of magic didn't feel anything like I'd experienced before. They flickered and fritzed out before I could truly feel their warmth. A lump formed in my throat and when I tried to swallow it down, I got a boulder sitting at the bottom of my stomach.

"What happened here?" My words were barely more than a whisper.

"This won't be easy for you, but I need you to suck it up."

The sleigh finally slowed to a stop and Konig jumped out. The animals were restless and jumpy. He unclipped their harnesses, and one by one, they dashed off into the forest. They were getting far away from here as fast as possible.

I wanted to do the same. My chest literally ached like I was having a heart attack. But I knew that's not what it was. Whatever was tearing up my heart was coming from the other side of that darkness. "I can't go in there."

Nuss jumped up behind me, holding one of Zucker's daggers at the ready in his good hand. "And you won't have to, ever. No one should be subjected to the atrocities in there. Now get behind me, princess. Konig and I have an old score to settle."

I knew he was too quiet back there. I climbed over the seat, but I didn't miss the anger flashing in Konig's eyes as I did so. I shook my head at him and looked away. "I can't, Konig. There's something terribly wrong in there. I thought you said you were taking me home."

"I have. Welcome to what's left of the Land of Spirit and Magic, Princess Clara." Konig bowed and behind him a gash of burning red rent the darkness open from the tops of the trees to the ground.

From inside, a melody played, a tune I almost remembered. It softly called to me, and I stepped from the sleigh. Men and women danced gracefully through my memory, and someone held me safe, but far away and long ago. I could almost remember, but the images faded like embers in this fiery gash.

My heart yearned to remember even as it ached. I had to know.

"Clara, no. You don't know what's in there. Stop." Nuss reached for me, but I pushed his arm away.

My legs didn't heed Nuss any mind. Where once I was scared, now I was mesmerized. It didn't matter that I was in bare feet in the snow, I felt no cold. I walked right past Konig and toward the gash. The closer I got the hotter my own crown charm burned as if it was an important part of that fire but coming from inside of me. It was glowing as bright as the tear in the world in front of me.

I reached my hand out and the magic inside of me swirled up. It had been a beautiful blue color when I'd been with my men, but now it matched the red light of this strange place. "Is this a portal? Like the one I came through to get here?"

Konig stepped up beside me on my right, and Nuss on my left. "No, Clara, it isn't. This shouldn't even exist. You mustn't go in there."

"She needs to see what happened to our world. Let her go." Konig's voice still carried his anger, but the magic here seemed to suck it up.

"You don't know what's on the other side. The Land of Spirit and Magic was destroyed. That's why this barrier is here. There's nothing there for you to see," Nuss argued. "I can't let you."

"Why don't you see for yourself, Nutcracker." Konig jumped behind both of us and shoved us into the glowing gash.

I spun and grabbed both Nuss's hand and Konig's shirt, dragging him with us at the last moment before we fell through the broken barrier.

My mind exploded with images of armies marching through the snow, animals being whipped while pulling machines of war behind them, Fae men and women murdering each other, and Viking axes smashing buildings, bodies, and everything else in their path.

The most ruthless of all were the magicians. They used their magic to tear people asunder, to make anyone who opposed them fall to their knees in pure agony until their heads exploded and feasted on the bodies of the animals that lay slain in the fields.

All but the Vivandiere — the Queen of Spirit and Magic, of the Steel Tree court. She was no longer the young woman who'd hidden the broken crowns around the realm on her adventures. She was a mother, a queen, and a magician. Instead of participating in the senseless fighting she'd tried to prevent, she took her children and disappeared, lost to the war.

I fell on my hands and knees into a pile of rubble. The broken pebbles scraped my hands, and only the thick blankets wrapped around me saved my knees. I couldn't breathe, I couldn't hear with all the high-pitched buzzing in my ears.

I turned my face to the side and vomited into a burned skeleton of a long dead plant in a broken pot. When I looked away to wipe my mouth, I saw the ruins of a once great castle. It was the only thing left standing in a barren wasteland.

There was no snow, but it was bitter cold, and the wind blew relentlessly. This... this is what was left of my home. Nothing but horrific memories and the relics of hubris.

Konig and Nuss tumbled through the gash a breath later and behind them, the rip in the barrier closed. Where it had been was now only more destruction as far as I could see. The two of them quickly rolled to their feet and Nuss punched Konig in the face.

It didn't take long before they were shouting slurs at each other and doing their best to beat the other into a bloody mess. I couldn't stand it.

I stood and held out my hands, drawing on the latent magic energy still in the ground, air, and ashes here. My voice boomed and echoed, "Stop."

They both froze and looked over at me as if I'd grown three heads. "No more fighting. No. More."

I turned my back on them and stumbled away, toward the only shelter from the biting wind. Small chunks of the castle remained, and someone had put a blanket across a tattered archway to serve as a door and windbreak.

"Clara, wait." Nuss ran after me, but I didn't stop for him.

I shoved my way into the stone room and found carpets, a

bed, a fireplace stacked with wood, and provisions on a shelf. I hobbled toward the shelf and grabbed up a jug filled with pungent liquid. I didn't care what it was. I needed to rinse out my mouth and get my bearings.

Nuss came flying into the room, Konig on top of him, wrestling him to the wall. What I hadn't noticed were the steel shackles bolted into the wall.

"I said no more fighting." I could hardly get the words out. Everything had drained out of me, even though I'd absorbed energy from this place. That wasn't exactly right. It was more like tired after eating and drinking too much. I was both full of that latent energy and exhausted from it.

Konig shoved Nuss up against the wall and clasped his good hand into one of the manacles. Nuss wasn't even fighting back. Konig then grabbed his broken arm, tearing the sling away, and closing the other on his bad wrist. Nuss cried out but gritted his teeth. I didn't even have the wherewithal to go to him.

I would do what I could to heal him as soon as I rested a little.

"My apologies, my lady." Konig gave me a little bow. "We weren't fighting. I was simply apprehending this enemy of the realm."

I lifted the jug to my lips and took a long gulp of potent wine. I'd meant to take a small sip, but I was suddenly so thirsty. Konig came over and gently lowered the jug, carefully taking it from me. "I'll not have you drowning your sorrows and getting drunk on me."

I knew I shouldn't, but I leaned into him and laid my head on his shoulder. Even if his were the only arms available to me, I needed this small comfort. Everything was wrong, it was all broken. This wasn't how the stories Drosselmeyer told to me and Fritz ended.

Konig stiffened at first, but then he wrapped his arms

around me. "I'm afraid this is only the beginning of the harsh lessons I have for you, princess."

"Don't you touch her, you bastard. We could be out there saving the realm from your greedy mother if you hadn't betrayed us. Let us go so we can get back to the duty you gave up on." Nuss hadn't ever sounded so enraged before. He was the calm, cool, and collected captain of the Nutcracker Guard. My hero, my protector.

Now when he needed me to save him, I couldn't. I didn't have anything left in me. I peered out at him and saw so much pain written in lines around his mouth and eyes. I mouthed the words I didn't have the energy to say to him. "I'm sorry."

"You're the one who gave up on me." Konig's words were controlled and measured. Though he addressed Nuss, he looked at me, lifting my chin so I had to meet his eyes. "I never stopped fighting for what was right, but you did, Captain."

"You turned on us and allied yourself with the fucking Mouse Queen." Nuss yanked against his chains. "The same woman who destroyed everything around us. I didn't give up on you. You forgot who and what you are."

"Never." He whispered that last word and then lifted me into his arms. In just a few long strides, he crossed to the bed and laid me down. I know exactly who I am. Consort to the Queen of Spirit and Magic."

He took my hand and kissed it. "Long live the Queen."

A COLD SNOWFLAKE

NUSS

$\mathcal{I}$ couldn't believe I'd fucking let this happen. I'd failed the princess and the entire Winter Realm by letting Konig steal her away from us when we were only one crown away from becoming the strongest bonded court in the history of our world.

I'd failed so utterly that if I wasn't so damn angry, I'd be ready to give up. The fire burning through my veins where my cool ice of a Snowflake Prince should be had me ready to tear the fucking chains out of this stone wall and strangle him where he slept beside my beautiful princess. Except I couldn't. This damned broken arm had me literally handicapped.

I slammed my good fist against the stone, and it hardly even made a sound. Never had I been in any place as desolate and bare as the ruins of the former Steel Tree Castle. Of course, I knew the land was demolished in the Mouse Queen's final attack, but this was so far beyond what I thought it would be like.

It hurt to even imagine how many lives and how much magic was lost here.

I couldn't allow Clara to stay here any longer than we already had. The sorrow seeping out of the land would eventually affect her and it could taint her magic. We needed her to be pure of Spirit and Magic just as she was now. Or how she was an hour ago before Konig had gotten his claws into her.

She was already drained. I saw the internal hurt in her spirit when she couldn't help me. Fuck. She shouldn't ever have to help me. It was my job to protect her. I was the captain of the Nutcracker Guard for Christmas' sake. I was doing a shitty ass job of giving her what she wanted and needed so far.

I couldn't even help give her the pleasure that would unlock her magic. She was never going to fall in love with me.

All the fantasies I'd had of the two of us searching out and finding the snowflake crown together and then consummating our bond in the most perfect of ways were gone. I was going to die here in the hell of the seven realms, never having experienced the pleasures of the flesh.

And what for?

Because the Church of the Christmas Star thought I was some kind of messiah? Because the king and queen of the Land of Snowflakes believed them and hadn't treated me like a son my entire life.

Fuck them.

If I had to do this whole thing over again, I'd have been right there in bed with Clara and the others that very first night.

Clara groaned in her sleep, and I strained against the chains keeping me from her. Konig was consummating his bond with her. No, that was a lie to myself. He was fucking her, enjoying her body, and showing her the pleasure I had not. Jealousy, guilt, and self-recriminations stoked the fire burning in my blood.

He had every damned right to bond with her and savor the

flavor of her cunt or sink his cock into her tight heat if she so chose him — he too was born under the Christmas Star.

"Shh. Settle the fuck down. She's just having a dream, asshole." Konig sat up from their little love nest and glared at me. "If you wake her, I'll kill you where you stand. She needs rest."

He crawled out of the blankets, stoked the fire keeping this hellhole warm, and sauntered over to me. "You thought I was fucking her, didn't you?"

I turned my face away. He would still know. He always had seen and understood me better than anyone else. Back in the days when we were all on the same side, he'd been my friend and confidant. His betrayal was the hot coals churning the fire in my blood.

Konig circled around, stalking me like the predator he was. He swiped his thumb across his mouth and then sucked the end of it as if it was covered in the most delicious nectar. "She is delicious and it's your own damn fault you haven't tasted her yet."

"You haven't either." He couldn't have. I would know. Whether she and I had bonded and consummated or not, we were connected. But here in the destruction of the Land of Spirit and Magic maybe everything was different. Clara was already broken. "I can feel her magic when she is aroused."

"Haven't I?" He smiled so smugly that I wanted to punch his teeth out. "Why do you think she sleeps so soundly now? I gave her the comfort and escape she needed."

"She doesn't need shit from you." I had so much more to say, but it wouldn't do me any good to argue with him. He had all the power, and I had none. How the tables had turned.

"Perhaps I can decide what I need and from whom." Clara approached us, her hair wild, her cheeks flushed from sleep, and only a blanket wrapped around her plump body.

Shit. "My lady, my apolo—"

"Not now, and not here." Konig grabbed Clara and held her, so she faced me, his arms wrapped around her waist and her throat. "Until you're ready to go up against the Mouse Queen and take her throne, you're going to do who and what I say."

Clara's magic surged up at Konig's commands. She leaned into him as if she liked the way he was being rough with her. Had he worked some dark spell on her?

"Princess, you don't have to do anything he says. You've already got the power of three lands, you can resist him if you want." I yanked on the chains holding me from her even though lightning shot through my broken arm. My pain didn't matter, only hers.

"She'll do what I tell her to, because we both like it when she does." He slid his hand up her throat until the very same thumb he'd sucked on earlier pressed against her bottom lip. "If I want her to drop to her knees and suck my cock, or yours for that matter, she would. Isn't that right, my queen?"

That telltale flush from her arousal spiked up her throat and cheeks and she nodded, opened her mouth, and licked the tip of his thumb. "I've wanted you both since the first moment I saw you in our great room. I thought it was all a dream then."

She dropped the blankets wrapped around her to the floor, displaying her beautiful body for the two of us. I hated that my cock responded when it was clear that something was wrong. Her magic wasn't just wisps swirling around like when she'd consummated her bond with the others. It literally pulsed like a heartbeat up and down her breasts, stomach, and thighs.

"What have you done to her?"

"This is all her, the real Clara you've been too chaste to see." Konig slid his hand between her thighs, and she arched into him. "I may be giving the commands, but she's the Queen of Spirit and Magic. This is her domain."

Holy Christmas star. She hadn't been drained of her power when we'd come through the rift and into her desolate land, she'd been absorbing the magic and power that remained, and now she was drunk on it. "Clara, love, listen to me. You can't take all this magic in. It's too much, you're not ready."

Her eyes snapped open, and the red magic of her land sparkled in her irises. "You're wrong, nutcracker. Do you think you haven't prepared me? All that I'm missing now is the bond with the land of the Snowflakes and the Land of Animals, and then I can complete my mission."

She walked toward me, slowly, like a seductress come to steal my spirit. This wasn't the Clara I knew and loved.

I swallowed hard past the lump of dread in my throat to ask this question. "To usurp the Mouse Queen?"

"No." She smiled, but not in that lovely uncomplicated way from her first few days here. This smile was the kind I'd seen on Zucker's face a hundred times, when he had sex on the brain. "That's never what I was here to do."

I didn't know what to do with that. Her magic was calling to that fire in my blood, and I was scared to death of this seductive magician she was becoming before my eyes. Since the night we were all born under the Christmas Star, those that fought against the tyrant magicians and later the Mouse Queen, believed the Stahlbaums were free from the taint of power that corrupted the rest of their ilk. The Queen of Spirit and Magic alone wasn't corrupted, and that someday her children would return and together we would bring the Winter Realm back to the peaceful land of the past.

Clara's magic was corrupting her before my eyes, spurred on by Konig's domination of her. He'd already proven he'd chose power, glory, and position over doing what was right. I could do nothing to stop her if she decided she wanted to take over the realm without the rest of us by her side.

Or just the Mouse Prince as her lone consort.

I couldn't let that happen.

I had never known what my role in her magic would be,

unlike the others whose gifts were so obvious. It was why I pushed hard to have courage, be a leader, and take on the most dangerous of missions, like passing through the veil between our worlds to bring her back to the Winter Realm. While I could access her power, I was no messiah or savior as my people believed.

But perhaps I could be her savior.

Only if I could access her magic, and I couldn't do that chained to the wall. "My lady, I am yours no matter your path. What would you have me do to serve you?"

Konig narrowed his eyes at me but continued to watch Clara's approach. My mouth became the desert and my blood the sun beating down on my spirit with desperate heat.

"I want only what you're unprepared to give me." She pressed her body to mine and for once in my life, I wished my clothes gone and to press my bare chest against hers.

Konig moved close, flanking her from behind. He leaned in and whispered in her ear. "Then take what you want from him, my Queen."

When she looked up into my eyes, they were clear, not clouded with magic. Perhaps I could still reach my Clara. I wasn't good with words like Tau and couldn't charm her like Zucker. But I had to try. I didn't even know what to say. But I would simply speak from my heart and rely on the power and magic of love.

She knew and understood that. Her bondings with the others had let me feel how deep her love ran. It was her life's blood, and that which made her magic so powerful. It was that which made us all believe she was the one who could save us all from the catastrophe we'd wrought upon our own realm.

Before I even had a chance to appeal to her, she grabbed the fabric of my shirt and tore it open, sending the buttons flying. Heat flared in her eyes, and she licked her lips. I shivered as she traced her fingers down my skin, and fuck if it didn't feel good.

Her touch was all I'd ever dreamed of. A trail of her magic sparkled down the path and spread across my skin. The pain in my arm lessened, although didn't go away completely.

She kept going down my stomach, and unbuckled my pants, tugging them down over my hips. My heart was ready to beat out of my chest and my cock stood tall and erect for her. The cool air of the barren castle ruins was no match for the heat of her body. If I wasn't chained to this wall, I would take her now and happily give up my vow of celibacy. It didn't matter anymore, none of my life as the Prince of Snowflakes meant a damn compared to the magic of being with her.

"He's dying for you to touch him. Can you see how much he wants you?" He grasped her hands in his and guided her fingers toward my cock.

Of course I wanted her, but why was Konig doing this? What was his endgame here?

Clara took a long steadying breath and dropped her hands. "No. Not without the Snowflake crown. Because without it, the sex will be meaningless to Nuss. We've waited what feels like a lifetime to make this connection between our spirits. I won't do it without the bond set in place between us."

Thank the fucking Christmas Star. I knew the real Clara was still in there, I knew it.

Konig nuzzled her ear and caressed her breasts. "Then you'll just have to come back to bed with me."

Her eyes fluttered shut and even behind her eyelids the red magic glowed. It returned to her skin and pulsed through her again. "I want the bond with you too, Prince of Animals. Where is your crown? Shall I use my magic to find them both?"

"Yes," I said.

"No," Konig growled. "The crown of the Land of Animals is buried somewhere so dark and deep, that it can never be recovered."

She spun in his grasp and placed her hand over his heart.

The pulsing magic poured from her into him until he stumbled back, breaking their connection. For a brief moment, I felt the anger in his spirit, but the love and confusion in hers.

"What are you hiding from us, mouse?" I yanked the chains, wanting so much to break free and stop this madness.

The anger faded from his face and was replaced with a smug smile. "Our luscious Clara's need for you is hotter than I expected. I'm going to have a lot of fun making sure you get to see every second of me fucking her, wearing this."

He reached inside of his shirt and pulled up a chain, at the end of which, the Snowflake Crown swung back and forth, sparking in the firelight.

Dear Reader~

Princess Clara and her Nutcracker Guards' adventures in the Winter Realm aren't over yet. Their story finishes in book three - Crowned.

CROWNED

CLAIMED BY THE SEVEN REALMS - BOOK THREE

For everyone who still believes in fairy tales, they're just dirtier now.

"You are enough to drive a saint to madness or a king to his knees."

— GRACE WILLOWS

CROWNS AND CHAINS

CLARA

I was home. Not back in the human realm I'd been raised in as a changeling, but my true home in Steel Tree Castle in the land of Spirit and Magic.

Of course, now the once beautiful and bustling keep lay quiet and in ruins, but that didn't matter. It was the magic of my people that made me feel welcome and warm.

And powerful.

A thousand generations of magicians had lived and were buried here. Their bodies may have been reclaimed by nature, but their spirits flowed, pulsing in every blade of dry grass, every cracked and broken stone, every cell of my body. It felt as if I'd been dehydrated for my entire life, and I was just now quenching my thirst. It wasn't water I needed to feel whole and hearty again, but pure unadulterated magic.

I wasn't the only one who the spirit flowed through. Konig, the once and future King of the Animals, and Nuss, the Prince of Snowflakes and captain of my Nutcracker guard, were as drunk on the magic as I was. I could feel every need, want, and desire they both had, and their feelings were mixing with my own in a way that was intoxicating and confusing.

That drunken feeling had lowered all of our inhibitions just as if it was spiked Christmas punch. It had me feeling amorous. But it had brought up old wounds and anger out of both Nuss and Konig. If I wasn't between them already, I'm sure there would be blood. There still might be.

There wasn't exactly any place for them to fight in this one small stone room of the ruins. On one side of me was the dark and mysterious side of this power struggle. Konig was my both my nemesis and my savior, my captor and the one to set me free.

But in front of me was the shining light that had guided me from the moment I saw him standing in my living room. Even chained to the wall, in pain from his still broken arm, and wearing little more than the armor of anger, he still tried to protect me.

I wanted both. I wanted to be with both and be what they both needed.

But they were mortal enemies and the only people standing in the way of me saving the Winter realm.

"Give the snowflake crown to the princess." Nuss balked against the chains holding him to the wall even though it caused him pain. The flurries of snowflakes swirled through the small room we'd taken shelter in, even though outside was dry as bones.

Konig dangled the sparkling charm on a silver cord from his fist. I expected a sharp reply to Nuss's demand, but he said nothing. Merely slipped the cord over his neck and tucked the charm into his shirt, as if he was the one who owned that bit of the Snowflake Kingdom.

I'd collected three pieces of the seven broken crowns of the Winter Realm, and bonded with the princes of those lands, claiming them as my consorts and their powers of the warrior, the peacemaker, and the seducer as my own. By rights I should claim the Snowflake crown too.

But there was something in the way Konig tucked that pendant close to his heart, and the magic passing between him and Nuss that stopped me from taking it. I could. Neither understood the breadth of power that surged into me the moment we crossed the Land of Spirit and Magic's border.

I could stop space and time, I could pierce the veil between realms, and I could make them bow at my feet. Lesser magicians than me had done that very thing. Some to crush this world under their boots, and others to try and save it.

While I knew I had these powers at my fingertips, I didn't actually know how to use them. Where's the Beginners Guide to Being a Winter Realm Magician when you need one?

Although... I caught Nuss's gaze with my own. Even in his current state of anger and hurt and arousal and what-the-fuckery, he and I were connected. We had been from the start and staring into his eyes, and indeed his soul, I knew we would be together in the end too.

Whatever that end may be. He had used my magic even before I understood that it existed. Could he teach me? Certainly not while being held prisoner.

I leaned back into Konig's hold, turning my face to his. "Do you not feel the bond between us all?"

Konig licked his lips before glancing down at me. "I not only feel it deeper than you know, sweet innocent princess, but I'm counting on it."

Nuss jerked against the chains again. "You would use it against us. Is no vow sacred to you?"

"None, Nutcracker. You taught me that." Konig's face went from soft for me, to a sneer for Nuss.

I don't know if it was the magic inherent in the land we stood upon, or if it was because my own powers were awakened, but the pain coursing between these two struck me as if a whole host of scarabs were buried in my chest and were digging to get out. I rubbed over the pain in my chest, but it was Konig who groaned.

He grabbed my hand and stilled it. "I wish I could save you from the pain. But I must teach you about the seedy underbelly of our world."

I gave Konig a sideways glance. "Oh my," I said making my voice melodramatically innocent. "You mean it's not all snowflakes and rainbows? I'm so surprised."

I understood this was no fairy story anymore. It never really was. Drosselmeyer had just made the Winter Realm pretty for a child. In reality, there was greed, betrayal, and war.

But I didn't believe it had to be that way. Somewhere in the lost memories of my life before I was stolen away from this world, there was a spark of the stories older and truer than the ones told to young children. Stories of when the Winter Realm embodied comfort and joy, spirit and magic, the beauty of what Christmas meant.

My mission to bring love, real love, back to my homeland surged through me. I could sense that the heartache and hardship that Konig wanted to show me existed. Just as well as I felt the punishing load of duty, obligation, and leadership thrust upon Nuss's shoulders.

If I was ever going to make this world and its people believe in kindness and love again, I had to start with these two. So at odds, and yet, even I could tell, they'd meant something to each other at one time.

They still did.

Asking questions was not going to get me anywhere. If Konig had something he wanted to show me about this realm, and it involved something that happened in his and Nuss's past, that's where I was going to get a deeper understanding of what had broken the relationship they had.

If I could repair that, then I wouldn't have to take the Snowflake Crown. Konig would give it to me. And perhaps help me find and claim the Animal crown too. Only then would our group be complete.

Because while the rest of my Nutcrackers held Konig in contempt, they too felt the connection with him. I'd heard them all bemoan his treachery. So much pointed to there being more to the story than a superficial betrayal. But they were not going to simply tell me.

What I could take advantage of was the pulsing arousal rising between all three of us. The moment Konig brought out the broken piece of the snowflake charm, everything changed. I wanted to have it, and Nuss so badly, I could practically taste it.

What I didn't understand was why Konig had his crown.

"I don't want to fight. You two might have a mad on for each other, but my feelings are different." I rubbed my palm down Konig's jaw, and a finger across Nuss's bare chest at the same time.

When I bonded with Leb, I got a boost in confidence from being a badass warrior. When I bonded with Tau and Zucker, I was filled with the gift of empathy, and the power of seduction. Their love both built me up and made me a better person. I could only hope that mine did something for them too.

Right now, I was using each of those advantages to try and soothe the anger and broken edges of the relationship between these last two important men in my life. I couldn't let go of either of them. They were mine, just as Leb, Tau, and Zucker were.

Konig grabbed both my hands, pulled me close, and held my wrists against my chest. "You're not as innocent as you were three short days ago, are you pretty princess?"

Nuss's gaze bored into me, waiting for my answer, even though he knew, quite intimately, everything I'd learned since he brought me to the Winter Realm.

The confidence and seduction given to me by my mates didn't allow me to back down from Konig's power play. "I have experienced quite a bit, yes. But you and I both know there is more for me to learn."

The demanding alpha burning inside of him had me wanting to ask for him to teach me, to guide me. Just the thought of having him command me sent a shiver through me straight between my legs.

The idea of wanting that was so discordant with the confidence and independence I'd embraced over the past few days. Yet the need was there, and it was being reinforced by the magic flowing between our spirits.

"Yes, there is. Both in and out of my bed." His gaze flicked between me and Nuss so quickly, if I wasn't so connected to him, I might have missed it. "Tomorrow, I'll take you to the dregs of our realm, and you'll see just how harsh life here can be for those not born with a snowflake in their hand."

I wanted to bring love and magic to everyone, not just the privileged princes. Perhaps it was the naivety Konig sensed in me, and not my inexperience. Could a society where everyone was treated with kindness and care even exist? It certainly didn't in the human world I grew up in.

Greed always got in the way.

Or fear.

I couldn't believe any of my mates, not even Konig, were greedy. They'd sacrificed everything for love. That's what gave me the strength to believe that I could do the same.

Which left fear. If the power coursing through me was any indication, what they feared most came from the Land of Spirit and Magic. The Mouse Queen had destroyed my land because of that fear. Had she also absconded with some of the power? That had to be why she held such a position over the realm.

What was Konig afraid of?

If I could figure that out, and help assuage it, his heart would be free to love again.

Konig still grasped my wrists in his hand, and I didn't try to squirm away. He had a deep need to be in charge here. I would start by giving him that.

"Tomorrow we will go to your people, and you can show me what you think I need to see. But not tonight." I didn't know how Konig or even Nuss would react to what I was about to do. "Tonight, I want you to bond the three of us together, King of the Animals."

Nuss had gone too silent as I spoke those last words. I could feel his emotions churning. But so were Konig's. His eyes went from fiery with passion to dark with need. He stared down at me, examining my very spirit to see if my words were meant only to manipulate.

"I told you the Land of Animal's crown is irretrievable, so I cannot bond with you." While his words said no, his spirit was reaching for me.

"I will find the crown. I have access to magic that can help me." The stories of the Vivandiere and the Animal crown were more vague in my mind than the others, although, I wasn't sure why. I'd heard it just as many times as the others.

Nuss sucked in a breath as if he was taking up all the air in the room. "You won't find it, unless the Mouse Queen wants you to. She's the last one to have it. But..."

Well crap.

Konig lifted one eyebrow, listening to what Nuss said, but didn't break eye contact with me. My heart went all ballistic and I realized, Konig knew what Nuss was about to say. This was all part of his plan to bring both him and I back to his lair in my land.

I swallowed hard and turned my face to Nuss. He was breathing hard, and he had so many mixed emotions, I couldn't read him. "But what?"

He looked at Konig instead of me. "But if you and I bond..."

Holy Christmas trees. Was Nuss saying what I thought he was saying? I couldn't spin fast enough to see what Konig's response was going to be.

He was smiling like a mouse who'd just tripped a trap and gotten the cheese. "Then by proxy, I'll be mated to the Princess too."

LOST IN LOVE

NUSS

"On your knees, Nutcracker." Konig unlatched the shackles holding my wrists tight against the wall and looped the links through another hook on the floor. He left some slack, not enough for me to escape, but so that I could kneel with my arms by my side.

I stared at Konig for a heartbeat, then two, then three. It was a wonder my heart still pushed blood through my body at all. I shouldn't even be alive. He should have killed me.

Instead, he's masterminded the perfect plan to truly break me and rebuild me into what he's always wanted. His puppet.

I didn't bend the last time he collapsed my world in on itself and I'd had to rebuild. When he left the guard and pledged his fealty to the Mouse Queen, he'd done his very best to convince me that she would bring our shattered realm back to its former glory. If I defied the Church of the Christmas Star and turned my back on the Land of Snowflakes, the Winter Realm would be saved. There would be no more inequity for the Land of

Animals, and she would vanquish the Magicians who ruled with too much power.

She'd taken care of the Magicians all right. Taken them out of existence. I hadn't been to the Land of Animals since, so I didn't truly know how his brethren fared, but it sure didn't seem like they were any better off. Not if what he was telling Clara was true.

Leb, Tau, Zucker, and I started the Nutcracker rebellion thinking Konig would be on our side. I'd thought he would see the error of his choices as the entire realm watched the Land of Spirit and Magic crumble before our very eyes.

He'd doubled down and become the Mouse Queen's captain, marching on each of our lands to ensure no one else would dare challenge her reign.

Sweet Clara still believed the best of him, that he wasn't here to strike the final blow in a long game betrayal. Even I hadn't seen this coming. She asked, with wonder in her voice, "You're going to... bond with Nuss so we can be together too?"

She'd just fucked both Tau and Zucker at the same time, letting them fill her up together, thus sealing the bond between the two of them as well as theirs with her. I was sure she thought the three of us would do the same. But I already knew that wasn't what Konig meant.

Konig bent his head to Clara's throat and kissed her. Her eyes fluttered shut and the magical feeling of her arousal skipped through the air to hit me right in the gut. Konig's demands couldn't send me to my knees, but Clara's need did.

He was going to use that against us both.

I didn't even move as he quickly secured the chains to the floor, taking away my slack. Then he returned to her, as if she was nothing more than his possession to flaunt and tease me with. But she was so much more, and I couldn't resist her.

Having the Snowflake crown here with the promise of bonding our bodies was too much for either of us to handle, and I dropped down before her, ready to do whatever it was she wanted. Even if it meant breaking my vow of celibacy until she possessed the Snowflake crown.

My body, my spirit, was meant only for her, that was my sworn duty. Even if I'd once wanted to share myself with another.

As he kissed her, she reached for me. The one thing I needed to bond with her was within my grasp and yet I still couldn't have her.

"You see, princess." Konig turned her body toward me once again and moved her so close all I had to do was lean forward and I would be able to kiss her soft cunt, ready and waiting for me. "You're going to give him just a taste of what he wants so that he'll accept me too."

She stiffened in his arms and a fiery glow of her inner magic burst into her eyes, like the lights on a Christmas tree igniting. Konig might think he was in charge, but Clara could make whatever she wanted happen. "No. I won't force him into bonding with you. Let him go."

He stared down at me over her shoulder and his next statement was for me and me alone. "But you see, he knows that only when all six of us are bonded, will you be strong enough to usurp the Mouse Queen. He wants to believe that only five will be enough, but it isn't. He'll bond with me to save you and ultimately himself. I'm just making the whole process more palatable for him."

Clara licked her lips, her own arousal warring with her need to fulfill her destiny. "That's not what I'm here to do. I know you all think it is, but even with the powers of Spirit and Magic flowing through me, I'm not meant to be the Queen of the Winter Realm. The stories all point to the Vivandiere being the one who should rule. She's the one you need to defeat your Queen."

She'd convinced herself she wasn't the one. That was something I could relate to.

She shook her head. "I can help heal our realm. That's my true purpose, I'm sure of it."

Fuck. Was this too a part of Konig's plan? Did his little mouse spies tell him that Clara didn't understand her true inheritance? If she didn't become the new Queen of the Winter Realm, we were all doomed.

Konig stripped off his clothes and pressed his body against hers. He wore nothing but my crown, and fuck if my body didn't respond to it. Seeing the only two people I'd ever lusted after, bodies intertwined, waiting only for me to seal the deal, was stronger than any vow.

I'd told myself long ago that the crush I had on the enigmatic soldier, also born under the Christmas Star but who was nothing more than a courtier's bastard son, was nothing more than a temptation. I could resist his allure because my church, my land, indeed my entire realm expected me to. But the two of them together? One promised to me, the other forbidden, had every cell in my body bursting with desire, magic, and pure need.

"Yes, help her heal our realm, Nutcracker." He caressed her soft, plump curves, cupping her full breasts, and walking her even closer to me.

Clara blinked, her long lashes fanning her face, waiting for me to give in. Konig would never give her the crown. I had no choice but to bond with him and give her my power through him. I simply didn't understand why he wanted Clara to usurp his own mother. He couldn't. So what was he getting out of this?

Would he use our bond to somehow take down the Snowflake court or the Church of the Christmas Star? Probably. And I'd be the one who'd given him that power.

But I would have also given Clara the power to become the

one true Queen of the Winter Realm. Not in the way that I wanted, that I'd fantasized about, that I'd been raised to believe was my duty and privilege alone. I would never have her luscious body to myself, never feel the magic of her spirit dancing with my own.

For her, and her alone, I would give up the promise of being her fated mate and give into the temptation of him. "Konig and I will take you, together, so that you can have the power of all six princes born under the Christmas Star. That is what is right for the realm."

The words burned, both searing and cleansing my spirit.

Clara's eyes lit up with the magic inside of her. "Can't you release him now? We're all doing as you want. Let's consummate this bond as equals."

I stilled, every cell on edge waiting for him to prove he'd had a change of heart.

Konig's jaw worked and ran a hand along her throat where he'd kissed her. "He's doing what you want, but if given the chance, he'll take you away from me, sweet Queen of mine. Won't you, Nutcracker?"

In a heartbeat. I could not lie to her, so I said nothing. We'd found our way to Clara without him, and I simply could not trust that he was doing this for the right reasons. If he wanted to help the rebellion against the Mouse Queen, why now?

"You see, he wants you. He knows this is the best way, but the snowflake savior can't help but be greedy. He wants you all to himself. He was bred to think you belong only to him."

Konig was right, even though all six of us bonded would make Clara an unstoppable force. It was why, during the war with the Magicians, I'd agreed to our pact to find her, and all become her consorts. I still bore the scars for that. Both on my heart and my back. No hate like the love of the Church of the Christmas Star.

Joining the Nutcracker Guard, finding the other princes and

Konig, had changed everything for me. Now Konig and Clara wanted to change everything again.

"Even when the others fucked you and each other in the Gingerbread Kingdom, he wouldn't, would he?"

Clara shook her head and pleaded with me in her eyes. She was too pure, untainted by the wars, to believe anything bad about any of the Nutcrackers. "No. He said only that we had to wait. Until we had the crown."

"And again, when you shared your body with both the Sugar Plum and Dew Drop Fae princes, he kept himself apart, didn't he?"

She said nothing this time. I bowed my head so she couldn't see the truth of Konig's words. Could I have joined in during either of her matings? Yes. But I didn't. I couldn't. Now I never would have her. Not truly.

"When and if you'd found the Snowflake crown, he would have found some way to have you all to himself when you consummated your bond with him."

Sweet Clara fell to her knees, face to face with me, her naked chest mere centimeters from my own, and cupped my cheek. "I don't think it's bad to need someone for your very own and want what's right for the greater good. That sums up most of my life."

The skipped beats of my heart made me dizzy. I did need her for my own and I also wanted to save the Realm.

Konig loomed up behind her and pushed his hand into her hair, turning her head so she was forced to break eye contact with me and look only at him. But his gaze flicked between the two of us. "Then you shall both belong to me. Now."

Konig was demanding love from each of us, and that shouldn't be how it works, but for tonight, it would be.

Clara nodded and got to her feet again. She pressed a soft kiss over Konig's heart and grasped my crown. Magic swirled in the air all around us and I was lost.

Lost to her, the once and future Queen of the Winter Realm. Lost to him, the Mouse King.

Lost to the Church of the Christmas Star, fallen savior of the Land of Snowflakes.

The burden of being the one tasked to save the spirits of everyone in the Winter Realm was too heavy for my shoulders. It always had been, and this was not the first time I'd faltered. I wouldn't wish the weight of this duty on the Princess, so why did I think I had to bear it alone?

Finally, I didn't. By giving myself to Konig, I was free.

I let my arms fall to my sides, as far as the chains would allow and dropped my head back, my face lifted to the two of them. "Come, princess. Let me show you the pleasure I've denied us both, as we bond with the Mouse Prince."

Konig's smile was meant to show me how pleased he was that I'd given in, that he'd won our battle after all these years. What it really did was break my heart and begin to rebuild it at the same time.

BROKEN BY LOVE

KONIG

I thought I could control my emotions, take what I needed from them both and use them to solve the real evils of our realm. The only reason I didn't have both Nuss and Clara on their hands and knees fucking each of them was because of the Queen's spell on my heart. My spirit wasn't mine to give away.

I had to be very careful how much of myself I allowed them access too. It would be hard enough to conceal my bond with them when I took the princess back to the Land of Animals, much less the Mouse Queen's court. I was dead if she even suspected my plans to destroy her rule. We all were.

So no, I couldn't fuck either of them the way I wanted to. But Nuss would be mine, after all these years and broken promises, he was finally mine as he always should have been. Just as Clara belonged to me too.

I wanted nothing more than to keep the two of them here, chained to the wall and tied to my bed so I could enjoy them when and how I liked. Maybe in another time and place I would have. But Nuss had more of an influence on me than even I realized until too late.

He was the messiah of the Land of Snowflakes, always ready to fucking sacrifice himself to save his people. Look at what the fuck I'd become.

For tonight I would lose myself in their bodies, pretend for just a few hours that they were both here with me because they wanted to be, and forget that in the morning I'd have to hurt them both. Just for tonight, they were mine and I was theirs.

"Yes, princess. It's time I got to see you come in person, rather than stroking my cock from a far." I pressed my hard length against the soft pillows of her ass and ran my hands down her throat, across her taut little nipples, and over the swell of her belly. I loved her plush curves but would never deign to think her stomach could be even more rounded with a child of mine.

No, she deserved a bright ginger terror of a boy, or a sweet little fae girl, even a golden-haired snowflake would be better in her life than a bastard of mine.

Maybe, just maybe, if my plans for her and our realm went even a little according to my plans, she could have all of those babies and more. And for once, the children of the Land of Animals could be their contemporaries and not the dirt under their feet.

She responded to my touch with a small sigh. "I knew you were with us when I bonded with Leb, and then with Zucker and Tau. I could feel your spirit, and your love."

Lust. What she'd felt was nothing even close to love, but that wasn't what she wanted to hear from me right now. My maudlin thoughts needed to wait for another time. Because none of that would happen if I didn't take care of bonding the three of us together.

Clara was already molding her body to mine. Her magic

drew me to her like a starving animal to a ready and waiting meal. If her spirit was the bait of a trap, I'd fallen prey to her.

Nuss's eyes were fixed on us both, tracking each move I made. It was killing him not to be able to touch her, but I understood better than most how the forbidden both turned him on and made him feel ashamed. He needed me to force this mating on him so his conscience could tell him that it wasn't his fault for breaking his oath to be with only her.

But oh, how playing this game turned us both the fuck on. "Look, my sweet, how hard our Nutcracker is for you. His cock is throbbing, and we haven't even begun to tease him with your body."

Nuss let out a frustrated breath and said nothing, but he couldn't hide his body's reactions. His suffering made this all the more fun... for me. "Let's show him what he's been missing when he made you both wait."

Clara grabbed one of my hands from her waist and guided it between her legs. "Yes, let's. I've been hiding that I'm a little bit hurt and mad that you wouldn't touch me."

Mmm. There's my girl. I saw how the human realm had beaten her down and quashed her worth. It was about time the feisty Queen of Spirit and Magic showed up. I had a deep need to dominate them both, but it wasn't even a tenth as delicious if I didn't have to fight for it.

After only a few days in the Winter Realm, she was more than a worthy opponent.

Nuss always had been. Which made having him here at my mercy all the more satisfying.

I trapped Clara's hand between her legs and used her own fingers to slide between her pussy lips. It took only a few strokes for her to relax into our foreplay and both our hands were slick with her arousal in moments. With each brush across her soft little clit, her breath hitched and so did Nuss's.

He licked his lips, and I mirrored the motion. He strained

against the chains holding his arms, and I don't even think he realized he was doing it. "Is this what you want, Nutcracker?"

I pulled our hands from Clara's wet cunt and drew her juices out along her thighs. But this taste wasn't for him. "Have you tasted her yet? Or have you denied yourself that pleasure too?"

I knew the answer to my own question. I'd been there for each of her bondings with the others and felt the connections as if I was the one fucking her. Her magic had connected us all, but Nuss kept himself apart, even as he stroked his cock, and we both came when she did.

"You know I haven't," he groaned out. What he left unasked was to allow him to do so now.

Not yet.

Instead, I brought her hand and mine up to her mouth and pushed our intertwined fingers into her mouth. Her legs faltered and she whimpered. I pumped my fingers in and out of her lips, watching Nuss's chest rise and fall and his cock bob as he flexed the muscles in his legs.

"Ask me if you can have the next taste of her, Nutcracker."

Red wisps of Clara's magic sparkled in the air around us, and Nuss responded like a raging bull. He thrashed against the chains. "Give her to me. Stop teasing us all and let me give her what she needs from me."

Yes, there was the fight in him I was after.

While I wanted to push my own cock deep into her, and make him watch me take her, I wanted even more to break him. I pinned her arm across her chest, grabbed the other to join it and whispered in her ear. "Don't move an inch or I won't give him what you both want."

Her throat bobbed and she tugged at my grip, testing me. Fuck, I loved this. "I do want it. Don't make us both wait anymore."

I squeezed her wrists tighter, put my feet on the outsides of hers so she couldn't spread her legs, and put my hand on her mound. She had to hold still as I slid my cock between her ample thighs. I wouldn't fuck her cunt, but her rich, plump legs, pressed together as they were, would be almost as tight. "Don't worry, he'll get his taste of us both. When he does as he's been told and asks for it."

Clara squirmed, clutching my cock tighter between her thighs. "I don't think he will."

I thrust my hips against hers until my crown slid through her wet folds and poked out right in front of Nuss's face. I hadn't thought I'd need to call on my own restraint, but fuck, just one thrust against her body and I was ready for so much more.

Another slow slide back and forth, and now my seed dripped from my tip. "Ask for it."

Nuss scowled, but his own cock had a bead of come pearling, ready to dribble down his hard length. Fine, I could do this all night. I'd happily make our sweet princess beg him to ask so that she could get off. Because none of us would until he asked for his turn with her.

I tsked and shook my head at him. "Your stubbornness will only torture her."

For the first time since I'd chained him to the wall, he finally fought back. "You think you can hold out against her pleas? You don't have the power to deny her. You'll give in before me."

Ah. There was the challenge I craved. I slid my cock forward and into my waiting hand. Clara arched her back, trying to position herself for my touch. She was going to get more than she bargained for. I bit her earlobe and then growled my words, meant for them both. "You don't get to fucking come until he asks for his taste. You understand me?"

Her whimper was answer enough. I thrust through her folds, cupping my cock so the head scraped across her clit over and over. She moaned, and Nuss groaned at the sound of her pleasure. I knew better than to think he'd ever ask for his own gratification. He wasn't wrong, even I wouldn't be able to withstand his willpower to deny himself.

He'd crumble under her need.

Unlike the other times when she'd bonded, her magic wasn't connecting us all. I couldn't feel her arousal or Nuss's like it was my own. Even as the sparkles of her power snapped around us, this wasn't consummating her bond with either of us. Yet.

If it took taking her to the edge and back a hundred times, I would. Just to hear him beg.

I thrust faster and faster, not allowing myself to pay any attention to the building need in my own system. I could get entirely wrapped up in watching Nuss getting harder, his breathing come in harsh drags, the very beat of his heart pounding in the muscles of his finely sculpted abs. But if I wasn't careful, Clara would come, and our fun would be over.

"Don't come, Clara. Don't you want his mouth on you?" Her body trembled and I slowed just enough to keep her right on the brink of orgasm. "Don't you want to see what it's like to have him worship your body as it should be?"

"I don't know…I—"

A little more and I would have her, which meant I would have him too. I released my grip on her wrists and slid my hand up to her throat. She leaned her head back against me and Nuss jerked on his chains, wanting to reach for Clara. So close to giving in, I could smell it.

I closed my fingers, not to crush her airway but to press against the pulse in her throat, beating staccato. "Tell him you want him to fuck you with his tongue. Tell him you need to come in his mouth. Tell him to ask me, princess. Now."

She shuddered and gulped, losing herself in the high of being told what to do. I'd remember every single reaction, everything her body responded to, all the things she liked for the day I could reward her for her submission.

"Say it, Clara." I closed my hand tighter and rocked my hips so my cock head stabbed against her clit. "Now."

"Please, Nuss. I need you. I've always needed you more than you do me. But please."

That wasn't what either of us expected her to say. Nuss's eyes went wide, and he blinked as if she'd slapped him across the face. His own magic, that he shouldn't have, shattered, his pupils went black, and that's when he broke.

Finally, deliciously, he broke. "No, my Queen, I'm nothing without you. Please, Konig, let me taste her, taste you both."

I thought I would feel joy when he finally gave in. But since there was only a black hole and spell where my heart should be, it shouldn't surprise me that even this was an empty victory.

With two easy steps, Clara's cunt and my cock were poised at the tip of Nuss's lips. I released her throat and grabbed the broken piece of the Snowflake crown I wore around my neck. Then I thrust forward once again, and into Nuss's mouth.

Our bodies finally finding each other, and the magic of consummating the bond, shot a spike of pure adrenaline-fueled arousal through us both and all my careful control went to hell. I came in the heat of his throat, well before I wanted to.

A visceral growl rumbled out of me, and I pulled out, not willing to give him more than that small part of myself. I pushed my cock back into the folds of Clara's wet cunt, blocking Nuss from touching me again. The rest of my seed spurted into my hand and the soft nest of her pussy.

It took me two deep breaths to get myself back under control. Clara was still lost in the haze of her denied orgasm, but Nuss stared up at me, my seed on his lips. For just one moment I wanted to take them both into my arms, hold them tight to me and share all that I was with them.

I could not. I grabbed Nuss by the hair and bent his head back. "I possess the snowflake crown. You willingly took my seed and so consummated our bond. You belong to me now."

"When didn't I?"

Fuck.

If I had a heart, it would have skipped several beats. "You were never mine, always hers. Give her what she needs so the bond between we three can be sealed."

I shoved his face into her pussy, needing to feel the magic of her orgasm again. Needing it to fill in the new fucking hole in my chest that wasn't supposed to be there. "Lick her clean and make her come, Nutcracker. That's your duty, isn't it?"

I didn't give him a chance to reply, but ground my hips against Clara's ass, getting myself hard again in the process. This time, her pleasure had to be my priority. Even if she didn't feel neglected, I had focused on Nuss first. I had to. I hoped someday they would both forgive me.

"Are you ready to come too, my delicious Queen?" I held Nuss fast to her cunt and she rocked her hips, writhing against his face. "You've been a very good girl and I think it's time we all felt the magic of your orgasm."

She grabbed my arms, sinking her nails into them hard enough to draw my blood. "I can't feel you like I did before. Please, I need you both. Please, love me, love me, love me, like I love you."

I had broken Nuss with my torture and games.

ClaraMarie Stahlbaum, Queen of Spirit and Magic, broke me with her love.

ALWAYS

CLARA

As soon as I climaxed, Konig stepped away, shoved my shoulders, and pushed me down to my knees. Nuss's legs and cock were covered in his own release and his cock was still hard. Without even a touch, he'd come simply from brining me to orgasm. How I wished that was part of our own bond.

It took our Mouse King only a moment to unlatch the arm restraints holding Nuss tight. But instead of releasing him all together, he turned and walked away. A chilly blast whirled into the room, and he was gone, into the freezing barren night.

Nuss wrapped his unbroken arm around me, and I curled into him.

I could sense the new bond between Konig and Nuss, but it wasn't the same as the one I'd forged with Leb, Zucker, and Tau. But exactly as they'd said, I also had a new and different connection with both of them. We were a circle of six, each enmeshed with each other. And yet, we were still incomplete.

Dammit. I know Konig said there was no way to get the

Animal's broken piece of the crown, but that's exactly what I was going to do.

I understood Konig had done this to give me more power and that he still believed I'd use that to overcome the Mouse Queen in her own land. But now that we'd fulfilled our roles to make that happen, everything was all wrong.

It wasn't that I regretted what happened. Although, it certainly wasn't the girlish fantasy I'd dreamed of when I thought about bonding with him. But even with the escalating amount of sexy times I'd experienced, this was the most erotic moment of my life.

It wasn't enough. I wanted love too.

That's what was missing.

Nuss had love in his heart for me, even though he was still keeping part of that shielded, which I understood. It was Konig's heart I was worried about.

There was no doubt that he belonged to me and I to him. I'd felt the draw between us, the connection we had was there even before I'd felt it with the others. He wasn't even guarding his emotions. There was something else terribly wrong.

"Shh, princess. It's okay, everything is okay." As his arm held me even tighter against his chest and it was then I realized that I was trembling.

"No, it isn't. We aren't connected like he thought we would be." Not only did I need to find that Animal crown, I needed to get Konig to give me the Snowflake crown too. This was all wrong and it was breaking my heart.

"No, but we are linked, even if it's not how you or I thought we would be. This will still work. You can become the Queen of the Winter Realm, my Clara."

I opened my mouth to protest that foolishness once again, but Nuss shook his head and shushed me. "I know what it's like to have the weight of grand expectations on your shoulders, and not believe you can fulfill the destiny thrust upon you.

Someday I'll take you to the Snowflake Court and you can see exactly what I mean. But believe me, Clara, when I say you will be Queen."

"But the Vivandiere..."

"Isn't here. You are, and wouldn't it be better to have a ruler who wants to heal the world with love, rather than a warrior always fighting for and defending her throne, anyway?"

I wasn't sure if the shivers running up and down my spine were from Nuss's words or the makeshift door into our ruined room opening with Konig's return.

"If wishes were sugar plums, we'd all be as sweet as the Princess. But they're more like snowflakes, aren't they? Come now, Clara. We have to leave before the rebels show up." Konig reached a hand down and I reluctantly let myself be pulled from Nuss's lap. "Put this on, we have a cold journey ahead."

He threw a bundle to me and walked back out the door. Okay then. I unwrapped the clothes and found a new dress, black as a starless night. But at least it would cover me, and it was better than the tattered blanket.

I slipped it over my head and wriggled my way into the bodice. It hadn't seemed form fitting when I'd examined it, but as I straightened it and got everything into its proper place, the material molded to my arms, chest, and waist. Not too tight, but more like protection of some kind.

"That's a magician's armor. Where in the world did he find that?" Nuss stared up at me and raised an eyebrow. "I haven't even seen any on the black market since the Queen destroyed the last of your people."

"A dress doesn't seem like a very practical outfit for battle." The skirts billowed around me, but I was already instantly warmer and surprisingly comfortable.

"It will respond to your magic and be what you need, when you need it. A uniform, a ballgown, protective armor, even a place to sleep, or to store your weapons."

I didn't really understand how to use my magic. But Nuss did. "Do your people have similar umm, magical armor?"

His eyes flicked back and forth while he processed my question. He didn't want to give me the straight answer. Even after all of this, he still guarded his secrets so close. "The people of the Land of Snowflakes do not have magic."

Good try, buddy. "But you do."

"Yes. Kind of. I have access to some magic."

Whoa. He actually admitted it? "Then why didn't you use it to get out of the chains? To stop Konig from taking us both? Why do you even need me?"

I was fired up and I didn't mean to say that last bit.

"Sweet princess, how could you still think I don't need you?"

"Pretend I didn't say that. I want to know about your magic, and mine." Konig was giving us this minute together before we left the Land of Spirit and Magic, but our time was running short. "We'll sort through our feelings later. But if you two, or rather all five of you, think I'm about to walk into a fight with the Mouse Queen, I need something to fight with. Teach me what you know."

That was a ridiculous request, and I knew it the second it popped out of my mouth. He couldn't teach me in minutes the power of a people who'd been gone for years and years. The magic flowed through my very cells, I could feel the tingles of it wanting to get out, to be used, but I was scared.

I had absolute power at my very fingertips, and what if it made me into the very thing the rest of the Winter realm had fought against? Maybe the Mouse Queen had been right to destroy my land and the magicians who would subjugate and use her people.

"You don't need me to do that. Besides, my magic doesn't work as yours does. I'm... it's not my magic."

Holy hot cocoa. It was mine. Nuss had access to my magic.

Mine. When he bit my lip and drew out my blood. When he pierced Fritz's skin. He was accessing Stahlbaum magic.

Duh.

I could either feel betrayed right now and worried that he'd been manipulating me, or I could put all my love and trust into him and believe with my heart that he was the good man I believed from the beginning.

But life wasn't black and white like that. I'd believed in Konig, and he'd done some pretty morally gray stuff. At his core, he was following his own code of justice and trying to do right by his people. Was Nuss?

The world around me went deathly silent. Nuss didn't move, Konig stayed away, and all that made way for the whoosh-whoosh of my blood and magic rushing through my ears. Who did I trust? With my heart, my body, my spirit, and so much more.

Nuss or Konig?

Could I trust either of them?

Yes. Absolutely. I couldn't even believe I was questioning that. Nuss was all that was good, but he wasn't fallible, and neither was I. Konig was fighting to right the wrongs in our realm, and I needed them both. The sooner I could get all six of us together, the better. Which meant I had some work to do uniting the broken pieces of the crown of the seven lands.

I would find the Animal Crown, I would claim the Snowflake Crown and I would...

A lump of fear mixed up in a lifetime of others telling me I wasn't even good enough to be a dancer, a sister, a daughter, or a woman at all, rose up in my throat. All I'd been told my whole life was that I shouldn't take up space, I should do as I was told and what society expected of me.

I'd rebelled in small ways, like not quitting dance lessons when the mean girls told me to. But even I believed I wasn't enough for that world.

It was only because I wasn't meant for the human life. I was born into the right life, but it had been stolen from me and I was going to damn well take it back.

"Clara, look." Nuss's skin sparkled with magic, or, no, wait. That was a reflection. Either way, it had him smiling for the first time in days. He gave a jerk of his chin indicating that I should look down at my dress.

The slick black material had gone red and satiny, just like my Christmas dress. Except instead of just making me feel pretty, this gown had me feeling badass. The warrior, the carer, the sensual charmer, the protector, and the commander, all rose up in me and I almost felt whole and prepared for anything.

Almost.

There was still a missing piece of my heart and walls to break down around another. But I knew what I had to do to make things right.

Konig opened the door again but didn't come inside. "Red. Why do you torture me so? Come on now. I have a lot to show you."

Hmm. He had a thing for red dresses, huh? I'd remember that. "Don't you mean to show us?"

"No." Konig sliced the air with his hand. "Our Nutcracker Captain will not be welcomed into the Land of Animals. Leb, Tau, and Zucker are not far and will rescue him soon. You and I are leaving now."

I had another protest on the tip of my tongue, but I shut my mouth. There were a lot of old wounds between Konig and the rest of my mates, and I thought that, more than his agenda, was sending him to rush us away. I wouldn't find the remaining crowns by standing here arguing with them.

Quickly, I bent and cupped Nuss's face in both of my hands. I kissed him just as I'd wanted to do all along. This wasn't chaste or innocent. I wanted him to know that even though we weren't bonded yet, he was still mine. His body, his spirit, and his love, they all belonged to me. When I finally pulled away, we were both breathing hard, and I wanted very little more than to strip my dress back off and show him just how much he meant to me. Instead, I looked deep into his eyes and pushed the magic I had access to into him. "Come for me, my love. I'll be waiting for you and the others."

"I will always come for you, princess. Always."

Konig pulled me away and out the door, but I heard the rattling of the chains as Nuss tried to break free. I also didn't miss how Konig's fists clenched and released over and over as we walked away from the castle ruins. He put on this dark warrior facade, but it bothered him to leave Nuss behind like that.

I took one of his hands and held it tight as he led me back to where we'd broken into the Land of Spirit and Magic. Neither of us was used to having anyone to lean on, and I would show him he could rely on me. He could have dropped my hand or refused it in the first place, but he didn't. He gripped it tight and didn't let go, even when we got to the red wound of the protective barrier meant to keep us out, or whatever was left in my land, in.

"Princess, we can push through here and come back out at the edge of the Christmas Tree Forest just as before. The journey to the Land of Animals will be long and the Queen's loyal soldiers will be on the lookout for us. If they find you, I'll have no choice but to bring you to her."

No choice. The way he said it hurt my heart. It wasn't with resignation or regret, but disdain. What power did this Queen have over him to make him do what she wanted even though he clearly hated everything she stood for. It was more than family obligation.

"I guess I'll have to face her eventually." I'd rather have the final crowns in my possession first. I wanted to be as ready as I could for this showdown.

"Yes. But I want to show you what we're fighting for first. You have the power to make a portal and take us wherever you want to go. I want you to try."

Oh. Is that how Nuss and Konig got to my home in the human world, and how I ended up in the forest? "Okay. Can you tell me what to do?"

"No."

Just no. No other explanation. Weird. "Okay. Let's see what I can pull out of my butt."

I thought hard about the night I'd come to the Winter Realm and realized Nuss had been trying to help me set an intention then. I hoped this was right.

I squeezed Konig's hand tighter and thought about going to where Konig lived. Wait, it needed to be more than that. We could end up in the Mouse Queen's castle. How about where he felt safest? No, no. He implied that the Land of Animals was a hard place to live. Maybe none of it was safe.

I took a deep breath and tried to search for the magic inside of me, the memories of the land where I once lived, and the love in my heart that was only growing day by day for the Winter Realm and everyone in it. But especially my mates.

A flash of red crackled in front of my eyes and in the next instant we were standing in some kind of barracks filled with soldiers.

The Mouse Army.

Before I could even blink or magic us out of there, the ones closest to us drew their swords and someone nearby said, "The prince has captured the last magician. We are saved."

Aw, rats.

FOR CLARA AND COOKIES

LEB

*I*f Clara was hurt, Konig was dead. Nuss probably already was. The rage of a thousand Gingerbread Vikings flowed through me, and I was prepared to go full on berserker on anyone in my path.

We were just at the border of the Sweet Fae lands and the Christmas Tree Forest and it had taken about a thousand years to get just this far. I was embarrassed by how long it took each of us to escape the mouse army's traps. Who knew those little shits could tie such tight knots?

Konig was long gone by the time any of us made it out of the cave, and all we caught was a glimpse of the sleigh flying off into the distant clouds.

Fucking flying reindeer? How the hell had Konig gotten his animal pals to take flight? When I found them, I was making every single one into a steak dinner, with a side of reindeer stew, and some tough, chewy jerky strips to fuel my war cries.

Unless of course they'd fly for me and then I was keeping

them as my new best friends. Not like the traitor horses who fled anytime we got near to them. Another of Konig's spells, I was sure.

Tau put a hand on my arm and drained away a tenth of my anger. We'd only gotten this far by guidance of the Dew Drop Fae assassins who'd tracked the escape of the mouse and his prey up to the borderlands. "I promise I'll help you kill every mouse, but first we have to find them. Keep your axe under control until we do. I don't want my own head chopped off in your berserker rage, my friend."

Anyone else and I would have already split them open and laid their ribs blood-eagle style on the field of battle. "I need to kill someone or something."

How could we have let Konig take her? I couldn't even imagine the horrors he must be inflicting upon her now. That was if he hadn't already turned her over to the Mouse Queen.

Zucker had gone completely silent, seething in his own guilt and anger. That was fine by me as long as he was ready to do his worst with those daggers of his when we found Konig. There was no pouting in love or war.

Now that we'd made it to the forest, we had to decide which way to go. We could go in the direction of the flying sleigh, but if it was me, I would have gone in several fake directions before going toward a real destination. Besides, they'd headed in the direction of the Land of Spirit and Magic, and we all knew there was nothing where the powerful court of the Stahlbaum's used to be.

"Lads, I say we heel it back to Mother Gingerbread and raise the Gingerbread Kingdom's army to march on Christmas Castle."

Tau shook his head. "The Dew Drop assassins are just over that ridge. We can signal them and make our way to the Land of Animals sooner if we use my people."

Zucker dropped to one knee and touched his hand to his

heart. "Don't you two feel it? Something has changed in our bond. He's cast a spell on both Clara and Nuss."

He took Tau's hand and brought it to his chest, Tau closed his eyes and bowed his head. It took only another moment before I felt the pain in my heart as well. What the fuck was going on?

Tau shook his head. "Konig doesn't have this kind of magic. Unless..."

Zucker rose and clasped a hand on each of our arms. "We don't know what he's capable of. Not anymore. His mother took down the entire Magician court. You don't do that without some magic on your side."

Not just anyone was born with affinity for magic, and the use of it was long outlawed in the realm. The fact that both Nuss and Konig might have magic at their disposal wasn't something I wanted to even consider. "Don't you think Nuss would have said something if he thought Konig had access to that kind of power?"

"Would he?" Anger like burned cookies passed through Zucker's eyes. "We know their history, and we only just saw our stalwart captain reveal his own affinity for magic a day ago. We three, that have consummated our bonds with her, are all we have now. We can't trust anyone else."

My axe felt heavier in my hands than ever before. "I will not lose my faith in Nuss. He's risked everything for her, practically died twice in the past three days to protect her. He wouldn't give in so easy."

"I wish I had your faith." There was enough pain in Zucker's words, eyes, and heart that the rage inside of me either had to explode or relent.

I relented, took the two steps over to my two favorite fae, and picked them both up into one big bear hug. "I trust no one more than you. Now, come, today is a good day to die."

"Mrph nrrght," Zucker said.

"Prfnr squrk," Tau added.

Luckily, I was fluent in bear huggenese since it was the love language of my mother and fathers. "I don't know and that sounds like a good plan."

I dropped them on their feet and gave each a moment to catch their breaths. "Now, ready to burn down the world? Oh, except the Christmas Tree Forest. I like the lights, and we'll need a new base camp."

Zucker wheezed a few more times. "Perhaps we save the razing for Christmas Castle, you giant ass Viking."

Hmm. Perhaps, but I was ready to destroy the whole damn realm if I had to. Unless we rescued Clara and Nuss, there was nothing for any of us to have faith and hope in. Once it was all gone, we could rebuild.

The pixies of Comfort and Joy didn't much like my plan either. A whole host of them flitted from tree to tree and then surrounded the lot of us, swirling around in a pixie tornado until we were pushed deeper into their land. "Settle down, you little bugs. I can't understand you with everyone flying around like angels with your heads cut off."

Three of them landed on my head and one sunk right into my beard. They yanked until I was forced to turn my head in the direction they wanted me to see. "What? Ouch. We don't have time for your—"

Well, shit. There was a scuffle going on maybe a hundred strides farther into the trees. Pixies swarming and tossing snowballs at our dear old son of a witch, Fritz. Looked like he was losing the battle, but pixies were going flying as he fought back and if that wouldn't piss off my luscious mate, nothing would.

I jerked my chin in Fritz's direction, quietly drew my axe up over my head, and went charging full speed ahead, my new war cry on my lips. "For Clara and cookies!"

The pixies split their ranks like the parting of the trees for an avalanche and guided me straight toward Fritz. Too late, he spotted me coming for him. He threw the cage he had in his hand at me, but he missed by a long shot. It did give him a one second head start, but the rat bastard's legs were a hell of a lot shorter than mine.

I tackled him to the ground, straddled him so he couldn't move and raised my axe over my head. It would be my pleasure to destroy the one person who could have made Clara's life in the human realm better and didn't.

He threw his hands over his face. "Wait, no. Stop, don't kill me. I know where ClaraMarie is."

Zucker and Tau ran up on either side of me, daggers and arrow at the ready, pointed at Fritz's heart. Tau poked the little shit in the middle of his forehead and scowled. "Talk or die, Prince Friedrich."

His throat bobbed as he swallowed down the terror. "I... I don't know exactly where she is, but I can tell you which way I saw that mouse warrior take her and your Nutcracker friend."

Zucker growled and I found I liked this darker side of the Sweet Fae prince. "We fucking know that much, you licorice eating motherfucker. If you've got nothing else for us, the pixies here are feeling a little blood thirsty."

A pink and a blue pixie floated up and over my shoulders and did quite the little fuck-you dance, buzzing and squealing in Fritz's face. I'd never seen an angry pixie before. They were the spirits of Comfort and Joy, so it wasn't exactly in their make-up to even be sad.

But being put into a cage and poked and prodded would make anyone spitting mad. "I can't understand a thing they're saying. I'm going to just assume it's their plan to gut you from cock to eyes and back."

"It's not, but let's go with that plan anyway," Tau said.

"Wait, no." Fritz squealed again. "You won't find her without me. I promise. The Mouse Queen told me, and I have the magic to take you there. I'm a magician you know."

"Ah, but I'm guessing you don't know what we did to all the magicians in the Winter Realm then, do you laddy?" I gave my axe a spin.

Fritz's sweat was turning to ice crystals on his face as fast as they formed on his upper lip and brow. "Fine. Fine. But you won't get into the Land of Spirit and Magic without me."

Spirit and Magic? Doesn't exist. Not anymore. "Once again, you don't know what you're talking about. You might have studied up on your Winter Realm current events and history while you were canoodling with the Mouse Queen."

"It does." Fritz frantically shook his head. "She's used a spell to hide what remains from you. But I can get through."

Tau pushed his arrow harder against Fritz's skull "What makes you think that's where Konig has taken Clara?"

"Because the Queen knows all his plans to try and usurp her and she's pissed. He wouldn't take my sister back to her before she can access her own magic. She can't do that without refilling her powers on our homelands."

Konig has plans to usurp the Queen? No. Now I knew this turd of a weasel was lying out of his asshole.

"Why are you telling us this? It is not just the threat of your life. The Queen will want you dead for spilling her secrets too. What's your angle?"

"I can, uh, see when I'm bested. Besides, she's my little sister." Fritz quit squirming and sighed as if this was all just a big inconvenience.

"I don't believe for even a second that you care about Clara. Try again, you tiny shit not even worth shitting out."

Zucker chuckled and dropped to a knee, pressing one of his daggers under Fritz's chin. That got the truth spewing from his mouth. "Before Clara fucking butted her nose in, the Mouse

Queen controlled the realm. But she's losing power. I'm not going to side with a loser."

Ah, now that was the real deal. "So, what you're saying is you have no loyalties, and you'll ally yourself to whichever side is winning at the moment."

His squirming started back up. I sat down on him a bit harder. His face turned red, and he wheezed out, "No, that's not it."

"I think it is." I gave him a little bounce, smushing him deeper into the snowy ground. "What was that you said about not trusting anyone, Zucker?"

"I'll happily slit his throat for lying, but I'll cut off his balls for being a shitty brother." Zucker pressed his blade into Fritz's skin, drawing blood.

The little shit cried out and somehow got his arm free from underneath me. He swiped at the drop of blood and closed his eyes. I thought at first he fainted, but then the telltale red swirls of a magician's spell rose up around us.

"Ha. I'm not as uneducated in the ways of the Land of Spirit and Magic as you though I was. Let's see how you like a taste of the old ways. Shall we?" Fritz rubbed his hands together and a portal opened up.

I'd only ever seen one other portal and that had led to the human realm, where the Princess had been hidden. This was nothing like the opulent room with its Christmas tree and strange dancing people. What I saw through the streak of red magic was a barren, burned and desolate land, with nothing as far as the eye could see, save some stone ruins.

"Say goodbye, suckers." Fritz rushed toward the portal, but Tau shot him in the leg, felling him like a squealing pig.

"Look, near the ruins." I pointed to a figure moving toward us. "Is that...?"

"It is. That's Nuss. But where are his clothes?"

Not only had he lost his captain of the Nutcracker rebellion's uniform, but there were chains dangling from his arms and legs. "I don't know, lads, but he looks like he could use some help. Let's rescue the captain and the princess and squash a mouse. Grab the shithead so he can portal us back from wherever the hell that is. The opening doesn't exactly look stable."

I turned to pull Fritz along on this little adventure, but he was gone. A few dribbles of red blood in the snow and then poof, nothing. I'd have to remember to kill him by choking him out next time. Magician blood was powerful stuff it seemed.

"Cover me, lads, I'm going in." I didn't know if I could get back, but I couldn't let Nuss be stuck in that barren wasteland alone.

"Cover you how?" One of them shouted back at me, but I couldn't tell which one as the portal magic sucked me in.

It spit me out the other side all disoriented and ready to blow cookies. I landed on my hands and knees in the dirt. Not just any old dirt, but the kind filled with fragments of bones.

In another moment Zucker and Tau landed on the ground next to me, and then two little pixies dropped right down onto my head. Heil, heil, the gangs all here.

Nuss wasn't more than a few strides away now and he stood over us, shaking in the freezing icy wind. "Welcome to the Land of Spirit and Magic."

Either I'd died on the way through the portal and this was the first step on my way to Valhalla, or Nuss had gone insane... or everything we'd been told about the destruction of Spirit and Magic was a lie.

WELCOME TO THE DARK SIDE

CLARA

*K*onig pushed me behind him and started just giving out orders. "You, you, and you. Guard the entrance to the barracks and make sure only those loyal to our cause come anywhere near. The four of you, board up every window and get this place locked down tight. We don't need anyone seeing the princess among us before we're ready. Everyone else, go about your business so we don't draw any added attention."

It took a minute for the ones he hadn't given specific tasks to stop staring at me and go back to whatever it was they'd been doing before we poofed into their lives. I gave them a little wave and that did it. Eyes went wide and looked away, spines stiffened and turned, and voices mumbled and rumbled expelling the brief moment of silence.

I had to assume we were in the Land of Animals, but this certainly didn't look like a castle. We were in a long wooden structure that smelled of bodies that had nowhere else to go. I should be afraid. This was the land of my archenemy, and I was surrounded by soldiers that were probably her army.

Another man in a uniform not unlike the black garb Konig was in stepped up and gave me a nod, but quickly looked away as if I was some kind of forbidden fruit. "Captain. We didn't expect you back so soon. It's only the sixth day of Christmas."

His eyes kept flicking back to me and I couldn't help it on about the fifth time, I winked at him. I'd blame Zucker later for turning me into a flirt. There was no way for me to know that the men in this building didn't want to eat me for dinner, so I shouldn't have done anything but hide behind Konig. The fact that I wasn't and had no intention to, I'd blame on Leb.

These soldiers were definitely Konig's mouse army, but uh, in manly man form. Did they like shapeshift into teeny tiny rodents? Blech. I'd rather think of them all as the strapping young warriors before me now than the mice who'd bitten at my clothes and skin back in the Christmas Tree Forest.

"Is it the sixth day? Damn, I guess it is." Konig rubbed the back of his neck and glanced over at me. "Halfway there. That doesn't give us much time, but more than I thought we'd have. No one has been punished in my absence, have they?"

Punished? What for? Maybe not capturing me.

"No, sir. She's been preoccupied with other matters. The Snowflake Queen is causing trouble and our Queen is on the rampage about some kind of pet being missing."

Pet? Why did I have the sneaking suspicion that meant Fritz? Gross.

Konig raised an eyebrow and frowned. "Interesting. You can fill me in later. Dismissed."

He waited just a few beats before turning to me. "Don't think you can charm the people here, princess. My army has been preparing for your arrival for a long time, but the rest of the inhabitants of the Land of Animals will not trust a magician in our midst. Even one as fabled as you."

Fabled? "There are stories about me?"

"Don't let it go to your head. Your family escaped a long and bloody war, but if it wasn't for the corruption of the magicians and their powers, we wouldn't have fought it in the first place."

I was here to help repair the wounds of that past. I know I was. "What happens now? You said you wanted to show me something here."

If Konig and his warriors were also rebelling against the Mouse Queen, I couldn't understand why they weren't working with Nuss and the Nutcracker rebellion. If their goals were the same, why not? Maybe what Konig wanted me to see would explain better than words.

"Yes. Remember I told you the armor would be whatever you needed? I need you to change into something less conspicuous. Think dingy and drab."

Yeah, my bright red dress did stick out like a sore thumb in the poorly lit, stinky, dirty building we were in. The people all wore black, and when I looked more closely most were a bit tattered too.

I closed my eyes and concentrated on what I needed. The color faded first in my mind and then when I opened my eyes, I saw that it was leeching out of the dress too. The original shiny black leather-like material reformed around me and the few people nearest us gasped.

Konig held out his hands. "It's okay. She's using this magic on herself, it won't harm you or anyone else."

The whites of too many eyes were on us and that made me falter. The dress ended up being something more like a robe or a cape than what I'd intended. But I guess it would work.

"You look ridiculous." Konig shook his head and half laughed. "But I think once you see what passes for clothing for the women of my land, you'll be able to adjust. Come on now."

He took my hand and led me through the building, not toward the front entrance he'd had the others close up, but to the back where a stairwell was hidden behind a rack of bunks. The steps led down into darkness, spiraling away. To where, I couldn't imagine.

"Now it's time you see how my people have been made to live on the scraps of the rest of the Realm." Konig lit a torch he pulled from the wall and as we went down the first few steps, I noticed the symbols for the Land of Animals etched into the stones.

"Are these like the tunnels under the Sweet Fae castle?" I'd have to remember each turn and try to make a map in my mind in case we needed an escape route later.

"Not exactly. We've been mostly living underground for generations, and we use tunnels like these for moving around in our day-to-day survival." He led me through several crossroads and down other tunnels. I could hear people, but didn't see anyone yet.

I didn't want to seem so completely ignorant, but even wracking my brain for some kind of memories, there was nothing about the lives of the people here. I had nothing I could do but ask. "Why do you live underground? Is it because of the cold?"

"We didn't always. Before the war with the magicians, we lived in the forests and the plains of our Land. Most of us were comfortable with nature and living off what we could forage and hunt, that was our way. The people of Animal didn't take more than we needed and lived simply."

"Until the war?" I didn't like that my ancestors ruined everything. Why were they such assholes, and what did that make me?

"The war came later." He paused for a moment and put his hand on the stones along one wall. "We were forced underground and into squalor when Christmas Castle was built."

I didn't like where this story was going but I was pretty sure, I already knew. "Who built it?"

"My people." We took another turn and were deeper underground than before. The voices I heard earlier were definitely getting louder. "But only because we were forced to."

"By whom?" This time I definitely knew. The story Konig was telling me was far too familiar.

"The courts of the other lands often squabbled and at some point, decided that there should be one Queen to rule overall, to make decisions in the best interest of everyone, not one particularly favored Land. But their lands all had castles and cities and no place to install a new court."

"What about the Christmas Tree Forest?" Ugh. Not like it would have been any better to take away the pixie's home.

"Don't worry, they took advantage of the wealth of resources there." We took one more turn, and I could barely see in the dark. Konig had to slow down while I stumbled along beside him.

There was light up ahead finally, and movement. We must be almost to our destination.

Konig continued his lesson. "Once upon a time, the forest was so thick with trees that you could barely walk through it, and the pixies numbered in the hundreds of thousands."

"Oh." With each turn of the tunnel and twist of Konig's history lesson my skin prickled from the inside out. He'd called me naive, and he'd been right. My life wasn't always easy, but I lived in a big house with servants and never wanted for anything more than respect and the love of those around me.

Konig didn't even have to finish his story. While I didn't know exactly what happened, it was obvious. Those with privilege and power had taken advantage of those without.

This should be called the Realm of Greed.

"Yes, exactly. It would take too much to clear the forest for the grandiose castle the Queens wanted. So they decided to use the wide-open spaces of the Land of Animals, not thinking that we were using it, simply because we hadn't created stinking messes of people forced to live in boxes."

I finished the story for him because it was obvious what had happened. "So, they took your lands and made you build the castle too. I suppose they told you it was for the greater good, didn't they?"

"Something like that."

"But what happened when the Mouse Queen became the ruler over the whole realm?"

"I'll show you."

The tunnel opened up into what I could only call an underground river port. If that river was a dark and stinky sewer. My eyes watered with the stench, and I threw my arm over my nose and mouth. No one else seemed even the slightest bit fazed by the stench. They were all simply going about their business, at market type stalls, moving cargo to and from the underground rafts floating on the river, and hustling about as if this was any other town. Just people, living their lives. In utter filth.

Except they weren't just people. The woman at the stall closest to us, selling wilted root vegetables, had the head of a lizard and scales on her hands. The nearest raft was being pushed along via a pole held by a man with antlers. Three little billy goats gruff circled the skirts of their mother, braying and biting at each other's tails.

"Welcome to the Land of Animals, princess." Konig drew me down the thoroughfare nearest the water and into the crowd. "Drop your arm and breathe through your mouth if you have to. I won't have you offending my people. They already know they stink, and there isn't much they can do about it."

"Sorry." I put my arm down and had to grip the side of my dress to keep it steady. Everywhere I looked, there was death, decay, and despair in the people's eyes. Each and every person, whether they looked human to me or not, seemed as if a huge weight was on their shoulders, as if they couldn't even imagine carrying one more burden or they would collapse under the weight of it.

It was unbearable to see this kind of poverty, and my throat burned, not with the stench, but with pain seeing how unbearable the conditions were for so many. I couldn't get more than a soft, horrified interjection out of my mouth. "Oh, Konig. Oh."

I knew there was poverty in the human world, but I'd been mostly sheltered from the worst of it. Seeing this made me feel bad about every meal I ever had, every stitch of clothing I owned, and made my own troubles seem so inanely trivial.

A small girl, with long, furry, floppy ears where her ringlet curls would be back home, trotted up to us and pressed a brightly colored fruit into Konig's hand. "Mama says this is for you."

She turned quickly and sprinted away to where a thin woman with matching furry ears stood next to a market stall. The woman gave a small wave and Konig held up the fruit and nodded. "Use your cloak and create a satchel, you're about to need it."

I willed the armor to give me a cloth bag over my shoulder, and Konig dropped the fruit into it. Another girl, and then two boys, a middle-aged woman, and an older man with a faded uniform and an eyepatch all approached us. Each had some small bit of food they gave to Konig, who handed it to me for the collection.

"But why are they giving you food? We should be finding something for all of them to eat." Their clothes were in tatters, and everyone was so thin. For the first time since coming to the Winter Realm, I was too aware of my own body.

The other women in the Gingerbread Kingdom and the

Sweet Fae Court were chubby like me. There had been easy food and drink available, and it was clear none had struggled for food. I wouldn't say Mother Gingerbread's life was easy, and a cold war going on between the two groups of Fae had to cause many a sleepless night, but no one's lives were as hard as these.

He accepted bits and bobs from more people and handed it over to me. "Because they're helping everyone in the community. No one has much, but they know the Mouse Army and I will redistribute what they give to make sure everyone has at least a little something to eat."

And here I was thinking I was going to do all the hard work of helping them. They didn't need me to be their savior, any more than I needed Leb, Tau, Zucker, Nuss, and Konig to be mine. We all just needed a little love and support, not rescuing.

We slowly made our way all the way down one end of this underground make-shift port and back again. I got lots of wide-eyed looks, and there were plenty of whispers and mumblings that were definitely people talking about me. I tried to make myself as small as I could, and smiled at everyone, but not too much. It was so hard to see the hardships of this kind of daily life.

"Why has no one from the other lands done anything?" Now more than ever I knew I wasn't here to take down the Mouse Queen. I didn't want some final battle where I ended up ruling over everyone. But I also didn't want the despair and animosity that seemed to have spread like cracking ice across the entire realm. Something big had to change.

"They think they are. No one can see past their own concerns. Nuss and the others believe that if they take down the Mouse Queen and install you as the new Queen of the Winter Realm, everything will be all flowers and candy. I needed you to see this, so you understand that what you're about to fight for isn't just about power."

"I don't want to fight anyone. That's not the solution. I'm sure of it." The people of the Winter Realm had been fighting for what seemed liked generations. First against my people, and then each other. More war wasn't going to fix anything.

"But you will, princess. You will."

SPELLS AND PROMISES

KONIG

*H*ope. That's what Clara was really giving to my people. She just couldn't see it.

Every eye was on her and they were enraptured. Wary, but so completely taken with her beauty, charm, and grace in the face of our shame. I hate that she had to see us this way, barely surviving as the dregs of society. The Animal people were once so proud and powerful, and now we are little more than chattel.

She may not think we need to fight to get our livelihood back, that she can fix everything with her spirit and magic, but I know different. She hasn't yet met either the Snowflake or the Mouse Queen. She doesn't have any idea how powerful and corrupt they both are. If given the chance, Nuss's mother would seize control of Christmas Castle and install the Church of the Christmas Star as the moral law of the land.

I grasp his piece of the crown through the fabric of my shirt. How the fuck Nuss didn't turn into some kind of egomaniacal despot is beyond me. Must come from the genes of his long-lost father.

Clara bent at the knee to interact with a small child fumbling with a dried bit of chicory root. The wee thing hadn't yet mastered her shift and in her nervousness, her little claws kept popping out. In her cute clumsiness, she accidentally cut both herself and Clara.

The crowd went completely silent around us.

Fuck.

Being in the Land of Spirit and Magic had recharged her, but Clara had no idea how powerful she or her blood could be. The world slowed, and I couldn't move fast enough to get to her side no matter how hard I tried. I pushed my body to get to her but watched the next sequence of events like a prophecy playing out before my eyes.

Our fast-healing ability meant the girl's scratch didn't hurt and would be gone in just a few minutes, but Clara couldn't know that. She carefully brought the child's hand up and gave it a soft, gentle kiss. Sparkles of her red magic crackled in the air around us all.

The cuts on the girl disappeared as if they'd never been there, and at the same time, the hollowness in her eyes filled in. Her skin cleared of the grime and sores from not having a proper place to wash, and her little fox ears and tail popped out, bushy and alert.

Clara didn't even seem to notice the cut on her own hand, The small bead pooled and began its dribbling path down the fine lines of her skin. Tears bubbled up in the child's eyes, and Clara reached up to wipe them away. The tiny tear ran down her hand and mixed with the blood.

I should have kept a closer watch, shouldn't have let anyone even get near to her. I forced the command out of my throat, but even my mouth wouldn't work fast enough. "Clara, no."

She turned her face to me, happy but surprised and

confused. She didn't understand. With her soft act of kindness, she'd ruined us all.

The Mouse Queen's connection to us would feel the shockwave of magic being used on one of her people. She would know Clara was here and I would be forced to bring her in.

I reached her too late, and yet still dragged her injured hand away. A mistake if ever I made one. The droplet of blood and tears splashed off her hand and into the river of sewage from the castle and keep above. Before all of our eyes, the water went from black and murky to red to crystal clear. The ever-present stench in the air that permeated our skin, hair, clothing, and food, lifted, leaving only the scent of fresh winter air.

The crowd around us gasped and it would take all of maybe ten minutes for the news of this to leak out of the tunnels and up to those fortunate enough to live in the keep around the castle. I grabbed Clara by the elbow and wrenched her up. "We have to go, now."

She didn't say a thing. I think she was as shocked as the rest of us that her magic had the power to create such an auspicious change. No one understood the catastrophic consequences.

Clara wasn't ready to face the Mouse Queen. I wasn't ready for her to. I didn't have enough time with her.

"Move, move." Few of the people who'd just witnessed this little miracle had ever seen the good that magicians could do. Most had only experienced the terrorism. I tried to drag Clara away, back into the dark passageways under the castle, but we were being slowly surrounded.

"Please, let us touch the princess. She can help my baby. Princess, look over here. Please, please, please." The cries were coming from every direction, and this was exactly what I didn't want to happen. How the hell they'd all figured out in that one instant that Clara was the lost princess of Spirit and Magic was incredible.

I hadn't lied to her. The story of how the lost princess would bring the best of us all back to the Winter Realm was legendary. If I didn't act fast, this was going to be the end of that tale, and any hope I had to pull my people back into the light and our freedom would be gone.

"Get out of the way. Go. Move." There were simply too many gathering around us, and someone was going to get hurt.

I pulled my sword from the scabbard at my waist and swung it over my head. But more importantly, I pulled upon the compulsion spell in my heart to command the people to my will. The Queen's fucking curse burned in my chest and changed my voice to almost a growl rather than words. "Get down or get out of the way."

The blizzard of people around us finally made way for us, but it was too late. Screams rang out from one end of the dock. The sounds of boots marching on the dirt and stone, all in unison, blotted out the individual cries of fear. The queen's guards were here, and they were headed straight for me and Clara.

"Get that armor up and protecting your body, princess. Here's comes that fight I warned you about." I shoved her behind me and faced the oncoming guardsmen. If I could deflect them, I would. It wasn't their fault they had to fight for my mother. I knew that better than anyone else.

Too many people were still about, and they were going to get hurt. A few men who had served in my army at one time or another stood in the path of the guards marching toward us. They knew better than to outright attack, but they were doing what they could to slow the attackers down. I pulled on the spell once again, because as much as I appreciated even the few seconds they could buy us, I would not have anyone else sacrificing for me. "Everyone go, hide, don't get in their way. Take care of yourselves."

Clara moved back to my side and flung the edge of her cape in front of us both. My compulsion should have worked on her too. Her own magic must have protected her. She was much more powerful than the bit of magic the Mouse Queen used.

Her magic shimmered red and then faded into an indistinct sort of brownish gray color that matched the ground and huts around us. Camouflage, perfect. "How did they know I was here?"

"You worked magic on an Animal." I dragged Clara over to hide beside a now empty food stall. We had moments before everyone cleared out and I needed a fucking plan. "The Queen can tell if any of her subjects are bespelled."

"I don't buy that. Wouldn't she have known when we bonded with Nuss? You and I are connected now."

Shit. "Not enough that she can tell."

At least, I hoped. She already knew about my feelings for Nuss. She'd used him against me more than once. If she sensed any kind of bonding, his spirit should block any presence of Clara.

She crouched beside me but kept peeking over the edge of the counter. "But I only did that magic on the girl like a minute and a half ago. They couldn't have gotten here that fast."

Logically, I knew she was right. The years of manipulation, trickery, and subterfuge from the queen kept me second guessing myself. "Then her spy network reaches farther than I thought and we're in deeper shit than I know how to get us out of."

"Can't we just run? Or can I use some of my magic?" She flicked her wrist as if trying to work a spell, but all it did was turn her armor from dirty gray to dirty brown.

"I won't have you hurting them. You don't know your own power." Damn it. This was not how I wanted any of this to go. I needed more time with Clara. She didn't have a clue what to do to destroy the oligarchy punishing my people. I wanted so much to believe that she could usurp my mother and change our realm for the better.

Deeper in my spirit, I hoped that just possibly she could destroy the spell on my heart. I wanted her to be mine, and I wanted to be free.

"I don't want to hurt anyone anyway, but I also don't want to die. Tell me what to do to keep them at bay until rescue comes." Clara closed her eyes and her magic snapped and sparkled around us. Some of it seeped into my skin, and very unhelpfully, my cock grew hard.

"Stop doing that, it isn't having the affect you want. There's no one to come for us, so your plan is moot."

New screams sounded from behind us, where my people should have been escaping into the tunnels. What now? I crawled to the next stall over and looked down the dock to see how many more of the Queen's guard were there surrounding us.

But what I saw coming toward us was no guard of the queen. Well, not the Mouse Queen anyway. Those fuckers. Strutting down the dock like he owned it was the biggest, meanest, dumbest friend I'd ever had in my life. He hated me now, but once upon a time, he'd taught me when to fight, when to fuck, and when to have a little fun.

I saw the exact moment Clara realized who was indeed coming to rescue us. Her eyes went all crinkly at the corners and she stood straight up, her dress going candy apple red again, and completely revealed our hiding spot. "Leb!"

The Prince of the Gingerbread Kingdom swung his battle axe over his head and somehow at the same time gave Clara a cute little finger wave and blew her a kiss. Blew her a fucking kiss. "We're here to rescue you, lass."

He drew his arm back and before I could yell at him to hold off, he flung the weapon straight for the head of the phalanx of soldiers. "No," my cry hung in the air as I threw myself out in front of the axe.

Mine wasn't the only 'no' hanging in the air. Clara screamed at the same time and threw her hands out, red magic swirling like a snowy squall. Everything around us slowed and then stopped, completely frozen. The people, the river, the Queen's guard. Even the axe that had been spinning head over end through the air, just hung there like an ornament on an invisible tree.

I didn't know if she'd slowed time, or literally frozen everything around us. Everything except Clara, me, and the rebellious Nutcrackers running toward me.

With nothing to stop me, I dropped and skidded across the stones. Leb went from an all-out run to a jog, until he caught up to his battle axe just hanging in the air. He knocked a fingertip on the sharp blade, and it made a solid thunking sound, but didn't drop. "You've learned some new tricks, princess."

Zucker and Tau caught up and stood on either side of Leb, looking first at his suspended axe and then at me. Tau frowned and pointed an arrow at me. "Are we sure it's not some stolen magic being used by him?"

Clara responded, but her voice was strained. "Nope. It's me. I don't really know what I'm doing, but I'm definitely the one doing it, and it's weirdly really hard. Oh, and also, I don't think I know how to stop."

I scrambled to my feet, wanting to help, but that was when Nuss appeared. He strolled out from behind the Queen's Guard, sheathing his sword at his side. I hated that my heart skipped a beat.

He'd been mine for a day, and now he was probably here to kill me and take back his piece of the crown. But he ignored me all together. Nuss strode over to Clara and brushed his lips across hers, while whispering something to her.

She was his first priority. Always was, always would be. That should hurt my soul, but it didn't. I was strangely buoyed knowing that just because I'd forced him to become my mate, he was still the same Captain of the Nutcrackers and the Prince of Snowflakes. Never wavering in his duty.

Clara shivered, and I could literally feel it as if I was the one quaking at his touch. Dammit, I was allowing their exchange to distract me. Now, when everyone was distracted by her magic, I could escape to fight another day. So why were my feet like blocks of ice?

Only when she took a deep breath, could I too breathe again, and the feeling came back into my feet.

Nuss strode over to me, looked me up and down and then grabbed me at the base of the skull with his uninjured arm, and pulled me in for a deep kiss. For one entire second, I forgot we were at war, that my life and my heart were forfeit, and that I'd left him naked and chained alone after we'd bonded.

For one whole second, I let him kiss me, reaffirming our bond, and declaring here and now with his actions, that we were together.

For one blink, one breath, one heartbeat, we belonged to each other, and the hurts of the past were erased.

Until Leb came over and slapped us both on the back. "About fucking time. Does this mean we get to stop hating this little fucker?"

Nuss pressed his forehead to mine and then took my hand and led me over to Clara, signaling to the others to join us. Tau and Zucker gave me looks like they still weren't sure, but did as Nuss instructed. We five surrounded Clara, but only I didn't belong. My mind said to run, my absent heart made me stay, even though I would likely suffer the consequences.

"Ooh, having you all so near certainly helps. Your gifts are saving me from feeling like I'm going to explode." Her shoulders dropped a little and the muscles in her hands released so it didn't look as though her fingers were trying to be claws.

Leb grinned and winked at Clara. "That's good, lass. I'd much rather see you explode from pleasure, on my cock."

I couldn't believe I was about to say this. "That's exactly what she needs to do. Bonding with all five princes will increase her powers five-fold."

"And you think she should bond with you?" Tau scowled at me, and Zucker had his hands on his sheathed daggers as if ready to draw them on me at a moment's notice. "Just because you've somehow tricked your way into their hearts?"

Clara shook her head, ready to refute their claims and stand up for me. Nuss was the same, although, I didn't know why. I'd treated him like shit.

I wanted to be everything they both believed in. But I wasn't. I was not the hero of this story. Even if I got her to usurp my mother and become the Queen of the Winter Realm, I wasn't the good guy here, and I never would be.

So before either of them could defend me, I spoke up instead. "And I would do it again. We have only a few days before I have to turn her over to the Mouse Queen, so either you're with me here and now, or I will cut each and every one of you down and take her to my mother now, because we will all have lost."

JUST WHO IS IN CHARGE HERE?

CLARA

When I'd first entered the land of Spirit and Magic, the empty places in my mind filled with magic and memories. I'd never been more at home than in the land of my mother. Even feeling that sense of belonging so deeply, there was still something missing inside of me.

A hole in my heart, dug there by absence from my realm and the wrongness of growing up in the cruelty of the human world had eaten away at my sense of self and worth. Little by little, finding these men, bonding with them, filled in the places inside of me that had been hurting for longer than I even realized.

Having all five of them, together, surrounding me with their love, affection, and power overwhelmed even the darkest parts of me. The worries that I would never be enough for anyone to truly love slipped away, fading, leaving only comfort and joy in their wake.

"No one is losing anything." The magical grip I had on the

world around us was all I had to hold the six of us together. I didn't know what would happen if I let go. "I just got you all together, so nobody is killing anyone. You got me?"

My magic crackled in the air. I didn't even know how I was doing any of this. It all just came out instinctually. I also knew I couldn't keep the world in this frozen state for much longer, because using the magic this way was exhausting. "If I release the soldiers without a plan, which I don't currently have and need all of you to help me figure out, they'll come after us. I don't want any innocent people here getting hurt."

I had no doubt my princes would keep me safe, and we could all escape, but the people who lived in such dire conditions already, didn't need to face any consequences of being left behind. Zucker and Tau still looked ready to murder Konig, and Leb was all that was standing between them.

My arms wobbled with the strain, and they dropped just an inch, but it felt like I was falling to some kind of intense gravity. My magic went a little haywire and Leb's axe fell to the ground with a clang. I glanced quickly at the line of soldiers, and I swear I saw them move. Just by millimeters, but still, I was losing control. "Oh crud. How about we all of us escape together, and then hash out the details of the rest of Konig's, umm, suggestion, later?"

I looked at each of my princes, and they nodded, one by one. "Good. Now nobody kill anyone, and let's figure out how to get out of here without anyone dying."

A muscle in my back spasmed and I almost went down. "Ouch, ow, ow. Oh no."

Zucker and Tau flanked me, one on either side, and wrapped their arms around my back supporting me. But too late, my magical hold had faltered and the world around us was slowly starting to move as if waking on a cold, snowy morning.

"Got any bright ideas, Captain?" Leb tipped his head at Nuss.

"No," Nuss said and shook his head. "But Konig knows the Land of Animals better than the rest of us. He should take lead."

The others grumbled and I think if anyone but Nuss had suggested that, they would have revolted. But we all trusted the Captain of the Nutcracker Guard with our very lives. "My hands are starting to cramp, so whatever you do, do it fast. I don't know how much longer I can hold on."

Konig pointed to a pile of stones near the water's edge that looked as if they used to be something but were now a rocky pile of trash. "Leb, use those ginger muscles of yours and move those stones directly into the path of the Queen's guard. Zucker, Tau, let Nuss support the princess, and help me move these stalls to surround them from the other sides."

Oh, I saw what he was planning. If we trapped the Queen's guard in a box of wood and stone, that should give everyone, including us, time to get away while they worked their way out. I prayed that the plan worked, but worried that the soldiers might still cause chaos after we were gone.

Nuss slipped between my arms and nodded to Zucker and Tau. "I've got her. Go to it."

They hurried away and the loss of such a close connection with them left me feeling weaker by the second. Nuss wrapped me tight in his arms and pressed his hips against mine. "Let's give you a boost to your magic, shall we, sweet princess?"

Ooh, I recognized that sparkle in his eye. I wasn't totally sure after last night that he would still have the same feelings about me, and I resolved once again that once the six of us were alone together, I would convince Konig to give me, or share with me, the piece of the Snowflake crown he had.

He wanted me to be strong enough to usurp the Mouse Queen and save his people, then he would have to see that letting Nuss and I bond directly and not only through him would only strengthen me.

Nuss bent down and pressed his mouth to mine, but a

shudder of pain shook my body, and my knees went out from under me. "Ack. I'm losing this battle. I guess that means no time for snuggling and kissing."

"Remember, your emotions are what fuel your magic, and none is stronger than the base emotions of lust or anger. So, you can either be mad at me for stealing a kiss, or you can remember just how much I want to bond with you." Nuss held me tight and kept me from falling both physically and emotionally.

I don't know why I was struggling to understand how my feelings were the key to my magic. Duh. It's how I'd healed him more than once, and how I'd found the crowns we had so far. There just seemed to be a disconnect between the two things in my mind still. Something was missing and until I figured that part out, instinct was all I had to go on. "Right. I choose door number two please."

I knew his touch now and wasn't shy with taking the taste of him that I craved. I stretched up to kiss him again, and bit at his lip like he'd once done to me. He hissed and held me tighter. "You've gained a bit of Konig's penchant for pleasure-pain."

"Hmm, no. I learned that one from you." Nuss has hidden his darkest desires for too long, and I was hungry for them. Aha, maybe that is what I got from Konig. Because even though Nuss and I couldn't be bonded until I got his crown, I still very much wanted him, and he wanted me. I think we both had put up walls between each other because of that crown, or rather lack thereof.

But I realized now, with our lips, bodies, and hearts touching, I was his and he was mine, with or without that crown. We were, and always would be, bonded in spirit. That more than anything else gave me the emotional boost my magic needed.

A whoosh of wind and magic spirited through the dank cavern and across the docks. I rose up and pulled out of Nuss's arms, although, I gave him another peck on the cheek. Then I walked toward where Leb was stacking the bricks in front of the Queen's guard.

Leb glanced over at me and then dropped the brick he was holding. I could see the reflection of my magic swirling around me in his shocked eyes.

"Blocking their path is only a temporary stop gap, and our new friends who live and work here may still have repercussions because of me." I walked over to the closest soldier and reached for him.

The tip of Konig's sword slid between my hand and the soldier's chest. "Princess, you don't know the power of your magic. These soldiers are under a compulsion spell created by the Mouse Queen. They can do nothing but obey her orders."

Zucker and Tau rushed over, their weapons drawn and pointed at Konig once again. I carefully wrapped my hand around his blade, feeling the sharpness of the blade against my palm. Slowly, pushed it down. "I told you, I don't want anyone dying today, and that means these soldiers too."

I pressed my hand to the soldier's chest and trusted my instincts. I thought of the love that each of my precious men had shown me and let it flow through me and into the heart of the man under the Queen's control. He dropped to the ground, not dead, but sleeping. I hoped.

"Princess," Konig's voice was a warning, with a dark promise of retribution behind it.

Knowing that he wanted to trust me, I gripped his sword tighter and let some of my blood spill over the blade. Then I forged ahead. My gift poured out of me now and I didn't even have to touch the others before wisps of red magic sunk into each of the soldiers.

They sunk to the ground, one by one. When the last fell, the world around us clicked back into normal time and space, as if a door to a noisy street had been opened. The fearful shouts of the people around us dimmed as they saw what I had done.

A woman, with the same horns as the little girl pointed and yelled, "You killed them?"

Someone else replied with so much anger and fear in their voice I couldn't tell if it was a man or a woman. "That's what magician's do. We can't trust her any more than we could her forefathers."

"She's murdered our Prince! Get her!"

"What? No."

I was so wrapped up in the magic that I didn't notice anything else going on around me. My heart dropped down to my stomach and my stomach jumped up my throat. Konig's blade was still in my hand, but he'd fallen to the ground along with the other soldiers.

"Time to go, lass. Leb grabbed me and threw me over one shoulder, then swooped up Konig and threw him over the other. He bolted for the tunnels, but the people blocked our way, shouting and shaking their fists.

Nuss yelled and pointed toward the boats on the river. "Go, I'll hold them off."

Leb pivoted like he was on ice skates and ran toward the water. Zucker and Tau fell in behind us protecting mostly me from projectiles of rocks and chunks of wood being thrown in my direction.

"Don't you let Nuss sacrifice himself. Let me down and I'll explain or freeze everyone again, or something." I reached my hand out and tried to summon the magic, but it fizzled at my fingertips.

Zucker saw my frustration and winked at me. "Don't worry, sweetness. We've been evading the people of the Land of Animals for a long time. Nobody is sacrificing themselves today."

I glanced over at Konig and hoped against hope, that was true for him as well. I had to trust that my men knew what they were doing and trust that they would save me from myself once again.

Leb jumped into an empty docked boat that would barely hold all of us if we squished together. He set me down, at the front, and I plopped right onto my butt. Had that use of magic really drained me so badly? I had no strength left. "Stay down, lass, and take care of Konig while we get the ginger out of here."

He slid Konig off his other shoulder and onto the floor next to me, depositing his head right into my waiting arms. His chest rose and fell as if he was just asleep, and my own breathing ratcheted down to match his.

An arrow flew and thunked into the top of the short mast in the center of the boat. It had a rope attached to it, and in the next moment, Zucker came swinging down into the boat on that very same cord. His landing pushed the boat further out into the water, and well beyond where anyone else would be able to reach us from the dock.

Tau shot another arrow and followed, but Nuss had run the other direction on the dock and I didn't yet see him anywhere. "Nuss, where's Nuss?"

I knew I didn't have much magical energy left, but pulled on the fear that was bubbling inside of me. I reached up and shot out one fizzling sort of firecracker that shot over the heads of the crowd. It was nothing more than a distraction, but it worked because all eyes went up as the light exploded into a shining golden star that illuminated the rocky ceiling of the cavern.

Nooks and crannies that were dark and shadowed lit up and on the far end, where the soldiers had come from, I saw something that had my anger boiling up instead of fear. Fritz.

He was crouched on top of a boulder next to a tunnel entrance, watching, and scheming. I knew that look as well as I knew he was up to no good. That rat.

"Everyone hold on, here comes Nuss." Tau shot another arrow with a rope, but this time toward the crowd. I heard it hit something wooden and then Nuss appeared at the edge of the dock, sprinting along the stones toward it.

I watched, forgetting about Fritz for now. The jump looked too far for even someone as strong and tough as Nuss, but he leaped into the air anyway, grabbing the rope, which Tau had tied to the little boat. Before I could even think to reach out with my magic to try and guide him in, the rope shredded from behind him, and he tumbled toward the icy water.

We'd all learned in the grotto that none of them could swim, and the icy water would make it even worse when the shock of the frigid river hit him. I shot my hand out again, but the magic didn't go beyond a glow in my hand. I was tapped. I'd already borrowed from my fear and was in spiritual debt.

The scream was bubbling up my throat and there was nothing I could do. Then, like a whole other kind of magic, Leb reached out past the edge of the boat and snagged Nuss by the jacket and tossed him into the boat. He skidded across the wood and kerthunked into the bow with me.

He blinked up at me and grinned like he'd just had the time of his life. I smacked him. "I thought you were about to die."

"Not today." He nodded over at Konig, who, though still unconscious, looked as if he was simply sleeping peacefully. "How is he?"

The boat lurched forward as Leb, Tau, and Zucker pushed poles into the water below and propelled us into the darkness of the tunnel where the underground river flowed. I didn't care where we were going, as long as we were all safe and together.

"I don't know yet." The words were hard to get out of my mouth. What if my misuse of magic had done exactly what his people were worried about, and hurt them all more than helped? "He's alive, but I don't know what I did to him. I only meant to break the spell on the soldiers."

"Because he is the prince, he is connected to all the people of the Land of Animals." Nuss reached over and pushed a lock of

Konig's hair aside. A warm snap of magic swirled around us and poured into my empty tanks. "But especially the soldiers of the Mouse Queen's army, even those ones that weren't under his command. Whatever you did to them, runs through their spirits to him."

"You're all princes of your lands. Is that true for each of you?" Would it be true of Fritz even if I was the only other citizen of the Land of Spirit and Magic left?

"No. The people of his land have a special connection to each other, unlike any other land. It's how he has the entire Mouse Army at his beck and call, why they shift for him and do his bidding."

"Because he commands them." I'd felt that very command over me too.

"No, because they trust him. The Queen by rights should have that same power, but she doesn't. That's what gives him that command. They are, for lack of better words, his pack and he is their alpha."

Oh. My heart thumped in my chest so hard I could feel it against my breast. I wished so much that I could have just found his crown and bonded with him in the same way as I had the others. There was so much missing in the link between us.

That was another reason my heart was going wackadoodle in my chest. Somewhere deep inside was a whisper of knowledge that I was afraid to say out loud, because I didn't know how the others would react. Konig was the alpha of the people of the Land of Animals, but he was also meant to be the leader, commander, and captain of our group. He was our alpha.

LOVE OR DESTRUCTION

CLARA

Our little river boat ride emerged out of the tunnel somewhere behind the castle keep. I hadn't actually seen Christmas Castle before and whoof, was it ever big and imposing. Whoever designed it, or rather had it designed, had definitely been going for big and dominating. If I could forget the history of why and how it was built, the actual architecture was lovely, like a storybook castle. And that made me hate it all the more.

How dare they use forced labor to create something so beautiful?

Leb, Zucker, and Tau steered the boat to the nearest bank where the river narrowed. Further ahead, it continued to get smaller and would quickly be impassable in a marshy, dank area. The lot of us had grown quiet in the dark tunnel, and now that we were out into the twilight of the day, I didn't know if it was safe to even talk. I leaned close and whispered to Nuss.

"Where are we going? We need someplace where I can try to heal whatever I've done to Konig."

Nuss also kept his voice low, and the others didn't speak at all, but communicated in the way a team who's been together for a long time do. "We should be safe here if we can find someplace to hunker down for the night. Not many venture to where the town's sewers empty out."

What? Ew. They just dumped their waste into the marsh? But I didn't smell anything so gross. Nuss gave me a knowing smirk and indicated that I should take a look around. All I saw was the crystal-clear, icy waters I'd accidentally created and snowy white ground leading into the swampy area.

Leb returned and picked up Konig again to carry him off the boat. "A day ago, this was a disgusting blight on the land. Your magic is renewing it."

We followed him off the boat and once we were safely on shore, they pushed the boat away to drift further downstream. I turned in a circle and couldn't believe even for a second that this was anything other than an untouched field with a small river flowing through it. If my magic could do this when I wasn't even trying, what could I do if I knew what I wanted to do?

"Come, we need to find shelter before the sun goes down." Leb turned and forged a path through the snowbanks toward the stone wall. It wasn't like there were any other buildings and only the icy marsh or wide-open plains for miles around. "At least the wall will act like a wind break, and I'm happy to do what I can to keep you warm tonight, princess."

We tucked ourselves against a decorative kind of pillar that looked like a tower of pine trees carved out of the stone. But a chill wind whipped along the ground and wall. My men might have been raised in the cold temperatures, but even they would freeze if we were stuck out in these elements. We needed shelter.

"My armor," I blurted out. "Konig said it could become a temporary place to sleep if I needed it to be."

"I have no doubt your magic can do whatever it is you want it to. We've never seen magic as powerful as yours." Nuss gave a small shake of his head and blinked as if searching his memory. "I have a feeling we're only experiencing the tip of the iceberg of your talents."

The awe in his voice warmed my cheeks. I shouldn't feel proud of a gift so easily corrupted in the past, but I promised I would use it as best I could. Starting with a place to keep warm.

I lifted the flowing black skirts of the cape-like dress and imagined in my mind what I wanted it to be. My magic snapped and sparkled, but nothing more happened. "I'm out of magical juice."

"We can help with that." Zucker and Tau approached me, once again flanking me on either side. I liked having them there and as a pair they leaned in, and each gave me a kiss. Tau on the corner of my mouth, and Zucker a place on my throat where my pulse beat against my skin.

Zucker nibbled his way up my neck and pressed his lips to my ear. "We have so many more delicious things to do to your body. Our claim on you has only just begun."

Eep. Yep, that did it. That snap and sparkle became just enough magic that my armor swirled and spun, whipping off my body. In a flash of a moment, it attached to the stones and turned into a domed tent, just big enough for the six of us.

The burst of magic also did something to Konig, and he grumbled and stirred. Leb set him down, leaning against the wall and his eyes fluttered open so he was looking directly at me. "I haven't missed all the fun, have I?"

He waggled one eyebrow at me, and his gaze went from my head to my toes and back. I glanced down and discovered I was butt naked. "Oops. I guess my armor can't be clothing and a tent at the same time."

Leb started laughing first, and then everyone else joined in too. It wasn't even that funny, but it was the break in the tension we all needed.

"Are you truly okay?" Tau pulled me into his arms. "We've been frantic since that rat kidnapped you."

His emotions roiled through me. I cupped his cheek and tried my best to reassure him with my touch. "I'm better than fine, and you don't have a hateful bone in your body. Can you find a way to let Konig back into your heart?"

The tension that had drained away spiked right back up. But this wasn't something we could ignore.

"You're asking a lot," Tau said, shaking his head. "How do you know he was ever there to begin with?"

None of them yet understood how much of each of them I could feel deep in my spirit. The tenuous bond with Nuss and Konig connecting all six of us together, didn't mean I didn't know how they were each feeling.

Nuss's fist opened and closed. If anyone had complicated feelings, it was him. But before I could say anything more, he answered for me. "He was. We wouldn't all feel so hurt and betrayed if he hadn't been. But we didn't have all the facts."

Konig groaned and tried to get up, but he wasn't strong enough yet, so he just waved his hand at us. "I'm right here, you know."

Leb gave Konig and then Nuss a stink eye. He was the easiest to forgive, but that didn't mean all was forgotten. "You don't answer our questions, Maus, so keep your mouth shut. Nuss, if you have all the facts now, please explain why we should forgive this dickhead of a betraying former friend."

Tau paced back and forth the whole two feet of space we had. "What can he possibly say that will make it okay that Konig led the god-damned Mouse Army on attack after attack of our Lands, destroying our homes, our food, and our families, until our Queen's submitted to her rule over the entire realm?"

Zucker fingered the daggers at his hips then pulled one and used it to point at Nuss. "Just because he's got your crown and taken you to bed, doesn't mean we can forgive the way he threw away every vow he made to fight by our sides. Fae, Vikings, and Snowflakes died at his hands, Nuss. Died, because he did what his mother told him too."

Nuss looked at Konig, then me then to each of the others. "Yes, we bonded, and I understand now it wasn't his fault."

Konig blanched. "Don't do that. I made my choices the same as the rest of you."

I wished that I could grab the whole lot of them up in a big hug, but I couldn't even move at the moment. I may have brought the five of them back together, but they needed to hash this part out on their own. I wasn't even around for the betrayal that broke up the band in the first place. But I had to intervene here. "That's not entirely true. Nuss and I can feel the spell on your heart."

Zucker, Tau, and Leb all turned and stared at me like I'd just said boogedy-boo. "If you all pay attention, I bet you can feel it through our connection too. Konig's action are not, and I'd venture to guess were not, entirely his own."

I didn't even really understand that's what the spell was I'd been breaking when I pushed my magic through the soldiers. The magic the Mouse Queen was using was compulsion to obey, and it had a grip on Konig too.

Tau shoved Konig in the shoulder. "Is this true?"

Konig didn't say a thing.

Zucker shoved him in the other shoulder. "Now is not the time to say silent. Tell us you've been bespelled by the Queen. That you were not in control of your actions when you marched on the Sweet Fae Court."

He didn't.

Both of my fae princes were hurt and this wasn't going to fix anything. "You must see that he can't answer that."

Nuss put himself in front of Konig. "I've felt it for a long time. I just didn't understand that's what I was feeling. Stop letting your anger put up the same wall I've used to deny my feelings and see what's already there. He didn't want to betray us. It's the Queen we should be angry with for taking our friend from us. The Mouse Queen who forced our mothers to their knees."

I added one final prod that I knew would have sway on them all. "If we're to make this land a better place, just as you've been fighting for all this time, you all must open your hearts to him too. You know we're better when we are all as one."

I looked over at Zucker. His eyes had gone stormy and angry again. His passion burned whether it was love or anger or a mixture of both. If he relented and accepted Konig back into his life, Tau would as well. "My sweet prince, you have so much love in your heart that you've had to keep hidden for too long. Would you ask another to do the same?"

Pain flitted across his face, and he glanced over at Tau and then up to the tented ceiling above us. "How is it that you believe in each of our hearts so deeply when you barely know us?"

It wasn't a real question, just something to deflect while he sorted through his feelings. I'd done that a time or two in my life as well. I wanted to give him the minute he needed, but I feared we had only tonight. If Fritz had found me so easily twice now, he would again.

I didn't want to believe he would hurt me to get ahead, but I had the proof of it from our life in the human world. So much more was at stake here in the Winter Realm than a silly business and a privileged family reputation. Fritz wouldn't care, just as long as he was in charge.

"The same way you believed in me before you ever met me." I pressed my hand over my heart and made sure my emotions were as bare and open as my body was to them. "I never believed in fate before all of this, but clearly there is more at work here than our own plots and plans. I don't know if it's some higher power, the Universe, or perhaps even the Christmas Star forging us together, but I do know it's important that we are one, united, bonded together forever."

Zucker was still not convinced. "How can we trust him if he's being controlled by the Mouse Queen? Her guard could be on their way here again right now."

"In this you can trust me." Konig sat up, his strength returning little by little. "Clara must usurp the Mouse Queen for my people as well as yours."

Tau laid his hand on Zucker's, pushing the dagger down to point at the ground. "We've seen what the Mouse Queen has done to her own people. I'm wary too, but you and I have already proven that love can overcome hate. Let's choose love."

My eyes stung and tears bubbled up on my eyelashes. Zucker groaned and wiped them with his thumb, then smeared them across his lips. "Even the pain in my heart cannot withstand the both of you. I will try."

Leb gave a whoot and thwacked Zucker on the back. "I would have held out in solidarity with you, lads, but you know this is what I wanted for all of us all along."

So much tension released from my muscles that the sparks flickered across my shoulders like pins and needles. The anxiety of knowing that the men I loved were angry with each other had blocked a deep flow of magic that was now available to me.

I stepped through the barrier they'd formed between me and Konig and knelt on the floor next to him. He'd said we all had to come together, that I had to bond with all five princes. Even him, though we didn't have his piece of the broken crown. The connection between him and Nuss would hold strong. Stronger if we reaffirmed that bond now.

All eyes were on us, waiting on me to make the first move. But I wanted Konig to be right there with me. He was the one who would bring us all together at last. "I know we can't truly bond without the crown from the Land of Animals, but take me anyway, make me yours."

Konig blew out a long breath and shook his head so imperceptibly that I doubted the others would see. Then he whispered so low that only I would hear. "I'm sorry."

I thought he was about to refuse me, but he grabbed me by the throat, flipped us both so my back was to the floor, and he was directly on top of me. The others shouted, but he held up his hand to them and growled low, like an animal. "She may never truly be mine, and we'll all be in danger the moment I give her my seed, but just for tonight, let us all be as we were meant, and claim our princess, once and for all."

I gulped for air, the silence of the others killing me. The determination in Konig's eyes never wavered. He stared down only at me, his back vulnerable to the others, waiting for them to submit to his request. No, it wasn't a request, but a demand.

This was the test of whether we could be as one, and if Leb, Zucker, Tau, and Nuss would trust him enough to be our captain. Without either, we wouldn't succeed in changing the Winter Realm. If love couldn't conquer all here, then it certainly wouldn't convince the rest of the people to let go of the hate and fear in their hearts.

That was what destroyed the Winter Realm.

Love was what would save it.

Starting with these five men.

TO PROMISE AND OBEY

NUSS

Konig clenched his fist and threw his fingers back open. "Kneel for me and your princess."

The others froze and I almost laughed at what they must be feeling. The first time Konig used the power in his voice to give a command was titillating. Especially to men like the fabled princes, who weren't used to taking orders.

I certainly wasn't. But where it should grate at me, and would if it was anyone else, there was a freedom in knowing that someone else was going to make sure everything was taken care of, done right, and that I didn't have to shoulder the responsibility for just a little while.

They'd learned to take them from me. They would come to trust Konig too.

Leb, Zucker, and Tau each looked to me, and my chest swelled with pride that they trusted me so much. I gave them a curt nod giving them my okay. They needed me to continue to be strong for them even when I already wanted to drop to my own knees just to please my mate.

The words in my mind sparkled with joy at the same time that they pricked me like sharpened icicles driven into my throat. He was mine and I was his, after years of having to deny I even had feelings for him. But sweet Clara never would be.

I shoved that pain away. If life as the captain of the Nutcracker rebellion had taught me anything, it was that very little in life was perfect. I'd take what comfort and joy I could from those around me that existed in this love like no other. The consequences of the rest would come later.

Leb gave me a big old Viking who ate the cookie grin and stripped right out of his clothes. He tossed them aside and dropped to his knees next to Clara's head. "I've been waiting for this for a long time, lass."

Out of the corner of my eye, I saw Leb's clothes wriggle and two tiny pixie heads pop out. Clara would be glad her faithful pixies were safe and sound, but now was not the time. I lifted my finger to my lips and gave them a little shush. They nodded and burrowed back into Leb's clothes, probably to nap. I looked forward to their kind of comfort and joy after we all bonded. I'm sure everyone would be hungry.

Tau gave Zucker a quick, but hot kiss that had my own cock paying attention. The two of them had invited me to their bed on more than one occasion, but that was never something that was allowed in my world. Now that I'd thrown off, was still in the process of shedding, the restrictions of the Church of the Christmas Star and their expectations of me, I had the chance to experience more than I'd ever thought I could.

Tau knelt across from Leb and Zucker stepped to my side. "Don't think for even a minute that I'd be jealous if you wanted to enjoy the indulgences of fae cock tonight too, my friend. Just say the word and we'll be there to make this bonding even more enjoyable."

He winked and tossed his own clothes aside to join the worship at Clara's altar. I would take him up on his offer, except for the glare that Konig gave me. For now, I belonged only to him and Clara. If and when we defeated the forces of evil plaguing our lives, there would be time for everything else later.

"Nuss." Konig barked out my name and fires lit inside of me back in the Land of Spirit and Magic rekindled. While I had so many deep feelings for him, our relationship would never be easy. For either of us.

I already belonged to him in bond. It was time I pushed for more.

Slowly, I peeled my shirt off my broken arm first and then my good one. "Are you ready to give her the snowflake crown so we can be truly bonded?"

Konig didn't like that at all. He growled again and I liked knowing that I could make his inner beast rise up. If he truly needed me to give in to him fully, like he did that first time, I would. He had my heart. Now we were on more equal terms, and I wanted his in return. But I also wanted Clara's.

I needed her. She was my destiny. Everything had changed, and Konig was just as much my chosen fate, but we both might die if he denied me Clara's true love. Because then I would have to fight him for it.

We stared at each other for a long moment, and no one else said anything. No one but Clara had seen this dynamic play out between us before and even for her this time was different. Yet she was the one who knew what to do.

She reached her hand up toward the crown. Konig growled but didn't take his eyes off me. He did squeeze his hand tighter around her throat. Not enough to harm her, but to keep her still. Sweet Clara resisted anyway.

Instead of snagging the crown from around his neck like I'd have, she pressed the flat of her palm against it, pressing it to his chest. "It's okay. It's already mine, isn't it, my King?"

King. Yes, that's what he was, and Clara understood that.

The rumble in his chest faded and the sharpness in his eyes turned to pure arousal. "Yes, my queen. So tell your captain to get his ass down her and kneel for us both."

Oh fuck.

As if that was an order I could deny.

Clara peered up at me through her soft lashes and said only one word. My name. "Nuss."

I'd been turned on before, but my cock was instantly rock hard and if I didn't rid myself of the rest of my clothes immediately, they might spontaneously combust. I ripped off my pants and literally tossed them over my shoulder, all the quicker to kneel next to my princess, my Queen.

Once we were all there, magic snapped in the air, and it sizzled through me. The others jerked and everyone's eyes went wide, but then hazy with lust. Clara's magic had just come out to play and she liked to play dirty.

Konig grabbed my hand and pushed it between my legs, getting me to wrap my fist around my cock, then stroked it a few times. "Watch them Clara. Their cocks are hard for you, their seed is for you along with their bond. I want you to watch them stroke themselves until they come all over you, while I fuck your sweet cunt claiming it for my own as well."

Fucking stars. I knew at some point if we fulfilled Leb's original plan to become her consorts as a group, we'd all perform some kind of sexual act together. This kind of group bonding was common among the Vikings, and the fae were certainly not shy about having full on orgies. But the Land of Snowflakes was reserved, and sex was behind closed doors and only with one's bonded partner.

The act of watching someone else fuck each other, like I'd done when Leb had bonded with Clara, was the first time I'd taken myself in hand while watching the sex act. It had been delicious with the touch of rebellion against the forbidden.

Leb took himself in hand next to me and cupped Clara's chin, turning her head to look at him stroking up and down his huge shaft. "My body, my heart, and my spirit are forever yours, lass."

She leaned into him, and we all got a surge of the love the two of them felt for each other. It had been a long few days and my injuries had taken a toll on me. Clara, feeling loved and loving in return was better than any food, drink, or rest to refuel me. The spark of magic I held inside of me was also powered by my emotions, ones that I'd carefully held in check. Until I'd found Clara and she'd bonded with the other princes.

When she'd bonded with Tau and Zucker at the same time, their gifts made it possible for the rest of us to participate through her magic, and I'd felt such pure satisfaction when I came in my hand, I couldn't imagine fucking her myself would be any better. Still, I craved her body for myself.

The two of them followed Konig's command, but in their own way. Instead of them each grabbing their own cocks for her, Zucker fisted Tau's and Tau wrapped his hand around Zucker's. They kissed each other, and then Tau said to Clara, "You made our love not only whole, but possible. You have always been, and will ever be, our Queen."

"It meant so much to me that I could be the catalyst to bring you together in a bond. You showed me how powerful and healing love can be."

I was the only one left to declare my feelings for her.

When Konig claimed our bond for himself and forced me to spill my seed for him, and take his own, a weight was lifted from my shoulders. I didn't have to be her consort and the savior of my people. I could no longer claim her, even though I wanted to.

The pressure of being the prophet prince of the Church of the Christmas Star was broken, and I could simply love for the sake of loving.

The emotions were too much. I wasn't used to being able to feel this way, and the words clogged in my throat. Konig locked eyes with me and shook his head. His hand was still on mine, and he squeezed his harder over mine, fisting my cock tighter. But then he let go and grabbed the back of my head and pulled me in for a kiss.

It wasn't gentle, and I gave as good as I got. Our teeth gnashed and our tongues dueled. I didn't want the same sweet love from Konig as I did from Clara. I wanted his hard to her soft, her spirit to his darkness, her magic to his power.

One without the other would never have been enough.

Never. Have. Been. Enough.

With Clara's hand on my crown over Konig's heart, his hand wrapped around my cock, and the magic of her love overflowing, I needed the link between us all to be complete. I pulled my hand from beneath his but made sure he didn't let me go. Then I reached between Clara's thighs and found her pussy wet and waiting.

She grabbed at my arm and held me tight to her cunt. "Nuss, I want you. I want to feel you inside of me."

"I know, but I want to hear you beg again. I want you begging for Konig's cock for yourself this time." I stroked my fingers through her wet folds, swirling the juices over her clit until she squirmed. Then I pulled away and coated Konig's cock with the very same.

"Please. Give me both of you."

"Not this time, my Queen. I've waited on the sidelines for too long and..." Konig trailed off. There was something more he was going to say and swallowed it back. I didn't like secrets now that we were here and all together, but I wasn't going to push him when he'd already given so much.

There was trepidation in his heart about being with us all. The Queen did have some kind of compulsion spell on him, and we were all in danger because of it. Only Clara's love and the pact we'd made all those years ago to take her together, would make him stay.

"And he's going to fuck you until you're begging to come." I finished for him and then guided his cock into her waiting cunt. Both of them groaned at the exquisite contact and Clara's magic burst out of her in pulsating waves. The three of us were locked together, and the sensations they felt poured into the rest of us.

I had to swallow a cry and grit my teeth not to come in Konig's hand right then and there. This was similar to what we experienced in the grotto, but tenfold. I could feel each of the prince's stroking their cocks as if it was my hand on my own cock.

Clara's cunt clamped down on Konig's cock and the pleasure they both experienced shot through my own spine and balls. We were all moaning and climbing closer and closer to orgasm uncontrollably. I was lost in the moment, rubbing Clara's clit like my life depended on it, feeling Konig's cock thrust in and out of her.

Konig was the only one in control and even his was near to breaking. "Don't a one of you come until she does. Clara, look at them, dying already to spill their seed on you, and claim you with it once again. Take it, take it all."

"Please, Konig, yes. I need everyone to claim me. Everyone." She looked at him, and then at me.

"Good girl. Then come for me and let your magic bond us all together." He fucked her fast and deep and her clit pulsed between my fingers. My own cock was ready to explode as Konig jerked it just as hard. We were both his, bonded, and claimed by him.

Clara threw her head back and her back arched up off the ground. She cried out something incomprehensible and her orgasm rocked not only her world, but all of ours as well. As one we all followed her into the bliss of her climax. We covered her breasts and belly with our releases. Her spirit and her magic skyrocketed out of her, filling the shelter with a deep red glow and a warmth like I'd never felt before.

Konig gave my cock several more strokes, pulling every last bit of pleasure out of my body. Then he smeared his fingers through my seed and pressed it between Clara's lips, until she was sucking on his fingers. A stronger link between the three of us solidified, and it overwhelmed me so intensely that another orgasm shot through me.

The dark smile Konig had on his face sent a deep satisfaction swirling dangerously close to the perfect place in my heart I kept sacred just for Clara. One without the other was never enough.

Never enough.

Was this real love? Was this the true destiny meant for me, and not what everyone else had always told me I was meant for?

As Clara moaned around Konig's fingers and he thrust into her, his hips jerking, locking his cock inside of her, I answered my own question. Regardless of what fate or destiny had chosen for me, I was choosing Clara and Konig, and Leb, Zucker, and Tau. They were the points of my perfect snowflake, unique, and beautiful, and that which made me who I was.

Konig finally let go and filled Clara's cunt with his seed, bonding the two of them in a way that didn't require a piece of the broken crown. For a brief flash, I saw the intricacies of the Mouse Queen's compulsion spell on Konig, and it shook me so deeply that my own heart skipped several beats and stole my breath. But as soon as I felt it, the feeling and the understanding slipped away.

But her magic had us all so connected that each of us could

feel the exact same thing as he did all the way down to the essence of our spirits. His mind overflowed with both pleasure and regret.

ONE MORE CLIFFHANGERY LINE

SACRIFICES MUST BE MADE

KONIG

*C*lara and Nuss were the wine I was drunk on. Because intoxication was the only good excuse for what I'd just done. I should have simply fucking given Clara the snowflake crown and let the two of them complete their own bond. The weak link I'd had with her through Nuss might have been enough.

She'd very clearly accessed the gift of command through me, and it was sexy as fuck on her. My hubris was in thinking she needed me to be strong. I had no idea the power within her, and never would have if she hadn't done everything in her spirit to bond with me, even without possessing the crown of my land.

While I could feel the link the Mouse Queen had to her through me, there was no hint of the compulsion spell. At least I'd gotten that right. Clara's magic was too strong for that, and she was still free, as were the others. But the queen would still know their whereabouts at any time, just as she did mine.

But until now, she had no way of knowing I wasn't completely loyal to her. She sure as shit did now. I would have to convince her otherwise. My chest burned as she squeezed my heart with her anger. That wasn't anything new, but I wasn't the only one who would suffer the consequences anymore.

I pulled away from my luscious princess and stood up and busied myself tossing everyone's clothes to them. I wasn't used to this kind of closeness. I'd been an outcast for a whole lot more of my life than I'd been in anyone's favor. I wasn't walking away, but I needed some space, which wasn't available as long as the six of us were together.

Zucker pulled on his pants and huffed. "One of these fucking times I'm showing the whole damn lot of you the value and intimacy in after sex snuggling."

"What the hell kind of heartburn did you give us, Konig?" Leb pounded on his chest as if this was nothing more than indigestion.

"I'm afraid our bond now allows you all to feel..." Fuck, I couldn't get the words out. The Queen's command that I couldn't talk about her compulsion over me and the details of her spell forcefully shut my mouth for me. I threw my hands up in the air and shook my head, angry that I couldn't express myself.

Clara was the first to understand. "I think we have to be careful with how we ask questions."

Nuss covered Clara with his jacket and nodded. "A life or death guessing game. I don't like it, and we will find a way to break the Mouse Queen's spell on you."

"Look, if we pay attention," Tau waved his hand in a circle indicating us all, "to sensations and emotions we're privy to through our connections with Clara and each other, it's not that hard to figure it out. The Mouse Queen is coming for us, and we've got to be prepared for a battle with her."

Leb smacked Tau on the back. "You definitely feel more than I do. I just want to rip my own fucking heart out of my chest."

That was the closest anyone had ever been to understanding how I felt every Queen-forsaken day. "He's not wrong. We don't have long before the Mouse Queen herself shows up. She'll be proceeded by more guards loyal to her. Either we stand together here and now and fight, or you all have to leave. Now."

"Hold up." Zucker eyed me. "Are you, or are you not a consort of the princess now? If you're on our side, then what you meant to say was that we all have to leave together, right?"

Clara pulled the jacket tighter around her. "Why can't I just break the spell on them like I did on the soldiers back in the tunnels?"

Seeing each of these men I once called friends and the princess so easily come to my defense after all I'd done to wrong them, hurt, but in a whole different way. As if I'd stretched an unused muscle for the first time in longer than I could remember. If I focused on Clara, I could contain the pain. "You probably could. But she would only call up more and more. Your magic isn't endless. You saw how it drained you after freeing that one detachment of her guards."

"The Mouse Army is ten times larger than any other in the land. You're saying she has control over all of them?" Zucker's question cut me to the core. She might only directly control a few soldiers at a time, but through me, she could command every citizen of the Land of Animals if she wanted. Not that I could tell them that.

"We six are not enough to stand against her legions." I said, deflecting. "She'll strike us all down before we can get her and Clara face to face. We can't afford to waste Clara's enhanced powers protecting us while we try to get to the Queen herself."

Clara looked around at each of us and took a deep breath. "What happens if she and I battle alone?"

Nuss sliced the air with his hand. "You should never be

alone with her. You must rely on us to support you, that's the power in having us as your consorts. We will protect you."

"But only you can cut her down and usurp her as the Queen of the Winter Realm. You're the only one strong enough." I knew full well that wasn't what she wanted to hear. She still believed she was no Vivandiere and would heal our realm with the magic of her love. While her love was even more powerful than I ever could have imagined, and I wished it were so that we needed only the beauty of her pure spirit to bring peace to our land, that was nothing but an innocent dream.

The room fell silent. It's not like they all didn't know what we'd been working toward since we trained together to fight in the Magician's war. This was why I had to give myself to her even though it put her in danger. They were all brave and strong, but none had ever had to truly sacrifice.

I had and I would again.

"I will go and stave off the Queen's advances. You all retreat to the Snow Queen's court. Call upon your armies and march on Christmas Castle as soon as you can gather your weapons. I will meet you again on the field of battle." I put every bit of command I had into those directives and a ripple of Clara's magic enforced my words.

"That's my girl." I cupped her cheek, and she drew close for a kiss.

"I don't want to let you go. You'll be back under her control, won't you?"

That wasn't a question I could, nor would, answer. "You don't get to let me do anything, my pet. But once we free the people of the Winter Realm and you are our Queen, I will let you spend the rest of the twelve days of Christmas on your knees, begging us all for orgasm after orgasm."

She blushed so beautifully and gave me a sad smile. "I'll be counting the minutes."

"Good. Then I'll leave you with this." I grabbed her chin and kissed her fiercely, knowing that this would be the last taste of her I would ever get. She was sweet and spicy, and I craved more and more of her. But this would have to be enough. Before I broke the kiss, I snapped the cord around my neck and pressed the broken piece of the Snowflake crown into her hand. I nipped at her lip and then whispered against them, "Take him and make him yours. Fuck him until he doesn't even know his own name."

I pulled away and gave the others a nod, not waiting for their responses. They all knew that I was right and what they needed to do. But Nuss followed me out.

He grabbed my shoulder and spun me, for the first time in a long time, towering over me. "You can't sacrifice yourself."

How I wanted to lean into him, let him be my protector too. That was never meant to be. I stepped back so I wasn't tempted any more than I already was. "Who says that's what I'm going to do?"

Nuss didn't let me get away with shit, he never had. He wrapped his hand around the back of my head and held me so that I couldn't look away. "You may have everyone else fooled, but we are bonded. I know your heart."

I wished that he could.

I let him hold onto me but gave him a stern look. "Clara is a strong magician and she'll have the people of the realm behind her. If anyone can free... my people, she will. You have to be there to help her do that. Promise me."

"No. Not without you. We need to break this spell the Mouse Queen has on you before we try to battle her." There was fear in his eyes, which was not something I was used to seeing there. Had I corrupted him too?

"Don't think you can start defying me now, Nutcracker." I pulled out of his hold and took his jaw in my fist, just as I did Clara's a moment ago. "You will give your heart and your spirit to the princess, but never forget, I took them first. You were mine before all others."

His breathing was harsh, and his chest heaved. "We will rescue you from the Mouse Queen. She's done enough to destroy all of our lives."

"No one can save me, except myself, Nuss." I was precariously close to the line of saying too much and I paused to try to let my meaning sink in without telling him anything more. "When the time comes, I know what to do, and I need to know that you will do what's best for the realm."

"Dammit, Konig." He understood all too well what I meant to do.

If I had my own heart, it would be breaking. I wanted more time with him, with Clara, with all of them. I'd missed being part of their brotherhood, and this one night was not enough. "You and I both know that sometimes we must sacrifice one, to save the many."

His eyes flicked back and forth between mine, studying me, warring with himself. "Where is your crown, Mouse Prince? Tell me so that Clara and I can reclaim your spirit."

Finally, he asked the right question, although he was the only one I could ever give this answer to. "Ask your father, Prince of Snowflakes."

He jerked away, shocked by my demand. He'd never known his father, but he and the others were headed to his mother's court, and now after all these years, he'd finally thrown off the mantle of duty that made him care what others thought about him. He would confront the Snow Queen and learn what I had when I stole the Snowflake crown from the Church of the Christmas Star.

He was not a messiah. He was half magician.

His father was the one who'd given the Mouse Queen the spell that compelled me to obey her, using the crown of the Land of Animals as the surrogate for my heart. His father was the reason I had betrayed everyone I'd ever loved, including myself.

Nuss would find out soon enough

I used this jolt to Nuss's system to break off. He would follow me if I allowed it. I pulled on my own bit of magic and shifted into my mouse form and sprinted away, finding a crack in the castle's stone to escape through.

It had been less than an hour since I'd bonded with Clara and the other princes, and the Queen was on the rampage. With every passing minute, she tortured me more to call me to her side and sent out minions to track me.

The sooner I got back to her side, the sooner she could be distracted. Which wouldn't be easy. She knew what I'd done. I just had to convince her it was for her benefit, and not a betrayal.

I scurried through the castle, listening close for every bit of intel I could find. Not all of her subjects lived in filth and poverty. The chosen few who got to live and work in the castle and it's keep appeared no worse off than those that lived in any other court. Except every single person lived in fear.

I garnered tidbits about the soldiers who'd been freed from her fealty spell, and how the docks were now barren in case she sent more soldiers. There was many a whisper about what Princess Clara had done with her magic, and speculation about whether she was dangerous or not.

Overwhelmingly, the stories surmised that she'd used her magic for good, and very quietly reproached the Queen for sending her guard to attack innocent citizens. She may be greedy and self-serving, keeping her subjects under her thumb so tightly that they couldn't breathe, but she'd rarely blatantly attacked them.

She didn't need to. Not when she could use me to compel them to her will.

Today would be the last day she would be able to do that.

The last thing I wanted was for Clara to have to kill any of my people because they were forced to fight for the Queen against her. If I had to die breaking the curse so that she waltzed right into Christmas Castle and squashed my mother under her boot, that's what I would do.

All that mattered was that no Animal ever had to serve or suffer for anyone else, ever again.

Outside the throne room, my mother's voice rang out so loud, it echoed through the hallways. "Give me one good reason why I shouldn't kill you now, my ungrateful son."

I shifted back into the warrior form she preferred and walked in as if I was returning from a war well won. My heart beat in her hand and she clenched it tight, poking her nails into the arteries and veins.

I dropped to my knees, the pain too much. The spell of compulsion forced the words out of my mouth even though I couldn't breathe. "Because I've set a trap for you to capture them all."

She glared at me but released her tight grip on my heart. "I know what you've done. Did you think I wouldn't feel the bond you forged with the princes? Why didn't you simply bring them to me? I hope you don't think you can rekindle your relationship with them without suffering the consequences."

I gasped for air and lifted one knee to lean on while I caught my breath. I wouldn't give her the satisfaction of seeing me sweat. She'd given me a glimmer of hope and hadn't even realized. She could feel my bond with the princes, but she hadn't mentioned Clara. "No, my Queen. They're the ones who will feel your wrath. I've practically handed them over to you. You can feel the link with them all now because of the bond. Can't you?"

"Yes. I suppose you knew that I would. Fine then. But I don't like being kept in the dark. You will keep me informed of their whereabouts and how I can capture them. I don't think I'll send you back out on your own until I have them and that girl in my dungeon."

The zip of the demand, skittered across my heart, and she set it back in the box carved of bones she kept it in. The lid snapped shut with a faint glow of red magic.

"Yes, of course. My apologies for making you worry." I'd seen this kind of demand coming and was prepared. "All the princes are now running home to their mother's courts to ask them to march into battle against you."

She stared down at me and sniffed the air, her only nod to her own animal nature. "Their puny armies can't defeat me. They have only a few soldiers while I have the entirety of the people of the Land of Animals. Every man, woman, and child will fight for me."

"Yes, they will." Unfortunately. But with Princess Clara at their side, they had magic. Much more magic than was at the Queen's disposal. Less when I finally broke the curse.

"So, you've laid a trap for them, and I'll have the means to crush each of those damn queens." She wiped at the remnants of my life's blood that had dripped down her arm. I clenched my jaw and took shallow breaths, so she didn't sense my utter disgust. "And then no one will challenge my authority ever again."

"Allow me to go and prepare our armies."

"No, no. You are not the bastard I thought you were. Come my sweet son and tell me more of your plans." She patted the cushion next to her and once again, I did as I was told. "My new pet will prepare the armies."

She signaled to a steward waiting on her every beck and call. In only a moment, the man returned with something I hadn't counted on. "You remember Friedrich Stahlbaum? The young man I sent to you for training. He'll be commanding the armies from now on as his thanks for my assistance in helping him come into his powers."

That little shit Fritz looked down his nose at me and grinned. "Toy soldiers always was a favorite game of mine."

I wouldn't give a fuck about Fritz, except magic he shouldn't have access to sparkled at his fingers, and he pointed them right at me. "But it comes in second to the pure joy of torturing one's little sister and breaking her dollies."

LONG KEPT SECRETS

CLARA

When Nuss returned without Konig, all the warmth in my body dropped out like icicles off the roof in a spring thaw. The crown, still in my hand, burned, making my hand throb, and I welcomed the pain. Because it was the same hurt each of us were feeling.

Nuss shook his head and looked anywhere but at each of us. The stronger connection between the five of us, sizzled and snapped, angry and sad. That was more than I could take.

"We will find his crown. We will break the spell the Mouse Queen has over him with it, and we will save him." I shed the coat Nuss had given me and called my armor back to me. Our little shelter fell down around us, and in the next instant I was clothed once again in my bright red Christmas dress. But this time, it clung to me in a way that protected my body from the elements and any attacks.

Except an attack of pixies.

My skirts fluttered and wiggled until Freunde and Trost

popped out from underneath. They flew up in front of my face and buzzed about like happy bees. "Hello, my little sweets. I'm so pleased to see you here and unharmed."

Leb held out his hand and Trost perched on his thumb. "There you are little ones. Got any cookies? We'll need to be well fueled to go off to war."

The two tinkled at each other, spun in a zippy little circle and conjured up a wooden plate filled with steaming hot cookies and mugs of rich coffee. One bite of the thick, bready treat and a place I hadn't realized was empty filled with comfort. "Thank you, friends. You are a miracle."

Freunde went from pink to bright red, smiling so wide it filled up their little face. They buzzed around saying something more and I took a sip of the coffee waiting for them to finish. "I have no clue what you're saying. Does anyone else?"

Leb chuckled. "They said you should know that the Christmas Tree Forest has always been neutral ground. But they don't like how the Mouse Queen treats their land as if it is a resource to be plundered. They want you to know, they're ready to fight with you."

Oh, uh. I remembered when they'd helped me fend off the mice in the forest. "Thank you, friends, but I don't want you to get hurt. I'm afraid this battle will be more than tossing snowballs at mice with me."

The two pixies looked at each other and laughed and laughed and laughed until I thought they'd fall out of the air. I looked at Leb to see if he could interpret and he just shrugged.

When they got themselves under control they put their heads together, chittered some more and then spun their magic once again. This time instead of cookies or a hot mug, a carved box appeared, decorated with a scene straight out of the Christmas Tree Forest on the lid. In the center of the carving was a woman with golden curls, a glowing red sword at her side, wearing a uniform. The Vivandiere.

She was placing a broken crown made of pine boughs and pure joy atop a tree with hundreds of pixies on it glowing like strings of lights. It looked exactly like an illustration out of one of Drosselmeyer's storybooks. But this was no story I'd ever read.

Nuss looked down at the treasure box and carefully reached out to take it from them. "Your mother, when she hid the broken crown of the Land of Comfort and Joy. I thought it was just a story. They hold no court, have no queen--"

His words trailed off as Freunde and Trost laid it in his hand and lifted the lid of the box on either side. It opened to reveal the shining pine bough crown tucked inside.

"No queen until now," Nuss finished and plucked the broken crown out of the soft downy bedding. "I believe this belongs to you, princess."

I took the precious gift and slid it and the Snowflake crown onto the chain around my neck, to join the other four. Six crowns, seven lands. How could I have ever thought I wouldn't need this one too?

"I don't know what to say, but yet again. Thank you."

This gratitude wasn't met with their usual giggles, but happiness none the less. They flew up to my face and Freunde kissed my right cheek, and Trost the left. A zip of magic warmed my cheeks, then down to my heart.

"Well, that's not something I ever thought I'd see in all my fae fucking days." Zucker grinned and gave Trost a little spin. "You just bonded with a pixie. Well, two of them."

"I did?" Wasn't that lovely?

"We all felt the same warmth of the magic you did. It's not quite the same as when we consummate our bond with you, but the result is the same." Tau gave a little nod to Freunde who returned his gesture with a loopty-loop in the air.

I still wasn't sure how that was going to help me defeat the Mouse Queen, find the Animal crown, and save Konig. Until I looked around at each of my men and saw them in a completely different light.

Before, thanks to Tau's gift of empathy, I'd been able to sense their feelings. But now, looking at each of them, I could very clearly see the absolute beauty of their spirits. As if I was reading a recipe, I could see their wants, their needs, their hungers, and what would bring them comfort, all written there as if by magic.

"This is how you know exactly what we all need all the time?" I gaped at the two of them and they both nodded back at me. "Huh. Well, I can see how that could come in handy."

What this ability showed me wasn't just superficial needs, but deep core ones. One that was very apparent in all four of my men, was an intense need for me. Not just my body and the ecstasy we could bring each other, although that was there, but also for my love. I was overwhelmed by how much I meant to each of them, and how much they all meant to each other.

Nuss however had a dark spot of pain and longing, and it wasn't only for Konig. I knew what he needed and hoped that I could fulfill his wishes before we had to fight the Mouse Queen. If I was going to make him happy, we needed to do what Konig instructed and get our butts to the Snow Queen's court.

"What's the fastest way to get to the Land of Snowflakes?" Walking would take far too long, and we'd be vulnerable to an attack, especially while we were still in the Land of Animals.

"Can you use your magic to open us a portal? That's how most magicians traveled back in the day." Tau made a wide swirling motion in front of us.

"I can try." I was going on pure instinct. One of these days, I was scouring the ruins in my land for some kind of magic manual. For the first time in more years than I could remember, a longing for my mother hit me across my chest like a cool ache. Perhaps if life had been quite different, she would have been the one to teach me how to use my magic.

I cleared my throat and closed my eyes, imagining what I wanted to happen. My magic snapped and crackled, and when I peeked a glowing tear in air hung in front of us. "How do we know it will take us where we want to go?"

Nuss grabbed my hand and dragged me to the portal. "It can take you anywhere you want. You just have to set your intention in your mind. Take us to the Land of Snowflakes, Church of the Christmas star. That's where the Snow Queen starts her days."

Nuss's mother. A flurry of nerves bounced around my stomach thinking of meeting her. I had a feeling she wasn't going to be warm and welcoming like Mother Gingerbread or the Sweet Fae Queen.

We stepped into the portal, Nuss first, then me with the pixies on my shoulders, followed by Leb, Zucker, and Tau. I didn't feel the same disorientation as before. This time it was like we'd walked through a door and stepped from one room to another.

An enormous imposing building made of pure ice stood before us, the sunrise reflecting off the hundreds of angles making the whole thing look as if it was carved of diamonds. The prism light of rainbows reflected off a courtyard of pristine snow. Not a flake was out of place.

"Welcome to the Land of Snowflakes." Nuss squeezed my hand and led us through the intricately carved archway and into the church itself.

I wasn't sure what I expected, but aside from everything being made of snow and ice, the inside was just like an older style church back home. There were vaulted ceilings and stained glass - or rather ice windows, rows of pews, and even an altar at the front. But where in our Christian churches there would have been a cross, instead hung an enormous shining, sparkling seven-pointed star.

Nuss practically marched me down the aisle to the very

front pew where a woman, dressed all in white, knelt with her head bowed. At our approach, she stood, and so did the women, also in white garb but with lacy head coverings and veils on, surrounding her.

"Good, you've returned." She said calmly, as if we'd just come back from a trip to the market for bread. She eyed me up and down and gave an approving sort of blink, head-nod combo. "And you've found your consort as foretold. I'll make the arrangements for the bonding ceremony. What happened to your arm?"

Beside me, Zucker snickered but Tau gave him a smack on the arm. Leb blew out a harsh sigh and Nuss squeezed my hand tighter. What in the world was going on?

"I broke it in the human realm, and it cannot heal here." He waited for her response, but she was a glacier and didn't move a centimeter.

"And I'm sorry mother, but it's a too late for the traditions of the church. We're already bonded to the princess. All of us." Nuss raised his chin, readying himself for the backlash of what he'd just said.

Because of my pixie spiritual sight, it only took me an instant to understand the relationship between Nuss and his mother, the Snow Queen. Her spirit was ragged with a thousand fears, and to protect herself, she'd become cold and harsh. I wanted to wrap her up in a great big hug and feed her cookies and hot chocolate, warm her with intimate conversation and assurances that she, and her son, were loved.

I think the cookies and chocolate part was coming from my sweet pixies, because she did not look like she'd eaten a cookie in an awfully long time. Unlike Mother Gingerbread and the Sweet Fae Queen, or even the majority of women I'd met in the Winter Realm, the Snow Queen was thin and hard lined.

At Nuss's words the veiled women gasped and murmured to

each other, but the queen simply raised one eyebrow and folded her hands. "That is not as we planned."

Zucker, Tau, and Leb each stepped up closer and laid a hand on Nuss's shoulders, physically showing their solidarity and lending him their strength. I squeezed his hand. I wanted to slap some sense into this woman, tell her to let the love she had buried deep in her heart for her son flow free, to wake her the hell up. But we didn't have time to heal wounds as deep as the ones between her and Nuss.

We had a war to get to. Which still wasn't what I wanted, but I wasn't sure what else we could do at this point.

Nuss stared at his mother for another moment, and I saw the resolve he had inside solidify. "Nonetheless, I am fulfilling my true destiny. I expect the Land of Snowflakes too not only support but celebrate that. But not today. Now we prepare for war."

The Snow Queen's spirit thawed just a tiny bit, and a bloom of respect for her son's commanding leadership grew inside. She could find out later that some of that was borrowed from Konig. She nodded in deference and the tight grip Nuss had on my hand loosened.

My turn. "Can you please contact the Sweet Fae Queen, the DewDrop Queen, and Mother Gingerbread? We need to gather everyone as soon as possible."

She snapped her fingers and one of the veiled women stepped to her side. "Send angels to the Queens. Tell them it's time for the reign of the Mouse Queen to end. They'll know what to do."

Oh, yeah. I could see the Snow Queen being a general in the Nutcracker army. She somehow already had everything organized for this war to happen. I was just glad she was on our side.

"Now, please come with me to the castle and we'll prepare

you and your... princess and... bonded mates as well." The Queen turned to leave but Nuss stopped her.

"First I need you to tell me about my father."

"Uh-oh." Leb said.

"You have no father."

Uh. Was he supposed to be an immaculate conception?

"I am not laying any blame on you for whatever may have happened in the past, mother. None of that matters now. You will tell me about why he knows, or knew, the location of the Land of Animal's piece of the broken crown. I won't lose Konig because of your secrets."

The Snow Queen looked around at the rest of us and gritted her teeth. She hadn't expected to be called out today. This should be fun. Freunde wiggled on my shoulder and gave my ear a little tug. Right, right, right. I didn't have to just stand here and watch this play out. Nuss was my consort, my love, and I could help.

I grabbed the Snow Queen's hand, and at first, she didn't want to give it to me, but I didn't relent. "I can see the love you once had inside of you. That's nothing to be ashamed of. Let it flourish again."

She shook her head and clicked her tongue, but I could see the ice breaking around her heart. She sighed, then waved the veiled women away. "Leave us."

The women looked around at each other like they didn't know what to do. "Go. Find the guards and have my armor prepared if you need something to do. Shoo."

They scurried away and when they were gone, the Queen sat. "I have carried this burden for so long, I don't know what I will do without it."

I sat next to her to lend her my support, hoping she would understand that I was here for her, even though we didn't even know each other. She patted my hand and gave me a wan smile. With a quick eyes-closed breath, she said, "I loved your father even though our bonding was forbidden. Except for you, my son, our messiah, nothing good came of our love."

Nuss knelt down in front of her. "I'm sorry this is so painful for you. I wish that it wasn't. Who was he?"

She set her chin and I watched her spirit swirl in her chest, trying to hide her own wounds. "You're half magician, but I never wanted you to know."

"That's why I have magic?" Nuss looked like he was about to fall over.

She nodded and so much more made sense. "Yes. But I hoped to hide that from you because the magic he gave you is so dark. Your father is the very same magician who betrayed his own kind and gave the Mouse Queen the spell she used to not only win the Magician's War, but that enslaved her own people to her."

Everyone in the room except for me whispered his name all at the same time. Some in awe, some in revulsion or fear, and one with a tainted love. "Drosselmeyer."

LETTING GO

CLARA

*D*rosselmeyer?

The man who wrote the fairy stories of the Winter Realm? The one I was supposed to marry?

Holy snowflakes. That made so much sense, but also how in the world did I not figure that out? I was absolutely flabbergasted. My mind swirled with so many questions that just created more questions. "Let me get this straight. Herr Drosselmeyer, the sweet storyteller and toy maker, is some kind of evil magician from the Winter Realm?"

All eyes turned to me and now they were as surprised as I was. The queen was the first to close her gaping mouth and reply to my question with her own. "Drosselmeyer is in the human realm?"

"I guess so? He's not any kind of magician. He makes toys and writes books for children. I... was engaged to marry him." That last part had my stomach roiling. Not because he was evil.

I just couldn't imagine being with him, not after I'd found my princes.

Leb got out his axe and gave it a fierce twirl. "That won't be happening, love. I'll cut him in two if he shows his face in our realm and even looks at you."

"I don't think he will." If he was planning on coming through the portal, wouldn't he have done that on the night of the party? But he'd given me a gift and left. He'd given me Nuss. Those were not the actions of a mad magician hellbent on subjugating the Winter Realm.

It was what a father trying to make amends might do though.

Nuss was too quiet, and I looked up at him. His spirit was a mess of confusion, the same as mine. "That's how I was able to open the portal and enter your world before the clock struck twelve on the first day of Christmas. Not some special messiah of the Christmas Star powers. Drosselmeyer, my father, helped me. My whole life has been a lie."

"No, son. You were born under the Christmas Star, and you will save our realm. The teaching of the church--"

"Stop," Nuss roared and swept the accoutrement from the altar. "You've lied to the Church, and you've all lied to me. You've tried to teach me that I was something so special that my duty was all that mattered in this life. But none of it matters. Do you want to know what does?"

He was seething and Leb, Zucker, Tau, and I let him.

The Snow Queen jumped up and paced back and forth before the altar. Her world was crashing down around her because of her secrets and lies. "Nuss, you must believe I did all of this for you. You're what matters."

His chest heaved, but his voice went dangerously quiet. "No, mother. You're wrong, and I doubt you'll ever understand. Your plan for me and the Winter Realm is just as bad as the Mouse Queen's, because you're greedy. You think this pristine privileged life we lead is the only valuable existence. But what is any of it worth without the love of a good woman or man."

She shook her head vehemently and pointed to the group of us. "Love is the lie, son. You think these rebels love you? They don't. They love what you represent. When we march on Christmas Castle, you're going to be a King. They'll worship at your feet."

"You think I care about worship?" He threw his hands up in the air, and sparks of blue magic shot out of his fingers like icy lightning. I'd never seen him do anything but access mine and Fritz's magic, and via our blood at that. This was definitely not mine.

The blue sparks struck the ceiling of the church, sending crumbles of ice raining down on us all. Nuss didn't even notice. "People are dying, mother. We're protected in our snowy hills with our churches of ice, guarded by the best dressed nutcrackers in all the kingdoms. But the rest of the realm is starving to death, being crushed under the boot of a despot."

The queen backed away, looking both afraid and ashamed. I joined Nuss up on the dais and put a hand on his arm, saying nothing, just showing him that I was on his side. He took several deep breaths and some of the anger faded. He took my hand and kissed it but had a few more words for his mother. This time in a calm, measured, yet still adamant tone. "That's what I fight for, that is why I lead the rebellion against the Mouse Queen, not because I want to be a King."

She'd been a pretty horrible mom, and I was glad he'd broken this lie of hers open. But she had been trying to protect her son. It had made her hard and skewed her view of the world.

She had been in love with Drosselmeyer once upon a time, and he'd left her in the wake of a war. So I understood how hurt she was inside. Not that it excused her actions. I wouldn't be allowing her to control or manipulate our lives anymore now that we all saw the truth about her.

But I also hoped she could either change, or step back and let Nuss lead his people and this rebellion for the good of everyone in the realm. "Can you let go of your fears and join us? Nuss is a great leader, protector, and his heart is full of so much love for this realm and his fellow citizens. Don't let your broken heart hurt others anymore."

She looked at me and she'd lost that stern no-one-is-good-enough-for-my-son look from before. She seemed lonely and plain scared now. "If you defeat the Mouse Queen in this coming battle, you'll become the new Queen of the Winter Realm. No one else has the magic to do so. Has Drosselmeyer trained you and orchestrated all of this?"

I thought about my last interactions with Herr Drosselmeyer on the night of the Christmas party. "I don't think his intentions with me were ever evil. He told me something strange about wondering if he'd done enough to prepare me."

"Prepare you for what? Does he intend to use your magic to send us into chaos once again?" The Snow Queen looked to Nuss again. "Can your Princess of Spirit and Magic fend off their combined magic? What if Drosselmeyer is coming back to support the Mouse Queen? We can't defeat that kind of power without a magician on our side."

All this talk of bringing magic back and using it for battle and destruction left me feeling cold. Magic shouldn't be weaponized the way they had. It should provide comfort and joy like the way the pixies used it, or even to live authentically like when the Animals used it to shift between forms.

"No. I think he wants me to make amends for his mistakes." His stories had not only been about adventure, but lessons in kindness, doing the right thing, and love. The Vivandiere had searched for the pieces of the broken crown but hadn't gathered them for herself. She'd left them hidden, and ready for whoever would need them someday.

Left them for me.

What was he trying to tell me?

"The stories are all true." I murmured the reminder to myself. If that was so, the crown from the land of Animals should be buried in the heart of their kingdom. I supposed that meant Christmas Castle. But that didn't seem like somewhere so deep it could never be retrieved.

The heart.

The heart.

The heart of the kingdom.

Konig was the heart.

Holy broken crowns.

I was making a huge intuitive leap, but I had to remember that this wasn't the human world and magic was possible here. Magic that could be used for good or evil. If I was wrong, then we were going to lose everything in this battle.

"Clara, what is it? Your magic is swirling, and I can feel your mind working." Nuss signaled to the others, and they surrounded me, blocking the Queen's view. That was good. I needed a little space from her erratic fear.

"We need to get back to the Land of Animals quickly, but I don't want to do anything that will put Konig in more danger. I have an idea, but we need a little bit of time. Can we distract the Mouse Army without putting either Konig's soldiers or ours in too much jeopardy?"

"The Snowflake army has been training for battle for a long time. It will be hard to explain to anyone why they can't directly attack, injure, or kill any of the Mouse Army, so I don't think we should send them in. But no one would harm a Snowflake nun. We can send them in to minister to the poor. That would throw the Mouse Queen off guard, and it's not like they'll be much use around her for very much longer."

"Yes, perfect, Nuss." I squeezed his hand and looked to the others.

Leb scratched his beard. "I think the Gingerbread Vikings could probably do something to keep them at bay. A bit of hide and seek. We did avoid surrendering to the Mouse Queen for all these years. I'm sure mother can hold out a bit longer."

"Perfect." I gave him a kiss on the cheek and pinched his butt as a promise for more later.

"The DewDrop assassins are trained in stealth." Tau folded his arms and gave a confident nod. "If I instruct them not to kill, but to do some espionage and gather intel, they will do as they're told."

Zucker cleared his throat, but I saw the twinkle in his eye at his idea for our plan. "The Sweet Fae soldiers aren't as skilled in the art of combat, but I'm sure they could, let's say distract, Konig's men and women with their charms long enough for you to create the sneaky masterplan I see you hatching."

"But what are we going to do about her?" Nuss hooked his thumb over his shoulder to indicate his mother.

She wasn't going to change overnight, and we definitely needed to make sure she didn't get over her shame once she was out of our site. "We do need someone to talk to the other queens. The Angel missives probably have them already freaking out, and we want everyone on the same page. Could she take care of that?"

"Yes. She can," Nuss said firmly. There had definitely been a power shift in the Land of Snowflakes. "Mother, it's time for you to step down. I will lead our people, including our armies today. I am asking you to be a figurehead as the revered queen. But if you can't accept that you need to say so now."

"It's time we take back our realm before Drosselmeyer or the Mouse Queen can use their magic to enslave us all." The Snow Queen narrowed her eyes and I saw her retreat to her cold facade again.

She wasn't going to like what I was about to say. I looked first to Leb, Zucker, Tau, and Nuss. "Do you trust me?"

I knew that they did, but I needed some reassurance because this was the scariest thing I'd ever set out to do, and it wasn't what anyone wanted from me. They nodded, and their spirits shined with their affirmations. "Good, because we're going to gather all the queens at the fields of Christmas Castle at first light. But not to battle."

"You think our show of force will get her to come to the table?" The Snow Queen asked.

I shook my head. "No, we're going to surrender."

Leb dropped his axe and the Snow Queen tripped over the altar step. Nuss took my hand and kissed it. "I see. You are a clever girl, my Queen."

His mother glared at us, but that was okay. Hers was not the love and approval I needed. "We can't win against the legions of the Mouse Army. Not when they're being compelled to fight with no worry for their own lives. As long as the Mouse Queen controls them and Konig, we're doomed."

"Surrender can't be the answer, princess." The Snow Queen didn't know me and had no reason to trust me. Even this little bit she was giving me by not outright challenging my plan was more than I could have hoped for with such a crazy idea at stake.

"No, but it will get me in front of Konig and the Mouse Queen, and we all know that's her goal. But that's how I'll recover the Animal Crown."

The Snow Queen gave me a different kind of look, like she didn't expect such a diabolical plan from me. "Then you can deal the killing blow and end her reign."

"We will end her reign." But it wouldn't be by killing her. I hoped.

"Good. Then let us make haste. Tomorrow morning, we march on Christmas Castle." She signaled that we should follow her and headed toward the same exit her ladies had gone through.

"There's one more thing I need to do before I'm ready." And it didn't involve her. I stood and stepped over to Nuss, and lifted his hand to my chest, where the Snowflake crown dangled with the others on my necklace.

His eyes went dark and sparkly, and he smiled. "Will you please excuse us, mother? We need the room."

Her face went white, and she coughed. Nuss gave her a look that I thoroughly enjoyed, and she huffed, then lifted her hem and hurried away.

Before she was even gone, Nuss lifted me into his arms and kissed me. Then he laid me on the alter and climbed up over me. "It's time we consummated our bond, princess."

Thank God.

DIRTY REFORMATION

NUSS

The pixies shot off, flying away at a blinding speed. In a rush of wings and snow, they erected barriers of intricate lace across the entryways, giving us privacy. This kind of bonding wasn't what they cared about, except for the joy it brought to us all. I'd thank them for their thoughtfulness and discretion with some gratitude of my own later.

This church had taught me to deny all that was decadent and pleasurable in life. They made me feel unworthy of the love around me while at the same time building me up into the image of what they wanted me to be. All under false pretenses. I wasn't some messiah, given magic by the Christmas Star to bring glory to the Land of Snowflakes, and today, I learned the truth.

I was going to destroy every rule they'd ever shackled me with and rebuild this institution into something worthy of my beautiful princess, my fellow nutcrackers, my mouse prince, and all that I genuinely believed in.

Zucker and Tau came up to the alter on either side of us, and Leb finished the circle by coming up at Clara's head. We were all feeling the absence of Konig, but I had to have faith that someday soon we would all be together. Until then, we'd do what he'd told us to.

I had to believe that consummating the bond with Clara while the Snowflake crown was in her possession would still bring her more power that she could then use to save Konig, save the Winter Realm, and save me.

I brushed a soft kiss across one of Clara's eyelids, and then the other. "You've been telling us all along that your purpose in the Winter Realm wasn't about usurping the Mouse Queen, nor war, nor rebellion. We weren't really listening. I, for one, held tight to my own agenda until I was forced to experience the real purpose for bringing you back the Winter Realm.

"And what is that my sweet Nutcracker?" Clara reached up and brushed a lock of hair out of my eyes. How in the world she had put up with the five of us not seeing her true essence all this time was beyond me.

"Your love." My heart pounded out a jingling staccato beat just being in her presence, knowing how deeply she felt for us and for her true home. I wasn't worthy of her, but I would spend the rest of my life making sure that I was. "This entire adventure, the rebellion, finding the pieces of the broken crown, rediscovering all the Winter Realm is and could be, it has all been about spreading love and repairing the wounds left on our realm from greed, power, and hate. I'm sorry I didn't understand that before."

Leb tucked his finger under Clara's chin and tipped her head back so she was looking up at him. "I don't know about the rest of these cookie crumbles you've been hanging about, lass, but I've always been lusting after your love. They're the ones who've had their heads up their arses."

While Leb's declaration was light-hearted and meant to

break the tension, it was clear that he wanted her to understand the depth of his love for her. He wasn't wrong either. It had been his idea in the first place that we all become her consorts in the fashion of the Gingerbread Viking society. When we'd made that pact, I'd agreed to keep the peace among us, but had been secretly wondering all this time if she should belong only to me and me to her. That was the church's prophecy. Such utter reindeer shit.

Choosing us all had not only made her stronger, but each of us as well. I'd never felt closer to anyone than I did Leb, Tau, and Zucker. Not even when we'd all trained and fought together in the Magician's war. We'd definitely bonded as brothers in arms when we thought Konig had betrayed us, but now I understood them at such a deep level, and I loved them. Not exactly in the same way as I felt about Clara and Konig, but it was an important love, and I was better for having experienced it. Mostly due to Leb's foresight.

His jest and declaration of love made Clara smile and relax. While I'd meant for my declaration to be serious, I also wanted her smiling and happy. There were likely some tears ahead of us in the morning. For now, we would revel in each other and bask in the delight of sharing her body and her love.

"Yes, my spicy Viking, I know. Thank goodness they have us to show them how to celebrate, hmm?"

"Hey now," Zucker said. "No one had to drag me kicking and screaming into falling head over heels for our princess. I do believe I was the one who suggested the group bonding sessions. And by bonding, I mean orgasms."

He waggled his eyebrows at us all and Tau rolled his eyes, but in a way that showed exactly how much he enjoyed his lover's teasing.

"Mmm-hmm." Tau jumped up onto the altar with me and Clara, leaned across us and gave Zucker a searing kiss, ending it by pulling his lip between his teeth and sucking on it. "That didn't have anything to do with how much you've wanted to see our Snowflake captain here lose all of his control and his mind when we finally got him into bed, would it?"

Zucker looked a little dazed by Tau's kiss and shook his head. "Uh, maybe?"

I was surprised by how much it warmed my heart to see them being free and easy with each other, especially when poking fun at my chastity. They'd had to hide the real nature of their feelings for each other, and apparently for me, for too long.

As had I with Konig.

No more.

Love was love no matter what, and Clara helped us all realize how much more important that was than any crown. If not for the magic within the broken pieces of the Winter crown that Clara needed, I'd destroy the damn thing so it would never control our decisions again.

"I only wish that Konig was here with us too. But he's given us this respite to so that we can come together under one banner and bring the people of the Realm together. I for one don't intend to fail in our mission. But first, I'm going to finally consummate the bond with my true Queen, right here, right now."

The nuns and my mother, and probably many a citizen of the Land of Snowflakes who'd been as indoctrinated as I had been, would see this as a desecration. Maybe that's exactly what we needed to throw off the oppressive yoke of the institution.

I was choosing to view the consummation of my bond with Clara as a new consecration of what I intended to make the Church into - all that Clara herself found holy. Which was kindness and love. That was the real spirit of what the Star represented. She was our guiding light.

Zucker smiled and said, "Glad to see the rest of us have

finally rubbed off on you, captain. It's about time you let us dirty you up."

What he didn't realize was that this act, with all of them here to witness and even participate in, would cleanse my spirit.

Clara magicked her armor into a softer cushion than the block of ice the altar provided, and within a second, she was completely naked beneath me. I sat back and worked to remove my jacket, but my arm didn't want to move in the ways I needed it to.

Tau was the first one to help. He halted the frustrated shake of my arm by grabbing the sleeves. "Allow me, Captain."

He carefully slid the jacket off my shoulders, and then went to work on the fastenings of my shirt. Under his stealthy hands, I didn't feel helpless or pitied, but as if this was part of a ritual I'd missed by denying each and every one of them access to my body.

Zucker jumped up and joined us, reaching for my waist. "There will be pleasure for us all, but for the time being, my inexperienced captain, allow us to show you how it's done. On your back."

He pushed me down, and Tau grabbed Clara up, handing her over to Leb. Then the both of them expertly stripped me. They slowly pulled off my boots, my uniform off my legs, my shirt from my arms, not with efficiency, but with soft teasing caresses so that by the time I was naked, I was also hard and panting, dying to be touched and tasted.

Zucker took my cock in hand and gave me a few hard strokes, something I'd done far too often on my own. Clara's soft gasp matched my own groan, and I could feel the magic sparking between the two of us. Tau signaled to Leb, and they positioned Clara with her knees spread open wide, straddling me, her pussy right above my cock.

"Lean forward, sweet thing. Let us make you feel good." Zucker notched the tip of my cock into her already wet folds and used my body as his tool to tease her clit. The Snowflake crown lit up and glowed with a shining blue light that swirled out, reaching for me.

Leb dropped open his belt and drew his huge cock out right above my head. "Come here, sweet lass and let me fuck your mouth. You'll get nice and wet from sucking on my cock."

I knew exactly how turned on I'd been when Konig had thrust between my lips. I watched as Leb fed his shaft between Clara's lips and holy fuck, he was right. In only a few short strokes, Zucker's hand on my cock was slick and sliding over and around the head, driving me crazy to be inside of her.

Her soft whimpers turned to pleading moans and I had to grit my teeth and clench my fists not to simply jerk my hips and shove my way into her waiting cunt. I'd waited so long for this, for her, and it was all so much better than I'd ever imagined when I'd fantasized about taking her on my own.

Zucker didn't relent, edging both Clara and I closer to coming. Our sweet princess shuddered and groaned, her first orgasm taking over her senses. The swirls of her magic rose up around her and that connection we'd all had in the grotto reconnected.

Her orgasm became ours, and only Zucker's hard grip on the base of my cock when she came kept me from spurting all over his hand. Leb though, grabbed her hair and pushed deep into her mouth. "Fuck, lass, that's it. I'm going to come in your throat, and I want to feel you swallow me down."

I watched Clara's throat work and swallow almost all of Leb's seed, but when he pulled out, some dribbled out her lips. I'd come watching her get fucked by these three already and seeing her take their seed had turned me the fuck on, even when I insisted it was from afar. This time, up close, and with my own cock so close to finally giving her my own seed, was more than I could handle.

I grabbed her cheeks and pulled her mouth down to mine,

kissing her, tasting Leb's seed for myself, and making her bond with him my own as well. She pressed her chest against mine and moaned into my mouth. I tried to push my hips up, to join us together, but Zucker chuckled and held me tight.

Clara broke our kiss and gasped for breath. "Please, I need--"

"Shh, sweetness, let us take care of everything."

And boy did they ever. I stared deep into Clara's eyes as they guided me into her and then sat her back so that she was fully seated on my cock. Then Zucker crawled up behind her, cupping and caressing her tits as he helped her slowly move up and down on my shaft. Tau jumped onto the altar behind Zucker and tucked himself tight against his back. The three of them moved together, creating a mind meltingly slow rhythm of bodies, thrusting, fucking, and driving us all into oblivion.

Leb moved to the side and pushed his hand between Clara's legs, cupping her mound in his palm and rubbed her clit with his thumb. With each touch, thrust, kiss, and caress, the magic connecting us all strengthened and grew, until we were all calling out each other's names.

Clara reached down and cupped my cheek as the magic rose up all around her. She brushed her thumb across my lips, before shoving the tip between my teeth. I gave her the delicious bite that I loved. I didn't need to draw her blood to make the magic work this time. My own magic, the part of me that had been suppressed for far too long, joined with hers and I was lost.

With one more thrust, both of our magics exploded out of us, my blue with her red, and our spirits were one. She closed in ecstasy and her inner muscles spasmed as she came on my cock. I didn't hold anything back from her or the others this time, and my own orgasm lightninged up my spine and I roared out her name as I filled her cunt with my seed.

Zucker and Tau both groaned out their own climaxes and I felt their seed on my legs. Leb even came for a second time and smeared the evidence of it across Clara's lips.

For the first time since she'd consummated the bonds with any of her consorts, all of our spirits swirled together, drawn out by the combination of our magic. While Konig wasn't here, both she and I sensed him with us. He knew exactly what we were doing and was pleased we'd obeyed his commands.

I wanted to stay like this with them all forever.

Someday, we would.

But today we had to rescue Konig and change the fate of the Winter Realm.

Clara collapsed onto me and laid her head on my chest for just long enough to appreciate the new bonds formed between us. My magic had mixed with hers, and she would now have the power of six of the seven crowns fully. Hopefully that was enough to rescue Konig and maybe, just maybe, find a way to uncovering the Animal crown too.

Konig deserved to experience everything I just did with Clara himself, not just through me or the sex act without the actual bond.

"I love you all so very much. I know what we're about to do is dangerous, so I just wanted to say that out loud so there is never any question of how precious and important your love is to me."

One by one, we each said our I love you's too and the star hanging on the ice wall above us shimmered and shined like it never had before.

REINDEER GAMES

CLARA

None of us wanted to, but we got up from our love making, all more determined than before to save Konig and the Winter Realm. Nuss led us to a small room off the main chapel with facilities to clean up. We performed those absolutions, helping each other wash and dress, all in silence as if we were performing an ancient ritual that only we knew. Then we left the church and entered the courtyard outside.

The town was so quiet that it felt deserted. All the quaint wooden houses frosted in banks of snow looked like the kind of winter village I used to see in shop's Christmas displays. I wouldn't even be surprised if a train tooted its horn and chugged in a circle around the outer boundaries of the village.

It all felt too perfect and not at all like home. The sooner we got back to the Land of Animals to put our family back together, the better. We'd ask the Queens to make the arrangements to march on Christmas Castle in the morning. I doubted they could get everyone organized any faster than that. But it didn't mean we couldn't sneak out into the night and be there, ready and waiting for the surrender.

"I don't want to spend the night here. I want to get as close to Konig as we can. If I open another portal, where should we set up camp for the night?" We couldn't go back to the swamp behind the castle, or really anywhere too close. If we were captured before the surrender, we might not get close enough to the Mouse Queen to rescue Konig and get the crown.

I wasn't a hundred percent sure what I was going to do after we got Konig back, but even that would be a win for today. My Nutcrackers were sure that me having all the magic was the key to overcoming the Mouse Queen. But without a battle, and I wasn't willing to fight lest people get hurt or even die, I didn't actually know how to make the Mouse Queen see how destructive her rule was.

Her greed had corrupted her, and I wasn't sure even love could conquer that.

But I did know that having all my consorts and my pixies did, in fact, make me stronger. The gifts I gained from bonding with them, the warrior spirit, the empathy, the charm, command, the spirit sight, and now Nuss's protective magic, were a boon to be sure. But it was their love that gave me the confidence to face the Mouse Queen down and try to save this Realm.

Nuss shook his head. "I don't think you should use your magic. We've seen how finite it can be. Powerful, yes, but it depletes quickly. You need to save every scrap of energy you have for tomorrow."

He wasn't wrong. The last time I'd used my magic to break the curse on the Mouse Army soldiers, had been exhausting. "How will we get back to Christmas Castle then?"

"With a little magic," Nuss said. He led us to the compound that must be the Snow Queen's castle, although it was much more demure than the other castles I'd been to. That surprised me. The Church was the most opulent building in the town by far. The Snow Castle was not dissimilar to the other rows of houses, except for being pure white, a few building lengths longer and with a courtyard of its own.

Around the side were stables, filled with reindeer happily munching on hay. A young man with blond hair not unlike Nuss's was there feeding the animals. When he saw us, and specifically Nuss, he went wide-eyed and touched his chest in a ritualistic fashion that I realized when he was done, was meant to be as if he'd drawn a star over his chest.

"Your highness, please forgive me. I didn't know you were here. I'm so sorry, I wouldn't have--" The boy stumbled over his words and bowed over and over, so flustered he was riling up the reindeer.

Nuss put his hand on the boy's shoulder. "It's okay. You don't have to either be nervous around me or supplicate yourself. It's I who should be apologizing to you for interrupting your work."

"Oh, no, your highness. I'm only a ... and you're...." He waved his hand toward himself, and then to Nuss, then made the sign of the star again.

"I'm the consort to the Queen. She's the one who deserves our praise and awe, not me." Nuss indicated me and gave a little bow just the like boy.

The boy took one look at me, my bright red dress, and he peed his pants. Literally. "You're the lost princess."

I knew I wasn't supposed to use my magic, but I used just a tiny bit to clean up his trousers and calm his excitable spirit. "I'm not lost anymore, and I want you to know how much I appreciate that you take such loving care of these reindeer. Is it okay if we hitch up a sleigh to use?"

He still looked like he was going to keel over or fall down at my feet, but I gave him a smile and let him get a hold of himself.

A moment later, he took a deep breath and nodded. "I'd be happy to prepare a sleigh for you, my lady."

He ran off and I whispered to Nuss, "Does everyone always act like that around you here?"

He sighed. "They've been taught to believe I'm some kind of messiah. I'm afraid it's going to take more than simple assurances and words to convince them otherwise."

Leb stuck his head between ours. "Once they find out what a sex god you are, they'll forget all about the other stuff."

It didn't take long before the boy had eight reindeer hitched up to a big red sleigh. He looked shyly over at me. "I thought you might like this one because of the color."

"You're right. I do." I wished I had some other way to show my appreciation for his thoughtfulness. All it took was that gratitude thought, and Freunde and Trost appeared. They spun around my head and conjured up a small square package wrapped in red paper and tied with a golden bow. "Perfect."

I handed the little box to the boy. "Thank you."

His eyes darted around like he was checking to make sure it was okay. But then he lifted the lid of the box and lifted out a star shaped chocolate, dusted in red and blue glitter. He sniffed it, grinned, and then popped it into his mouth. "Mmm. Sweet dewdrop, my favorite flavor."

Tau snorted and tried to cover it with a cough, but Zucker just straight out laughed. "Kid, I think you've got a little fae in you."

Nuss blushed. Blushed. Then he dismissed the young man with another thanks and sent him back to his work.

Nuss rubbed the closest reindeer's muzzle and it leaned into him, then looked at me. "Will they fly? If we're going to make a statement, this is as good a way as any to arrive on the field of battle. And if Konig is there and can see us, he'll know we're there for him."

It was perfect. "Let's find out."

In another few moments we were airborne, with Nuss steering the bright red sleigh over the snowy landscape. We left the Land of Snowflakes behind and with every minute and mile closer to the Land of Animals, my heart pinged with pain for my Mouse Prince.

This time I better understood the landscape of the Realm and felt the pull to the Land of Spirit and Magic. Someday soon I would take all five of my consorts and my pixies back to my homeland and rebuild a better and kinder Kingdom. The kind filled with little ginger headed Viking princes and princesses, sweet Fairies, gentle Dewy Fae babies, proud Snowflakes, and rascally little warriors.

We landed in the icy field outside Christmas Castle, and I was surprised to see gathered troops already. I should have known the Gingerbread Vikings would be the first to answer the call. I met Mother Gingerbread with arms outstretched and she clasped me into a bear of a hug. "I sure hope you know what you're doing, lass."

I leaned into her. "I'm not entirely sure that I do."

"Auch, well. We'll help you figure it out." She held me out at arm's length again and looked me dead in the eyes. "We're behind you come hell or high snow. It's time this Realm had a good dust up. We haven't had one since your mother left."

She guided me toward her tent and the scent of spices warmed me down to my spirit. "You knew my mother?"

We all followed her inside and sat down beside her mates, who were sharpening their weapons to ready for battle. She stopped and gave each man a kiss and then sat on a cushion and indicated ones for the rest of us to rest on.

"Grand adventures the Vivandiere and I had in our youth before the Magician's wars. She saw them coming, you know. That's why she broke the Winter Queen's crown and hid the pieces. But now you're here and have them all gathered up again."

I shivered and bit my lip. "All but one."

"Aye. But you'll get it. That's what your plan is all about, isn't it? Surrendering to the Mouse Queen to get back the final crown and control all the magic in the realm?" She looked at me sideways as if testing that I knew what she was talking about.

"Yes." Although, that wasn't my main objective. Even though it probably should be. Was I being selfish not focusing on the larger mission at hand of saving the whole Realm from the corruption and greed that had overtaken it? I knew I'd only scratched the surface of what my magic could do. How much more powerful would I be if I had all seven crowns and the love of the princes, pixies, and people?

"But what do I do once I have the magic?"

Mother Gingerbread's brow wrinkled with her frown. She glanced around the room and caught the eyes of her men. They each nodded in turn and got up and left. Then she said to my consorts, "Lads, we have some Queenly business to discuss, your mate and I. Would you excuse us?"

I held out my hand to them, not liking being away from them even by a few feet. "Whatever you need to say, you can say to them as well. We are as one."

Mother Gingerbread smiled, as if that had been a test. "Right you are. Now listen to me. This realm has been ruled by powerful women for as long as history reaches back."

I didn't know that. How could I?

She lowered her voice. "It wasn't until men decided we needed a ruler over us all, someone who could control all the power, that our ancestors began to fall into chaos. They should have left it to their Queens."

"That's not how I heard it. I thought the Queens were squabbling and they chose a Queen over the whole realm to help settle those squabbles."

"Cookie crumbles. That's propaganda left over from the Magician's war." Her voice wasn't quiet anymore. She was getting riled up and the gift of the warrior in me matched her energy. "So now you tell me, ClaraMarie Stahlbaum, Crown of Steel Court, Queen of the Land of Spirit, knowing you're descended from Queens, do you really think that when the time comes, you won't know what to do?"

I shrugged. I hadn't been raised in the Winter Realm to know my own history nor was I brought up by a Queen. Everything I knew about being a confident woman I'd learned here in the past few days, and mostly from the way my men treated me, how they trusted me, and how they made me feel.

"You've been tested repeatedly, and you've fought for everything you believed in from the second you got here. Trust me and trust your men. We all believe in you."

"As do I," the SugarPlum Queen stood in the doorway to the tent. Behind her was who I had to assume was the DewDrop Queen. She gave me only a reverent nod and yet, I very much felt her support like a warm hug around my heart. I understood now where Tau got his empathetic powers. Except hers seemed to be able to project her feelings to others too.

The Snow Queen was the last to enter, and with a whammy. "Your mother hid you from this Realm to keep you safe. I hope you will use that gift now for the good of all."

I took a deep breath and nodded. "That's what I'm here to do."

"Good. Because the sun is rising and it's time we went to battle. Even if it's only for show. I just hope whatever you have planned works." She swirled around, her snowy white skirts sparkling in the rays of sunlight from outside.

We followed her out and I couldn't believe the incredible army of people that stood gathered on the field. Most were dressed in the same uniform of the Nutcracker, but there were also ballerinas, Vikings, and flower capped fae dotting the field.

The Snow Queen raised her arm over her head and a staff of

ice formed in her hands. She shouted and the sound echoed across the field. "To our new Vivandiere. May she save us all."

Every single person on the field, Snowflake, Fae, and Gingerbread alike, replied in response with their own war cries. But then Nuss held out his hand for the staff and the Snow Queen lowered her chin and handed it over.

He lifted the staff in the air, and it filled with his blue magic. He shot a bolt of it into the sky and shouted. "Today, we march not in the name of war, but in the name of love. May the Christmas Star bless us with victory."

Then her grabbed me in his arm and kissed me like there was no tomorrow.

BROKEN SPELLS

KONIG

I felt the moment Clara, Nuss, Zucker, Tau, and Leb returned to the Land of Animals. Their bonds were even stronger, and their emotions washed over me. I'd had to hide my arousal when Nuss had finally consummated his true bond with Clara. Their combined magic had gone straight to my cock and had me so fucking hard for hours.

I struggled against the ropes tying me to the throne while Fritz laughed and poked at the already open wounds on my chest. He was the kind of magician we'd gone to war to defeat. One taste of power had corrupted him completely.

I couldn't imagine what would have happened if he'd gained access to the Land of Spirit and Magic like Clara had. My mother had only taught him how to draw on the latent power he had inside of him, and already he was greedy for more.

I would suffer his small tortures for now because it distracted him from the real battle coming our way.

The Mouse Queen stood at the windows overlooking the

front of the castle. "Time for you to earn your keep, little magician. Come, see the gathering armies for you to destroy."

Fritz rolled his eyes at me, then joined her at the window. "A pittance against the might of the Mouse army. Hardly worth my time."

While he puffed himself up, Fritz was nothing more than a cruel, inexperienced boy. I would enjoy killing him later. Or if that displeased my Queen, my true queen, Clara, I'd happily keep him in the dungeon, where the bugs could eat away at his body, slowly, over years.

"You won't defeat those Queens standing up here talking about it." I chastised them both. They knew they needed me and that's what I was counting on. "Your pet's games will cost you the throne if you let them, mother."

Her ire at me might be raised at the moment, but I was still her son and most trusted captain. Only because of the spell of course. I needed her to think I was still on her side.

The Queen sighed. "Shut up. You can do nothing. Konig, it's time to destroy your little friends."

That wasn't actually an order and so I didn't move. I needed a minute to think. The news of Drosselmeyer threw me off guard. I couldn't allow her access to his magic again. I had hoped I could wait on my plans a little longer to give Clara and the Nutcrackers the chance to usurp the Queen even without my crown.

I hadn't counted on her having a cutthroat ruthless magician of her own. Drosselmeyer had disappeared after he'd given my mother the Crown of the Land of Animals and the spell to use it on me. His betrayal of his own people at the end of the Magician's war would send anyone into hiding. It seemed he was coming back now to do it again. But he wasn't here yet and that gave me a very short time to take advantage of the only thing I could do to stop the Mouse Queen.

"I want you to send the entirety of the Mouse Army onto

that field and destroy every living soul upon it. Now." The power of the compulsion spell she had over me, and thus the soldiers of the Land of Animals, whooshed through me sending her orders out en masse. Even the two guards holding me went wide-eyed and walked out the door.

Fuck. "My Queen, you wanted to bring the other queens to heel. You cannot show them your might if they are dead."

"Hmm. Yes, but I've changed my mind. Once they are gone, I will install new obedient queens in their places. Then we won't have to worry about rebellions anymore." She didn't even bother to look at me, her attention drawn to the field of battle.

I would end her reign here and now. I could only pray that breaking her spell now would free the soldiers that were already heading toward the field of battle from their destructive orders. I busted the cords binding my wrists and reached for my dagger.

"Hold." The Queen held up a hand.

I froze and so did my armies. Had she caught me before I'd even started?

"What is that?" She pointed out the window, toward the battlefield, where the Queens were gathered to direct their armies in the battle. Clara's bright red dress stood out among the blue uniforms and the white snow like a beacon.

"That is the prin--" I couldn't finish my word. The Queen had forbidden me from calling Clara the princess. I cleared my throat again. "That's Clara Stahlbaum."

Fritz snorted. "We can see that. What is she doing?"

What in the fuck was she doing? There was only one reason to be waving a huge white flag and if she was doing what I thought she was, I was going to kill her myself. I couldn't answer.

The Mouse Queen rubbed her hands together. "My, my. Yes. She is surrendering. Looks like your little girlfriend is afraid of the might of my army. Friedrich, go get her and bring her to me. I should like to see Konig chop off her head."

Fucking fuck.

Fritz grumbled but made the trek down to the castle gates and out onto the field of battle. If I had a heart, it would be pounding so hard that everyone would be able to hear it. I watched the little asshole ride out on a horse while the contingent of soldiers he took with had to run on foot alongside of him.

When they approached Clara and the Queens, I strained the limits of my shifter hearing to try and catch even a speck of what they were saying, but it was simply too far away. What I did see was Fritz draw a sword and Leb come at him with his battle axe overhead.

Clara held up a hand and stopped both in their tracks, not with magic, but a single look. She had certainly grown in both confidence and power.

I didn't like what happened next. Clara stepped away from her Nutcracker guard and the Queens and submitted to having her wrists tied. Then she followed along behind Fritz's horse as he trotted too fast for her to keep up without stumbling along. I was going to kill him with the rope he'd used to tie her up.

After I was sure she made it into the castle without being harmed. If she was hurt, or worse, before she got to the throne room, I'd kill him on the spot, the consequences be damned.

I paced while my mother continued to calmy stare out the window. I couldn't stand it and sent stealthy mouse spies to track her progress and well-being even though she'd be in front of me in less than ten minutes.

Fritz seemed to actually understand his assignment and hurried back. When they walked into the room, I lost all sense of self preservation, crossed to her, shoved Fritz aside and untied her wrists. Neither of us said anything, but I saw her examine my wounds, and her eyes glisten with tears.

CROWNED

I wanted nothing more than to wipe them away and tell her everything would be all right. But it wouldn't and the Queen pulled on her spell. "Bring her to me."

I watched my own hands grab her by the arm, as if they weren't my own, and my feet obeyed, marching her to stand across from the Queen at the window.

"Hello, Clara. Come to supplicate yourself to me? You can't save your lover, you know. I control him and his heart, silly girl."

Clara said nothing, but a flash of red burst out from the necklace at her throat, and the Mouse Queen took a stumbling step back. She glared at Fritz. "You bound her powers like I showed you, didn't you Friedrich?"

The Queen looked Clara up and down with narrowed eyes, and I was thoroughly enjoying seeing fear in her eyes for the first time in an exceptionally long while.

"Of course. I'm not stupid." He scoffed and examined his fingernails like nothing bothered him. But I could feel Clara's powers rolling off her like an avalanche. Fuck, I hope she had a plan to use them really damn soon, because the facade wouldn't last long. If she did, there was the slimmest of chances I wouldn't have to die today.

"Yes, yes. Good." She waved her hand as if his words were of no consequence. "Now some lessons must be learned, and punishments meted out. Perhaps that will help you remember who your Queen is."

With another wave of her hand, the guards snatched up Fritz, tying him up just as I had been. He shouted and struggled against them, but he hadn't spent his years fighting or even training for battle like my soldiers had. He was no match for them and in a second, they had him pinned to the ground under their boots.

Ah, this lesson wasn't for Clara.

The Mouse Queen tipped her head to the side and studied

him. "What a silly stupid pet you are. How could you think I would ever trust a boy magician to rule by my side?"

"But you said you needed me, that you couldn't be the queen you needed to be without me." While Fritz squealed like a child, I inched closer to Clara.

If she had access to her magic, why hadn't she used it yet to take down the Queen and usurp her. I needed her to fulfill her destiny and sooner, rather than later, so that we could be together.

"Yes, that's true. You helped me find where Drosselmeyer's been hiding, much easier than if I'd had to get it out of your sister. With his power at my disposal again, no one will threaten my reign. Ever."

Drosselmeyer? That had been her end game with stupid Fritz? Shit. Now would be a good time for Clara to do something. I looked at her, pleading with my eyes for her to act. But was I wrong? Did she not have control over her magic?

If not, I needed a backup plan right the fuck now.

I risked a whisper while the Queen was occupied with Fritz. "Use your powers, my Queen and end her."

She shook her head and just as quietly replied. "Not until I have your crown."

The legends had said that the one who possessed all seven pieces of the broken crown and put it back together with love in her heart would be the new Queen of the Winter Realm. My hope that I could live through this final battle was misguided. I always had to die so that Clara could rule.

She didn't know what she was asking, and yet, I would still give it knowing she was the one woman I would trust with the care of my people. But if even the slightest thing went wrong when I pulled out the crown and gave it to her, like say I blacked out and couldn't protect her from the Queen's wrath, it would all be for naught.

She needed the rest of her consorts and now.

"That old man? He's weak and lecherous. I can be much more useful to you than he ever could. I know the human world and it's got so many more resources and technology than this realm. We can slip back and forth and plunder until both our coffers are overflowing."

I glanced at Fritz still wiggling around on the floor. He too was a magician, albeit one who knew nothing of how to use his own powers. But I did. I'd watched both Clara and Nuss use theirs and knew what I had to do.

Spill his blood to access the purest magic inside of him.

The Mouse Queen turned her back on Fritz and went back to Clara. "Kill him Konig. I'm tired of his whining and I don't need him anymore now that I have his more enticing sister."

"With pleasure, my Queen.'

I moved to Fritz's side and put my finger to my lips to keep him quiet, making it look like I was trying to free him. He smiled and nodded. Until I pulled out my dagger and slit his fucking throat.

He gurgled and flopped around like a stuck fish, but it was too late for him. The Queen jumped at the noise and turned just in time to see me slap my hand into the pooling blood. The portal opened wide, tearing the time and space in the throne room open like the wound in Fritz's throat.

The Mouse Queen shook her head and rolled her eyes, like I was a stupid, selfish child throwing my own tantrum. She didn't understand that this portal wasn't for me. Good. "What have you done? We could have used him for more than one portal for you to--"

Her tirade ended abruptly when I ignored her, reached through, and grabbed the first arm I could find. I yanked and Nuss came tumbling through. We fell together, him on top of me, and while I knew I shouldn't, I grabbed him and kissed him one final time.

Our teeth gnashed together, and I thrust my tongue into his

mouth, wanting his taste to be the last on my lips. Then I broke the kiss as fast as it had started and ordered, "Quickly, grab the others and stop the Mouse Queen. Now."

He blinked and gave a couple quick shakes of his head and then jumped up and back through the portal.

"Konig, what have you done? You would betray me for your lover? Stupid boy. You would have grown up freezing and starving to death before my eyes if I hadn't wormed my way into this position of power. I lived without everything a decent person should have for far too long and I will never live like that ever again." She marched toward me with her face twisted in fury.

I pointed my dagger at her and scooted away. "You could have made our world great, mother. For once the Animals wouldn't have to live in fear and subjugation. But you were greedy."

"Don't you chastise me." The spell flickered through me again, and any other words I had for her were gone.

I couldn't give her another opportunity to command me or our people to obey her psychotic orders ever again. With Nuss here and the others on their way, Clara was safe, and I could fulfill both our destinies. Even if it wasn't the one I'd hoped for.

I turned the dagger toward my own chest and just as I plunged it into the center, Zucker, Tau, and Leb came through the portal, followed by the Queens, an army of angry pixies, and a harem of Vikings, weapons at the ready.

Finally, they were here to protect Clara and when I gave her the crown of the Land of Animals, they would end her reign. I could die knowing they would take care of my people in their newfound freedom. I twisted the blade, hooked it on the crown buried where my heart should be and pulled it out. The dark compulsion spell swirled around and around, syphoning out through the wound, and fizzled like the wick of a burned-out candle.

"No, Konig, no!" Clara screamed and just as before in the tunnels below the castle, time and space slowed. Except for the six of us.

"You stupid, stupid boy."

Ah, I was wrong, seven.

The Mouse Queen shifted, but not into a small creature as she was meant to be, but as one huge and deformed body with seven heads. She reached for the broken piece of the Animal crown and laid the bloody mess on one of her heads.

My vision tunneled and I reached for her. The crown wasn't meant for the Mouse Queen. I needed Clara to have it.

Tau shot the evil bitch in that head's eye, and she screamed, but continued moving forward, crawling faster and faster toward Clara.

With my last breath, I shouted at her. "Don't even think that you can touch my princess."

She whipped around and glared at me. Her voice squeaked out like a monstrous version of what she'd been before. "I told you never to call her that."

She had.

And yet I did.

The spell was broken.

If only Clara had my crown, I could have died in peace.

PARTING IS SUCH BITTER SORROW

CLARA

Konig's eyes looked directly at me, but his spirit was gone. He'd broken the spell the Mouse Queen had over him and all her people and sacrificed himself to do it.

With his death, my heart shattered. The pain of it burned away the love and magic inside of me and I exploded. My dress became flames, my body a weapon. Without care for my own safety, I grabbed the dagger from Konig's limp hand and marched directly toward the grotesque monster the Mouse Queen had become.

Nuss was already attacking the queen-thing. His sword sliced through the air, but with every angry slice of his blade into her flesh, one of her heads bit at him until he fell to her onslaught. Leb's battle cry sounded, and his axe flew through the air, striking down one of her heads.

She screamed again and shook with rage and pain. The

severed head wearing Konig's bloody crown fell to the ground and still she didn't die. Zucker swept in and snagged the crown from the mess and tossed it to Tau. Her great wriggling tail slapped Zucker so hard, he went flying across the room and smacked hard against the stones, slouching in unconsciousness.

Tau grabbed the crown in mid-air and rolled out of the way of another slash of the Mouse Queen's tail. He landed at my feet and pressed the crown into my hand. "The final crown is yours, my lady. Don't let their deaths be in vain."

The other six gruesome mouse heads looked directly at me and in unison said, "Give us the crowns, give us the magic."

The magic.

The magic that didn't belong to her, or me, or any one person, but all the people of the Winter Realm.

I looked down at the seven crowns, at the broken pieces that represented each of the unique lands that made up this realm. I tore the chain I wore and let each piece of the crown fall into my hand. One by one they joined together, the puzzle forming a Queen's crown, until only one final empty spot remained.

The mouse queen rushed toward me, and both Leb and Tau tackled her. Tau held her down and Leb broke one neck and then another and another, until only the final head remained. She shifted, trying to reclaim her form of a woman, her body was battered and torn up, half skin, half fur, but still fighting.

With a final snap, I laid the broken piece of the crown of the Land of Animals into place, and the crown reformed in my hand. The magic contained within the seven pieces exploded into the red sparkling magic of the Land of Spirit, the blue electric fire of the Land of Snow, the sensual purple of the Land of Sweet, the bright green of the Land of Flowers, the spicy orange of the Gingerbread Kingdom, and the brilliant golden rays of the Land of Animals. The rainbow that made up the diverse lands of the Winter Realm glittered and sparkled, accented by pretty pink starbursts that calmed and comforted my heart, filling me with pure joy.

This was the magic of the Winter Realm. Beautiful and perfect, whenever part came together as one.

I held the key to controlling all this magic, all this power. All I had to do is set the crown on my head and the Winter Realm would be mine, just as it's princes were. I could end the Mouse Queen's cruel rule and make things right for all the people of the land.

But...

I wasn't meant to usurp the evil queen, punish her for her crimes against her people, or even kill her. Even though that's what everyone wanted me to do.

I wasn't the Vivandiere.

I wasn't the loving daughter, nor the put-upon sister of the human world I'd left behind.

I wasn't even the pudgy girl who wanted nothing more than to dance.

All of those roles were the opposite of all the lessons I'd learned on this adventure back to my true home and my true self.

I was a woman who thought she would never be loved until she met her five princes. A woman who'd had that love taken away before she even got to truly experience it.

Just as Mother Gingerbread said I would, I felt the love and knowledge of my ancestors before me, and I knew what to do.

I was the princess of the Land of Spirit, where love, not hate, was meant to be. The magic never belonged to my people. They'd somehow corralled it and controlled it over the years, and that too was greed that caused corruption. I had to set that right.

Just as Konig made his choice to reclaim his true self, I would too.

CROWNED

I set the crown of the Queen of the Winter Realm on my head, but not to take the power, not to control it. I chose in that moment to give the magic back. Back to the land, back to its people, where it belonged. Never to be used or abused again.

When everyone had power, no one did. When we were all equal, we were free.

The fire of hatred, anger, shame, and greed subsided as a mighty wind of love, comfort, and joy whipped through the room, and the walls around us, along with the ceiling above us blew away, leaving us access to the wide-open sky.

The stones of Christmas Castle, built on coerced labor, and for all the wrong reasons, crumbled and melted away under our feet and it was if the castle had never stood. We stood in soft fields of snow, dotted with bushes and trees. The castle keep washed away and left only the people who'd been in the buildings standing around wondering what happened.

Some of the swirls of magic seeped into the people around us, but still more of the light floated out toward the armies on the field. As they each received their gift of magic and power, they laid down their weapons and embraced those around them. Even the Queens joined together hand in hand, and Mother Gingerbread led a cheer that spread all across the lands.

Snow fell down on us all and with each snowflake, the magic contained in the crown seeped away. I used the last bit of magic contained in my tumultuous emotions to heal those around me.

I pushed the snow toward the Mouse Queen and as it touched her fur, the monstrous heads disappeared, and a small mouse was all that was left.

She scurried away, leaving bloody footprints in the snow. I didn't chase her, I had no need to find her now. There were more important matters for the Winter magic to take care of.

I directed the snow to fall on Konig, Nuss and Zucker next. I let my spirit flow into theirs and find the connection between us all, as faint as they were.

Zucker rose first, shaking his head and looking around like he'd only just woken from a dream. Tau rushed over and pulled him into his arms and that link clicked back into place.

Nuss awoke next and Leb helped him to his feet. He made his way over to me and pulled me into his arms. They were both healthy and whole again. "You've saved us all my Queen."

I shook my head and let the first of my tears fall. "Not all of us."

I fell to my knees beside Konig's body and covered his chest with my own. He'd sacrificed everything for this realm, for his people, and for me. He'd made the ultimate sacrifice for love and if I had a modicum of magic left in me, I would curse him for it.

I couldn't breathe, only weep. Nuss dropped to the ground beside me and put a hand on both my head and Konig's. "This can't be. We were supposed to save him. Nothing else mattered. It was my job to protect him, and I let him down again. I'm so sorry, my King. I'm sorry."

Leb, Zucker, and Tau knelt with us, and Tau joined our hands. Just as when we all experienced pleasure together, our link connected our pain. My heart broke five times over and it would never heal.

The people living in and around the castle began a procession past us, grieving the loss of their prince, their king, their protector. While this was a day for rejoicing, it was also a day of sorrow.

The little doe-eyed girl from the docks approached us from the line of mourners and came right up to me. She touched my tears and pressed them to her own eyes. "If I give the magic back, my lady, will you use it to give Konig his life back?"

"Oh, honey. I wish it worked that way. But only you can use the magic inside of you now. So, use it to make something beautiful in this life and perhaps if we all do that, we will honor him and his sacrifice."

She shook her head and her own tears streamed down her face. She wiped them away and pressed her wet hands to my face. But when nothing happened, she cried even more.

My sweet little pixies appeared, and they flitted around us all, wringing their hands not knowing what to do. Milk and cookies weren't going to provide very much comfort today. Freunde sat on the little girl's shoulder and nuzzled her ear. But Trost made a strange nosedive for the ground and went headfirst into a pile of snow.

"My lady, what're they doing?" The little girl pointed to where Trost had gotten lost, and in an instant, Freunde followed them in. We could see their lights wiggling around under the snow, and finally, Leb got frustrated waiting for them to reappear, and he started shoveling scoops of snow away with his hands.

When he uncovered them, I thought at first they'd conjured up another present. I just wasn't up for gift giving. But then I saw that the box they had wasn't pretty and tied up in a bow, but instead was made of bones. They'd had a tough time getting it out of the drift because a small, raggedy mouse had a hold of it too.

The Mouse Queen.

She smacked Freunde and Trost away and shoved the box toward me.

I reached for it, but the little girl held my hand back. "My lady, no. That thing is evil."

I patted her hand and picked it up anyway, then held it up and let the snow fall on it, washing the evil away. Because I could feel that what was inside wasn't evil, but magic instead. When I turned back, the little mouse was gone and there were only tiny footprints in the snow.

Carefully, I lifted the lid, and my heart skipped a beat, then another and another, until I had to finally remind myself to breathe. Inside was a heart, made of golden magic. It beat ever so slowly, but it did beat.

I looked at my men and it took me a minute to find my voice. "All together now."

We five reached into the box and as one, we lifted the heart and pressed the magic into Konig's chest. I held my breath and closed my eyes. "We love you, my Mouse King. Come back to us now and complete this bond. We need you."

I heard the others' sighs of relief before I opened my eyes. I was met with the sparkling eyes of the final piece of my heart. He pulled me down to him and into a long kiss. I think he would have let me go on kissing him forever if my tears hadn't dripped all over us both.

"Don't cry, my Queen. I want your laughter, not your tears."

I did let out a small laugh and hugged him tight.

Leb grabbed us all up into his great big arms and held us tight as one. "Well, I for one want her orgasms."

The others groaned and then laughed, and a final bit of magic passed between us all, linking all of our hearts back together again.

We helped Konig up and the people around us gasped, cheered, cried, and laughed. Somewhere nearby, music that sounded a whole lot like some of the jauntier Christmas carols from the human world, started up and soon there was merry making and reveling all around us.

Though most were in celebration mode, the Queens had their heads together. The Snow Queen approached us, and I could see trouble coming. Nuss tried to fend her off, but I wrapped my arm around his waist and tucked myself against him. "It's okay, let her come. We'll deal with her together."

"Nuss, Clara," she said, giving a little bow.

"Mother, this isn't court, you don't have to--"

She held up a hand. "I will just the same, thank you very much. You may have changed life here in the Winter Realm, but it will take some time to get used to it."

I gave Nuss a squeeze. He too was going to have to get used to not caring so much what his mother said, thought or wanted.

"Fine. Then what is it that you need?"

She gave a thank-you-very-much jerky nod of her head. "We'd like to know if Clara isn't the Winter Queen, and the Land of Spirit and Magic--"

I interrupted her this time. "It's just the Land of Spirit. The magic belongs to us all now."

"Fine. And the Land of Spirit," she made a face as she paused the beat for where the words 'and Magic' should have been said, "is, umm, non-habitable at the moment, will Clara step into the role of the Queen of the Land of Animals?"

"No." Nuss, Konig, and I all said it emphatically at the same time.

The Snow Queen frowned and looked uncomfortably between Nuss and Konig. "Then he will be the, uh, King?"

I could feel Nuss's ire rising up again, so I stepped in, so he didn't have to say anything more to her. "For a while, we're going to let the people of the Land of Animals heal. When they're ready, they'll decide who they want to be their leaders."

"That's not how it works in the Winter Realm. They need a Queen."

"Do they though?" They'd been hurt long enough by people in power. Maybe they needed a break. Either way it wasn't any of our decisions. Only Konig should have a say.

My favorite little girl ran up and tugged on my hand. "I'll be Queen."

Konig chuckled and gave her head a gentle stroke. "Okay, love. That sounds like a good plan. But let's iron out the details when you come of age and can control your shift, hmm?"

She nodded and ran back to her mother. "I'm going to be Queen, mama."

The Snow Queen rolled her eyes and stomped her way back to the other Queens. She must have reported what we'd decided, and the other women laughed, and Mother Gingerbread gave me an approving smile.

THE END OF INNOCENCE

CLARA

*P*ixies and messenger Angels flew through the air, and Freunde and Trost pulled me to follow them. They buzzed and squealed, and I vowed to learn to speak their language now that we weren't searching for crowns and fighting an evil queen. "Leb, what are they saying?"

"Basically, there's a party in the Christmas Tree Forest and they want us to join them there. There's something they want to show us."

Nuss gave a little whistle, and our reindeer came trotting over still attached to the sleigh. Konig rolled his eyes. "It's no animal carved work of art, but I guess it will do."

Nuss picked Konig up, in a princess hold, and carried him over to the sleigh and carefully deposited him into the soft blankets, wrapping him up snug as a bug in a rug. Zucker, Tau, and Leb all conveniently looked up at the sky or across the field when Konig scowled. But the way our King leaned into Nuss's touch, he secretly liked being taken care of that way.

I'd venture to guess no one had ever done anything of the sort and I was already making plans to do lots of taking care of him. In and out of the blankets.

The rest of us climbed in and it took quite a while for us to make it to the Christmas Tree Forest because so many wanted to greet us and cheer us along the way. But there was no more flying for us now that I couldn't magic us up into the sky.

When we finally made it to the heart of the forest, the party was in full swing. There were adults talking and dancing, and children running around with cookies in their hands. It reminded me so much of the night of the Christmas party at my human home that my chest and heart gave a little contraction.

Tau took my hand and gave it a kiss. "I can feel your heartache. Do you miss that world so very much?"

I thought for a moment and shook my head. "No. This is where I belong. That world never appreciated me for who and what I am, and I don't even mean being a magical queen. I do wonder about my father though. I did love him."

Was he even my real father? I doubted I would ever know since no one else from the Land of Spirit was still around. Unless of course Drosselmeyer found a way to come through the portal. Pins and needles creeped down my spine worrying that he might still have the power to do that.

I still didn't think he was evil, but he might have been at one time and his energy didn't belong in the Winter Realm anymore. But with the magic now dispersed across the land perhaps there was no more portal between our two realms.

Freunde and Trost circled me and while one pushed my shoulders, the other tried to drag me by the arm. "Where are we going my little loves?"

Tau and I went along to where they pulled us, and the others followed close behind. We were just outside the main circle of trees where the revelry was in full swing. But in another few steps, I recognized one particular tree. A few of the lower branches were broken from where I had fallen along with Nuss only a few days ago.

This was the tree we had portaled through. And if I squinted at it close, looking between the branches, there was electric light from the lamps in the Stahlbaum house's living room. My stomach dropped a little and I took a step back. But Nuss dragged me back forward. "The portal is here but without an intention it's not entirely opened. We can observe until the final hour of the twelfth day of Christmas."

"But look, the tree is still up, the living room still has remnants from our Christmas party. It looks as though it's only the next day. Christmas Day."

"Yes, lass." Leb said. "Remember, time moves differently between the realms. At Christmas each of our days is a mere two hours in your world."

"What day is it here?"

They all glanced around at each other as if I'd asked what the square root of pi was. Zucker even made calculations on his fingers. It had been a terribly busy few days and it seemed we'd all lost track. Konig was the only one to speak up.

"The ninth day of Christmas."

My true loves gave to me... let's see... oh, I was so getting five golden rings made up for them. But then I remembered. The ninth day of Christmas my true loves gave to me, nine dancers dancing.

I wondered if I could get the ballerinas of the Sweet Fae court to do a dance with me that ended with a partridge in a pear tree. "So, it's Christmas afternoon. Father should be having afternoon tea."

Suddenly, through the branches I saw someone wheeling my father into the living room and one of the maids bringing in a tray of tea and biscuits. The man pushing my father's chair sat, so that his back was to the old grandfather clock, the one Herr Drosselmeyer had given us.

But I had a clear view of my father, and he looked... happy. He was lucid and animatedly talking to his visitor. That brought a gentle tear to my lashes, and I didn't bother to wipe it away. He was going to be okay. I almost hoped he wouldn't remember that Fritz and I were gone, and he likely wouldn't.

He and his visitor laughed and talked, but eventually my father yawned, and the maid came and cleared the tea away. She returned and rolled my father away, but he no longer had that tired lost look on his face. I was glad and sad all at the same time.

The visitor rose and turned, finally toward the clock, which gave us a straight view of his face. It was Herr Drosselmeyer, but he looked so much younger, and he had a new twinkle in his eye that absolutely reminded me of Nuss.

He looked directly at me, and I gasped. He wasn't supposed to be able to see through the tree, was he? He tipped his hat to us and put his hand over his heart. Then he opened his jacket, and revealed a blue, sparkling, snowflake, beating along with his heart. He patted it and held his hand there, in a gesture that expressed sadness and love.

Nuss touched his heart. "I felt that. Although, I don't think it was actually meant for me."

"It wasn't," I said. "But your mother probably isn't ready to hear this story."

Herr Drosselmeyer nodded and walked out of the living room so we could no longer see him. The Stahlbaum house fell silent, and the living room began to darken as twilight fell. Soon, the only thing visible in the house was the twinkling lights of the Christmas tree.

We returned to the party, but along the way back, the pixies pointed to other trees, and I caught glimpses of more portals. These were in that same window-like state, and the quick views that I saw weren't of homes like mine, but exotic lands. Someplace warm with a lot of sun, that I'd definitely like to visit someday for a vacation from the snow, and another filled with thunderclouds and trees with branches filled with the flowers of Spring.

I caught up to the others and asked, "Are there other realms? Like say the Summer or Spring Realm?"

"Of course, lass. There are seven realms."

"There are? I only know of four seasons, what are the others?" I was fascinated by the idea of other realms and wondered if we could even visit.

Nuss answered with, "There's also the Twilight and Shadow Realms."

"But that's only six."

Konig supplied this last answer with a dark frown. "The Lost Realm."

Fascinating. I felt like I needed to go to Winter Realm elementary school to catch up on all that I'd missed living in the human world. "Ooh, that sounds creepy and ominous. How do you know about it if it's lost?"

"There's still legend and lore about it. The magicians used to have a whole field of study dedicated to finding the Lost Realm, thinking there must be power and magic to be had there. I found text in the ruins of Steel Tree Castle."

Well, that was a downer discussion for another day. We rejoined the revelers and the party in the Christmas Tree Forest lasted well into the tenth day of Christmas. Which was both fun and exhausting. Those pixies could party, man.

On the last two days of Christmas, we as a group, travelled around to the different courts, visiting the Queens, Mother Gingerbread, and finally the Land of Animals. They'd set up a new market where the old castle had stood, and it was thriving.

Animals who'd been in hiding for years had come out, and all the men and women who'd been enlisted as soldiers had the opportunity to build new lives. It wasn't going to be all sunshine and snowflakes. There were years, generations even, of trauma that needed to be healed.

But the other lands helped how they could. The contingent of Snowflake nuns that Nuss had sent to help the poor had an uphill battle. Not only because there were so many who'd been living in poverty for years, but because very few Animals trusted any Snowflakes.

I thought maybe we'd make our forever home in the Land of Animals, but Konig said no. He didn't want any of his people to harbor any resentment for non-Animals deciding they could just take up some of the land for themselves, even if they were bonded and mated to him.

"Where should we settle down then, or will we roam from Land to Land the rest of our days? That sounds exhausting to me." Zucker was stretched out in the back of the sleigh, with Tau tucked into his shoulder.

Leb nodded and patted his axe on his hand, which had become his main thinking strategy. "No, we should find a place to build a long house and begin the work of filling it with many children."

"That doesn't exactly sound like work to me. But I agree the sooner the better. We haven't had a moment alone to bond with our Queen." Konig gave me a come hither look and it was something I couldn't refuse.

Nuss grabbed me up and threw me over his strong shoulder. His arm still hadn't healed, and it seemed unless we took him back to the human realm, it may never do so. I used a bit of my magician's armor, which seemed to have some if its own inherent magic in it, to create a more permanent sling. Even with only one arm to use, he wasn't any less my protector or lover.

"Yes, we need some privacy and a place of our own, because otherwise, I'm going to be getting more lessons in lovemaking here in the back of the sleigh in the middle of the prairie. So, whoever has a suggestion, speak up now."

No one said a thing.

"You guys just want to watch while Nuss learns the fine art of cunnilingus, you dirty bastards," Zucker finally said. "And I for one am ready and willing to teach him."

"Wait," I squeaked out. "I know of a slightly run-down castle in the Land of Spirit that could use a good solid family to move in and fix it up."

Even while I was hanging upside down over Nuss's back, I could see that all of them liked the idea. Leb jumped into the back of the sleigh with Zucker and Tau and settled himself in for the ride. "Sounds like the perfect place. As long as we can build a room with a bed made for six, I'm game."

That sounded simply perfect to me.

We took off in the direction of the Land of Spirit, and this time when we got close to the boarder, there was no more wall, and no more magic barrier. The ruins of the castle were still as they were when I left, but the zip of magic was gone.

But where the land had been barren, windswept, and cold before, trees and plants had started to take root. The land was already beginning to recover. As we pulled up to the bit of castle that still stood, I noticed something on the side of the room we'd stayed in before.

I hopped out of the sleigh and walked around the building to where a courtyard opened up. In the center was a Christmas tree made of shiny steel. My family's namesake stood tall and proud, even in the face of destruction around it.

Around the base of the tree was a stack of brightly wrapped Christmas presents. I looked back to my men, but they didn't seem to know anything about them.

I carefully unwrapped the first present and found a gingerbread man and a gingerbread house inside. I showed it to Leb, and he smiled and gestured for me to go on.

The next boxes had a sugar plum, and a dewdrop flower in

them. They were beautiful and altogether too deliberate to be coincidental. Who had left these for us?

I opened the next two boxes and indeed found a mouse king and a nutcracker. Of course.

But what was going to be in the final box? It was the biggest and wrapped in shining red paper. I lifted the lid and found two dolls inside. One an adorably chubby ballerina, and the other...

I lifted the beautiful doll out, and she was dressed as the Vivandiere. There was a chain around her neck, with a stylized crown of gold and rubies, similar to the one my mother had left for me.

There was also a note, and it read.

Welcome home, princess.

WANT JUST a little more of the Winter Realm?

Grab a special bonus chapter I've written for Clara and her consorts available ONLY to my Book Dragons on Patreon or my Curvy Connection newsletter subscribers!

Want to read more curvy girl Why Choose Just One stories?

Check out Grumpy Wolves in The Fate of the Wolf Guard series now.

ACKNOWLEDGMENTS

Special thanks to my Mushroom Mastermind, M. Guida, JL Madore, Dylann Crush, Bri Blackwood, and Claudia Burgoa, for being great friends who know that believe in me and help me keep calm and carry on, even when I think I've screw up my career or have planned the impossible.

Big thanks to my proofreader, Chrisandra. She probably hates commas as much as I do now. All the remaining errors are all my fault. I'm sure I effed it all up somewhere.

I am so very grateful to have readers who will join my on my crazy book adventures. I know this isn't what I typically write - no dragons, no wolves, no witches... but there will ALWAYS be curvy girls getting happy ever afters!

Without all of you, I wouldn't be able to feed my cats (or live the dream of a creative life!)

Thank you so much to all my Patreon Book Dragons!

An enormous thanks to my Official Biggest Fans Ever. You're the best book dragons a curvy girl author could ask for~

Thank you so much for all your undying devotion for me and the characters I write. You keep me writing (almost) every day.

Hugs and Kisses and Signed Books and Swag for you from me!

- Helena E.

- Alida H.
- Daphine G.
- Danielle T.
- Stephanie F.
- Jessica W.
- Cherie S.
- Marilyn C.
- Katherine M.
- Kelli W.
- Mari G.
- Stephanie. H.

Shout out to my Official VIP Fans! Extra Hugs to you ~

- Jeanette M.
- Kerrie M.
- Michele C.
- Corinne A.
- Evie B.
- Frania G.
- Hannah P.
- Nicole W.
- Sandra B.

ALSO BY AIDY AWARD

Dragons Love Curves

Chase Me

Tease Me

Unmask Me

Bite Me

Cage Me

Baby Me

Defy Me

Surprise Me

Dirty Dragon

Crave Me

Dragon Love Letters - Curvy Connection Exclusive

Slay Me

Play Me

Merry Me

The Black Dragon Brotherhood

Tamed

Tangled
Twisted

Fated For Curves
A Touch of Fate
A Tangled Fate
A Twist of Fate

Alpha Wolves Want Curves
Dirty Wolf
Naughty Wolf
Kinky Wolf
Hungry Wolf
Flirty Wolf - Curvy Connection Exclusive
Grumpy Wolves
Filthy Wolf

The Fate of the Wolf Guard
Unclaimed
Untamed
Undone
Undefeated

Claimed by the Seven Realms
Protected
Stolen
Crowned

By Aidy Award and Piper Fox
Big Wolf on Campus
Cocky Jock Wolf

Bad Boy Wolf

Heart Throb Wolf

Hot Shot Wolf

Contemporary Romance by Aidy Award

The Curvy Love Series

Curvy Diversion

Curvy Temptation

Curvy Persuasion

The Curvy Seduction Saga

Rebound

Rebellion

Reignite

Rejoice

Revel

ABOUT THE AUTHOR

Aidy Award is a curvy girl who kind of has a thing for stormtroopers. She's also the author of the popular Curvy Love series and the hot new Dragons Love Curves series.
She writes curvy girl erotic romance, about real love, and dirty fun, with happy ever afters because every woman deserves great sex and even better romance, no matter her size, shape, or what the scale says.
Read the delicious tales of hot heroes and curvy heroines come to life under the covers and between the pages of Aidy's books. Then let her know because she really does want to hear from her readers.
Connect with Aidy on her website. www.AidyAward.com get her Curvy Connection, and join her Facebook Group - Aidy's Amazeballs.

Printed by Amazon Italia Logistica S.r.l.
Torrazza Piemonte (TO), Italy